# SUMMONER
## BOOK TWO

# SUMM✪NER
## BOOK TWO

# The Inquisition

## TARAN MATHARU

Hodder
Children's
Books

## HODDER CHILDREN'S BOOKS

First published in Great Britain in 2016 by Hodder Children's Books
This edition published in 2017 by Hodder and Stoughton

1 3 5 7 9 10 8 6 4 2

A C atalogue record for this book is available from the British Library.

ISBN: 978 1 444 92424 4

Typeset in Garamond by Avon DataSet Ltd, Bidford-on-Avon, Warwickshire

Printed and bound by Clays Ltd, St Ives plc

The paper and board used in this book are made from wood from responsible sources

Hodder Children's Books
An imprint of Hachette Children's Group
Part of Hodder and Stoughton
Carmelite House
50 Victoria Embankment
London EC4Y 0DZ

An Hachette UK Company
www.hachette.co.uk

www.hachettechildrens.co.uk

For Rob, the bravest man I have ever known

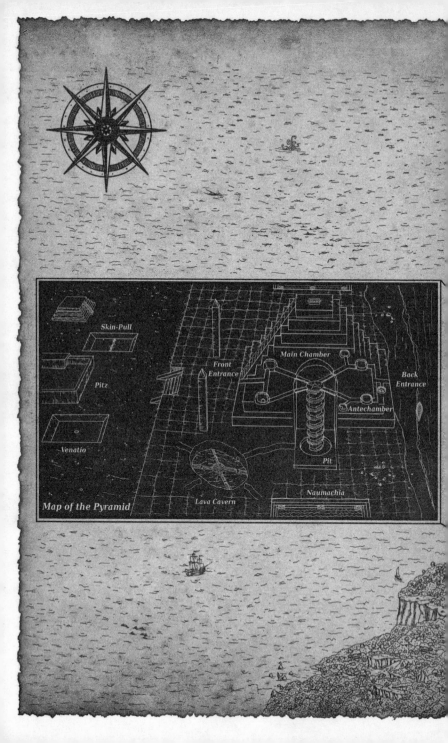

Skin-Pull

Pitz

Venatio

Map of the Pyramid

Front
Entrance

Main Chamber

Back
Entrance

Antechamber

Pit

Lava Cavern

Naumachia

# Map of Hominum

Elven Lands

Akhad Desert

Pelt

Beartooth Mountains

Faversham Forest

Boreas

Corcillum

Antioch

Vesanian Sea

Vocans Academy

Raleighshire

Orc Jungle

The Pyramid

The Warren

The Waterfall

The Swamps

# 1

Fletcher opened his eyes, but all he saw was darkness. He groaned and nudged Ignatius, whose claw was splayed across his chin. The demon complained with a sleepy mewl, before tumbling on to the cold stone beneath them.

'Good morning. Or whatever time it is,' Fletcher mumbled, flaring a wyrdlight into existence. It hung in the air like a miniature sun, spinning gently.

The room was bathed in cold, blue light, revealing the cramped, windowless cell that was paved with smooth flagstones. In the corner lay a latrine, a simple hole in the ground that was covered by a jagged piece of slate. Fletcher stared at the large iron door embedded in the wall opposite him.

As if on cue, there was a rattle as the small flap at the bottom of the door eased back and a mailed hand pushed through the gap. It groped around for the empty bucket that sat beside the door. The sound of gurgling followed and the bucket was replaced, sloshing with water. Fletcher watched the flap expectantly, then groaned as he heard the echo of footsteps walking away.

'No food again, buddy,' Fletcher said, rubbing a crestfallen Ignatius under his chin.

It wasn't unusual; sometimes the gaoler just didn't bother bringing food. Fletcher's stomach growled, but he ignored it and reached for the loose stone he kept beside his bed to scratch another notch in the wall. Though it was hard to tell the time with no natural light, he assumed that he received food and water – or sometimes, like today, just water – once a day. He didn't need to count the hundreds of notches on the wall to know how long he had been imprisoned – he knew them by heart now.

'One year,' Fletcher sighed, settling back into the straw. 'Happy anniversary.'

He lay there contemplating the reason for his imprisonment. It had all started that one night, when his childhood nemesis, Didric, had cornered him in a crypt and tried to murder him, gloating about his father's plans to turn the entire village of Pelt into a prison.

And then came Ignatius, from out of nowhere, burning Didric as he advanced, giving Fletcher time to escape. The little demon had risked his own life to save Fletcher's, even in the first moments of their bond. In the aftermath, Fletcher had become a fugitive, for he knew Didric's family would lie through their teeth to frame him for attempted murder. His only consolation was that if it hadn't happened, he might never have made it to Vocans Academy.

Had it really been two whole years since Ignatius entered his life, and he first set foot in that ancient castle? He could remember his last moments there so clearly. His best friend

Othello had earned the respect of the generals and convinced his fellow dwarves not to rebel against the Hominum Empire. Sylva had cemented the peace between their races and had proven herself and the other elves worthy allies. Even Seraph, the first commoner to be elevated to nobility in over a thousand years, had impressed his fellow nobles during the Tournament. Perhaps most satisfying of all, the Forsyth plot to create a new war with the elves and dwarves, in order to profit their weapons business, had been foiled completely. It had all been so perfect.

Until Fletcher's past came back to haunt him.

Ignatius gave Fletcher an owlish blink from his amber eyes, sensing his master's despondency. He nudged Fletcher's hand with the end of his snout. Fletcher gave him a halfhearted swipe, but the demon dodged out of the way and nipped the tip of his finger.

'All right, all right.' Fletcher grinned at the boisterous demon, the pain distracting him from his misery. 'Let's get back to training. I wonder what spell we should practise today?'

He reached under the pile of straw that was his bedding and removed the two books that had kept him sane over the past year. He didn't know who had hidden them there for him, only that they had taken a great risk in doing so. Fletcher was eternally grateful to his mysterious benefactor; without the books he would have been driven mad with boredom. There were only so many games that he and Ignatius could play in the tight confines of the cell.

The first was the standard book of spellcraft, the same one they had all used in Arcturus's lessons. It was slim, for it

3

contained only a few hundred symbols and the proper techniques for etching them. Before, Fletcher had only been vaguely familiar with them, so he could pass his exams – preferring to focus on perfecting the four main battle-spells. Now, he was able to picture every single symbol from memory, and could etch them in his sleep.

The second book was thick, so much so that whoever had hidden it had removed the leather cover to make it more easily concealable in the straw. It was James Baker's journal, the book that had started Fletcher on his path to becoming a trained battlemage. Within its pages, Fletcher had found a dozen new spells, diligently copied by the late summoner from the walls of ancient orcish ruins. Moreover, Baker had studied scores of orcish demons, detailing their relative power, abilities and statistics. Now Fletcher was an expert too. Perhaps most fascinating of all, Baker had compiled all of his knowledge of orcish culture, including their strategies and their weapons, in the journal. It was a veritable treasure trove of knowledge, which Fletcher had devoured in a few days, only to immediately begin again and hunt for details he might have missed.

These two volumes were all that distracted him from the deafening silence of the outside world. Every night, he dreamed of his friends, wondering where they might be. Did they battle on the front lines while he rotted in the bowels of the earth? Had they been killed by an orcish javelin or a Forsyth dagger?

But the most torturous thought of all was knowing that his adoptive father Berdon was close by, in the village above him. He remembered when the prison transport had brought him back to Pelt in the dead of night. He had peered through the cracks in the armoured wagon, desperate to catch a glimpse of his childhood home. But before he could get a proper look, the gaolers threw a sack over his head and dragged him away.

As Fletcher lapsed into miserable silence once more, Ignatius growled restlessly before snorting a tongue of flame that singed the straw beneath them.

'Wow, we are impatient today!' Fletcher exclaimed, powering up a tattooed finger with a blast of mana. 'OK, you asked for it. Let's see how you like the telekinesis spell.'

He allowed a thin stream of mana through his fingertip, the spiral symbol glowing violet until a strip of air shimmered above it. Ignatius began to back away, but Fletcher whipped his hand at the mischievous demon, curling the ribbon of energy around his belly and flinging him upwards. The demon splayed his claws and dug them into the ceiling, showering Fletcher with a trickle of dust. Before Fletcher had time to react, Ignatius hurled himself down, twisting in midair like a cat with his claws and tailspike pointed at Fletcher's face. It was only through a desperate roll that Fletcher avoided it, then spun on his heels to find the room cast in darkness. Ignatius had slashed the wyrdlight during his attack, snuffing it out like a candle.

'So, that's how you want to play it,' Fletcher said, powering up his index finger, the one without a tattoo. This time, he etched in the air, using one of the rarer symbols he had learned from Baker's journal. He twisted his finger so it was pointed directly at his face.

The cat's-eye symbol looked almost exactly like its namesake, a thin oval within a circle. Through trial and error, Fletcher had learned the spell had no effect until its light was shined into his retinas.

The glowing symbol gave away his position, as did the flash of yellow that soon followed, but Fletcher rolled to the side so Ignatius would lose him in the darkness. He could feel his eyes slowly changing, his pupils elongating into feline slits. It was not long before Fletcher's vision brightened and he could make out Ignatius's figure, crawling towards his previous position like a lion stalking a gazelle. Though Ignatius had far better night-vision than Fletcher did, in the pitch black of the cell even the demon was struggling to navigate.

'Gotcha!' Fletcher yelled, diving across the room and bundling the demon into his arms. They tumbled back into the straw, and Fletcher laughed uproariously at the demon's barks of protest.

The door burst open and the room filled with light, blinding Fletcher's sensitive eyes. He scrabbled to hide the books beneath the straw, but a boot kicked out, slamming into the side of his head and throwing him against the wall.

'Not so fast,' a voice rasped.

There was the tell-tale click of a flintlock being pulled back and Fletcher felt the cold metal of the weapon's barrel pushed against his forehead. As the effects of the spell faded, he could make out a hazy, hooded figure crouched beside him, holding an elegant pistol.

'One twitch from you, and I blast you into oblivion,' said the voice. It was hoarse, like a man dying of thirst.

'OK,' Fletcher said, slowly raising his hands.

'Ah-ah,' the figure tutted, pressing the muzzle harder against his temple. 'Are you deaf? I've heard of what you can do with those tattooed fingers. Keep your hands by your side.'

Fletcher hesitated, aware that this would probably be his best chance of escape. The gunman gave Fletcher a husky sigh of exasperation.

'Rubens, give him a little taste of your sting.'

Fletcher caught a flutter from the depths of the man's hood, then a bright red Mite buzzed out and alighted on his neck. He felt a sharp pain, then a cold sensation spreading through his body.

'Now I know you won't be playing any tricks,' the figure croaked, standing up so he was silhouetted against the torchlight from the open doorway. 'Speaking of which, where is that Salamander of yours?'

Fletcher tried to twist his head, but it seemed locked in place. At the mention of the word Salamander, Ignatius stirred from beneath him, and Fletcher knew that the demon was preparing to attack. He quelled Ignatius's intentions with a stern pulse through their mental link. Even if they managed to overpower the man, Fletcher wouldn't be able to crawl out of the cell door, let alone pull off an escape.

'Ah, he's in the straw there. Well, keep him quiet, if you want to keep your brains inside your skull. It would be such a shame to kill you, after all the preparations we have made.'

'Pr-pr-preparations?' Fletcher managed to stutter, his tongue clumsy and numb from the Mite's venom.

'For your trial,' the figure replied, holding out a hand for Rubens to perch on. 'We delayed it as long as we could, but it seems your friends have been very persistent in their petitions to the king. A shame.'

The figure stowed the Mite within the confines of his hood once more, as if he could not bear to be apart from him. The skin of his hand was smooth, almost feminine, with carefully manicured fingernails. The man's boots were made from hand-stitched calfskin, with fashionable, figure-hugging trousers above them. Even the hooded jacket was made from black leather of the finest quality. Fletcher could tell the stranger was a wealthy young man, most likely the firstborn son of a noble.

'I will allow you one more question, then I must take you to the courtroom. Take your time, so the paralysis can wear off. I don't want to have to carry you there.'

Fletcher's mind flashed to his friends, to Berdon, and to the state of the war. But he had no way of knowing if the stranger would have the answers he sought. Did they know each other? He pictured the other summoners that he had met at Vocans, but none of them had a hoarse voice. Could it be Tarquin, playing a cruel trick on him? One thing was for sure: his opponent would keep the upper hand as long as he remained anonymous.

'Who. Are. You?' Fletcher asked, forcing each word out through numbed lips.

The fact that he could speak at all meant that Rubens had pricked him with only a low dose of venom. He still had a fighting chance.

'Haven't you worked it out yet?' the stranger rasped. 'That *is* disappointing. I thought you would have guessed by now. Still, I do look quite different than when we last spoke, so you are hardly to blame.'

The figure crouched again, leaning forward until Fletcher's vision was filled with the dark confines of his hood. Slowly, the man pulled it back, revealing his face.

'Recognise me now, Fletcher?' Didric hissed.

# 2

Didric leered with a lopsided smile, leaning back so his face would catch the light. The right side was waxy and mottled red, with the edge of his lip burned away to reveal a flash of white teeth. His eyebrows and lashes were gone, leaving him with a wide-eyed appearance, as if he were constantly alarmed. Patches of his scalp were almost bald, covered only by a sparse scattering of hair that pushed through the melted flesh beneath.

'Beautiful, isn't it?' Didric said, stroking the ruined skin with a long, tapered finger. 'The night you did this to me, my father paid through the nose for a summoner to be brought in to perform the healing spell. Lord Faversham, as a matter of fact. Funny that he was unknowingly cleaning up his own son's mess, wouldn't you agree?'

Fletcher was dumbstruck, though whether it was the paralysis, or shock, he didn't know. How had Didric heard about Fletcher's supposed relationship to the Favershams? A lot had changed in a year.

'In truth, I should probably thank you,' Didric said, brushing the long hair on the unburned side of his head to cover the melted scalp. 'You are the reason for both the best and the worst things that have happened to me this past year.'

'How?' Fletcher choked, watching Rubens crawl on to Didric's chest. Didric wasn't a summoner . . . was someone else controlling the Mite, to trick him?

'It's all thanks to you, Fletcher.' Didric gave him a lopsided smile and flared a wyrdlight into existence, casting the room in electric blue light. 'It is a phenomenon that has occurred only once before in recorded history, though legends of it have always pervaded the summoning world. A magical attack that brings the victim close to death will occasionally pass the gift on to them. Something about the way the demon's mana interacts with the body. Your Salamander's flames may have charred my vocal cords and ruined my face, but they imparted a priceless gift as well. For that, I thank you.'

'There's no way.' Fletcher's mind reeled from the implication.

'It is true,' Didric stated, stroking Rubens's carapace. 'It happened with another noble family, centuries ago, in a sibling argument gone wrong. Manticore venom, straight into the younger brother's bloodstream. A lethal dose that should have killed him. Instead, he inherited the gift.'

Didric grinned at the horror on Fletcher's face. He was enjoying this.

'Come, it is time for your trial. Don't worry, you'll be back in your squalid hole soon enough. I can't wait to lock you back in here and throw away the key.'

Fletcher staggered to his feet, swaying slightly as his muscles shivered and tensed from the venom. A trial . . . justice, finally?

He felt the faintest glimmer of hope, for the first time in what felt like a lifetime.

He pointed his tattooed palm at the straw, where Ignatius was hiding. The pentacle on his skin burned violet, and the demon dissolved into threads of white light that glided into his hand. It was best to keep the demon infused within him, so nobody could separate them. He didn't want to imagine being imprisoned without his little companion.

'You first,' Didric said, jerking the pistol towards the open doorway.

Fletcher stumbled out of the cell. For a moment he delighted in his newfound freedom, enjoying the feeling of walking more than a few paces in one direction. Then the cold tip of the pistol's muzzle was pressed into the back of his neck.

'Try not to make any sudden movements. I wouldn't want to blow your head off before the fun begins,' Didric snarled, as they walked down a long, stony corridor. Doors identical to Fletcher's own cell were embedded in the walls. It was deathly quiet, the silence broken only by the echo of their footsteps.

Didric halted him at a staircase also built into the wall. On either side, the corridor stretched for hundreds of feet, before disappearing into gloomy darkness.

'We keep the most dangerous prisoners here, people like you – rebels, murderers, rapists. The king pays us handsomely to keep them here, against the cost of a bucket of water and one meal a day. It's a beautiful thing.'

Fletcher shuddered, imagining what it would be like being alone in the cell, with no Ignatius, books or spells to keep himself sane, and the knowledge that he would never leave there again.

He felt a flash of pity for the lost souls trapped inside, horrendous though their crimes might be. Then he realised that he could very well be joining them soon, forever entombed in the deep bowels of the earth. Icy tendrils of fear gripped his heart.

'Keep moving,' Didric spat, prodding him up the stairs. They spiralled upwards as they did on the inside of a dwarven home, though at intervals there were barred doors, with a guard holding them open. On and on they went, until Fletcher's knees ached under the strain. He had tried his best to exercise in the confines of the cell, but so many months without walking or enough food had left him weak and malnourished. He did not know if he could survive another year in such conditions, let alone a lifetime.

Didric pushed him through a large set of doors at the top of the staircase and into a crowded courtyard. Around them, guards formed up in rows, performing musket and bayonet drills. Their uniform was a wasp-like black and yellow, a mix of chainmail and light leather. There were enough of them to be Didric's own private army.

Fletcher gulped in deep breaths of fresh air. He revelled in the light of the open sky once more, feeling the gentle warmth of the sun on his face. His head spun with vertigo at the expanse above him, but he opened his arms wide and felt the cool breeze on his skin. It was heavenly.

Didric shoved Fletcher ahead of him and they made their way through a large set of iron gates and on to the street. Fletcher was surprised to find that he knew where they were. He turned and took in the prison behind him, recognising some of the features built around it. It was Didric's former mansion.

'Love what you've done with the place,' Fletcher said drily.

'Yes, the old stomping ground. It was time for an upgrade, what with my new station in life. What do you think of our new quarters?'

Didric pointed upwards. The village of Pelt was built at the base of the Beartooth Mountains' largest peak. It shadowed the village at sunset, towering over them like a vast monolith. Fletcher followed Didric's finger and saw that the tip of the peak no longer existed. Instead, a castle had been built in its place, all crenellations, towers and arrow slits. Cannons lined the walls, the black holes of their barrels menacing the village, as if they might open fire at any moment. It was more a fortress than a home.

'The safest place in Hominum, stocked with enough supplies to endure a siege of ten years. The elves could betray us, the orcs could invade Hominum – the prisoners could even take over the village, and it wouldn't matter. The greatest army in the world couldn't breach those walls, even if they could climb the sheer cliffs on either side.'

'You sound paranoid, Didric,' Fletcher replied, though Didric's words had taken him off guard. 'Like you have something to hide.'

'Only our immense wealth, Fletcher. My father doesn't trust the banks. He should know, he used to be a banker.'

'A crooked moneylender does not a banker make,' Fletcher replied. The boy stiffened but prodded him on, ignoring the jibe.

As they walked down the deserted streets, Fletcher saw poverty everywhere.

Many of the houses and shops were empty shells, while others had been converted into jails. Rough, dirty faces were pressed against the bars, silently watching Didric's strutting figure with hatred in their eyes. The entire place stank of misery and desperation; it was a far throw from the industrious little village Fletcher had grown up in.

Didric's father, Caspar Cavell, had become the richest man in the village by lending to the needy and the desperate, tricking them into signing ironclad contracts that would end up costing them far more than they borrowed. It looked as if the Cavells had called in all that was owed, taking their debtors' savings and kicking most of the citizens of Pelt out of their homes in order to build the prison.

Disgusted, Fletcher slowed and flexed his fingers, fighting the temptation to punch Didric's face in.

'Move,' Didric snarled, slapping Fletcher across the back of the head with his free hand.

Fletcher burned with anger, but his hands were still numb. The paralysis was dulling his reactions. Even if he were at his best, he doubted his chances at wrestling away the gun pressed into the small of his back. He would have to wait.

They reached the front gates which led out of the village, and Fletcher's stomach lurched. Berdon's hut was gone! But that was not the only thing unusual about the scene. The area around the front gates had been flattened, with racks of pikes, bayonets and swords replacing the houses. Stranger still, there seemed to be a queue of men lining up by the gates in front of a long, low table piled with red uniforms.

No. Not men.

'Dwarves!' Fletcher breathed.

Hundreds of them, even more than he had seen at the dwarven war council. They wore traditional dwarven garb – heavy leathers with canvas shirts. They seemed rougher than the dwarves Fletcher had encountered before, their braids loose and uneven, the clothing stained with mud, grime and sweat. Their faces were dark and brooding, and they talked among themselves with low, angry voices.

'They've just marched over Beartooth to collect their new gear,' Didric said, smiling, 'after two years of keeping the northern front safe from the elves. It's taken a long time for the elven war to end, though I wish it was longer. The peace talks were delayed when the elven clan leaders saw the state of that she-elf after the Tournament at Vocans. She was your friend, wasn't she?'

Images of the broken and bruised figure of Sylva came unbidden to Fletcher's mind, but he held his tongue. He knew that he couldn't trust anything Didric told him about her.

'My lord!' a guard shouted, bringing Fletcher back to reality. 'This reprobate tried to murder you. It isn't safe. Let us escort him for you.'

'Did I ask for your opinion, bootlicker?' Didric spat, brandishing the pistol. 'Do not presume to speak to me unless spoken to first. Get back to work.'

'As you wish, my lord,' the man said, bowing low. Didric shoved him away with his boot, sending the man sprawling in the mud.

Fletcher was disgusted by the way his nemesis held himself, as if he were above them all. He turned on Didric as the final vestiges of paralysis left him.

'You have the guards calling you lord?' Fletcher said, layering his voice with contempt. 'I bet they laugh at you behind your back. You're nothing more than a jumped-up gaoler, you pompous arse.'

For a moment Didric stared at him, his face slowly turning red. Fletcher suspected nobody had spoken to him like that for a long time. Then, to his surprise, Didric burst out laughing. The hoarse cackle echoed across the courtyard, turning heads as Didric heaved with mirth.

'Do you know why they call me lord, Fletchy?' Didric gasped, wiping a tear from his eye. 'It's because I *am* a lord. Lord Cavell.'

## 3

Fletcher stared at Didric in horror. Suddenly, small details he had overlooked came into focus. The heavy signet ring on Didric's little finger. The uniforms of the guards, so specifically coloured and heavily armoured; they *were* Didric's private army – a privilege the king afforded only to the nobility.

There was even a coat of arms sewn on to the chest of Didric's jacket, depicting the bars of a jail, with two crossed swords behind them, emblazoned in the same yellow and black that his soldiers wore. A fitting emblem.

Didric cocked his head, obviously taking pleasure in Fletcher's dismay. Fletcher, in turn, tried to remain expressionless, though it was almost impossible. He was overcome with disgust.

'While you have been rotting away in a prison cell, I have been at Vocans, in my very own luxurious suite. No commoners' quarters for me,' Didric boasted, his lopsided smile widening. 'Lord Forsyth was kind enough to give me Rubens, a demon that had been in his family for generations. Of course, it is not my only demon, but it got me started. In fact, you might be interested to know that the Tournament is in just a few days' time. I really should be training, but I couldn't miss this – not for all the world.'

'Let's just get it over with,' Fletcher snarled, looking around for the courthouse. 'You talk too much.'

'Oh very well. I'm surprised you're in such a hurry to get back to your prison cell. If I were you, I would savour the next few hours of fresh air and natural sunlight, Fletcher. It will be your last.' Didric pointed the way, before pressing the pistol into Fletcher's back.

The courthouse had been converted from the old village hall, a large oval-shaped building complete with a steeple and large oak doors. Its walls were freshly painted in white and the sigil of the Judges was emblazoned over the door – a black gavel and block that loomed ominously as Didric led him through the wide open doors.

The inside of the room reminded Fletcher of a church, with low benches on either side, filled with people. At the end of the centre aisle, two guards stood waiting with chains and manacles. Behind them, a grim-faced judge, resplendent in black robes and a powdered white wig, stared out from a high table.

'It was genius to convert this place into a courthouse,' Didric whispered out of the corner of his mouth. 'Now we can take the accused straight from sentencing to prison. Of course, it's never usually this full. You've drawn quite a crowd!'

Fletcher tried to ignore the staring faces on either side, crushed with self-consciousness in the solemn silence of the room. He realised that the clothes that clung to his body were barely more than stinking rags, for there was little he could do to wash with the limited water they gave him in prison. His hair hung in greasy locks around his face and his adolescent beard and moustache grew in sparse, scruffy patches. He imagined if he looked in the mirror, he would hardly recognise himself.

Didric led him down the aisle as if he were part of some macabre wedding party, proudly displaying his captive. Fletcher darted quick looks to his left and right, hoping to see Berdon, but if he was there, Fletcher could not find him. Finally, they reached the pulpit.

'Chain him,' the judge ordered in a high, reedy voice. Fletcher allowed the guards to shackle him to the floor, like a bear being baited in a pit. Soon, they would unleash the hounds.

He stood in silence, waiting for what was next. He had no cards to play here, no way out. His best bet would be to try to escape after the sentencing. It might be difficult if Didric took him back to his cell personally. Even so, Fletcher knew one thing. He would rather die fighting than be left to rot in that cell.

'Bring out the defence.' The judge motioned at the doors to his left. A guard knocked twice, then opened the doors with a ceremonial flourish. A tall, battle-scarred man in blue officer's uniform stepped through.

'Arcturus!' Fletcher cried, all sense of decorum forgotten. Arcturus gave him a grim smile and a tiny shake of the head, as if to tell him to be quiet.

'Silence,' the judge ordered, pointing a long, bony finger at Fletcher. 'One more outburst from you and we shall have you gagged.'

'My apologies, your honour,' Fletcher said, as Arcturus

came to stand beside him. 'I did not mean to disrespect your courtroom.'

'Hmm, very good,' the judge replied, lifting his glasses and peering at him down a long, aquiline nose. He looked surprised at Fletcher's civility. Perhaps he was used to far less courteous treatment from those on trial.

'Be that as it may, I will have order in my courtroom. Is that clear?'

'Yes, your honour,' Arcturus said, cutting Fletcher off before he could say anything else. His message was clear. Fletcher was not to speak again.

'Who will act as the prosecution?' the judge asked, shuffling some papers on his desk.

'I will, your honour,' Didric announced, turning to face the crowd.

'Ahem. That is very . . . unorthodox,' the judge said, as Didric strutted to a table and chair on the left side of the room. 'But not outside the realm of the law. I should remind you that you will be unable to testify for the prosecution, should you choose to represent yourself. Is that understood?'

'It's an open and shut case, your honour. The sworn testimony from the two witnesses will be more than enough to convict this villain, whether I take the stand or not,' Didric replied, smiling confidently at the watching assembly.

'Very well,' the judge said, shaking his head with disapproval. 'Will the prosecution and the defence be seated. Guards, bring out the first witness!'

Arcturus and Didric sat down on their respective sides of the courtroom, leaving Fletcher chained to the floor in front of the

21

judge. The guard waited until everyone was settled, then opened the side door with an officious bow. For a moment Fletcher did not recognise the young woman who stepped through the door. But then she glanced at him with a sneer, and he saw who it was.

Calista had changed since he had last seen her, advancing on him in the crypt. Her hair, once a raggedly shorn mop, had grown out and glossed into an elegant wave of black. She had chosen a baby-blue dress, edged with lace and frills, giving her an almost doll-like appearance. Her face remained hard and pinched, as it had always been, but she – or a stylist – had gone to great lengths to powder and paint it, softening her features and smoothing her skin.

Even the way she walked had changed, her usual bow-legged gait seemingly gone as she took her seat at the podium beside the judge. Now that she was in full view of the crowd, she bit her lip and edged away from Fletcher, as if she was afraid of him.

Fletcher knew that he was in trouble. They had turned the tomboyish guardswoman into a wide-eyed innocent. How could he convince the judge that it was in fact Calista, along with Didric and Jakov, who had attempted *his* murder? The spectators were already muttering to themselves and looking at Fletcher with accusation in their eyes.

'I will remind you all that the final decision rests with me, as do all matters of criminal law. There will be no jury or trial by peers – that is reserved for military courts. As such, I will have no discussions, no side-taking in the crowd. Should you wish to do so, I suggest you leave my courtroom.' The judge gave them all a stern look, before turning to the podium next to him.

'Now, my dear, are you ready to begin?'

Calista nodded, twisting her hands in her lap. Didric rose and went to stand beside her, leaning nonchalantly against the podium.

'I'll keep this simple, so as not to have Calista up here any longer than she has to be. Just focus on me, Calista, and ignore everyone else. There's nothing to be afraid of. Just tell the nice judge what happened on the night I was attacked and it will all be over soon.'

Calista lowered her head demurely, hiding her face from the courtroom with a curtain of black hair. It was a masterful performance, one that would have almost convinced Fletcher himself, had she not flashed a sadistic smile at him from behind her tresses.

'Didric, Jakov and I were standing watch at the village gates, that night,' Calista said, with just a hint of a tremble in her voice. 'We saw Fletcher leaving his hut, carrying a heavy book. There was a soldier selling one just like it in the market a day earlier, and we assumed he had stolen it and was going to hide the evidence. So, we followed him in the dark, to the graveyard, of all places. When we confronted him, he claimed to have bought the book—'

Didric interrupted her with a raised hand.

'Please take note that the investigation found a significant amount of money sitting in the defendant's room on the night of the incident, unspent. It is unlikely that he ever purchased the book. We can add theft to his list of crimes.'

'One . . . count . . . of theft . . .' The judge scribbled at his desk with a swan-feather quill. 'Quite the deviant we have here.'

'Indeed, your honour. We confiscated the money, naturally,'

Didric said, winking at Fletcher. 'My apologies for interrupting you, Calista. Please continue.'

'Thank you, Lord Cavell,' Calista said, a theatrical quiver in her voice. 'Foolishly, we chose to believe Fletcher's story. He then told us that he was going to use the book to attempt to summon a demon and asked if we would stay and watch. We thought it would be funny, so we did . . .'

She was trembling now, darting quick, fearful glances at Fletcher. He had to admit, she was a good actress.

'I don't know how, but he did it. There was so much noise and light, it was like the world was about to end! That was when it happened.'

A single tear trickled down her cheek. The judge handed her a handkerchief from the high table and murmured, 'Go on. Tell us what he did.'

Calista gulped and set her jaw, wiping the tear from her face. She pointed at Fletcher, her finger quivering with emotion.

'He turned on us, tried to kill us!' she cried, leaping to her feet. 'He hated us, blamed us for every misfortune he had ever suffered. It was as if he had gone mad! I remember how he laughed as he herded us into the chapel, our swords useless against his demon's flames. And when I started crying, he focused on me, telling me I would be the first to die.'

She stepped down from the podium and stalked towards Fletcher, keeping her finger pointed like a pistol.

'*Ladies first*, isn't that what you said?' she hissed. 'You monster!'

Calista turned and buried her face in Didric's chest. He patted her shoulder while she heaved with fitful sobs, each one more dramatic than the last. Fletcher rolled his eyes in disgust, earning himself a glare from the judge. Calista let Didric go and made a final, impassioned speech.

'It was only when Didric – brave Didric – stepped in front of me, that Fletcher left me alone. Didric tried to reason with him, but it was useless. All of a sudden the demon attacked Didric's face with fire. Even as his hair was ablaze, Didric managed to fight it off, scaring Fletcher down the passageway beneath the chapel. It was then that Didric fell unconscious and cracked his skull. We carried him back to his father's house. The rest you know.'

The judge steepled his fingers, giving Calista a contemplative look. Despite her sobbing, her face was dry as a bone and her cheeks were puffed with excitement, flushing red. For a moment, Fletcher thought the judge sensed her deception, but then the old man smiled at her kindly and thanked her for her testimony. She gave Didric a deep curtsy, before departing the room without a backwards glance.

'Bring out the next witness!' the judge ordered.

# 4

Jakov had grown in the two years that Fletcher had been away, the last vestiges of puberty gone, to leave a Herculean giant. His arms were made up of thick slabs of muscle that shifted like the haunches of a horse, and he walked with the top-heavy shamble of a jungle gorilla. The guard now wore Didric's black and yellow uniform, and the horizontal stripes accentuated his broad and powerful chest.

'Please be seated, Sergeant Jakov,' Didric said, pulling his chair out for him. 'My first question is, can you confirm that Calista's story is entirely truthful and accurate?'

'I can, milord. Hearing her was like reliving that night all over again.'

'Good. I know you are a busy man, so we don't need you to tell it again in your own words. Please explain what happened after Fletcher's murder attempt.'

'Right you are, sir,' Jakov said, tugging his forelock. He took a deep breath and began to speak.

'After we delivered Didric to his father, I went to wake

the rest of the guards. We found the door to Fletcher's home barred. Once we had broken it down, we encountered resistance from Fletcher's adoptive father, Berdon. He damn near killed us – he's almost as big as me you know – but I managed to disarm him. Some of the boys got a little . . . overexcited at that point. Let's just say Berdon didn't do much blacksmithing for a while after that night. Bones take a while to heal.'

'You animal!' Fletcher growled, hatred bubbling inside him, caustic and hot. He knew they wanted to make him angry, so he would act out in front of the judge. But the words were out before he could bite them back.

'One more word out of you, Master Fletcher!' the judge said, knocking his gavel against the desk for emphasis. 'One word, and it's back to the cells, where you can wait to hear the verdict.'

Fletcher bit his lip until he tasted hot blood, trying to stop himself from crying out at the unfairness of it all. Images of them beating Berdon's unconscious body flooded his mind, and he could not shake them from his thoughts.

'After that, we confiscated all the possessions in the property as evidence. In the fighting, the fire from Berdon's forge somehow spread. His hut burned to the ground that night.'

Fletcher felt hot tears running down his cheeks. He sank to his knees. In one night, the man he loved most in the world lost everything. All because of him.

'Your honour, I don't understand what this has to do with the charge against the defendant. Can we get to the point, please?' Arcturus's voice was tight and angry.

'I agree. Thank you, Captain Arcturus.' The judge nodded.

'Lord Cavell, unless you have any actual evidence to present, I find this line of questioning entirely irrelevant. Is there any?'

'No, your honour. I think Jakov has said his piece,' Didric replied.

'Very well. You may go, Sergeant Jakov.'

'Thank you, milord.'

The big man eased himself from the podium and walked out the side door. Just before he was out of sight, he gave Fletcher a sarcastic little wave. Fletcher looked away, but his gut twisted with a fresh wave of fury. He held it in, knowing that Jakov's testimony was intended to goad him into a reaction.

'Is that all then, Lord Cavell?' the judge asked, shuffling his notes.

'It is, your honour. The prosecution rests. As I said earlier, I believe you'll find this is an open and shut case. I recommend a minimum sentence of life in prison.'

'Thank you, Lord Cavell. I will take this under due consideration,' the judge said, though his eyebrows creased with annoyance.

A low hum of conversation permeated the room as Arcturus stood and collected his notes.

'I guess all my preparation for training as a judge paid off, huh, Fletcher,' Didric croaked as he made his way back to his chair. 'Although, one look at that fuddy-duddy makes me glad I ended up going down a different path.'

'Like they would ever let a monster like you become a judge,' Fletcher replied, hatred dripping from his words.

Didric's shoulders stiffened and he turned back, despite a stern cough from the judge.

'Remember, Fletcher, it's *my* prison,' Didric hissed, his eyes blazing with madness. 'If you think withholding food is the worst I can do, your imagination is severely lacking.'

'Lord Cavell, I must ask you to return to your seat,' the judge ordered.

'Actually, your honour, I would prefer it if Didric stayed.' Arcturus strode forward and lifted Fletcher to his feet. The firm grip on Fletcher's shoulders steadied the erratic beat of his heart. He took a deep breath and met the judge's gaze.

'Very well. Lord Cavell, please take the stand,' the judge said, waving Didric back to the podium.

'Would it be unorthodox if I was to bring Sergeant Jakov and Private Calista back in as well?' Arcturus proposed.

'It would be, but it is within the realm of the law. But let me ask this first: as I understand, you are not a qualified lawyer, Captain Arcturus. Why is it you who is defending the boy?' the judge said.

'I defend him because nobody else would, for fear of reprisal from the Triumvirate. Cowards, all of them.' Arcturus shook his head, his voice bitter.

'I am sorry, I am not familiar with this term, *triumvirate*,' the judge said, furrowing his brow.

Fletcher was curious – he was also unfamiliar with the term.

'Lord Cavell, Lady Faversham and Lord Forsyth have close ties in politics and business. That is what the three families have come to be known as,' Arcturus replied.

So Didric was in cahoots with the Favershams and the Forsyths. Fletcher almost smiled to himself. How fitting. All the people who hated him most in the world, working together to bring him down. He should have known.

'Perhaps they would not represent him because it is so obvious he is guilty,' Didric said loudly. 'No lawyer in his right mind would take a case like this.'

'Quiet!' Arcturus snapped, turning on Didric. 'I did not speak during your plea. I would appreciate it if you afforded me the same courtesy.'

Didric rolled his eyes, holding up his hands in mock surrender.

'Bring in Private Calista and Sergeant Jakov,' the judge ordered. 'And fetch chairs for them too.'

It took but a few seconds for the guard to bring them back in. Fletcher suspected they had been listening at the door.

'Let's get to it then, shall we?' the judge said. He sniffed irritably as the guard dragged two chairs beside the podium, making a loud grating sound against the floor. 'State your case and I shall give you my verdict.'

Fletcher watched the three onstage, wondering what game Arcturus was playing.

He had never told Arcturus, nor anyone else, the full story of what had happened that night. Kicking himself for it, Fletcher sank into an even deeper despair as Arcturus began to speak.

'I want to first point out to the honourable judge, that there is no evidence whatsoever to support Private Calista and Sergeant Jakov's claims, other than their testimony. Therefore, we must conclude that should their story be proved inconsistent, the judge must acquit Fletcher of all charges. Is that right, your honour?'

'Well, that is a very simplistic interpretation of the law,' the judge harrumphed. 'If you cast sufficient doubt over their story, yes, I will be more inclined to find Fletcher innocent. However, you must also provide an alternative version of events, with proof.'

'Thank y—' Arcturus began.

'Keep in mind that the matching testimony of three individuals is very powerful,' the judge interrupted. 'There must be significant doubt, Captain Arcturus. Significant indeed.'

'Very well, your honour,' Arcturus said, bowing his head with respect. 'In that case, I shall begin by proposing a very different set of events that night.'

Clasping his hands behind his back, Arcturus turned back to the three witnesses.

'On a cold evening, two years ago, Fletcher befriends an old soldier. As I understand, his name is Private Rotherham, also known as Rotter to his compatriots on the front lines. He was the man who was initially in possession of the summoner's book. The two are drinking in the local tavern when Didric accosts them, accompanied by Jakov, and demands the book in exchange for a paltry sum that was never agreed to in the first place. Do you deny these events, Didric?'

'I believe the proper form of address is Lord Cavell,' Didric said, crossing his arms and challenging Arcturus with an obstinate glare.

'Lord Cavell,' Arcturus said, forcing the words out through gritted teeth. 'Do you deny the charges? I have found several witnesses who would swear to it. It looks as if not everyone in the village would take your money, even those your father bankrupted.'

Didric flushed with anger, but kept his fury in check,

responding in a measured voice.

'I do not deny the charges. We did meet in the tavern that night, though I would debate with you whether we had agreed on the sale or not.'

'Regardless,' Arcturus said, turning to face the crowd and speaking louder. 'There was an altercation between the four gentlemen, resulting in Didric attempting to kill Fletcher with a concealed blade. I ask you again, *Lord* Cavell – do you deny it?'

'It was self-defence. The madman was choking me,' Didric said, waving his hand as if it were barely worth mentioning. 'In fact, it only proves that he already had the intention to kill me, not to mention an even greater motive to do it, given what transpired that night.'

'I am glad that you brought up self-defence,' Arcturus said, pacing to the other side of the room. 'For that will be very relevant later in the case. Now, given that Rotherham and Fletcher were friends and had even fought side by side, why would you be so surprised that Fletcher was later found in possession of the book?'

'I didn't say that, Calista did. She hadn't been involved in the fight, so she didn't know. I guess that was her reason for following, not ours,' Didric replied smoothly, the good side of his face half crooked with a confident smile.

'So why did *you* follow him then?' Arcturus asked.

'Curiosity. A boy going to a graveyard in the middle of the night is suspicious, don't you think?'

'Nothing to do with getting revenge for him beating you in that fight the night before?' Arcturus pressed. Fletcher tried to hold back a bitter laugh, but the garbled snort that resulted earned him a severe look from the judge.

'No,' Didric responded, leaning back and crossing his arms again.

'Well then. I guess we'll just have to trust you on that. I find it curious that you and Jakov would not mention your fight to Calista, given the several hours you must have been together, but I'll leave that for the honourable judge to consider,' Arcturus said.

The judge huffed, then, after a shrug, scribbled something in his notes.

'So then, at the graveyard,' Arcturus said, tapping his chin. 'Despite you having almost disembowelled him the night before and there being no love lost between you, Fletcher invites you to watch him attempt to summon a demon? There was no argument, no bad blood, when you surprised him there?'

'I am a forgiving person, Captain. I didn't threaten him and he certainly didn't threaten me – not with two armed guards behind my back. Obviously, he was planning to set the demon upon us, so he acted all nice until he had the demon under his control.'

'Ah. Control. I'm glad you brought that up. Tell me, what is the first thing you learn in summoning lessons at school, after infusing and your introduction to the ether?' Arcturus asked.

'Demonic control . . .' Didric admitted, a flash of doubt crossing his face for the first time. Fletcher couldn't help but smile. This line of questioning was obviously not one the bully had expected.

'Do you really think, within a few minutes of summoning a

demon, that a novice such as Fletcher could make it attack you? Without provocation, no less?' Arcturus demanded, waving at Fletcher as if he were an incompetent. For the first time, Fletcher was glad of his filthy appearance. It certainly didn't paint him as an expert summoner.

'As I'm sure the judge is aware, controlling a demon is nearly impossible for someone who has just summoned their first one, especially when that person has had no previous knowledge of the art,' Arcturus continued, raising his eyebrows.

'Yes, this is true,' the judge said, after a moment. 'That *does* merit some thought.'

'Maybe there was something in the book that taught him how to do it properly,' Didric suggested, though his face had lost some of its colour.

'I have here a copy of the same book, for evidence,' Arcturus said, striding back to his desk and pulling out a thick sheaf of papers from a satchel he had brought with him. He slammed it on the table with a weighty thump, releasing a puff of dust. 'I can assure the judge that there are no instructions on demonic control within its pages. Shall we take a recess for you to read through it, your honour?'

The judge looked at the tome in horror; it would take days for him to read it all. Fletcher couldn't help but grin at Didric's crestfallen expression. The arrogant boy had shot himself in the foot by preventing a real lawyer from speaking on his behalf. Only a summoner of Arcturus's experience would have thought of that line of argument.

'I'll take you at your word, Captain,' the judge said, clearing his throat. 'I agree that it does cast some doubt over the prosecution's version of events, but one might also argue that Fletcher is naturally gifted. I will, however, take it under due consideration. Please move on to your next point.'

'Certainly, sir. I will now question each witness in turn. I also ask that they do not speak until I tell them to,' Arcturus said, clasping his hands behind his back and stepping in front of the three witnesses.

'Now, I want you to go into as much detail as possible. Let's start with you, Private Calista. Tell me, what happened at the graveyard? What did Fletcher use to summon the demon?'

'I . . . can't really remember,' Calista said, momentarily taken aback. 'It was two years ago, you know.'

'I do know. Just like you know exactly what he said and how he said it, on that night. But you don't remember the tools he used? You witnessed a demon-summoning, but it didn't seem a memorable event to you?' Arcturus asked.

Calista looked over at Didric for help, but he stared ahead, his eyes fixed on Fletcher.

'I think . . . he just read from the book.'

Fletcher kept his face as straight as possible, though inside he was rejoicing. Didric had obviously never told them how novices usually summoned their first demon.

'Anything else?' Arcturus asked.

'I don't remember . . .' Calista said, her voice wavering.

Didric's face was emotionless, but Fletcher could see the muscles of his jaw clench.

'How strange. You described everything else in so much detail. Does that not seem unusual to you, your honour?' Arcturus asked, his face a picture of innocence.

'It does indeed,' the judge said gravely, writing a note on the paper in front of him.

'Perhaps Jakov can shed some light on the subject,' Arcturus mused, touching a finger to his lip.

Jakov's mouth hung open, his eyes darting around the room as if looking for clues.

'For heaven's sake,' Didric blurted. 'He used a scroll and a leather mat with a pentacle on it, like every other summoner before him. Why are we continuing with this farcical line of questioning?'

'Lord Cavell!' the judge snapped, banging his gavel against the table. 'You will be quiet!'

'My apologies, your honour,' Didric said, holding his hands up in surrender. 'I was just impatient to tell my side of the story.'

'Not. Another. Word,' the judge ordered, punctuating each syllable with a stab of his finger.

Fletcher felt a flash of hope, as he finally understood what Arcturus was trying to do. Didric had already fallen into his trap.

Arcturus continued to address Jakov. 'Is that so? He read from a scroll and used a leather mat to summon the demon?'

'It's like Didric said,' Jakov said slowly, looking desperately at Didric for confirmation. 'I remember it now.'

'Ah, good. I'm glad we have all that sorted,' Arcturus said, nodding to himself. He began to walk back to his podium, then paused, as if he had just remembered something.

'Lord Cavell. Where do you think he got these two items? I thought he was given only a book by the old soldier?'

Didric glared at Arcturus, and Fletcher could see the boy's

mind working as he considered what to say. Didric had not prepared for this.

'I have no idea,' Didric replied, looking at the ceiling as if deep in thought. 'If I was to speculate, Fletcher was given those items as well. The soldier stole a summoner's satchel, which would definitely have contained a summoning leather of some kind. The same with the scroll.'

'Can you describe the scroll?' Arcturus asked. 'Perhaps tell us what colour ink was written on it. How large was the scroll? How white was the paper?'

'You are not testing the validity of my story, Captain. You are simply testing my memory,' Didric said, then sat back and smiled as if he had scored a point.

'Nevertheless, please indulge me,' Arcturus said, giving Didric an innocent smile.

'The scroll was obviously an orc's, written in their language. I remember it very clearly.'

Fletcher wondered for a moment how Didric knew of the scroll's original owner. Then he remembered he had told Inquisitor Rook that the scroll was of orcish origin, in front of the entire class. Anyone could have told him that . . . he only hoped that was all Didric knew about it.

'The ink was dark in colour, that's all I can remember. The size was also difficult to judge, since each end was rolled up. The graveyard was too poorly lit to tell how white the paper was. Does that answer your question?'

'It does. But saying the ink was dark – surely any writing would need to be dark, in order to be read. You're absolutely sure you can't give us any more detail on the colour of the ink?'

'Do you really think that a murderer's innocence can be proven because I can't remember the exact colour of ink on the scroll? You should stick to war, Captain – you make a poor lawyer. It used dark ink and that's all you'll get from me.'

'You're quite sure?' Arcturus said.

'Completely,' Didric replied, folding his arms defiantly.

'And you, Jakov. Do you corroborate this story?' Arcturus asked, striding over to him.

'Yes, sir,' Jakov mumbled.

'Calista, has that description reminded you of anything?'

'I think there was a scroll and mat like that, yes,' Calista muttered.

'So, to summarise. Didric and Jakov say that Fletcher used a rolled-up paper scroll of indeterminate size, written in dark ink to summon the demon, as well as a leather mat with a pentacle on it. Calista now corroborates that story,' Arcturus announced.

'Yes, Captain, that is quite clear,' the judge said, reading through his notes. 'Can you please let me know where you are going with this?'

'Of course,' Arcturus said. He strode over to his rucksack and withdrew an item, brandishing it in the air for all to see.

'I give you . . . the scroll.'

# 5

After an entire year, Fletcher had almost forgotten how grisly the summoning scroll actually was.

The scroll was a single sheet of yellowed, leathery material. The orc lettering was formed by roughly raised lines on the surface, so that even a blind man could read it using touch alone. The faintest trace of Baker's pencilled translation was etched below, barely visible to the naked eye.

'This scroll, if you can even call it that, is nothing like the object Didric described. There is no ink to speak of, no rolled edges on either side, nor is it made of paper or anything even resembling it,' Arcturus announced, his finger pointed at Didric in accusation. 'It is in fact made from someone's skin. The victim would have had the lettering carved into their back, then once the wounds had healed and scarified, the skin would be flayed from them and dried to form this disgusting object.'

There were gasps of horror from the crowd. One man ran out of the courtroom, holding his hands over his mouth. As the sounds of his retching permeated the room, others followed, tripping over themselves to get into the fresh air. Not all of them made it outside in time.

'Guards, get someone to clean that up,' the judge said, his own face turning a tinge of green. 'We will take a brief recess.' He hurried down the steps of his podium and disappeared through the side door.

Didric had gone pale, but he kept completely silent. As he stared at Fletcher, the colour rushed back to his face, his shock turning into anger.

'Fletcher,' Arcturus said, squatting down beside him. 'Are you injured? Have they hurt you?'

'I'm fine. It . . . it's good to see you.'

Suddenly, Fletcher felt awkward, his words tripping from his tongue. He wasn't used to kindness . . . not any more. His body shook and he felt briny tears trickle down his face. He hadn't realised how lonely he had been until that very moment.

Arcturus squeezed Fletcher's shoulder.

'We're going to get you out of here. You're sorely missed.'

'How are the others?' Fletcher asked.

'We haven't seen Sylva since the Tournament. She was flown back to her home country as soon as King Harold got word of her injuries. He was furious, as were the elves of course.' Arcturus paused, then took a deep breath. 'Berdon has been thrown in jail on some trumped-up charges. They can only hold him for a few nights, so don't worry. Didric just didn't want you to see him. He denied you even that shred of comfort.'

'That snake,' Fletcher growled, grinding his knuckles into the floorboards. 'I'm going to get him if it's the last thing I do.'

'Careful,' Arcturus said, looking around in case anyone had heard. 'We're at a murder trial, remember.'

'What about Othello?' Fletcher asked.

'Othello's at Vocans. Atilla and a young dwarf girl, Cress, joined the academy this year. In fact, they are preparing for their first Tournament as we speak. Othello stayed on to make sure their transition went smoothly – he turned down his commission to do so. It means he will be able to lead the dwarven recruits, so in a way it is ideal.'

Arcturus looked over his shoulder as the judge returned to his seat, the green tinge gone from his face.

'Othello misses you terribly. It is thanks to his family that we are having this trial at all. They petitioned the king to make sure you had a hearing and managed to secure you a judge that hadn't taken a bribe from the Triumvirate. Trust me when I tell you that there weren't many left.'

'Wait . . . about the Triumvirate—' Fletcher began to ask.

The judge rapped his desk with the gavel, turning the room silent once again.

Arcturus gave him a look that said, *Later*.

'Captain, it is clear that there are some discrepancies in the story presented by the witnesses and the prosecution. Do you have any more evidence to present?'

'I do, your honour,' Arcturus said, striding back to the witness podium. 'But first, I would like to ask the witnesses a few more questions. Please reply in turn – from Jakov, to Calista, to Lord Cavell. Is there anything you would like to change about your story?'

Jakov's eyes flicked to Didric, who gave an almost

imperceptible shake of his head.

'No,' Jakov said.

'I can't remember. No,' Calista muttered, looking at her hands.

Didric stood, addressing the room in a loud, confident voice.

'I would like to say that this orc scroll proves nothing. The memory is a fickle thing; your line of questioning simply led me to describe it in that way.'

'Yes, that was because you had never seen the scroll before. It was not your memory I was leading, it was your lie,' Arcturus replied, raising his voice so the crowd could hear. 'Now answer my question.'

'*Obviously* I did not see the scroll as well as I thought I did,' Didric said in a bored voice. 'But my story still stands. You cannot summon a demon without a pentacle made of, or inscribed on, organic material. He had a summoning leather. I saw it.'

Arcturus grinned, clapping his hands together with finality.

'You're half right, Lord Cavell. You *do* need a pentacle formed of organic material to summon a demon. Can you think of what Fletcher would have had on his person that matched that description?'

'Wait . . .' Didric stammered, his eyes flashing with recognition. But it was too late.

'It was, in fact, the book itself!' Arcturus announced, reaching into his pack and withdrawing the book cover with a flourish.

It was same one that had been removed from the journal Fletcher had left in his cell. The leather was dusty and wrapped around what must have been the copy of the original, but he recognised the pentacle on the front.

'Another lie,' Arcturus continued, shaking his head. 'I can have witnesses flown in – Dame Fairhaven and Lord Scipio himself – to corroborate that Fletcher told them he used these two items to summon the demon. Will that be necessary, your honour?'

'No, Captain, I believe you. Please give us the version of events as you see it.'

Arcturus turned his back on the crowd, this time directing his line of argument to the judge.

'One night, prior to the night in question, Didric assaulted Fletcher and suffered an embarrassing defeat at his hands, losing much standing amongst his peers. The following evening, he or one of his companions spotted Fletcher going to the graveyard. Didric gathered his accomplices and followed, arriving *after* Fletcher summoned his demon. Seeking revenge, they attacked Fletcher, whose demon reacted instinctively in defence of his master. As the victim, rather than the aggressor, Fletcher ran away. If he had truly wished to murder Didric and his friends, he would have stayed to finish the job, once he had the upper hand.' Arcturus paused, as if something had just occurred to him. 'This was nothing more than a repeat of the previous night's events. Didric attacks Fletcher and is defeated when Fletcher acts in self-defence. There is a pattern here. Consider that, your honour, when coming to your verdict.'

The judge blinked slowly at Arcturus, as if deep in thought. He leaned back in his chair and rubbed his head with his gavel. The room was absolutely silent, every eye focused on the old man as he closed his eyes. The minutes ticked by, the silence weighing heavily on the room. For a moment, Fletcher thought the judge had fallen asleep, so he jumped with shock when he suddenly spoke, his eyes still closed.

'I have come to a decision. Fletcher Wulf, you are accused of the attempted murder of Lord Didric Cavell. Please stand to receive your verdict.'

Fletcher struggled to his feet, forced to hunch awkwardly as the chain attached to his manacles was too short to allow him to stand upright.

This was happening too fast; he had barely begun to process it all. His future hung on a knife's edge, a yawning chasm of despair on one side, an unknown future on the other. He could feel his pulse rushing in his ears as his heart throbbed, so loud that he barely heard the words that came from the judge's mouth.

'I find the defendant . . . innocent of all charges.'

Fletcher collapsed to his knees. He could feel Arcturus pounding him on the back with joy, hear the uproar of the crowd behind him. It was so surreal. He hadn't realised before, but he had never really believed he would be found innocent. Yet somehow, between Othello's family and his teachers at the academy, he had been saved from a lifetime of imprisonment, and more besides.

He looked up at Didric through tear-filled eyes, blinking through the blurry haze. It was strange, but his nemesis didn't look angry. In fact, he was simply frowning, as if mildly annoyed by the verdict.

'Order, order!' the judge bellowed, as the spectators continued to yell in the background. Slowly, silence resumed, the noise dying down with each blow from the judge's gavel.

But one sound remained. A slow clap, coming from the back of the room. It continued, getting louder as it approached them. The judge made no move to quell the noise, furrowing his eyebrows and watching with interest.

'Very well done: most entertaining,' came a sardonic voice.

Inquisitor Rook strode into view, a lopsided sneer on his face. He wore the uniform of the Inquisition, a long black coat not unlike a cassock, with a military flair. Fletcher felt his stomach twist with dislike at the sight of the man. Rook was a racist and a bigot, and bore a deep hatred of Fletcher.

'I must say, you've outdone yourself, Arcturus. A masterful performance. For a second there I thought you had lost but, my oh my, did you turn it around at the end.' Rook continued clapping slowly, smiling and nodding to the crowd.

'Ahem, Inquisitor Rook. I would ask that you be seated so that I can release the boy. You have no jurisdiction over a common-law court. This is not a military tribunal.' The judge's voice was firm, but it had an edge of fear to it that Fletcher didn't like.

Rook nodded thoughtfully to himself, walking past the podiums and allowing his fingers to trail along them.

'I understand, your honour. Forgive me for intruding, but I would not remove the manacles just yet. I have another charge to bring against Master Wulf here.' Rook's eyes flashed menacingly as he spoke, though his face remained a picture of innocence.

'This is preposterous,' Arcturus growled, striding in front of Rook. 'What possible charge could you have to bring against the boy?'

Rook sauntered back as a group of soldiers trooped into the room, carrying a set of heavy chains.

'The worst crime of all,' he snarled, grasping Fletcher by the back of his neck. 'High treason.'

# 6

They took Fletcher to a holding cell, complete with a table, chairs – even a washbasin and soap. They removed his chains, holding their noses, then left the moment he was free. As soon as the door closed, Fletcher began to scrub his face and wash out his long, greasy hair. It was amazing to have more than a small bucket of drinking water to work with.

After ten minutes of pawing at his scalp, he moved on to the rest of his body, darting quick glances at the door in case anyone came in. As he jumped up and down to dry off, he dipped his jerkin and breeches into the basin for good measure, to wash away a year's worth of dirt and grime. By the end, the water was a filthy brown colour, but Fletcher felt renewed.

He summoned Ignatius, and pulled the imp into his arms. His wet skin was all gooseflesh, but the warm Salamander flattened himself against Fletcher's chest, breathing a toasty gust of heated air across his face.

'We're not out of this yet, Ignatius. But at least you don't share my fate. If I die you'll fade back into the ether, safe and sound.'

Ignatius mewled miserably and wrapped his tail around Fletcher's bare midriff.

'Don't worry, we'll get out of this somehow.' He tugged at the Salamander, but Ignatius stubbornly held on.

'Come on, little guy, I know you're happy to walk around buck naked all day, but I'm not. The guards would get quite a show if they came in now.'

Ignatius slipped off reluctantly and contented himself with exploring the confines of their new cell, sniffing suspiciously at the chairs, as if they might suddenly attack.

As Fletcher struggled back into his sodden clothes there was a knock on the door and Arcturus strode in, his face grim and pinched with worry.

He gave Fletcher a forced smile and said, 'You look like a drowned rat. God knows what Berdon's going to think when he sees you.'

'He's coming?' Fletcher said, hardly able to believe it.

'Yes. His case was right after yours. After Rook's little performance, the judge was inclined to release Berdon temporarily to see you today, even though he must spend the next two nights in jail. A silver lining to a very dark cloud.' Arcturus pulled up a chair and sat in front of him.

'Arcturus, thank you,' Fletcher said, clasping Arcturus's hands. 'For everything. You've given me back my life.'

Arcturus gave him a fleeting smile, but soon his face was dark and foreboding once again.

'I wouldn't speak so soon. It's bad, Fletcher. You're accused of killing Lord Forsyth's troops, in support of a failed dwarven rebellion. They have evidence – witnesses that say both you and Othello were at the scene, even evidence that you harbour anti-royal sympathies. I'm told Othello was arrested a few nights ago . . . I didn't even know he was here. I'm sorry Fletcher, this is all my fault. They distracted us with Didric's trial, while they planned this one.'

Fletcher collapsed in a chair and buried his face with his hands. Somehow, the accusation hadn't sunk in until now. Ignatius nudged his leg, growling with worry.

'Out of the frying pan, into the fire,' Fletcher murmured, filled with the dread of returning to his cell. 'I remember that night. We were there, Arcturus.'

'That's not the worst of it. The Inquisition run all military trials and, as an officer cadet of the king's army, you are eligible for one. Not to mention the fact that there will be a jury, who I suspect will have all heard of your murder charge, if they haven't been paid off by the Triumvirate—'

'Hang on, tell me more about the Triumvirate,' Fletcher interrupted.

'As I said, it's Lord Forsyth, Lady Faversham and Didric,' Arcturus replied grimly. 'Didric met them when Lord Faversham came to heal his burns, and he found out they own the exclusive weapons contract to the northern frontier. Faversham introduced Didric's family to the Forsyths – they were allies from the beginning, before you even set foot in Vocans. Together, the three families now run most of the prisons and weapons manufacturing in Hominum – which is why they're aggressively anti-dwarven. They're determined to do anything to drive them out of the firearms business.

Unfortunately, they have the Inquisition and the Pinkertons deeply in their pockets, and the friendship of old King Alfric.'

'An evil alliance if there ever was one,' Fletcher muttered.

'Yes, and a powerful one. They also have a particular vendetta against you. Somehow you managed to offend all three families, what with Didric's face, foiling the Forsyth-led plots last year and your supposed claim to be Lord Faversham's son.'

'How are we supposed to get out of this?' Fletcher asked, running his hands through his wet hair.

'The only way we can win this is by proving beyond a shadow of a doubt that you are innocent, so that the jury will find it impossible to convict you. Now tell me, what do they have on you?'

But Fletcher didn't get a chance to reply. The door burst open, revealing the burly figure of Berdon. Fletcher barely had time to stand up before he was wrapped in a bear hug, lost in his adoptive father's scent of leather and coal-dust.

'Son . . . my son . . .' Berdon sobbed.

He pulled away and grasped Fletcher's face, examining it through sparkling eyes.

'You're taller. Almost up to my beard,' he said, half laughing and half crying. 'You're a man now. Still can't grow a proper moustache, though.'

Fletcher grinned and hugged him again, unsure of what to say. He couldn't find the words to describe how much he had missed the amiable giant.

'There's so much I have to tell you,' Fletcher murmured.

'Your friend, Othello, has told me all of it,' Berdon replied,

50

ruffling Fletcher's hair. 'A year is a long time, and I've been working with his family to get you a fair trial. I hear you're quite the warrior.'

Fletcher shuffled his feet and shook his head with embarrassment.

'Othello's father, Uhtred, is a decent blacksmith,' Berdon continued, filling the silence after a brief pause. 'You're a good judge of character, son.'

'They're good people,' Fletcher said, nodding through blurred eyes. 'I wouldn't have made it through Vocans without them.'

Berdon took the seat behind Fletcher and began teasing out the tangles in his hair with a comb from his pocket. Ignatius sniffed suspiciously at his feet, unsure of what to make of the big man. Berdon looked down and ruffled Ignatius's head, leaving the demon with an affronted look on his face. He spat a puff of smoke, and Berdon chuckled as the Salamander stalked off, his snout in the air.

'Haven't seen this little tyke in a while. I hope you've been looking after him,' Berdon said.

'More like he's been looking after me,' Fletcher said, warning Ignatius to behave with a thought.

Arcturus, who had been sitting awkwardly next to them, coughed politely.

'I'm sorry to interrupt, but the trial starts soon and we've had no time to prepare your defence. Othello and his father will be joining us at the trial. They have told me what happened the night of the dwarven council meeting.'

'Best get you cleaned up while you speak with Captain Arcturus here,' Berdon murmured. 'You never were one for self-grooming.'

'Thanks . . . Dad.' The word felt unfamiliar in his mouth, but Berdon's huge smile told Fletcher he had said just the right thing.

'May I?' Berdon asked Arcturus, pointing at a slim knife scabbarded on his belt.

'By all means.' Arcturus smiled, handing it to him.

Berdon brandished the knife, then trimmed away Fletcher's wispy moustache and beard with deft swipes of the blade. He considered Fletcher's long hair for a moment, then shrugged and handed the knife back to Arcturus.

'We'll deal with the length later,' Berdon said, lifting the comb once again.

Arcturus cleared his throat and for a moment Fletcher thought he saw a tear in the man's eye. He turned away to sheath his knife, and Fletcher wondered if he was mistaken, for when he looked back it was gone.

'Let me recap, and you can tell me anything Othello and Uhtred might have left out,' Arcturus said.

'Go ahead,' Fletcher said.

'You and Sylva followed Othello when he snuck out to attend the dwarven council meeting. Someone betrayed the meeting's location and Lord Forsyth's men gathered outside to ambush them, under the pretence of preventing a rebellion. You were able to warn the dwarves before the soldiers could attack, but killed five men as you, Sylva, Othello and Atilla made your escape from the area. Atilla was injured and you carried him to the infirmary at Vocans, guided by Captain Lovett through her Mite, Valens. On the way, a young soldier accosted you

52

but was incapacitated thanks to the Mite. Does that about cover it?'

'That about covers it . . .' Fletcher replied, wracking his brains. It was hard to think clearly with Berdon combing his hair. It brought back memories of when Berdon had done the exact same thing as they sat by the warm glow of the hearth in their old hut, listening to the crackle of its flames.

Sensing Fletcher's mood, Ignatius returned and gave Berdon a reluctant lick across the knuckles. Then he snorted and spat, pawing at his tongue with his claws.

'Coal dust,' Berdon said, grinning at the little demon. 'It'll put hairs on your chest.'

Ignatius buried his head in the basin-water to wash out his mouth, then tumbled on his back and retched at the taste of the murky brown liquid.

Fletcher laughed at the demon's antics, but then Arcturus's grave expression brought him back to reality.

'Can you think of anything else? Anything at all,' Arcturus asked.

'Grindle and four of his men might be witnesses,' Fletcher said, thinking of the huge thug that had tried to kill Sylva and later attack the dwarven council meeting. 'I doubt they will use them though, they're an evil-looking bunch. There's no other evidence I can think of – we'll only know when we get in there.'

Arcturus shook his head, rubbing his eyes as he tried to think. 'I've had no time to prepare our case. They'll execute you and Othello for this, Fletcher. That's the only punishment there is for treason – hanging or beheading.'

Fletcher's stomach twisted at the reminder. He caught himself

53

rubbing his neck and forced his hands back to his lap. Beads of cold sweat formed on his back, and all of a sudden his chest felt tight and constricted.

'They want to take down you and the dwarves in one fell swoop, I know that much,' Arcturus continued. 'Even the whiff of a rebellion will have the dwarven council arrested and every dwarven weapon and forge seized. The Triumvirate's weapons business would lose its biggest competitor, leaving only Seraph and his family to contend with. They'll throw all of their resources at this. We just need time to come up with a plan.'

As he spoke, there was a knock on the door from one of the guards.

'Fletcher Wulf. They're ready for you.'

# 7

The courtroom was even more crowded than it had been before, but despite this, a hush hung in the air. A double row of benches had been added near the judge's high table, where ten men and women sat, resplendent in red robes. They watched Fletcher with animosity, as if he might attack them at any moment.

Behind Fletcher, there were generals and nobles on the front rows, adorned in their military regalia. A cloud of smoke stained the air above, as many of them puffed on long-stemmed cheroots, whispering in each other's ears as if they were at the theatre.

Lord and Lady Faversham were sitting on the front bench. Lord Forsyth was seated close by, his large, imposing figure taking up two spaces on the bench. Beside him sat an elegant blond lady who Fletcher could only assume was his wife. Didric and his father were nearest to Fletcher, dressed in velvet suits, with heavy gold rings weighing down their fingers.

All of them tracked Fletcher and Arcturus with hate-filled eyes as the guards shackled him to the floor again. He resisted the urge to shudder and instead lifted his chin; he would not give them the satisfaction of seeing his fear. Arcturus returned their gaze levelly, though Fletcher could see his hand trembling.

'Be upstanding for Inquisitors Damian Rook and Charles Faversham!' a guard shouted.

Rook swept into the room, followed by a hook-nosed man with dark eyes and jet-black hair. His skin was as pale as Rook's was jaundiced, and he was so skinny as to be bordering on the skeletal. The two Inquisitors took their seats at the high table and stared regally around the room.

'I haven't been in the same room as my father and half-brother since I was fifteen years old,' Arcturus murmured, nodding at the dark-haired Inquisitor.

Fletcher stared at Charles, comparing the man's face to his own. If Arcturus's theory was correct, Fletcher was Lord Faversham's illegitimate son, just as Arcturus was, making Charles their half-brother. He saw little resemblance to his own face, though Charles's hair was as thick and black as his own.

'Bring in the co-conspirator!' Charles snapped in a high, reedy voice.

The doors slammed open and Jakov entered the room, pulling Othello behind him. The dwarf was festooned with chains, so many that he could only shuffle a few inches at a time. There was a dirty rag gagging his mouth and an eye was swollen shut, bruised the ugly purple of an overripe plum.

Uhtred followed at their rear, his face dark with anger. He walked with his fists clenched, the swinging gait of a man ready for a fight.

'What have you done to him?' Arcturus demanded, as Jakov shackled Othello next to Fletcher.

'He was insubordinate,' Jakov grinned, 'so we gave him a few love taps and a gag to keep him quiet. It's the only thing these half-men understand.'

'Leave it, Captain,' Uhtred growled under his breath, pulling Arcturus aside. 'There's no use reasoning with these animals. Let the jury see, maybe it will elicit some sympathy.'

'I doubt it,' Arcturus whispered, as Jakov nodded to one of the jury members and sauntered out.

'Only one of us can speak in the boys' defence. I think you would be best placed to do it, after the job you did at the last trial,' Uhtred said, giving Othello a rough kiss on the top of his head. 'I won't watch. I don't trust myself to keep calm. It was all I could do not to rip that brute to shreds. Good luck . . . I'll see you when it's over.'

Before Arcturus could reply, Rook cleared his throat; the room went from a gentle murmuring to silence. Fletcher caught one last look at Uhtred's receding back, then the side doors were slammed shut.

'Ladies and gentlemen, thank you for coming,' Rook proclaimed, sweeping his hand theatrically. 'It is not often that we Inquisitors have the chance to preside over a case of treason. After all, it is the most heinous of crimes, punishable by death.'

This time, Fletcher felt a strange dullness at the threat of death. Somehow, it seemed a better fate than spending his life imprisoned in that cell.

'I want a swift trial today; I know we all have places to be,' Rook said magnanimously. 'We, the Inquisition, will act as prosecutors and arbiters in this case. It will be up to the jury to decide the guilt of the accused. If you don't mind, we will get straight to the point. Inquisitor Faversham, please state the facts.'

Charles looked down his nose at Fletcher, shuffling his notes.

'During a night-training exercise, five of Lord Forsyth's men were murdered. One had burns on his face, consistent with a Salamander attack, a rare demon owned exclusively by Fletcher. We believe that he was accompanied by Othello Thorsager, who helped perpetrate the massacre.' Charles pointed at the shackled dwarf, who could do nothing in response but stare back. 'It was an attack motivated by the desire to overthrow King Harold, the first step in a dwarven rebellion. If Fletcher had not been arrested for the attempted murder of Lord Cavell, we might be in the midst of civil war right now.'

'An arrest that was not justified,' Arcturus countered. 'Fletcher was cleared of all wrongdoing. Lord Cavell is fortunate that he has not been charged with attempted murder himself.'

'Ah, Arcturus, you speak at last,' Charles sneered, holding up a hand as Rook took a breath to shout at the captain. 'Do us the courtesy of holding your tongue until after we have given all of our evidence.'

'Then get on with it, rather than talking about disproven accusations.'

Charles ignored him and stepped down from the high table.

'We have three pieces of evidence. The first, the weapon Othello Thorsager used in the attack. The second is proof of Fletcher's affiliation with dwarven dissidents. The third and final piece of evidence is witness testimony. I believe that these three pieces shall prove their guilt, with a swift beheading of both perpetrators to follow. Though I know Inquisitor Rook is keen to suggest the more . . . traditional death by way of hanging, drawing and quartering. Perhaps fortunately for the accused, the method of execution shall be decided by the jury.'

Fletcher saw Othello's clenched fists, and he gave Fletcher a wide-eyed look. It was a terrible death, one that did not bear thinking about. Fletcher changed his mind. Imprisonment didn't seem so bad after all.

'Captain Arcturus, do you have any evidence, or witnesses, to call upon?' Charles inquired innocently, his eyes sparkling with malice.

'Since the charges were only brought against Fletcher an hour ago and I was unaware of Othello's arrest, I don't think you'll be surprised that I find myself unprepared,' Arcturus said, sarcasm dripping from his words.

'If I remember correctly, you were petitioning King Harold himself for Fletcher to have a swift trial. I thought you would be happy!' Charles said, equally sarcastic.

'There is a big difference between a year and an hour, as you well know, Charles. Fortunately, witnesses and friends are flying in, and they are not too far away.' Arcturus glared up at him. 'At least one of them shall speak on Fletcher and Othello's behalf, if they received my message in time.'

'Excellent!' Charles said, clapping his hands together. 'Then you won't mind the prosecution giving evidence first. Before we begin, I would like to pay my respects to King Harold.'

There was a smattering of applause, and Fletcher's ears pricked up. Charles smiled and continued:

'And of course, I cannot forget his illustrious father, the founder of the Inquisition, leader of the Pinkertons and overseer of the Judges – old King Alfric.'

Fletcher turned around to see two men in the crowd, sitting beside the Triumvirate. He had barely noticed them before, for they were dressed in much the same way as the other nobles in the crowd, but now he understood the meaning of the circlets resting on their heads.

'Less of the old,' Alfric called out in a cracked voice, eliciting an appreciative chuckle from the crowd.

Alfric's son, King Harold, looked to be in his thirties, the same age as Arcturus. The gold circlet he wore rested on a mantle of wavy blond hair, above a handsome face and piercing grey eyes. In contrast, old King Alfric wore a silver circlet, with a long mane of white hair and an aquiline nose. He stared impassively around the room, though his eyes narrowed when they settled on Fletcher.

'Now, I will call upon Sergeants Murphy and Turner, the lead investigators, to bring in the first piece of evidence,' Charles announced, accompanied by a barked order from Rook.

Othello growled beneath his gag as the two Pinkertons came into the room, brandishing a small object wrapped in a white cloth. They handed it to Charles, flashing Othello and Fletcher a nasty smile. They did not linger long, instead doffing their peaked caps to the jury and strolling back out through the side door.

Charles waited until they had left the room, then pinched the white cloth between two fingers.

'Our first piece of evidence,' Charles cried, removing the cover with a flourish. 'A tomahawk, belonging to Othello Thorsager!'

# 8

The room descended into smattered conversations and the front row leaned closer for a better look. Othello was yelling through his gag, his beard and moustache trembling as he tried to tear it through with his teeth.

'That's a lie!' Fletcher shouted on his behalf, despite Arcturus's attempts to quiet him. 'That was stolen from us weeks before, when those two monsters broke Othello's ribs.'

'Weeks before what?' Rook asked, holding his hand up for quiet. The chatter silenced almost immediately, and Fletcher found himself under the scrutiny of the entire room.

'Weeks. Before. What?' Charles repeated.

'Before … the attack happened,' Fletcher replied, his mind racing. What had he just done?

'So you know when the attack happened? You admit you were there?' Charles demanded, sensing weakness.

'That's not what I'm saying,' Fletcher answered lamely.

Arcturus lay a hand on Fletcher's shoulder and gripped him so hard that he had to force himself not to wince.

'I told Fletcher when and where the incident allegedly happened. Does that answer your question?' Arcturus said, staring Charles down. They stood there for a moment, like two wolves vying for supremacy. It was Charles who broke eye-contact first, though he went on the attack as soon as he did.

'The murder weapon bears the emblem of the Thorsagers, so it could only belong to a male member of the family. Both Othello's father, Uhtred, and his brother, Atilla, provided alibis for where they were on the night in question. Although Othello is a student at Vocans, the staff there could do no such thing for him. As such, it is quite clear that it was Othello who slaughtered the soldiers.'

The jury examined the object with interest, some whispering to one another. Fletcher knew this wasn't good.

'Thank you, Inquisitor Faversham, very compelling. Please bring out the next piece of evidence,' Rook said, scribbling something down on the paper in front of him.

This time, Charles did not call anyone in. He removed a simple card from a pocket in his uniform, brandishing it high for all to see.

'This is a membership card for the Anvils. It was found among Fletcher's belongings after his arrest. We were lucky to find it – his room had been ransacked by a mysterious benefactor,' Charles said, raising his eyebrows at Arcturus. 'After watching the last trial and seeing the scroll in the defence's possession, I think it's safe to say we know who did it.'

Fletcher felt a twinge of confusion. The card had been given to him a long time ago, on his very first day in Corcillum. He knew little about the Anvils, only that they were a group of humans who were sympathetic to the dwarves and campaigned for their rights.

'What does that have to do with anything? I was given that two years ago,' Fletcher said, despite a hiss of frustration from Arcturus.

'Inquisitors, would you give me a brief recess to speak to my charges?' Arcturus asked, though this time he didn't clamp his fingers on Fletcher's shoulder.

'Yes, why not?' Rook said in a cheerful voice. 'Maybe it will teach young Fletcher to keep his mouth shut. Not that it will matter in the end; it will be shut permanently before the week is out.'

Arcturus bowed stiffly and hunkered down beside Othello and Fletcher, waiting until the room was awash with conversation before he spoke.

'Fletcher, in the year since you were imprisoned, there have been explosions and attacks on Pinkertons and civilians. Every time, the evidence has pointed to the Anvils.'

Othello grunted loudly, jerking his head.

'Sorry, Othello. I'll remove it, but you must promise there will be no more outbursts, from either of you. You'll have a chance to defend yourselves after the Inquisition has made its case.'

Othello spluttered as the gag was cut.

'That tasted like a gremlin's loincloth,' he gasped, spitting the gag away from him.

'Why don't you explain to him the significance of the Anvil card?' Arcturus said, handing Othello a flask from his hip. Othello took a few deep gulps, then turned to Fletcher.

'It's good to see your face, Fletcher. I only wish our reunion was under different circumstances.' He gripped Fletcher's arm and drew him closer. 'There's a lot that's happened while you've been . . . away. Tensions between humans and dwarves have never been higher, and it's all thanks to these supposed attacks by the Anvils. Membership of their organisation is now illegal and many of their leaders have gone into hiding.'

'Why are the Anvils doing this?' Fletcher asked. 'Surely it's only making things worse?'

'We believe there is a traitor in the Anvils, the same person who told the Forsyths about the council meeting and got us into this mess in the first place,' Othello whispered.

Rook cleared his throat.

'I thought you said "brief", Captain,' he said, tapping his wrist.

'Listen to me, now that I have you together,' Arcturus whispered, ignoring Rook's gaze. 'There's no time or reason to fabricate a story. You have no knowledge of the events and you will remain silent throughout. Is that understood?'

'Now, Captain,' Rook ordered, waving the guards over. Arcturus stepped back, his hands raised in surrender.

'See, that wasn't so hard,' Rook laughed, shooing the guards away. 'I think the card speaks for itself, wouldn't you agree?'

Fletcher tried to ignore the nods coming from the jury. Were he and Othello already guilty in their eyes, or was there a chance?

'Bring in the witness. He will give his testimony and then I shall question the accused,' Rook ordered, before turning to Arcturus.

'You may make your defence tomorrow, Captain, but if you wish to put anyone on the stand, he or she must testify today. We will get all the questioning out of the way so we can have a quick verdict in the morning.'

Arcturus's jaw clenched but he remained silent. Fletcher wondered who Arcturus's witness could be. Seraph, perhaps?

Jakov led a soldier into the room, wearing the charcoal uniform of the Forsyths. Fletcher did not recognise him, but didn't think he was one of Grindle's soldiers. They had all been hard, muscular men, while this one was young and skinny, barely older than Fletcher himself. He took his seat at one of the witness podiums.

'State your name for the jury,' Charles ordered.

'I am Private John Butcher of the Forsyth Furies,' the soldier said in a confident voice. He stared straight ahead, ignoring Fletcher and Othello.

'Tell me, John. What did you see on the night in question?'

'We were on a night training exercise, when we heard gunshots. Five men were dead when my squad arrived, so we searched for the attackers. I was separated from my group in the darkness. That was when I saw them.' John finally looked at Fletcher and Othello, pointing to each of them with a steady finger. 'I held them at musket-point, hoping reinforcements would arrive in time. It was then that I was paralysed by a Mite's sting and they escaped. That's the last I saw of them. My squad found me several hours later.'

'Thank you, John. That will be all,' Rook said. John stood and saluted, before marching out of the room. Fletcher watched his stiff back with a heavy heart. He recognised the boy now. The worst part was, it was all true.

'That concludes the prosecution's evidence,' Rook said, lifting his notes to read aloud. 'In summary. We have the motive – membership of the Anvils for Fletcher, and as for Othello . . .' He paused, then lifted another sheet of paper. 'Well, Othello, he has a rap sheet as long as my arm. Assaulting a Pinkerton, resisting arrest, spreading anti-human propaganda. A known troublemaker.'

'Circumstantial!' Arcturus said loudly, looking to the jury.

'Nonetheless – motive!' Rook growled, daring Arcturus to disagree. Fletcher's heart sank further as Rook handed the sheet of paper to the jury to pass around. Othello was guilty of none of those charges. He had simply taken the blame, and the beatings, for his twin brother, Atilla.

'We know the murder weapons, from the burns on the bodies from Fletcher's Salamander to the discovery of the Thorsager tomahawk,' Rook continued, nodding at the weapon on the table. 'Finally, we have a reliable witness who places them at the scene. Now, we shall interrogate the accused. Guards, bring the dwarf to the witness stand!'

Othello struggled to his feet as the shackles were removed, then shuffled to the podium. He glared at Rook, his moustache bristling as he wrinkled his lip in disgust.

'Where were you on the night of the attack?' Rook asked, steepling his fingers.

Othello stared at Rook defiantly. He crossed his arms with a clatter of chains.

'Why did you attack those men?' Rook demanded, leaning forward. 'Did you plan it, or was it a spur of the moment killing?'

Othello's gaze never wavered. He was like a statue, unblinking and still, but for the steady rise and fall of his chest.

'Well, it looks as if your gag did the trick, Jakov,' Rook said, braying with laughter. 'He's been struck dumb!'

There was a soft chuckle from behind, and Fletcher turned to see old King Alfric smiling.

'Still, he does look at me in a distinctly disrespectful way, wouldn't you agree, Charles?' Rook said, the humour suddenly gone from his tone.

'He does indeed. Incredibly disrespectful. Slovenly in appearance, too. Beard unkempt, hair all over the place,' Charles replied, rubbing his chin. 'His grooming does not show this courtroom the respect it deserves.'

They were play-acting now, Fletcher could tell. It was like watching a poorly performed pantomime, and it filled him with dread – this was preplanned.

'Jakov, why don't you come here and give it a trim,' Charles said, beckoning the large guard over.

Othello's face paled. He tried to stand, but Charles slammed his hands on to the dwarf's shoulders, keeping him in the chair. Ordinarily, the brawny dwarf would have had no trouble escaping Charles's grip, but the chains impeded him, leaving him swaying back and forth.

'You can't!' Fletcher shouted, tugging at his manacles. 'It's sacrilege to cut a dwarf's hair!'

He heaved on them until the metal bit his skin, thin rivulets of blood trickling down his fingers.

Arcturus turned to King Harold, but the monarch sat in silence, his arms crossed. Lord Forsyth, Didric and Lady

Faversham were grinning with savage abandon, and old King Alfric was whispering excitedly into Didric's ear.

'This is against his civil rights,' Arcturus said, appealing to the jury. 'This is illegal!'

'Dwarves have no rights,' Rook laughed, as Jakov walked to the podium. 'We shall make him presentable for the court. A haircut never hurt anyone.'

'You will not do this!' Arcturus bellowed, his finger flashing blue as he raised it. The click of the muskets gave him pause, and the guards shuffled forward, the guns pointed at his chest. He sank to his knees beside Fletcher as Jakov withdrew a curved blade, stepping beside Charles and Othello.

'Don't watch,' Arcturus whispered, gripping Fletcher's wrist to stop him pulling at the sharp metal cuffs. 'They want to see you suffer.'

Fletcher stared at Othello as he struggled, jerking left and right and gnashing at the hands with his teeth. It made him look like an animal, and the jury shook their heads in disgust.

'I am beyond suffering,' Fletcher replied at last, dry-eyed. All he felt was anger, raging hot within him. He could barely stop himself from blasting the manacles from his hands and charging the podium. But he knew it would be suicide, and exactly what his enemies would have wanted.

Jakov's meaty palm held Othello in place as the blade was raised.

'Hold still,' he growled, grasping the dwarf's beard. 'Wouldn't want an uneven haircut, would you.'

Othello's head dropped to his chest, the fight gone from him as the first cut was made, the *snick* of the knife sharp in the silence of the room. He held Fletcher's gaze as a tuft of hair floated to the ground.

A slow tear trickled down his cheek, but Othello did not cry out. The blade flashed again and again, and each time it felt as if it had been stabbed into Fletcher's chest. That tear was the last. Othello bore the rest of the assault in stoic silence, and Fletcher willed him all his strength and courage.

'Good enough, Inquisitors?' Jakov said, stepping back to admire his handiwork. The beard was trimmed now, almost as short as Rook's.

'Hmmm. The ponytail. I'll keep it as a souvenir,' Charles said, lifting it with his hand. Othello closed his eyes as the knife swished again.

'Perhaps I should fashion it into a shaving brush,' Charles laughed, flicking it back and forth like a horse's tail.

'Far too dirty for that,' Rook replied, wrinkling his nose in disgust. 'Now the moustache. All of it – I've always wondered what a dwarf looks like witho—'

But he never finished his sentence. The doors at the back of the room slammed open, unleashing a gale of rain and whistling wind. A Griffin stalked through the doorway, emerging from the darkness with a screech. There was a uniformed rider astride it, her black hair plastered across pale cheeks. She lifted the goggles from her face, to reveal a pair of grey eyes that surveyed the scene with cold anger.

'Captain Lovett,' Fletcher breathed, hardly believing it possible. The last time he had seen her, she had been in a coma, only able to communicate through her Mite, Valens.

Lovett rode down the centre of the room, leaving a trail of

dripping water and ignoring the aghast looks from the crowd on either side. Still astride the regal beast, she stopped beside Jakov and snatched the knife from his hand. Rook, momentarily lost for words, suddenly found his tongue.

'Captain Lovett. How dare you ride into a court of law! Dismount at once or be found in contempt!'

Lovett let the knife fall to the floor, a look of disgust plain on her face.

'I can't,' she said.

'Can't, or won't?' Rook snarled, standing up from the high table.

'Can't,' Lovett replied, tossing her hair. 'I'm paralysed from the waist down.'

## 9

As Rook spluttered, unsure how to respond, Lovett turned her gaze to Fletcher. She gave him a barely perceptible nod, then walked her Griffin, Lysander, over to the jury.

'I am here to tell you that Fletcher and Othello were *not* complicit in the crime. They were defending themselves from being attacked by ten men, and they barely escaped with their lives. The dwarf had been shot and Fletcher was carrying him to safety. My own Mite, Valens, stung a soldier who had captured them, allowing them to get away.'

'You helped them escape?' Rook roared, slamming his fists on the table. 'After the murder of five soldiers?'

'I saved them from being slaughtered in cold blood, after merely protecting themselves from a group of soldiers who were hunting dwarves for sport.' Lovett's voice was clear and confident, her gaze moving steadily across the jury.

Charles held up a hand and wagged a finger, smiling and shaking his head.

'Not so fast, Captain Lovett. I have it on good authority that you were in ethershock until a few months ago . . . hence your unfortunate paralysis. How could you have seen the events that night?'

'Through Valens, my demon. I was able to learn to see through his eyes without using a scrying stone, as have others before me.' She lifted her chin and stared back, defiantly.

'Preposterous. Only the most skilled of summoners are able to master that technique,' Charles said, waving his hand dismissively.

'Yes,' Lovett said simply. Charles pursed his lips, but could think of no reply.

'Well, if this is true, we could test it right now,' Rook laughed.

'Please do,' Lovett replied.

Rook paused for a moment, staring at Lovett's face over clasped hands. Her eyes bore into his, daring him to challenge her.

'Let us assume that you are able to scry without a Corundum crystal to aid you,' Rook said, examining his nails. 'Your testimony is worthless, regardless of this ability. Or should I say, precisely because of it.'

'Why is that?' Arcturus asked. 'There have been other cases where evidence has been given based on what was seen while scrying.'

'Yes, but that was because they saw it with their own two eyes, on the stone itself. Lovett claims to have seen it all in her mind's eye, as it were. There is no precedent for this and I rule it inadmissible in court. You are dismissed, Captain Lovett.'

'This is ludicrous,' Arcturus shouted, striding up to the podium.

72

'It is *law*, Captain. I make it, you follow it.' Rook couldn't help but smile as Arcturus's face reddened with rage.

'Jury, please disregard Captain Lovett's statements,' Charles said, pushing Arcturus back to his table. 'And Arcturus. Speak in that way again and we will hold you in contempt of court, leaving the criminals to defend themselves.'

Arcturus stood rigidly, his arms crooked as if he could barely prevent himself from tackling Charles to the ground.

With visible effort, Arcturus turned away, instead grasping Othello by the shoulder and leading him back to Fletcher. The dwarf stared at his feet in silence, avoiding his friend's eyes. He looked smaller somehow, diminished. The stoic dwarf, who had borne so much, had been broken.

Fletcher's hatred for his tormentors simmered inside of him. They had all the power, and he had none. This trial was a farce, the verdict a foregone conclusion. Even as he raged, his thoughts were preoccupied with one, frightening realisation: he was going to die, and there was nothing anyone could do about it. Berdon . . . Sylva . . . he would never see them again.

'I won't stand for this,' Lovett said, crossing her arms.

'Yes . . . I can see that,' Rook said.

He grinned at his jibe, and Fletcher heard Lord Forsyth snort with laughter.

Captain Lovett ignored him and turned to the jury.

'Listen to your conscience, not these charlatans,' she said, pointing a finger at the two Inquisitors. 'These boys are victims of circumstance, nothing more.'

'That's quite enough, Captain,' Rook snapped. 'My patience wears thin. One more word . . .' He nodded at the nearest guard, who raised his rifle, the barrel wavering slightly under her griffin Lysander's steely-eyed gaze.

'Now, do you have any other witnesses that you would like to call forth, or can we call it a day?' Charles asked.

Captain Lovett turned to Arcturus, and Fletcher heard her whisper.

'Sir Caulder was held up by the guards outside.'

Arcturus paused for a moment, then shook his head.

'No . . . that is all,' he announced, then turned to Lovett and said in a low voice. 'It won't make a blind bit of difference, no matter what he has to say.'

Rook grinned as he caught Arcturus's words and raised his gavel.

'Well, it's nice to see that we are in agreement on that point. Court is adjourned until tomorrow morning, when we will hear your defence. We should have a verdict by the afternoon . . . and the convicts dead by evening.'

They didn't let Fletcher stay with Othello, though he knew that he was not far away when they threw him back in his cell – he could hear Uhtred's angry bellows through the wall. The words were muffled, but there was the splinter of broken furniture and yells from the guards. A few moments later, Jakov burst through the door, and Uhtred was hurled to the ground at Fletcher's feet.

'You can calm down in here,' Jakov snarled, wiping a trickle of blood from his face. His lip was cut and a red bruise was blossoming on the corner of his jaw. 'Raise your hand to the guards again and I'll give you the same beauty treatment I gave your son.'

Fletcher advanced on him, flaring a fireball into existence as he did so.

'Get out,' Fletcher snarled. 'Or *I'll* give *you* the beauty treatment I gave Didric.'

The door slammed shut before Fletcher had even finished speaking. The fireball spun above his finger and for a moment he was tempted to blast the door apart. Unlike the steel entrance in the underground cell, this one was made of wood.

'Thank you, Fletcher,' Uhtred groaned, dragging himself up into the chair. He clutched his side and winced, turning his back on the door.

'He's a monster, both inside and out,' Fletcher growled, absorbing the fireball's mana back through his fingers. He would need all the mana he could get if he had a chance to escape, but now was not the time.

'Come here. I have something to tell you.' Uhtred's words came in short bursts – his injuries had to be worse than Fletcher thought: beneath his beard it was difficult to see the damage his brawl with Jakov had wrought. Fletcher pulled up a chair and sat beside him.

'I won't let you and my son die here. I have a plan,' Uhtred growled. 'We're going to break you out.'

Fletcher couldn't think of a reply, but his heart sank. No good could come from this.

'The dwarven recruits are not far from here. I will fetch them and we will storm the village.'

'Don't even think about it,' Fletcher said in a low hiss, looking fearfully at the door. 'The consequences would be catastrophic. All the goodwill you have won with King Harold, gone. The end of peace between dwarves and men. You would throw this country into civil war, and you would lose.'

'No, Fletcher. Our soldiers have been armed and trained now. We have Othello here to capture demons for our own summon—'

'So what?' Fletcher snapped, cutting him off. 'You forget, I heard your debate at the war council. Nothing has changed since then.'

'But it has, Fletcher. We will take Didric's castle. It has enough supplies to last a decade and the king would not waste his troops laying siege to it. The cannons will be enough to dissuade an attack from Hominum's flying battlemages, the Celestial Corps, and we can use the money there to trade with the elves. We will carve out our own kingdom.' Uhtred's eyes were unfocused, but his words shocked Fletcher to the very core. The dwarf had believed in peace, like Othello, but something was broken within him now. Fletcher only hoped he could repair the damage.

'What about Thaissa and Briss, and all the other dwarves in Corcillum? Have you considered what would happen to them?'

Uhtred was silent, twisting his callused hands in his lap. Fletcher continued.

'Arcturus and Lovett are here, do you think they would stand by idly as you openly rebel? Or would you kill them too? The king and his father are also present, not to mention dozens of nobles, each one a powerful summoner in their own right. As for the castle, it's heavily defended day and night because of the convicts. If you say the Celestial Corps can't beat its cannons, what hope do your dwarves have? Your soldiers would die bravely, but it would be dwarven blood that stains the earth tomorrow, and none other.'

Uhtred blinked, tears running down his face. The anger that had gripped him so tightly abandoned him, leaving only pain behind.

'I have failed my people,' Uhtred gasped, his broad shoulders heaving. 'I have failed my son.'

Fletcher put his arm around the dwarf's hefty shoulders. It filled him with fury to see the Thorsagers brought so low, but he pushed that feeling aside. It was compassion that was needed now.

'Don't let what those scumbags did to Othello jeopardise everything you and he have achieved. This is what they want. Remember, the king—'

'The king has abandoned us!' Uhtred bellowed, hitting the table with his fist. 'He watched! He watched as they did that to my boy. My brave, kindhearted boy.'

There was a polite cough from the doorway behind them. Fletcher froze, the hairs on his neck standing on end. If it was a guard, their conversation was enough to have Uhtred executed for treason right alongside them. He powered up his telekinesis finger, keeping his back to the door. One blast would be quick and dirty enough to incapacitate whoever it was.

'Come now, Fletcher. If you attacked me now, you really would be committing treason. Unfortunately for you, a young battlemage would have little chance against a king.'

Fletcher spun to see King Harold, leaning against the door.

His eyebrows were creased in consternation but there was a glimmer in his eye that Fletcher couldn't place.

'I'm sorry about what happened in there. If I could have prevented it, I would have. If you let me explain, you will understand,' Harold said.

'Please do,' Fletcher replied, struggling to keep his tone civil. The monarch's authority barely deserved his respect, if beneath that authority such actions could go unchallenged, let alone unpunished.

'There can be no explanation for your indifference,' Uhtred said, standing up and limping past Harold.

'Uhtred . . .' Harold began.

'You can speak to me tomorrow, after the trial is over. I'd like to hear your explanation, with the death of these innocent boys on your conscience,' Uhtred growled, slamming the door behind him.

There was an awkward silence in the room, as Harold stared after the dwarf. Finally, the king sighed deeply and pulled up a chair beside Fletcher. He removed the circlet from the cap of golden curls on his head and put it on the table, before rubbing his temples.

'I am going to tell you a story, Fletcher. A story that you may have heard some, but not all, of,' Harold said, his eyes closed. He spoke in a low voice, as if wary of being overheard.

'When I was but a boy, Hominum was in trouble. My father had raised taxes so high that the poor could barely feed themselves and even the nobility had to tighten their purse strings. He spent the money on frivolous things – great feasts, statues, paintings – he even built a sumptuous palace in the centre of Corcillum. The people were unhappy, the nobles even more so. It was not a question of *if* a revolt would happen, but *when*. So, he abdicated his throne to me, just as I graduated from Vocans. Taxes were cut, the common folk had a new king and peace was restored once more.'

Fletcher was vaguely aware of the tale, but he did not understand how this had anything to do with the trial.

'You see, I am king in name alone. My father holds all the power. He controls the laws through the Judges and manages the army and nobility through the Inquisition. He can put down any troublemakers via the Pinkertons. When he gave me the throne, he believed I would do as I was told: and he had those three branches of government in place in case I did not. It was a publicity stunt, nothing more.'

Fletcher was stunned. In that instant, the king had diminished somehow. His presence weighed less heavily on the room.

Harold opened his eyes and gave Fletcher a level look.

'My father is a bigot, a racist and a sadist. Yet, I . . . I grew up among tutors and scholars and was raised by my dwarven nannies.'

Fletcher had heard the stories about old King Alfric and the anti-dwarven laws that had existed during his rule. But to hear his own son speak of him in that way was shocking . . . the old king must be a real monster.

As Harold wrung his hands, Fletcher couldn't help but feel uneasy. Why would the king tell him all this? He had no desire to be a pawn in someone else's game.

'I even spent a great deal of time with the elves on diplomatic missions, back when we were at peace,' the king continued.

'I am nothing like that man, though we share the same blood. Sometimes, I wonder if my mother's death is what made him so hateful . . .' Harold's voice trailed off, and they sat in silence for a while longer.

'I feel for you, truly. But I find it difficult to believe. What about the agreement with the dwarves, and the peace with the elves? What about the war? They say those were all your policies,' Fletcher asked, unable to hold himself back.

'The king's council. It was my way of clawing back some power. I tricked my father into creating it, telling him the council would help deal with the boring, administrative tasks involved in running Hominum.' Harold chuckled to himself and rapped his knuckles on the table.

'A voting system was introduced, one that my father, Alfric, believed he could control, given his friendship with most of the council. But I had my own allies. As their parents died from old age and from protecting their borders, my younger friends inherited their positions. I managed to push through these new laws using that conduit. That was why last year's Tournament was so important – it was my father's idea to offer a council seat as a prize. If one of Zacharias Forsyth's children had won, the balance of power would have swung in my father's favour, for the Favershams and Forsyths remain on his side. I owe you thanks for preventing that.'

'What does this have to do with Othello and our trial?' Fletcher asked.

'My father still believes I am as hateful as he and his friends are, that the laws I have introduced are for reasons of practicality, not morality, even if he disagrees with them. If he knew the extent to which I am against him . . . he would start a civil war and take power once again. I am trying to hold Hominum together, and the safety of its people balances precariously. We are barely holding off the orcs as it is. If there were civil war between my father and me, or if the dwarves were to rebel, or the elves to decide to invade, our armies would fall and the orcs would rampage across the Empire, slaughtering everyone in their path.'

'So you can't get involved in our trial, because your father would get suspicious if you did. You can't give us a pardon?'

'I can only give pardons to the nobility, but yes, even if it *were* possible, I could not, not without a good reason,' Harold replied. 'But, I am not here just to explain my actions. I have to tell you what will happen if Othello is executed tomorrow. The generals, nobility and common soldiers would be told a dwarven officer had been found guilty of murdering five men and committing treason. The dwarven recruits would find out that an innocent dwarf, the son of the great Uhtred Thorsager himself, has been executed for defending himself against a group of racist soldiers. Can you imagine what would happen?'

'There . . . there would be riots . . . the humans and dwarves would murder each other,' Fletcher gasped, horrified. He had been so concerned for himself and for Othello, he had not realised the wider ramifications of the trial.

'The dwarves would be slaughtered, but not without first putting up a fight that would cripple our army,' Harold said grimly. 'The elves might end their alliance, after seeing what we did to the dwarves. And all the while, the albino orc would be gathering his forces, ready to send his hordes at our beleaguered and distracted army. All this, from one dwarven death. Yet all the Triumvirate can think of is their damned weapons business and getting their revenge on you. All my father cares about is putting the dwarves and elves in their place. I'm damned if I help you and damned if I don't. It's civil war with my father or a dwarven rebellion.'

'Is there nothing you can do?' Fletcher asked desperately, grabbing Harold's hand.

The king looked sadly at Fletcher, and grasped him like a drowning man.

'There is nothing I can do. But there *is* something you can do.' His eyes bore into Fletcher's, burning with hope.

'I'll do anything. I'm a dead man anyway,' Fletcher said. It felt good, to have a purpose, a plan of any kind. For a moment, he allowed himself a flicker of hope.

Harold took a deep breath.

'Confess to treason tomorrow. I'll make sure your death is quick.'

# 10

Fletcher received no further visitors that night. When sleep would not come to him, he summoned Ignatius and they played together, a stupid game of tag around the table that left Fletcher with bruised shins but gave him a welcome distraction from what was to come.

But by the end Fletcher could do little but sit in silence and watch as Ignatius slept, glad that the slumbering demon could not sense the despair that had taken hold of him.

Jakov and his guards came early, banging and shouting as they entered the cell, expecting to drag a terrified convict from his bed. Instead they found Fletcher standing alone beside the door, ready for what the morning would bring.

Despite the early hour, the courtroom was full of people, with more nobles and generals in the crowd, even some soldiers. It did little to assuage Fletcher's nerves, but he reinforced his resolve with thoughts of the consequences of inaction.

What he was about to do would exonerate Othello of all crimes. It would cheat the Triumvirate of their victory and prevent a war that would tear the Empire apart.

All it would cost him was his life.

Arcturus looked haggard as he took a seat at the defence table, a great pile of notes and papers clutched to his chest. Captain Lovett looked no better, seated behind him on the front bench, uncomfortably squashed between Zacharias Forsyth and old King Alfric, with a rickety wheelchair close by.

As Rook and Charles waited for the crowd to be seated, Othello was dragged into the room and manacled beside Fletcher. This time, he stood proudly, head held high, eyes blazing with defiance.

Fletcher worried whether Uhtred had told Othello of his plans. Whether he might still go through with it. The threat to his son's life had put a lot of strain on the goodhearted dwarf ... it would be best for Fletcher to make his move now, just in case.

'Othello, I need you to promise me something,' he murmured, keeping his voice low. 'The king came to see me last night. He's on our side and has a plan. I don't have time to tell you what's going on, but whatever happens, you have to go along with it.'

Othello raised his eyebrows and gave Fletcher a trusting smile. It was strange to see so much of Othello's face. His jaw was strong and square beneath the remaining stubble, like the edge of an anvil.

'I'm glad someone has a plan,' Othello whispered back. 'After my dad's ... *outburst* last night, they punished us by banning Arcturus and Lovett from seeing us – I heard them arguing with the guards outside my cell. My father can't even attend the trial.'

Othello curled his lip with anger, shooting a hate-filled glance at Jakov. He whispered out of the corner of his mouth, 'Are you sure we can trust the king?'

'We have no other choice,' Fletcher replied. 'I doubt anything Arcturus and Lovett could say will make a difference.'

Othello glanced at the defence table and shook his head.

'They look like they've been up all night. I'm willing to roll the dice.'

Fletcher gave Othello a sad smile, wondering if there would be a chance to explain himself before his execution. He took a deep breath.

'I have something to say!' he yelled, twisting his body uncomfortably against the chains so that he faced the crowd.

'Fletcher, be quiet,' Arcturus growled, his tired eyes widening with surprise.

Rook banged his gavel as the room began a murmured discussion, with many of the crowd standing, to better see which prisoner had spoken.

'I'm sad to say I agree with Captain Arcturus,' Rook sneered. 'We have no time for impassioned speeches and grandiose last words. Keep your tongue still or Jakov shall gag you as he did the dwarf.'

'I want to confess,' Fletcher said, turning back to him.

'Don't do it,' Arcturus yelled out. 'We can still win this, we can still wi—' His voice was muffled as he was tackled off his feet and slammed into the ground; Jakov's bulky frame straddled his chest and a meaty palm clapped over his mouth.

Another guard stepped purposefully towards Lovett, but there was no need. Fletcher could see Zacharias Forsyth whispering in her ear, and the glint of something sharp and metallic pressed against her ribs. It only strengthened Fletcher's resolve. He hated these bloodless, indifferent men – they were nothing but empty vessels, slaves to their own desires.

'Say that again,' Charles said, his voice breathless with excitement. 'Say it so the whole room can hear it.'

The room was loud again, and Fletcher felt the combined gaze of the most powerful men and women of Hominum. He did not flinch – it needed to look convincing.

'I confess to the murders of the five men,' Fletcher bellowed, shocking the crowd into silence. 'Yes, that's right, *I* did it. It was me and no other. I stole Othello's tomahawk that night and went out looking for trouble. Little did I know Othello had seen me take the axe and followed me.'

He stuttered, the words he had rehearsed so carefully like hot coals in his mouth. With every syllable, he brought himself closer to death.

'Af— After he had tracked me for almost an hour, the soldiers saw him on their patrol and decided that a dwarf would make for good target practice. I heard the gunshot and went to investigate. When I arrived, I saw that they had shot Othello through the leg.'

He took a deep breath, knowing the next words would condemn him. Yet, in the final act, his nerve returned, and he spoke with conviction once again.

'I killed them all while he was barely conscious on the ground. I did it in cold blood – they didn't even see me coming. Othello had nothing to do with it. I am the guilty one here.'

The words rang in the silent room.

Rook scribbled furiously, barely looking up from the table.

86

But Charles's glee faded from his face, as he realised what was happening.

'The . . . the dwarf. He also . . .' Charles stuttered. There was a curse from behind and Fletcher allowed himself a grim smile, recognising Didric's throaty tone.

'We must confer,' Charles said, seizing the gavel from the high table and banging it against the side. He hurried up the steps and there was a hushed conversation between the two Inquisitors, but Fletcher could not hear it over the whispers of the crowd. He noticed a great deal of glancing at the Triumvirate and the old king Alfric, confirming his suspicions. Othello was the real target for the trial. His own death was just the icing on the cake, and now they would find it a poor meal.

Suddenly, a new voice broke through the crowd.

'We have our verdict.'

It was one of the jury, a tall, imperious-looking lady with grey, scraped back hair and tortoiseshell spectacles. She held a small pile of torn paper in front of her, and Fletcher's heart skipped a beat at the sight of it. The jury had voted while the Inquisitors were distracted.

'A moment, if you please,' Charles said, holding up a finger.

'We do *not* please,' the jury lady snapped. 'You would do well to remember that it is the defence's turn to speak, and Fletcher has clearly dismissed his representative and pleaded guilty. It is we who make the decisions in this courtroom and we may rule whenever we like. I only ask whether the dwarf has anything to say, before I read it out.'

Othello hesitated, looking searchingly at Fletcher's face. After a moment he looked away, indecision creasing his brow. For ten beats, the future of Hominum rested in the hands of a single dwarf. Then he shook his head, unable to say the words aloud.

'In that case, our first ruling is this. We find Othello Thorsager . . . not guilty. He is a victim of circumstance, nothing more.'

Othello barely reacted, instead gripping Fletcher's wrist and drawing him close.

'What was the plan?' Othello whispered. 'This doesn't make any sense.'

He stared into Fletcher's eyes with sudden intensity. This time, they told the truth that Fletcher's mouth could not.

'No . . .' Othello said, tightening his grip as Fletcher's eyes began to water. Fletcher did not need to be strong any more. Othello was safe now.

'You said there was a plan,' Othello croaked, grasping Fletcher's clothes like a drowning man. 'The king was going to save you.'

'This was the plan,' Fletcher said, smiling bitterly at the dwarf through blurred eyes. 'You'll understand one day. This is bigger than us.'

The jury's verdict hit his ears, each word like a hammer blow to his chest.

'Fletcher Wulf is found guilty of all charges. He shall be hung by the neck until dead.'

# 11

The verdict echoed in the rafters like a death knell, and Fletcher supposed it might as well have been. Silence weighed heavily on the room; some people were shocked, others waited for his reaction.

Then a string of curses erupted from the very back of the hall. Fletcher turned and saw the familiar, lopsided figure of Sir Caulder stomping down the centre of the court. His wooden leg clunked against the stone floor as he made his way to the front of the room, never ceasing his tirade of expletives.

'What the hell are you doing?' Rook yelled, banging his gavel. 'Guards, expel him from the court at once!'

'Dammit, I have something to say and I'll hamstring any guard who comes near me,' Sir Caulder growled, unsheathing a short sword from a scabbard at his waist. He was in his old uniform – steel chainmail with the silver and blue surcoat of the noble house he had once served. The guards hesitated, instead raising their muskets.

Zacharias Forsyth shook his head in disgust, then sprung to

his feet and turned to address the crowd.

'Would you give this foulmouthed old man a platform to spew his ramblings? The trial is over – let us leave him to his mad thoughts.'

But Zacharias had clearly misjudged the crowd. Eager for more entertainment, they ignored him, some even calling for him to be seated. King Harold stood and glared out at the onlookers, until silence reigned once again.

'I am inclined to agree with Zacharias,' he announced.

Fletcher's heart sank. Why would Harold take Zacharias's side? Had this all been a ploy, to get him to confess?

'But . . .' the king continued, 'I knighted Sir Caulder and appointed him as weapons master at Vocans Academy myself. He is a good man, and of sound mind. Out of respect for a knight of the realm, we shall hear him out.'

He sat down with finality, and Zacharias was forced to join him, unable to publicly contradict his king. Fletcher sighed with relief and turned his gaze back to the old weapons master.

'Thank you, my king,' Sir Caulder said, inclining his head. He cleared his throat, then began to speak in a loud, clear voice.

'Twenty-one years ago, I entered the service of the Raleigh family, protecting their ancestral homeland of Raleighshire. The estate was on the outskirts of a village which bordered the jungle and suffered frequent raids from the orcs, but was easily defensible. There was only one way the orcs could enter into our territory – a mountain pass, where my fifty men could hold off an army of orcs if need be. For years I defended that pass, with nothing more than a few skirmishes.'

His voice hitched and he paused, taking a moment to compose

himself. Fletcher didn't get it. Sir Caulder was buying time, but for what, Fletcher did not know. Was he stalling, so that Uhtred could get his dwarves into position? Fletcher glanced at the entrance doors, hoping against hope that they had not gone ahead with such a foolish plan.

'It was a night like any other. The sentries were awake, the sentinel torches were lit. There was no movement from the tree line. We didn't know it was happening until a dying servant staggered through the back entrance of our mountain camp with a javelin in his belly. He told us that orcs had appeared out of nowhere, slaughtering the entire county. By the time we arrived it was too late. The family and villagers were dead or dying and a hundred orcs were bearing down upon us. I was the only survivor of the attack.'

Sir Caulder brandished his hooked hand, for all to see.

'I lost a hand and a leg, but that was nothing compared to the loss of life that night. Every man, woman and child in the village beheaded, their skulls piled in the village square. The Raleigh family and their servants, impaled on spikes and left to rot on the jungle border, a warning to the Empire to stay out of orc lands. They were barely recognisable by the time they were cut down and laid to rest.'

Inquisitor Rook groaned aloud and stared up at the ceiling in exasperation.

'We have all heard this story before, Sir Caulder, it is the event that set the war in motion, after eight years of bad blood. I have no patience for an old man reminiscing over his past failures. Get on with it.'

Sir Caulder glared up at the pale-faced Inquisitor, but with visible effort turned back to the courtroom.

'That mountain pass was the only obvious way to enter Raleighshire. But there was another. A secret passage under the mountain, known only to the Raleighs and their friends. Someone betrayed them. They are probably in this room right now.'

His words were quiet, without accusation, but they caused the room to fill with the low buzz of whispered debate.

Zacharias leaped to his feet, his finger outstretched at Sir Caulder like a loaded pistol.

'You dare stain the memory of Edmund and his family with your lies?' he hissed, the fingertip glowing blue. 'I should kill you where you stand!'

King Harold laid a hand on the angry lord's shoulder and gently pressed him down into his seat.

'Please, Zacharias. Let the man finish – he was the only witness to our best friend's death.' He turned to the audience. 'It is true what Sir Caulder says. Many noble children played in that secret tunnel. I remember, we would dare each other to see who could go deepest into the jungle before running back to the safety of the hidden entrance. Edmund always got the furthest.'

He smiled at the memory, and Fletcher could see nods of agreement from some of the other nobles. It didn't seem much of a secret to them.

'It was my fault that we did not leave enough men to protect the passageway,' Sir Caulder lamented, rubbing his eyes as if he were holding back tears. 'Hell, it should have been blocked up years ago. It was my fault. That is why I never denied the accusations levelled at me, that I had been derelict in my duty.'

There was a murmur of sympathy for the old man, and Fletcher could not help but feel pity for him. It was an easy mistake to have made.

'I'm glad you were able to get your failings off your chest – I really do hope it makes your miserable life more bearable,' Rook said, spreading his hands wide. 'But this has nothing to do with this trial. Leave, before I have my Minotaur drag you out by the hair.'

'Oh, but it has *everything* to do with Fletcher. This trial has been a farce from the beginning,' Sir Caulder said, stomping up to the witness pulpit. 'The Inquisition have no authority over the boy. A jury cannot charge a noble-born with a crime; only the king can judge them.'

He took his place and looked expectantly at Charles, who was advancing on the wiry old man and beginning to speak.

'You are, if I am not mistaken, referring to Fletcher's claims that he is the illegitimate son of my father, and my—'

'I claimed no such thing!' Fletcher yelled.

'My half-brother. A preposterous assertion that, even if it were true, would not make Fletcher a noble-born. Just a bastard.'

Sir Caulder shook his head and laughed, then swatted at Charles with the flat of his blade, sending the Inquisitor stumbling out of reach.

'As much as I would love to expose your father's indiscretions, Fletcher is *not* one of Lord Faversham's bastards – if you'll forgive the term, Captain Arcturus.'

Arcturus, who had finally managed to extricate himself from Jakov's clutches, simply shook his head, ashen-faced.

'No. I will admit that, for a while, I believed Fletcher might very well have been your half-brother, Inquisitor. But it was only after I spoke with his adopted father, Berdon, that I discovered his true heritage,' Sir Caulder said, raising his voice so the entire crowd could hear.

'I was told last night that Fletcher was found naked in the snow, just outside of this very village. There was no note, no blanket or basket. What parent could leave their child like that, to die of exposure? Why outside a village as remote as the village of Pelt, so far removed that it lies on the elven border? What I am about to tell you will explain all of these things, and more.'

For the first time, Sir Caulder looked at Fletcher. There was sorrow in his eyes, even a hint of regret.

'As I lay with my limbs shattered in the mud beside the Raleighs' home, a demon flew from their bedroom window. Lord Raleigh's Gryphowl, clutching something in its claws.'

He looked at Fletcher expectantly, but all Fletcher could return was a confused shake of his head.

'What was it? A letter? Money? A Gryphowl is barely larger than the bird it is named after, it couldn't be carrying much else,' Charles scoffed.

Sir Caulder gave Fletcher a rueful smile.

'A baby boy. No more than a week old and naked as the day he was born.'

# 12

Fletcher could barely think with the noise that erupted around him, the shouts of angry men and women drowning his thoughts. He fell to his knees and covered his ears, trying to understand Sir Caulder's story. With a racing heart, he turned over each fact, ignoring the clatter of the gavel and Zacharias's roaring.

He knew it was nothing more than a last ditch attempt to save him, but he couldn't help entertaining the idea for a moment. If he *was* Raleigh's son, it would explain his ability to summon – found so rarely in commoners who were unrelated to the nobility. The timelines added up, more or less. But that was all. Just like Arcturus's theory that he was his half-brother, there were huge holes that needed to be explained . . . as Rook was eager to point out.

'This is laughable,' Rook said, as the noise died down under the steely gaze of King Harold, who had stood once again to silence the crowd. 'Even if we were to believe you – and we have reasons to suspect you would lie to protect Fletcher – why would that baby have ended up on the northern border, when Raleighshire is the most southern point of Hominum? What possible reason could Edmund Raleigh have to send his child there?'

'Because he didn't know who to trust!' Sir Caulder growled, slamming his fist against the pulpit. 'Somebody wanted his family dead, some ally of theirs had led the orcs right to their door. Lord Raleigh knew his son wouldn't be safe anywhere in Hominum, so he sent him to the only place he knew that even the king himself couldn't touch. To the elves.'

'And then? The demon left him in Pelt because it got lost?' Charles scoffed.

'Lord Raleigh had died. The gryphowl was fading back into the ether, as all demons with dead masters do, no longer tethered to our world. It wasn't going to make it to the elven border; I bet it was lucky to get as far as the Beartooth Mountains,' Sir Caulder stated plainly, and Fletcher could see several nobles nodding in agreement. 'So it left the boy as close to the border as it could, in a place where he would be discovered – just outside the gates of Pelt. Naked and alone, but crying loudly enough for a local blacksmith to find him.'

It made sense, Fletcher realised, if you took a leap of faith. But the boy could have been sent anywhere – an orphanage, a friend's house. Would Lord Raleigh truly have sent his son to the elves? And that was if Sir Caulder was telling the truth in the first place. Fletcher shook his head. It was not enough, even if he hoped in his heart of hearts it was true.

'Why?' Charles blurted. 'Why would you not tell anyone about it? About the baby, the secret entrance, all of it!'

Sir Caulder sighed and lowered his shoulders, avoiding

Fletcher's eyes. He hung his head, the courage gone out of him.

'I was afraid. Afraid that if I tried to tell anyone, the betrayer would kill me to avoid suspicion. Afraid that if they found out the boy had escaped, they would go looking for him. That was why I took the post at Vocans, in the hope that he would somehow find his way to the Academy. And he did.'

There were cries of alarm as Zacharias stood suddenly, shrugging off King Harold's hand as he advanced upon Sir Caulder.

'I don't believe a word of it. You've concocted this story to save your friend's skin, at the expense of my dead friend's memory!' He bellowed the last words into Sir Caulder's face, slamming his hands on either side of the podium. Sir Caulder did not even blink, instead calmly wiping a fleck of spittle from his face.

'That is up to the king to decide. He can believe Fletcher is a noble and pardon him from this trumped up charge for the sake of his parents. Or he can do nothing and let him die,' Sir Caulder said. He met Zacharias's gaze, until the noble turned away in disgust.

'Do you believe this, Harold?' Zacharias asked in disbelief. 'The man is clearly mad. Do not besmirch Edmund and Alice's memory so this old crackpot can save the life of a murderer.'

Fletcher could see hope in King Harold's eyes as he stood and, with a deep sigh, joined Zacharias in front of the high table. Fletcher felt that hope reflected in his own heart.

Before Harold could speak, Sir Caulder made one last plea, his voice trembling with emotion.

'My king. I loved the Raleighs as if they were my own flesh

and blood. I owe them my life and more, for my failure as their protector. I do this for them, so their child may live, not out of loyalty to a student.'

Harold held up a hand, silencing the old man.

'It is a tall tale, one that I wish I had heard many years ago,' King Harold remonstrated. 'We started a war over the events of that night. To tell an incomplete version of that story verges on treason.'

'Hear hear,' Zacharias said, nodding in agreement.

'But . . . I cannot in good conscience kill the lad, even if there is no way of proving his heritage. You, Zacharias, of all people, will understand that. I deem the boy a noble, and give him a full pardon, for the sake of the memory of Edmund and Alice Raleigh.'

It was over. Sir Caulder's ruse had worked. Fletcher felt a flood of relief and Othello's hand thumping him on the back. His first thought was of Berdon. There was so much he needed to tell him. He felt faint with happiness. Somehow, he had won.

But then, a cold, wavering voice cut through the air.

'There *is* a way of proving it.'

It was the old king. Fletcher turned to see him being helped up by Lady Faversham. Now that he saw her in full view, Fletcher could tell she had been very attractive in her younger days, with delicate cheekbones and a cascade of silver hair falling to her waist. Her eyes, however, showed that her beauty was only skin deep, for they were filled with hatred.

'The Raleighs had a unique demon, handed down over generations, before it was killed a few hundred years ago. That is why the crest on Sir Caulder's uniform bears the image of a Manticore, is it not, my son?' old King Alfric continued, taking a long cane from beside his seat and hobbling over to stand beside the others. Was this the man King Harold was so afraid of? The wizened elder before him did not seem so formidable an opponent.

'Do you remember the old tale of a second son who was stung by his older brother's Manticore and inherited the gift through its venom? Not unlike our friend Lord Cavell, who became a summoner when he was burned by the flames of the criminal's Salamander,' old King Alfric said, nodding at Didric.

'King Alfric, I beg—' Arcturus began, but was silenced by a kick to the ribs from Jakov.

'Eventually, that older brother died in the first dwarven rebellion, leaving the second son as heir,' Alfric continued, ignoring Arcturus. 'From then on, all of the firstborn children of his descendants, the Raleighs, were immune to Manticore venom.'

'That is a fable, a story,' Harold said, smiling at his father good-naturedly. 'Even Edmund did not believe it. A thimbleful of Manticore venom is enough to kill ten men. Only a Manticore's master could survive such a sting, and even then, only if it was administered by their own particular Manticore, in the same way that a Mite or an Arach's owner is immune to their demon's venom.'

Fletcher could tell Harold was speaking for the crowd's benefit, though he already knew it from his demonology lessons. At the time he had thought it a useless piece of information. How wrong he had been.

'Do not presume to lecture me like an incompetent child,'

Alfric snapped, limping up to Fletcher and examining his face. His eyes were cold and calculating, and they flashed with sadistic intent.

'This boy should by all rights be executed – a punishment well befitting his heinous crime. I should not indulge your fantasy. It is preposterous to believe that this common guttersnipe is the son of the great Edmund and Alice Raleigh. The stink on him alone is proof enough for me.' Alfric chuckled to himself and turned back to his son.

King Harold's smile faded slightly, and he gave Fletcher a worried glance.

Despair gripped Fletcher's heart once again, tightening with every second, like a vice. He swayed on his knees, and only Othello's steadying hand kept him from falling.

'I have a proposal,' Alfric said, tapping his chin and gazing up at the rafters. 'Let us administer the sting. If the boy dies, well, he was never Raleigh's son and deserved the death that the jury prescribed. If he survives . . . you have my permission to pardon him.'

Harold reddened at being spoken to in such a manner. After all, he was king, and a full-grown man. He did not need his father's permission to do anything. For a moment Fletcher saw him struggle with a decision, then he slumped his shoulders and gave his father a curt nod. He could not openly defy his father, not in such a public setting. Not yet.

'I must object,' Captain Lovett said, still seated on her bench. 'A Manticore's sting is a terrible death. It could take hours, all the time in terrible agony.'

'Then we shall give him a full dose!' Alfric snarled.

'That should kill him quickly enough.'

'That is not what I meant . . .' Lovett started, but was cut short by Alfric's raised hand.

'Fortunately, there is a summoner in this room who owns a Manticore. Is that not so, Charles?' Alfric said, pointing at the dark-haired Inquisitor.

'A gift from my mother, when I joined the Inquisition,' Charles Faversham said, bowing his head. 'I believe you, in turn, gave the demon to her.'

'I did indeed give it to my cousin,' old King Alfric said. 'I cannot deny that I have missed Xerxes, he was a favourite of mine for a good few years. Why don't you summon him? I bet he hasn't had a chance to sting something for a while.'

'Yes, my liege,' Charles said, falling to one knee. He clicked his finger at one of the guards, who went behind the high table and brought him a long tube. With practised ease, Charles slid out a roll of leather from within and unravelled it on the floor.

He lay his hand on the pentacle embossed upon it and closed his eyes, brow creased with concentration. The pentacle hummed into life, glowing a dull blue that shone even in the well-lit interior of the courtroom. Threads of white light appeared, knitting and merging into a formless mass that slowly took shape. In moments, an enormous creature had materialised, and Fletcher's breath caught in his throat.

Xerxes was as large as a thoroughbred horse, towering above Fletcher. His limbs and body had the musculature of a lion, covered in a thick pelt of dark, violet fur. His mane was black and shaggy, but interspersed between the hairs were vicious spines that rattled as the creature shook its leonine head. He had a short, wide-mouthed muzzle, but his eyes seemed almost human, the irises a soft blue that bore into Fletcher's own with hungry curiosity.

But all this was nothing compared to the black, scorpion tail erupting from the base of its spine, waving hypnotically like a snake about to strike. A droplet beaded on the glistening sting, yellow as pus and twice as viscous.

'Ahhh, there's the little scamp,' Alfric said, shuffling closer and caressing the Manticore's tail. 'A beautiful specimen. I am glad you have cared for him so well.'

'*Little scamp*?' Othello uttered. 'It's a monster!'

Alfric's eyes snapped to Othello.

'Guards, get the dwarf away and someone hold Master Wulf down. I want muskets on Captains Arcturus and Lovett. Their sentiments for the boy might make them do something they would regret.'

Fletcher heard the click of flints being pulled back as the guards raised their weapons. Othello swore as Jakov gripped him by the hair and dragged him away, the chains scraping along the floor. But Fletcher saw nothing but those strange, hypnotic eyes, as the Manticore took a step forward.

'I suggest everyone watch closely,' Charles said jovially. 'It is not often you see Manticore venom in action, especially not a full dose. Although those of you with weaker stomachs might wish to leave the room.'

The sting swayed back, bending like a bow at full stretch. It froze, perfectly still, as Xerxes waited for instruction from his master. Charles held up his hand, ready to give the order.

The Manticore purred with excitement, then there was a grip

on Fletcher's arm and he heard Didric's voice croak in his ear.

'Hold still. We wouldn't want him to miss now, would we?'

Another, larger hand reached over his shoulder and tore open his jerkin, ripping the threadbare fabric to leave his chest exposed.

'Your sacrifice is in vain, Fletcher,' Zacharias hissed, and Fletcher felt his hot breath on the back of his neck. 'You have done nothing but delay the inevitable. The dwarves will be put in their proper place, one way or another. It is a shame that you will not be there to see it.'

The two nobles pulled Fletcher's arms apart, until he thought his shoulders would pop out of their sockets. He kneeled there as the Manticore took a final, deliberate step forward.

'The prisoner is ready, my liege!' Charles cried, his voice high with excitement. 'Shall we begin the *test*?'

'Do it,' Alfric said simply.

Charles's arm swung down and the sting came with it, hissing through the air. There was a grisly pop as the point broke through the skin below Fletcher's sternum, and he cried out, for it felt like he had been run through with a sword. Then the bulbous sting pulsated as it injected the venom.

He sagged to the floor, feeling the liquid seethe within him, like acid in the blood. The pain gripped Fletcher then, as if the flesh within him was being cooked from the inside. His nerves screamed with agony, and his muscles seized and spasmed, leaving him kicking and twitching on the cold floor of the courtroom.

He could feel a blackness approaching and welcomed it with open arms. Anything would be better than this suffering. Even death.

As the blessed relief of unconsciousness took hold, he heard Didric cackling, as if from a great distance away.

'Goodbye, Fletcher Wulf!'

# 13

The pain was almost gone, just a dull throb in the darkness. It would be so easy to let go. To be infinite and nothing, all at the same time. To be free.

But something called to him, in the endless black. Another soul, lost, as he was. Ignatius.

There was love there. It kept Fletcher from falling, though he leaned out over the abyss. Ignatius was calling to him. He felt their bond, unravelling, weakening. But Ignatius would not let go. The final thread held strong, and it pulled him back from the brink. Fletcher opened his eyes.

The walls and ceiling of the room were made of smooth, raw wood, patterned with the whorls of the grain beneath. There was no door to speak of, simply an opening that led into a dark corridor. Strangest of all, the room was lit by jars of tiny, glowing balls of yellow light that flew randomly within, like wyrdlights.

He was lying in a bed of sorts. Thick, deer furs swaddled him like a baby, cocooning him in a chrysalis of warmth.

'You're awake.' A soft, lilting voice spoke.

A face sporting a pair of bright blue eyes appeared above him, and he discovered his head was resting in someone's lap. Hair the colour of white gold tickled his chin, and he realised he was looking at Sylva, upside down.

'Sylva!' Fletcher blurted, then winced with pain as he sat up. His body ached, as if he had just woken from a fistfight he had lost. Badly lost.

'Relax,' Sylva said, pushing him back down with a gentle touch. 'You took a full dose of Manticore venom. Let me do the talking.'

Fletcher lay back down, relaxing in the softness of her lap. He felt her fingers tease the unkempt locks away from his face, then a soft sponge wiping at his brow.

'You're lucky you were so close to our border. We used elven medicine to purge the venom from your body. Something that even the healing spell Hominum relies on so heavily could not fix.'

Fletcher smiled up at her and this time she allowed him to sit up gently and swing his legs from the side of the bed. He was on a strange shelf, which appeared to have grown out of the wall itself. A thick patch of soft, green moss served as a mattress on the top of it.

For a moment he reddened as he realised that he was wearing a simple blue doublet and trousers, with soft felt slippers on his feet. He wondered absently who had dressed him, hoping that it had not been Sylva.

'It is good to see you,' he said at last, throwing his arms around her. She hugged him back and they sat there for a while, revelling in their reunion.

Fletcher took in his old friend. Sylva wore a green velvet tunic, edged with fur and embroidered with leaping stags, the detailing as intricate as the finest of paintings.

Fletcher wasn't sure if it was because he hadn't seen a girl his age for more than a year, but Sylva seemed to him more beautiful than she had ever been, especially in her traditional elven garb. Avoiding his frank gaze, she jumped from the bed and gave a sharp whistle with her fingers.

Sariel bounded through the door. The golden-haired Canid was larger than when he had last seen her, and she sniffed at his feet excitedly. Fletcher avoided the temptation to stroke her, knowing the implications of caressing another person's demon. Instead, he held out his hand for her to sniff, and she brushed his fingers affectionately with a wet nose.

The brief demonic contact reminded him to summon Ignatius, and the Salamander materialised with a joyful chirp. Fletcher gathered him into his arms and pressed the demon's warm body against his chest.

'So ... your medicine saved me. I'm not a noble after all,' Fletcher said, breaking the awkward silence.

He felt a twinge of disappointment. For a moment, he had thought he knew who his real parents were.

'Not exactly. I know it's a lot to process. King Harold is waiting for you, he'll explain everything. Do you think you can walk?' Sylva asked.

'I can try.'

He swayed uneasily on his feet when he stood, so Sariel slipped her snout beneath his arm and nudged it on to her back, while Ignatius took his customary position around Fletcher's neck. He leaned against Sylva and they hobbled out of the room.

Sylva led the way, taking one of the jars from the walls and shaking it. Within, tiny fireflies floated around, though a few of them sat at the bottom, feeding on a glutinous liquid.

'Nectar,' Sylva explained as she saw Fletcher peering at the jar. 'We use it to trap them before dusk, then release them in the morning. No smoky torches for us.'

But Fletcher was barely listening, for they had stepped out into the light. He staggered again, but this time it was nothing to do with his fragile state. They were thousands of feet above the ground, on a thick branch as wide as the largest of tree trunks.

All around him, there was a network of similar structures, with broad, oaky leaves big enough to roof a house. He turned to see they had walked out of the inside of an enormous tree, the trunk thicker than the tallest building in Corcillum. All around, other trees, just as large as the one he stood upon, stretched into the sky. The entire scene was bathed in dusky orange light, for the sun was setting.

'The Great Forest. Our home,' Sylva said proudly, leading him out over the broad pathway.

On mossy branches above and below, Fletcher could see other elves, walking sedately back and forth. Several paused and stared at him across the way, some waving, others shaking their heads. He wondered when they had last seen a human. As for him, he had never seen an elf other than Sylva, and he found it fascinating that they all shared her fine bone structure and pale hair.

'Watch your step,' Sylva said, pointing to a bridge that connected one branch to the other. It was constructed from strange, vine-like roots, twisting together to make a footway, complete with railings on either side. It felt solid under his feet, as if it had been carved from stone.

They walked in silence for a time, as the golden light of the setting sun filtered through the canopy. Their journey took them closer to the ground, though Fletcher wished they would go all the way to the top, so he could look out over the Great Forest and catch a glimpse of the Beartooth Mountains.

Finally, they stopped, and Sylva called over a nearby elf when they reached the next branch, speaking in a lilting language. The elf bowed respectfully, then leaped on to the branch below, as nimble as a squirrel.

'Forgive my elvish,' Sylva said, reddening. 'I was tutored in many languages, even orcish runes, but the other high elves have not been so fortunate. I sent him to fetch your King.'

'Not at all,' Fletcher replied with a smile. 'I liked it.'

They were on a smooth, flat branch, only a few hundred feet from the ground. Sylva led him to the edge, where they sat together, looking out at the forest floor.

'I wanted you to see this,' Sylva said, waving out at the plains below.

Herds of deer moved slowly beneath them, a countless procession of thudding hooves. Along the edges, great stags clattered their antlers as they ducked and dodged, vying for the attention of the does who grazed nearby.

They were a mix of greys, browns and white spots; small deer, large deer and great, heavy-horned moose that stomped past.

The ground was covered in a thick layer of bright green moss, the same that had made up the mattress of his sickbed. The deer seemed to enjoy it, trimming the top layer like grass and chewing it slowly into pulpy cud, staining the edges of their mouths with green.

'These are the riches of our people. The Great Herds of the forest. We raise every species of deer under the sun,' Sylva said, her hand outstretched at the deer below.

Fletcher turned to look behind him, and saw an endless host of deer, fading into the depths of the forest. There must have been thousands of them – of all different sizes and breeds, from barking, muntjac deer with their long, tusk-like upper teeth, to red deer jousting back and forth as they interlocked their heavy crowns of antlers.

'Look at those fawns, there's at least a hundred of them,' Fletcher said, pointing to a group of deer on the edge of the herd. They were tiny, barely larger than a wild hare.

'Where are their mothers?' he asked.

'Those aren't fawns, they're pudus,' Sylva laughed. 'See the two spikes on some of their heads? Those are the males' antlers.'

'Oh,' Fletcher said, marvelling at the miniature creatures. 'You really do have every species.'

'The herds give us everything we need: furs and leathers for clothing and blankets, meat and milk for our tables, bones and antlers for carving, sinews and rawhide for our bowstrings and stitching. We even render their fats for tallow, making soaps, candles and glues.'

She pointed to the far edges of the herd, where Fletcher could see elves astride the same elks he had seen in Ignatius's memory, as large as horses but with splayed antlers that they tossed and jostled each other with. Ignatius yelped in recognition, startling the riders below.

The elves carried bows on their backs and long, supple sticks tipped with lassos, which they gently waved to scare wandering deer back into the herd. Their hair was long, streaming over their shoulders in waves of sable, russet and hazel, unlike the elves Fletcher had seen in the trees. They wore wolfskin cloaks, with the wolves' upper jaws resting on their brows like helmets.

'Our wood elves keep them safe, healing their injuries and helping to deliver their young, guiding them down the safe paths and protecting them from the predators of the forest.'

As Fletcher watched, a large bird swooped in from above, alighting on an elf's wrist. It dug its talons into a thick leather wrist guard, and the elf offered it a morsel of raw meat as a reward.

'You keep eagles as pets?' Fletcher asked. 'Why?'

For a moment he wondered if he was being too inquisitive, but Sylva answered readily enough. She seemed pleased he was so interested in the culture of her people.

'We keep foxes too, as you do with dogs. But an eagle is strong enough to carry off a wolf if need be, and they keep watch for the hundreds of packs that forever roam behind the herds. But we can never keep all the deer safe, there's just too much food in one place.'

Fletcher watched a nearby wood elf whip his pole down, slipping a lasso over an errant fawn's legs and pulling it back to the safety of the herds like a trussed chicken.

Fletcher was going to ask more, but someone cleared his throat behind him.

'Thank you, Sylva, for bringing him,' King Harold said,

settling down beside them. 'I'll see you at the council meeting.'

'Council meeting?' Fletcher asked, but Sylva simply smiled at him and gave him a squeeze on the shoulder as she got up to leave.

Then she was gone, leaving Fletcher alone with the king.

# 14

'So, Fletcher. You're still with us,' Harold said. They were sitting, watching the deer herds below. The sun was near set, casting dappled shadows over the busy ground, and Fletcher heard the mournful howl of a wolf in the distance.

'It appears so,' Fletcher replied, avoiding the king's eyes.

'It was touch and go for a while there. I didn't think you'd make it. You were writhing in pain for most of the night.'

'I owe the elves a great deal. And you, it seems. I can't imagine how you convinced everyone to send me to the elves for healing, once you found out I wasn't immune,' Fletcher said dully.

'Oh, no. You're immune all right. But pump enough toxic, acidic liquid into someone's body and he'll not walk away easily, immune or otherwise. You should have died within minutes with that dose, but after the first hour of twitching on the floor, we knew. All the elves did was flush the venom from your system.'

Fletcher was stunned. He was immune. He was a Raleigh. It seemed unreal. Impossible.

'I have pardoned you, but you should also know that your guilt is still being debated by the other nobles, and you may experience some animosity in the future,' Harold continued. 'Most agree that you were only defending your dwarven friend. You can be sure which side your cousins are on, of course.'

'Cousins?' Fletcher asked, still dazed.

'The Forsyths. Your late mother and Tarquin and Isadora's mother were identical twins, Alice and Josephine Queensouth – twins run in the family, it seems. Your father, Edmund, married Alice, while Zacharias married Josephine. We were all childhood friends, back in the day; everyone knew they would end up marrying . . . But that's not what I have come here to talk about. I want to talk about your inheritance, or rather, the lack thereof.'

Fletcher remained silent, both elated and saddened by the news. His parents *had* wanted him. He had not been abandoned to die . . . but to live. Yet, he would never meet them, never hear their voices.

'I don't care about my inheritance,' Fletcher mumbled. 'I was just fine before.'

'Be that as it may, you deserve to know what happened to your family's estate. As their closest relatives, the Forsyths inherited all of your parents' money, lands and properties.' Harold paused awkwardly, clearing his throat. 'Given your supposed crime, they have said you shouldn't be alive and therefore don't deserve any of it back. I disagreed. So we came to an agreement. They will keep all the money and the fertile lands in the centre of Hominum. In exchange, they have given you back your homeland. Raleighshire.'

Fletcher's eyes widened.

'What does that mean?' He knew so little of Hominum's lands, and barely anything about the Raleighs.

'After your parents and their people died, the buildings fell into disrepair and the outlying villages were abandoned,' Harold said, shaking his head with sorrow. 'Other than the troops protecting the mountain pass and the not-so-secret entrance, there's nary a soul for hundreds of miles all around. It's a wasteland, really. But it's yours, to do with as you wish. It is the least I could do, after the sacrifice you made for me. I will not soon forget it.'

Fletcher nodded. It didn't seem real to him. It was land – which had been there before and would be there long after he was dead. What difference did it make who owned it? Nobody even lived there.

'I have something else for you. How can I explain this?' Harold said, rubbing his eyes. 'Have you ever wondered how demons are passed down from generation to generation in noble families, even when the parent dies far from home? The demon should fade back into the ether upon their master's death, correct?'

Fletcher nodded.

'We summoners know the risk we run, always fighting one war or another. So, a summoner will always leave the summoning scrolls for their demons with a trusted friend, so that in the untimely event of their death, their child can be given the scroll and summon the demon back from the ether. In your father's case, I was that trusted friend.'

Harold got to his feet and Fletcher joined him, unsure of

himself. The king reached into his pocket and withdrew a roll of parchment, tightly bound with a red ribbon. From his other pocket, he withdrew a summoning leather, complete with a keyed pentacle embossed in the centre. He laid it down carefully a few feet away from them, in the middle of the branch.

'Edmund's Canid died in the attack, as did your mother's Vulpid. But the Gryphowl that carried you to Pelt; that one may be alive, somewhere in the ether. Here is its scroll. The summoning leather has a keyed pentacle; as you know, you need one when summoning a demon from the ether.'

Fletcher's hands trembled as he untied the ribbon, careful to not tear the dusty material as he unravelled it. The ink was faded, almost to a dark brown, but the words were clearly legible.

'I would infuse your Salamander first,' Harold suggested, before Fletcher could begin to read. 'It's not unknown for a newly summoned demon to attack an unfamiliar demon, before it is fully under its master's control.'

Fletcher nodded, remembering how Ignatius had attacked Didric unbidden. Reluctantly, he infused Ignatius in a flash of violet light.

'Begin,' Harold said, nodding with approval.

'Doh rah go si mai lo go.' Fletcher's voice grew more confident with each word spoken, growing louder and louder until the deer directly below scattered in confusion. 'Fai lo go di ai lo go.'

The pentacle flared with purple light, and Fletcher's vision became saturated with colour, just as it had years ago in Pelt's graveyard. A violet orb appeared above the star, expanding until it was as wide as a carriage wheel, spinning slowly. There was a roaring sound, and Fletcher could hear the shouts of startled wood elves as the entire deer herd began to canter down the plains, fearful of the flashing lights and noise.

'Lei go si mai doh roh!'

As the last words were spoken, the orb blinked out, leaving a fluttering creature in its place.

'My apologies!' the king laughed as the wood elves below hurled what could only be elvish curses at them.

But Fletcher was ignorant of it all, for the new consciousness in his mind was like nothing he had ever encountered. While Ignatius's psyche was a gentle mix of emotions and intentions, this creature's mind was as sharp as it was fast, flitting from thought to thought with absolute clarity.

The demon was much like a barn owl in appearance, with a heart-shaped face, white plumage on its underside and tawny brown feathers above. But unlike an owl, it had four feline legs, complete with a cat's tail, ears and claws, as well as fur intermingled within the fluffy plumage. Most endearing of all, it had round, expressive eyes as blue as Sylva's, which it focused on Fletcher with curiosity.

'The Gryphowl is exceedingly rare, so you may not have heard of it before,' Harold said, edging away from the demon as it emitted a disgruntled screech. 'As you might have already guessed, it's rather like a hybrid of owl and cat, at level four. Your father named her Athena.'

'She's beautiful,' Fletcher breathed, exerting the control he had learned at Vocans. Grasping his connection with Athena, he pulsed his intentions to her, allowing her to read them as he could hers.

The Gryphowl cocked her head to one side then, with a flap of her wings, settled on Fletcher's shoulder. She was careful not to grip too hard with her paws, for they were tipped with a razor-sharp mix of claw and talon. As Athena sensed a twinge of pain from Fletcher, they retracted back into her paws with a soft *schick*.

'You should probably infuse her, before anyone sees,' the king said, looking around warily. 'The elves have requested that any foreign demons must be infused at all times. I would have waited, but I wanted to gift you the demon before Zacharias laid claim to the scroll. I wish you well of her.'

Fletcher was disappointed, for he wished to get to know the demon better, but nevertheless pointed his palm above his shoulder. The pentacle flared violet until he could feel its outline, hot against his skin. With a mental tug, Athena dissolved into threads of white light that shot into his palm. He staggered with the powerful euphoria of the first infusion, as his consciousness merged with hers like the meeting of two rivers.

Within him, he felt his pool of mana grow twofold, and the threads that connected master and demons seemed to braid themselves together. He felt more powerful, the electric energy pulsing along the connection like a beating heart.

As for the psyches of the two demons, they remained apart from each other, unable to sense each other's thoughts. Still, *he* could sense their intentions, as they watched the world through his eyes.

His mind felt very fuzzy, pulled in all directions by the combined consciousness of two demons. He remembered Seraph had once described a summoner who had dozens of

Mites. He couldn't imagine how confusing that would be.

'Good!' Harold said, snatching up the summoning leather and propelling Fletcher along the branch before he could catch his breath. The sun was almost completely set now, and the king released a large ball of wyrdlight, which illuminated the branch ahead as they walked.

Still dazed from infusion, Fletcher saw other lights wink into existence on the branches around them, illuminating the elves that still wandered above. But these were not wyrdlights.

Luminous mushrooms, previously just common frills of brown that had grown along fissures in the mossy bark, glowed with a fierce, green light. Above, blue shone out from the undersides of the branches – glow-worms with incandescent strands of silk dangling like blue gossamer. Even as he marvelled, the fireflies ascended from the wood floor below, a drifting cloud of orange sparks that swirled around them. It was a kaleidoscope of colours, which cast the entire network of branches in an eerily shifting light.

'Amazing, isn't it?' the king said. 'Edmund wrote about it to me, years back. He was often in the Great Forest then, negotiating a trade agreement with the elven clans. Bows, leather, furs and medicines – all were much-needed commodities in Hominum. He dreamed of a society where elves and men could walk each other's lands, with free trade and movement for all. Of course, it all fell apart when he died.'

Fletcher listened closely, eating up every morsel of information he could about his parents. He wished he knew what they looked like. With a twinge, he realised that, in a way, he already did. Had he seen Zacharias's wife in the crowd during the Tournament and the trial? It was hazy in his memory, but he could just about picture a blond lady, sitting close beside Lord Faversham. He supposed he had inherited his dark hair from his father.

'Can you tell me more . . . about my parents?' Fletcher asked timidly.

Harold gave a deep sigh, leading Fletcher on to a bridge to another branch.

'Edmund was my closest friend and Alice . . . well . . . if things had gone another way, she might have been *my* wife. But, I could never get in the way of their happiness. You're all that's left of the two people I loved the most.'

Fletcher looked into Harold's face and saw sorrow there. Perhaps a sadness that he had kept hidden for a long time, even from the nobles he considered friends. It would not do for a king to show his emotions.

Fletcher had always imagined the king to be a calculating, indomitable figure. Instead, he found a kind-hearted man with a deep sense of morality, but who was utterly alone and powerless to make the changes he dreamed of.

'I wish I could help you,' Fletcher said. 'I can fight them in the open, while you work against them in the shadows. But I am just one boy. There's not much I can do.'

'You're a Raleigh now – there's plenty you can do,' Harold disagreed, as the branch they walked upon ended at a large hollow in the centre of a particularly thick tree trunk. 'The first of which is casting your vote as a member of the council, a right you earned when you won the Tournament. The elven clan chiefs and the dwarven elders will be in attendance too. It's the first time this has happened in the history of our peoples.

It's time to solidify the alliance of men, dwarves and elves, once and for all.'

Fletcher gulped as they walked into the shadowed entrance of the trunk.

'When will that be?' he asked.

'Right now.'

# 15

Just inside the entrance, two elves stood against the walls, barring the way with their swords, each as long as a spear.

Fletcher recognised them from his blacksmithing days as falx swords, made up of an unusually long handle that could be gripped with two hands and an even longer meandering blade, shaped like the end of a bow.

The curved edge gave them an axe-like quality, with the long handle giving the sword extra leverage for swinging and parrying. They were fearsome blades, and if he remembered correctly, they were the chosen weapons of the elven people.

'It's OK, let them through.' Sylva's voice came from the darkness beyond.

She stepped out of the shadows. Fletcher was surprised to see that she had her own falx strapped to her back, as well as a supple bow and loaded quiver. Her hair, usually loose and flowing, was now knotted into an oiled, single braid that fell over her shoulder and down to her navel, with a jade stone set on the end to weigh it down.

But what drew Fletcher's eye most was not her weapons, but the lamellar armour she wore. It was made up of hundreds of rectangular pieces of leather, each one pierced in four corners and laced to those around it. It hugged her body closely, flexing and loosening with each step she took towards them. Her limbs were protected by thigh, shin, shoulder and wrist guards, and the entire ensemble had been lacquered to shine dark green.

'Well, we are here for a war council.' She blushed with a rueful smile, seeing Fletcher's admiration.

Harold gave her a respectful nod and walked on, through the darkness of the passageway and into a room lit by flickering torches. Sylva followed behind without a backwards glance.

The room was as large as the dining hall at Vocans, with a domelike ceiling and walls completely bare but for the entrance they had walked through, and a few dozen torches. In the middle of the room was a large, round table of polished wood, with a strange, cloth-covered object as tall as a man in its centre. The table was surrounded by high-backed seats, each with a standard affixed above it. Most were occupied – some by men and women, others by elves and, closest to Fletcher, dwarves. They had all turned to look at the newcomers. Fletcher shrank under their gaze.

'Fletcher, your seat is here,' whispered a familiar voice. Othello's face peeked out from behind one of the chairs, his clipped beard strange compared to the row of grizzled dwarves to his right. He grinned as Fletcher broke into a smile, but held a finger to his lips.

Fletcher looked at the seat beside Othello, to find the blue and silver insignia of the Raleighs on the standard above it.

It was so strange to suddenly have a history, even a family crest. He knew he would never grow accustomed to it – not least because it had a Manticore emblazoned across the centre. He took a tentative seat as both Sylva and King Harold walked around to find their places.

Harold sat down to Fletcher's left, in between Alfric, Zacharias and Lady Faversham, who were carefully avoiding Fletcher's eyes. There were four generals with lamb-chop sideburns and thick moustaches sitting closest to the elves. They sat with ramrod backs and stared straight ahead.

A hawkish noblewoman Fletcher did not recognise nodded to him. She was thickset and sported red hair shot with silver. Beside her a dark-skinned nobleman completed the human contingent, though he only stared at Fletcher beneath hooded eyes. Fletcher found it hard to believe that he was now as highborn as these nobles were, and was considered their equal.

To think, just a few hours ago he had been thought a common murderer, condemned to a brutal death. He felt a shudder of horror pass through him, and within him, Ignatius's consciousness squirmed at his discomfort.

Athena did not react at all. Perhaps his father had trained her not to allow her emotions to cloud his own.

To his right, Othello, Uhtred and five white-haired dwarves sat in stony silence, waiting for the meeting to begin. It seemed the father and son had been made elders in the past year, perhaps for their respective contributions to the alliance with Hominum, or the high standing they held among their peers.

There were ten elves, including Sylva, who must have been representing her clan chieftain father. All were high elves and all but three were female. Each of them wore the same heavy armour Sylva did, though the colouring varied to match the banners above their chairs.

'Well, now that we are all here, let us begin,' King Harold announced in a loud, clear voice, banging his fist on the table for attention.

Fletcher was stunned by the change in the man. His voice had taken on an edge and his authority suddenly weighed heavily on the room.

'We have three problems to solve today. The first, and most pressing, is the morale problem – among dwarves, men and elves alike.'

He pointed at Sylva and softened his tone.

'You elves delayed our alliance for almost a year, because you were angry at the injuries Sylva sustained in our end of year Tournament, and at the hands of a council member's son, no less. This animosity remains, in both wood elf and high elf alike. Do I tell a lie?' he asked.

'No, you are quite right,' Sylva said, standing and looking at the other chieftains. 'Though I have done my best to explain that *all* the students were put at equal risk.'

'Quite so,' Harold said, waving his hand for her to retake her seat. Sylva narrowed her eyes as Zacharias and Alfric exchanged amused glances, but sat back down. Harold was an excellent actor.

'As for the dwarves, the terror attacks by the Anvils have caused much hatred between our peoples. I tried to assuage dwarven anger by rescinding the population and property laws, but it has had little effect,' the king continued.

'What use is being allowed to own our own land if your nobles will not sell to us?' one of the dwarven elders asked in a quavering voice.

'If they own the land, it is not my decision who they sell or rent it to,' Harold replied. 'Most nobles are reluctant to part with their lands at the best of times. I am no tyrant, they can do as they wish.'

'The population laws are little use when our menfolk are away training,' Uhtred added. 'Fewer dwarven children have been sired this year than any other.'

Harold sighed loudly, then moved on, ignoring him.

'Humans have their own reasons to hate the elves, after the expensive war you forced us into. If this gets any worse, there will be infighting among our soldiers. Dwarves, men and elves, at each other's throats. A disaster that could lose us the entire war. Do you agree that this is a serious problem?'

There were nods of assent from around the table.

'I'm glad we can agree on something,' Harold said, easing himself back into his seat. 'The next two problems can be explained better by another. Lord Forsyth, if you please.'

Zacharias stood and turned to the entrance.

'Send in the boy!' he shouted.

There was the rasp of blades being uncrossed, then a dark-haired young man stumbled into the room. He was skinny as a rake, so much so that his garments hung from him like a ship's sails on a windless day. His eyes were sunken, and he was tanned a deep, dark brown, as if he had been working in the sun all his life.

'Freshly escaped from an orc internment camp,' Zacharias

said, dragging the boy into the torchlight. 'Fourteen when he joined up, fifteen when captured and sixteen now. For two years he's been one of their slaves, carrying their firewood, catching their fish, building their monuments, making their weapons.'

The boy avoided the watchers' eyes, instead looking at his feet.

'Like a gremlin, but bigger, weren't you?' Zacharias barked, making the boy jump. 'Go on, speak up.'

The boy opened his mouth, but all that came out was a nonsensical stammer. Zacharias slapped him on the back of his head, and the boy cringed.

'To think you were once a Forsyth Fury. Snivelling wretch! Speak or I'll beat it out of you!'

He raised his hand threateningly and the boy spoke, the words tripping over his tongue in his rush to get them out, his accent as thick and common as Fletcher had ever heard.

'There were ten of us, doin' the 'eavy liftin' when the gremlins couldn't manage it, sire. Me and nine other lads. But there was another. A woman. Noble, I reckoned. Older too. Ain't never got a good look at 'er – the orcs kept us away from 'er cage mostly. 'Alf starved, she was. Never said a dicky, not even when I snuck 'er some food. Gone mad, bein' alone so long. But 'er clothes. Officer's uniform, from the old days. That's 'ow I knew she was one of your lot.'

There were whispers from the nobles, then the red-haired noblewoman stood and spoke in a soft, lilting voice.

'Elizabeth Cavendish. It must be her. She and her demon, a Peryton, went down behind enemy lines twelve years ago. Ophelia, could it be?'

Lady Faversham looked up, for she had been in deep thought.

'You are right, Boudica. I never saw Elizabeth killed; it was the Peryton that was struck by the javelin. She could be alive, though she fell from a great height. I only wish I had been able to fly to her aid, but the Wyvern riders were in full pursuit. Perhaps they kept her. Tortured her. To discover our secrets.'

'Rufus's mother,' Othello whispered.

Fletcher remembered the small, mousy-haired boy from Vocans who had followed Tarquin Forsyth around like a lost puppy. His mother, a noblewoman, was thought dead, while his father was a commoner.

'We cannot allow her to remain in orc hands. It would be unseemly, to leave one of our own out there. She was popular among commoners and nobles alike, thanks to her marriage to that common servant.' Disdain dripped from Ophelia Faversham's words and she curled her lip. 'It would do well for morale, and her two sons, if we were to rescue her.'

'Exactly,' Harold agreed. 'Well said, Ophelia.'

An elven woman stood. She was powerfully built, with a strong jaw and hair so finely braided that the strands hung in dreadlocks around her head.

'This noblewoman is no concern of ours. Save this for your own council meeting.'

Her voice was heavily accented, but clear enough.

'Please, Chief Cerva,' Harold implored. 'A victory for Hominum is a victory for all. Are we not in this together?'

Cerva stared back, unimpressed.

'We will not risk elven lives on a foolhardy rescue mission, if that is what you ask of us,' she stated simply.

'It is nothing like that, I assure you. Please, allow us to present our plan, and if afterwards you are dissatisfied, we shall assuage your doubts.'

Cerva returned to her seat, but kept her arms crossed.

Harold paused then, allowing silence to settle over the room.

'Our next problem is perhaps the most shocking. Something new. Something that could spell doom for us all, allied or not. Lord Raleigh, would you be so kind as to remove the cloth from the container there?'

It took a few moments for Fletcher to realise Harold was speaking to him. Lord Raleigh. Was he ever going to get used to that? He stared at the object for a moment then, realising he had no other option, climbed on to the table.

The wood creaked underfoot and there was a mutter of annoyance from one of the elves, but he eventually reached the cloth-covered cylinder. He gripped the sheet and tugged it away, hearing the slosh of water from within as the cylinder rocked on its base. He did not know what he had expected to see, but the cries of disgust from the room echoed his own.

A creature lay within.

# 16

It hung there, suspended in a greenish liquid that continued to slosh back and forth. It had been pickled to preserve the flesh, and a ragged hole could be seen in the centre of its scrawny chest.

'What is it?' Cerva asked, her voice tinged with a mix of horror and curiosity. 'A demon of some sort?'

'No,' Harold said gravely. 'Not a demon. It is an aberration, a monstrosity. A strange mix of orc and gremlin, created by some dark art unknown to us.'

Fletcher examined the creature. It looked somewhat like a gremlin, for it had the same droopy, triangular ears, elongated nose and bulbous eyes. The fingers were long and nimble like a gremlin's too, with a similar, if less exaggerated, hunch. It even wore a loincloth of the same design.

Yet it was far too large, standing at a height somewhere between a dwarf and a man. Its mouth was filled with sharp, yellow teeth, and it sported thick canines in its lower jaw that reminded Fletcher of a juvenile orc's tusks. Its build was on the skinny side, but the cords of muscle that wrapped its limbs left no doubt that the creature was an agile fighter. The corpse's skin, grey like an orc's or a gremlin's, had shrivelled slightly in the liquid.

'We call them goblins, and they are breeding them by the thou—' the king began, but was interrupted by Uhtred.

'Thousands?' the dwarf cried. 'We are barely able to hold off the orcs as it is. Numbers were our greatest advantage!'

'What weapons do these goblins use?' Sylva asked, leaping on to the table so she could examine the creature more closely.

'The same ones as orcs, so far as we know,' King Harold said gravely. 'Clubs studded with volcanic glass, javelins, rawhide shields, stone-tipped spears, that kind of thing. As Uhtred said, it is their numbers that worry us. Even with the addition of dwarven and elven troops, they may already outnumber us.'

'How did you find out about them?' Fletcher asked, his face flushing. Yet Harold answered him readily enough.

'The boy. Boy, what's your name?' Harold asked, snapping his fingers. Fletcher was momentarily taken aback by Harold's rudeness, but then realised he was still acting.

'Mason, sire,' the boy mumbled.

'Mason here brought that body with him. He took one when he escaped. Clever boy, aren't you, Mason?'

'If you say so, your majesty,' Mason said, lowering his head respectfully.

'Mason tells us that he saw them spawning from eggs of all things, deep within the orcs' jungle caves. The one you see is full-grown, one of the first specimens. Sexless beneath those loincloths.'

'How many of these early specimens are there?' Uhtred asked, directing his question to Mason.

'I can't rightly say, beggin' your pardon, mister. Maybe a few 'undred,' Mason said, after a few moments' thought. 'They mostly stay 'idden underground, tendin' the eggs and such. Them eggs 'ave been cookin' for a long time, 'cos the goblins come out full-grown – I've never seen no babies runnin' about. Some of the eggs must be years old, from the dust and muck on 'em. Once this batch 'atch, there might not be another for while.'

'Well, at least that's something,' Uhtred said.

'Indeed.' Harold nodded gravely. 'Which brings me to the next part of the meeting. These eggs must be destroyed. Lady Cavendish must be rescued. Our peoples must be unified and morale improved. The question is how?'

'Leaving aside the morale problem, we cannot mount an all-out assault on the orcs,' Cerva said as Sylva stepped down from the table. Fletcher followed Sylva's example, glad to be away from the pickled corpse. Cerva did not wait for him to be seated before she spoke again.

'You need open ground for your soldiers' muskets and the orcs would be fighting in their own territory. It would be a slaughter.'

'I agree,' one of the generals said. 'Lady Faversham, can't your flying summoners mount an assault?'

Ophelia turned to the general and gave him a withering look.

'Mason tells us he was kept deep in the jungle. He only escaped when he was swept away by a river, using the goblin's corpse as a flotation device. Is that not so, boy?' She barely waited for his nod before continuing.

'That far in, the Celestial Corps might be spotted before we were even halfway there, and the shamans would fly their Wyverns out to meet us. Their airforce is stronger than ours, though we are faster. Even if we managed to reach the target, we would only be able to land at the site for a few minutes, then fly out again before the orc shamans mobilised their Wyverns and caught us up. But there would not be nearly enough time to search the caverns, destroy several thousand goblin eggs and break out a prisoner, especially with half of Orcdom alerted to our presence.'

At her mention of Wyvern riders, Fletcher's mind flashed to one of the long, tedious demonology lessons with Major Goodwin, where he had learned about them for the first time. They were enormous, scaled creatures, sporting two powerful legs, batlike wings, a long, spiked tail and a horned, crocodilian head. At level fifteen, they were considered the most powerful demons in the orcs' arsenal, an exception to the belief that orc shaman demons were generally weaker than Hominum's. There were only a dozen or so of them, but even Hominum's Alicorns, Hippogriffs, Perytons and Griffins were no match for the fearsome beasts.

For the first time, old King Alfric spoke. Fletcher steeled himself and tried not to glare at the man who had tried to kill him.

'My dear cousin is right,' he said, nodding at Ophelia. 'If we lost the Celestial Corps we would lose our only air defence. Then the Wyvern riders could run rampant without the corps to harry them if they chose to raid Hominum.'

'So, that's not an option,' Harold said, though his tone

suggested that he had already known this. 'But I have a solution. It is a risky plan, one that we would need a unanimous decision on. I propose we send in four teams of graduates from Vocans – to go behind enemy lines, rescue Lady Cavendish and destroy the goblin eggs. As battlemages, they will be powerful enough to defend themselves effectively, whilst also being in small enough numbers to pass through the jungle undetected. We cannot risk our experienced officers – the soldiers need their leadership on the front lines.'

Harold paused to see the council's reactions, but this time the silence was one of surprise rather than disinterest. Fletcher's mind raced, contemplating the plan. It could work, true – but it was so, so dangerous.

He already had an idea of who would be sent on this fateful mission – and a kick from Othello under the table told him he wasn't the only one. He met Sylva's eyes across the room. Her gaze was impassive, but he could see the muscles of her jaws were clenched.

'They will each be given a guide to lead them,' Harold continued blithely, 'and once they have completed their mission and are out of the caves, the Celestial Corps will fly them out of there.'

Again, silence. Harold's carefully rehearsed speech was not having the desired effect.

'But that's not all,' the king said. 'We can unite all three races behind a common purpose. Lord Forsyth. If you would be so kind.'

Zacharias stood and removed something from his pocket, holding it up to the flickering torchlight, so that all could see.

It was a purple crystal, carefully polished and cut into a flat, round gemstone.

'Corundum crystal. Scrying stones, fulfilmeters and charging stones are all made from it. Up until a few weeks ago, it was one of the most expensive and rare elements in Hominum. No longer.'

Zacharias tossed the crystal across the table, as if it was worthless.

'The Triumvirate invested in mining operations to supplement Hominum's limited supplies of sulphur, the key ingredient of gunpowder. We came across a large deposit of corundum instead. Enough to put scrying crystals in every barracks, tavern and village hall across the country, with more to spare.'

If he had expected a reaction from the table he was disappointed, receiving only blank stares.

'Congratulations,' Sylva said, with only a touch of sarcasm.

'Don't you understand what this means?' Ophelia said, surprised by their lack of interest. 'Every person in Hominum can use the scrying crystals to see what is happening on the front lines. It could be a huge morale boost.'

'Yes, from the perspective of only one demon for each crystal,' Othello said. 'And they wouldn't be able to hear a word – only the demon's owner could do that.'

'But they would see elven, dwarven and human troops fighting side by side,' Uhtred said, warming to the idea.

'But that only helps in the long run,' Cerva interjected. 'The elven and dwarven troops will arrive on the front lines within a few weeks. We need to solve these racial tensions before they arrive. If we don't, there will be infighting between our soldiers, mark my words. One tavern brawl could spiral into an all-out race war.'

'Well that is the second part of my plan,' Harold said, jumping to his feet and addressing the entire table. 'The mission takes place *before* these troops arrive, and it shall be transmitted to human, elf and dwarf alike through the Triumvirate's scrying stones, generously provided by Lord Forsyth here. Most importantly, with dwarven and elven graduates, our peoples will see that we are all in this together, and that orcs are the true enemy.'

Harold paused again, allowing his words to sink in.

Fletcher considered the plan. It *was* risky, and it could hurt more than it helped. There were no guarantees that the different races would get along during the mission – he thought back to all the race rivalry that took place at Vocans. One slip-up and there could be rioting on the streets.

'Our three races are branches of the same tree,' Harold said, gazing earnestly at each person around the table. 'This could be the beginning of a new era, where man, dwarf and elf can live in peace, side by side. Never before have we had an opportunity like this. Let us seize it, together!'

'I have a question,' Sylva said, raising her hand. 'Who are these graduates you speak of? The only elven summoner is . . . me.'

'Yes, well . . . that is part of the reason why I have gathered you all here.' Harold coughed, his bravado replaced with a sudden awkwardness, the mask slipping for the briefest of moments. 'We are in the infancy of the diversification of

Vocans. You are the only elven graduate and Othello is the only dwarven graduate.'

'I see,' Sylva replied, her voice pensive as she considered him carefully.

'We would need both you and Othello to undertake this mission,' Harold said. 'Lord Raleigh would be another candidate; his common roots and noble heritage would appeal to the people of Hominum. That would also make it fair – one from each of our respective councils. We will also allow one first-year volunteer to join each team. It is my hope that Atilla and Cress, the two dwarven first years, will do just that.'

Silence lay thick in the room. Then whispers began, as the dwarves leaned together and discussed the proposal. There was a shaking of heads. Across the table, Fletcher heard Cerva's angry muttering.

'If the mission failed, it would do more harm than good,' she growled, clasping Sylva's forearm. 'It's a risky mission as it is. Your father would never forgive us if his only daughter died.'

Fletcher looked to Harold. Sweat trickled down the king's temple, plastering golden hair to his forehead in sodden curls. He flicked his eyes to Fletcher and gave the smallest of nods.

It was time to stand and speak. But was it the right move? All he knew was that the alliance was crumbling, and the hatred between their races was near boiling point. Sooner or later, it was going to spiral out of control. One more attack from the Anvils, one more argument gone bad, even a racially charged comment could set it all off. But sometimes, doing nothing was the greatest risk of all.

'I will do it,' a voice said, cutting through the hushed debate.

It took a moment for Fletcher to realise it was his own. He gulped as all eyes turned to him once again.

'I am not afraid,' he continued, standing and knuckling his fists on the table. 'Hominum will not back down from a fight.'

He *was* afraid, but he knew they were the right words as soon as they had left his mouth. Cerva bridled at the unspoken accusation.

'The elves are not afraid either,' she said, lifting her chin. 'Sylva is the best of us. I cannot speak for her, but the clans will support her decision.'

Sylva stood to face Fletcher, looking at him with a cool, calculating expression that made it clear that she would not make this decision on the basis of their friendship. Fletcher stared right back, trying to convey a confidence he did not feel.

'The dwarves will not let you down.' Fletcher breathed with relief as Othello growled from his right. 'If Hominum's people wish to see a dwarf fight the orcs, I shall be glad to show them.'

Uhtred snatched at his son's sleeve, but it was too late, the words had been spoken. Othello gave Fletcher a grim nod, and Fletcher clasped his wrist in gratitude.

'Agreed,' one of the white-bearded dwarven elders said, after a quick glance at the others.

Sylva looked unmoved, her eyes flicking from Zacharias Forsyth, to Ophelia Faversham and old King Alfric. It threw a shadow of doubt over Fletcher's heart. Whose plan was it really? Something didn't add up. Why would Lord Forsyth give away all those valuable crystals for free, when all he cared about was profit? He didn't care about uniting the races: the dwarves were his main competitor in the weapons industry, and a war with the elves would mean continued demand for weapons on the northern front.

Stranger still, Ophelia seemed to be supporting the decision, despite the fact that she was just as invested in the weapons industry as Zacharias. Perhaps they finally understood just how dangerous a race war would be for the safety of Hominum.

Even as Fletcher tried to wrap his head around their bizarre behaviour, Sylva finally spoke.

'So be it.'

# 17

'I'm not doing it,' Fletcher said, as Captain Lovett leaned out of her saddle and pulled him up behind her.

'Too late,' she laughed, grasping Fletcher's hands and putting them around her waist.

It was the next morning, and they were on a wide tree branch, with Lysander pawing at the bark beneath his claws, ready to take off. Before, Fletcher hadn't minded heights much, but now he knew he would be flying above it, the ground seemed a long distance away.

The other riders were down below, Arcturus included, ready for the long flight to Vocans so that they could watch the Tournament. He could see Sylva among them, the only elf in a sea of humans and elderly dwarves. He felt anxious about what had happened between them at the council meeting, but had not spoken with her since, instead being ushered back to his room by an impatient elf servant and, after a night of uneasy sleep, had been woken by Lovett that morning.

Sylva would always put her people before their friendship,

and the memory of her attempted alliance with the Forsyth twins at Vocans came, unbidden, to his mind. He could hardly blame her for feeling that way, but the reminder of her priorities at the council meeting made his chest tighten.

'Are you sure you're OK taking me back to Pelt first?' Fletcher asked, trying not to look down.

'Of course. Between you and me, I don't like spending time with the Celestial Corps, though I am still a member,' Lovett said over her shoulder. 'That's why I volunteered to teach at Vocans. Ophelia Faversham is as unpleasant as any corporal I have served under – though she prefers to go by the title of Lady, thinks the rank sounds too masculine. I'll stick with *Captain* Lovett though, so don't go getting any ideas!'

'I'm a captain too, you know,' Fletcher grumbled, trying to focus on the square of Lovett's back. 'I won the Tournament after all.'

'I forgot about that!' Lovett laughed. Fletcher smiled, for he had never seen her laugh before. Her voice, usually so steely and resolved, had become warm and inviting.

'I think—'

But Fletcher never got to tell her what he thought, because Lysander had launched himself from the branch, and the world had turned a blur of brown and green. The Griffin swooped and jinked between branches, and Fletcher felt the bottom fall out of his stomach, then somersault. Lovett whooped with unbridled joy, urging Lysander on to greater speeds.

With a few last thrusts of his great wings, the Griffin burst through the foliage at the top, the thick, waxy leaves slapping against their faces. Then they were out in the dawn air, the morning sunlight pale but warm against Fletcher's skin.

In the distance, the Beartooth Mountains loomed, their jagged peaks stretching into the sky like the fangs they were named after. Despite their heady ascent, Fletcher felt a sudden calm wash over him. A sea of green stretched out beneath them; the treetops waved in the breeze, accompanied by the gentle creak of moving boughs. It was breathtaking.

'I never tire of flying,' Lovett exclaimed, rubbing Lysander's neck. 'How are you doing back there?'

Fletcher gazed at the vista around him. Even when he had peered out of his bedroom window at Vocans, he had never been this high, nor seen more of the world he lived in.

'*I* would never tire of it either,' Fletcher said, leaning back in his saddle. His fear had dissipated, replaced by a sudden desire to move, jump, feel something, anything. He was alive and free and his own man at last.

He wanted to summon Ignatius, so he could share the moment with him. But it was risky, there was barely any more room on the saddle. Yet, there was another who could join him for his first flight, and he pointed his hand into the air. His palm flashed with a brief pain as the pentacle burned violet, then Athena burst into existence with a purr of exhilaration, zooming around Lovett and Fletcher in a flash of white and brown. As Lysander turned his head to look at the new arrival, she regained her composure, settling on her master's shoulder and gazing serenely back at him. He reached out to stroke her and felt a twinge of jealousy from Ignatius. The emotion was hidden as swiftly as it had appeared, but Fletcher lowered his hand.

'I remember Athena well,' Lovett said, her tone suddenly

sombre. 'I was at Vocans with your parents, Fletcher. Of course, they were much older than me. You should know that they were good people. Edmund and Alice were always kind to me, making sure I was looked after, since I was the youngest at the academy. And Arcturus did that too, of course.'

'Arcturus knew my parents?' Fletcher asked.

'Yes. He was the first commoner to come to Vocans. Edmund, Alice and I were the only ones who truly accepted him.'

'He might be disappointed, now that he knows I'm not his half-brother,' Fletcher said, his mood taking a turn for the worse. He had always known he could rely on Arcturus to come through for him, as any older brother would. Would Arcturus still care about him, now that he knew the truth?

'I think he would love you all the more for it,' Lovett said reassuringly, looking at Fletcher over her shoulder. 'Your parents died only two years after they graduated, and it hit Arcturus hard. He got that scar searching for the orcs that did it.'

'I didn't know that,' Fletcher said, looking down at his hands. He felt an affectionate nip on his ear, as Athena tried to cheer him up. Feathers brushed against the back of his neck as she rubbed up against him. It comforted him to think that she would have done the same thing to his father, long ago. She was the only connection he had to his past life.

His resolve strengthened and he turned back to the task at hand. Sir Caulder and Berdon would want to know he was OK.

'Take us to Pelt, Captain,' Fletcher said, gripping the saddle and pointing at Beartooth's highest peak. 'Let's see how fast this Griffin can go.'

*

143

As they spiralled slowly in their descent, Fletcher was surprised to see new structures built outside Pelt's gates. Ramshackle huts spread out like scattered pebbles, poorly constructed from mud, straw and sparse branches. There was a clearing in the centre, where a host of men and women had gathered, and Fletcher could see Berdon's imposing figure standing at their head, with Sir Caulder by his side. In front of them stood a line of Didric's guards, their yellow and black uniforms stark against the muddy ground.

'Land there,' Fletcher shouted, pointing his finger between the two groups.

As they neared the crowd, Fletcher could hear yells of anger; he saw pitchforks, bricks and spades held high. Trouble was brewing, and they were going to arrive right in the thick of it.

Lysander landed in a spray of mud, spattering the guards closest to them as Fletcher leaped to the ground, leaving Lovett to take off again and circle above, her steely gaze leaving no doubt as to whose side she was on. Athena followed in her wake, ready to swoop down at the first sign of trouble.

'Lord Raleigh,' one of the guards shouted, 'I respectfully ask you to stand aside. We are here on orders from Lord Cavell. These squatters are to leave his lands immediately.'

Fletcher ignored him and walked closer to Berdon and Sir Caulder. He raised his palm and Ignatius materialised beside him, spitting a warning plume of flame as the nervous guards began to raise their muskets.

'What's happening?' he asked, wishing that he had his khopesh with him.

'They're trying to turn us out,' Berdon said. 'This is our settlement.'

'And we aren't leaving,' one of the women from the crowd bellowed. 'You won't make us homeless a second time.'

There was a cheer of support from those around him, and the mob surged forward, stopping just short of Berdon's arms. Fletcher recognised her as Janet, the leatherworker who had made his jacket.

'Most of Pelt have been living in this settlement since Didric and his father called in their debts to build the prison,' Berdon explained to Fletcher as they looked on. 'But Didric was granted the land we built on when he was made a noble and he's been trying to get us off it ever since.'

'I had no idea,' Fletcher murmured, shaking his head in disgust.

'It's not going to end well,' Sir Caulder grunted, pulling his sword from his scabbard and prodding at the closest of the angry villagers. 'Those guards will start firing any minute. Berdon tells me this is the first time they've brought their muskets.'

'Aye, son, I think this is revenge for your victory at the trial,' Berdon agreed, then peered over his shoulder. 'I can't hold them back much longer.'

Fletcher looked at the approaching soldiers. He was to blame for this; he had to fix it. But how?

The homes around him were nothing more than filthy hovels, for the penniless villagers could not afford proper building materials. There was no well for water, no walls to keep out wolves and thieves. The villagers themselves wore ragged, dirty clothes, their unwashed faces streaked with grime. Even Berdon

145

was poorly dressed, and Fletcher could see now that he had lost weight too – his once meaty frame turned to lean, corded muscle.

This was what Didric had reduced them to, turning once proud hunters and artisans into slum-dwelling vagrants. And now, left with no more than a roof over their heads, Didric would take away even that from them.

'He'll pay for this,' Fletcher whispered, as a stone arced over his head. It landed a few feet from the guards, but suddenly muskets were raised high and fingers tightened on triggers.

'They can't kill all of us, lads,' Janet bellowed again. 'Our homes are all we have left!'

'It's not worth dying over!' Fletcher shouted. The mob's shouting reduced to a murmur as they turned their eyes on to him.

'We have nothing else,' Janet replied, curling her lip and spitting to show her contempt. 'Without these "homes" we'd be begging for food on the streets of Boreas, if the Pinkertons don't run us out of the city first. Half of us will freeze to death before the year is out.'

Her words struck Fletcher hard. It was so easy to think that they could rebuild their lives, find jobs elsewhere. Yet he could still remember that fateful night two years ago, when he himself had been forced to leave Pelt. The fear, the doubt. Even then, he'd had money, clothes, weapons. These people had nothing. He wished that he could help them, but he had barely anything to give.

'Cat's got your tongue has it, *Lord* Raleigh?' Janet mocked. 'That's right, we know all about your heritage now. Get off your high horse and stand aside. This is where we make our stand. There's nowhere else.'

But there was. The realisation dawned on him, like sunlight breaking through the clouds. It would be hard work, and he would not be there to help them. But he owed these villagers. Owed Berdon.

'Wait! There is somewhere you can go!' Fletcher shouted. Ignatius snarled as the guards took a step closer. 'Raleighshire. You can resettle there.'

Silence descended, broken only by the clinking of metal from the guards' uniforms.

'There are abandoned villages there. Land for hunting, rivers for fishing. It's warm, on the jungle border. You can rebuild. Start anew.' Fletcher spoke rapidly, for there was another bark of warning from Ignatius as the guards moved forward once again.

'You think we'd be safer, near the jungles? With orc raiders coming over the border every day, slaughtering us? I'd rather take my chances right here, right now,' Janet hissed.

'You know me, all of you,' Fletcher said, addressing the crowd. 'I will be the liege lord of the lands you live on. I swear I will do my utmost to keep you safe and secure, when I return there.'

Ignatius scampered up his leg and on to his shoulders, and Fletcher took Berdon and Sir Caulder by their arms.

It was time to change tactics. 'You can die here, like stubborn fools,' Fletcher said, walking towards the crowd. 'Or you can follow us, to a new life. It's up to you.'

Fletcher pushed through the mob, walking away from the soldiers. He felt their eyes on him as he brushed past, and he hoped they couldn't see the red blush of fear burning the back of his neck. Had it worked?

Berdon spoke loudly in his deep baritone voice as they broke out of the gathered people.

'Those who would come with us, gather your things and meet me at the edge of the encampment. Take only what you can carry, for the road will be long. The rest of you, I shall see in the afterlife.'

Fletcher, Berdon and Sir Caulder walked on, not looking back. They heard the squelch of footsteps behind them, but if it was more than a few, Fletcher couldn't tell.

'How many are following us?' Sir Caulder whispered out of the side of his mouth, grunting with effort as he wrenched his peg leg through the mud.

'No idea,' Berdon murmured back. 'Don't look. Give them a few minutes.'

They walked on, through the last of the hovels, until they stood alongside the mountain path that led down from the village. There were no gunshots, but they kept their heads facing forward, looking out into the valleys below. The sun was still rising in the distance, bathing the treetops in golden light.

'If it's all right with you, I'd like to go with Berdon here, back to Raleighshire,' Sir Caulder said, his voice tentative, barely louder than a whisper. 'It's where I belong, and I don't think I'll be safe at Vocans after what I said at the trial.'

'You're welcome to, of course. You know, I didn't get a chance to thank you. You took a great risk, telling that story,' Fletcher said to Sir Caulder.

'Think nothing of it, my dear boy. It was my duty. I am glad that I was able to save you, even if I was unable to save your

148

parents all those years ago. Can you forgive me?' His voice quavered, and Fletcher remembered that, though a capable warrior, Sir Caulder was an old man, nearing the end of his years. He could imagine how terrible his guilt had been, kept hidden for so long.

'There is nothing to forgive. The past is the past,' Fletcher said. 'I will focus on the family and friends I have left, you included.'

He paused and turned to Berdon, who was staring out at the sunrise, avoiding his eyes.

'You know you're still my dad, right?'

Berdon closed his eyes and smiled, the tension dropping from his shoulders.

'There are some things I have to do soon,' Fletcher went on, putting his arm around Berdon's broad back. 'Things that will take me away from you. But I promise I'll come home. We can found the new village together, far away from the hellhole this place has become.'

'I'll hold you to that, son,' Berdon said, wrapping Fletcher in a bear hug that made his ribs creak.

There was an awkward cough from behind them, and Fletcher peered over Berdon's shoulder to see a crowd of people standing there, their belongings piled high on handcarts and a lone, rickety wagon. Janet stepped out from the crowd, her face briefly shaded as Lysander's shadow glided by.

'Well, you've convinced us. Now stop this soppy rubbish and tell us how to get there.'

# 18

Fletcher's demons ignored each other on the flight to Vocans, despite being inches apart – with Athena on his shoulder and Ignatius around his neck. It wasn't that they didn't like each other. Fletcher could tell it was a strange sense of uncertainty, compounded by competitiveness.

The journey was quiet, with little conversation between him and Lovett, though it would have been hard to speak anyway, with the wind snatching away the few words they did attempt. He tried not to dwell on the events of the past few days, for it deeply unsettled him and left him plagued by self-doubt. Even thoughts of Berdon were bittersweet, for their reunion had been short-lived and their parting as painful as the first time he had left him.

Instead, Fletcher busied himself with watching the land below, sweeping into the horizon like a slow-moving patchwork quilt of yellows, browns and greens, broken by threads of blue and grey as roads and rivers wended their way across the plains.

It was almost nightfall when he saw the dark facade of Vocans in the distance, and as they circled down to land in the courtyard, he realised how much he had missed the crumbling old castle.

'You'd better hurry if you're going to catch the end of the Tournament,' Lovett said as they landed, propelling him towards the doors. 'I'll unsaddle Lysander, you go on ahead.'

'Thanks for the ride. I'll see you in there,' Fletcher said. 'Sorry I was such poor company.'

Lovett tutted and waved him away.

'Don't worry about it.'

He hurried through the double doors to find the atrium silent as a grave, his footsteps echoing in the empty space. It was strange, to be back. It had been a year, the longest year of his life, but it felt like only yesterday he had walked these halls. Somehow, he felt more at home at Vocans than he had back in Pelt.

Funnily enough, having both Ignatius and Athena on his shoulders barely hampered him, though Athena took the opportunity to stretch her wings and fluttered into the air, gliding above and keeping watch for potential dangers. Ignatius yawned at her, then wrapped himself more closely around Fletcher's neck, as if to let her know that she was wasting her time.

Soon Fletcher was pacing down the stairs and along the corridor of cells. He could hear the roar of the crowd reverberating along the cold stone walls, rising and falling as a battle for supremacy was waged on the sands of the arena. As he neared the entrance, Fletcher realised it must be the final round, for the cells were empty, with all the contestants but the two in the arena having been knocked out of the Tournament.

His entrance went unnoticed by the spectators, so focused were they on the events below them. Nobles, generals and servants alike added their voices to the chorus, yet now Fletcher could make out one name being chanted.

'Didric! Didric!'

In the sweltering heat of the arena, two figures whirled around each other on the sand, jabbing and parrying as they sought an opening. There seemed to be no demons present, the rules of the final round set up as a trial by combat, just as Fletcher's second round with Malik had been in his own Tournament.

Didric was armed with a long, thin rapier on a basket hilt, designed for fencing rather than killing orcs. His blond hair was plastered across his head as he sweated in the sweltering heat of the arena, and a stain of dried blood crusted his lips and chin, the remains of a nosebleed recently staunched.

His scarred face grinned in a savage rictus at his opponent, the once flabby body now lean and hard, extending and rescinding with the practised ease of a trained swordsman.

The other combatant was clearly a dwarf, with a long wave of red hair that lashed the air as they dodged and countered, one hand clutching a spiked bangle as a knuckleduster for striking and parrying, the other wielding a short, wedge-shaped blade on a carved bone handle that Fletcher recognised as a seax.

The dwarf took a few steps back against a sudden flurry of blows from Didric, then lashed out with a foot to send a spray of sand into his face. As Didric spun away, pawing at his eyes, the dwarf took the opportunity to dodge sideways into open space, for they had been pressed up against the wall of the arena.

Fletcher was surprised to see the beardless chin of a female dwarf, her eyes as green as Othello's, with a smattering of freckles across the bridge of her button nose. She wore no veil as other dwarven females did, but he recognised the spiked bangle in her hand, a torq, the female equivalent of the dwarf male's tomahawk.

'Fletcher, down here,' Othello shouted, and Fletcher saw him waving, a few steps down.

Fletcher made his way to Othello's side and took a seat, never taking his eyes off the two fighters as Didric closed in once again, spitting words under his breath. Fletcher could not hear what they were, but he could tell from the way the girl's eyes widened that they were offensive.

'What's her name again?' Fletcher asked, as the girl parried another blow with her torq and swept her seax at Didric's legs, forcing him to leap awkwardly over her blade.

'Her name is Cress. Should have won this contest already – Didric wasn't trained to fence a dual-wielding fighter. See his nose? She got him in the face with her torq, but Rook deemed it a non-killing blow. Typical.' Othello pointed at the black-clad judge in the corner, his eyes glittering with anger as Cress's seax slit the cloth of Didric's uniform at the neck, the flesh beneath untouched thanks to the barrier spell.

'Come on,' Othello bellowed, his voice lost in the crowd as they booed Didric's poor defence. 'A neck blow is fatal!'

Rook shook his head, pursing his lips. Despite the obvious support for Didric from the almost entirely human crowd, several booed his decision. Noticing the lack of dwarves present, Fletcher nudged Othello.

'Where's Atilla? In the infirmary?'

'No,' Othello replied. 'He and Cress . . . let's just say they don't get on. After he lost to Didric he stormed out.'

Below, Cress swept at Didric's stomach, forcing him to hunch over to avoid it. As he did so, her torq came thrumming through the air, leaving spiked indents in his face and producing a resounding crack that Fletcher heard even over the screams from the crowd. Didric dropped like a stone, spread-eagled on the floor. Even so, Rook gave it a full ten seconds before finally nodding his head, to a smattering of applause from those around him.

'Cress wins the tournament!' he said, clapping twice before letting his hands drop to his side. He leaped into the arena as Didric regained consciousness, and helped the woozy boy to his feet. Cress stood proudly, wiping her brow, seemingly unconcerned by the lack of celebration around her.

Clearly, the attacks from the Anvils had done their work. The anti-dwarven sentiment seemed worse than when Fletcher had first arrived at Vocans. Most of the crowd were already dispersing, disappointed that their champion had lost the battle. Othello shook his head as the room began to empty. It was a poor celebration of a well-earned victory.

'Watch out – the twins are here,' Othello whispered.

Tarquin and Isadora were climbing the stairs ahead of them with a sweaty Didric in tow. The trio stopped a few steps below, staring Fletcher and Othello down.

'What a touching family reunion,' Didric mocked, earning himself a punch on the arm from Tarquin. He caught the hateful look Fletcher gave him, and they stared each other down. It was all Fletcher could do to stop himself from shoving Didric back down the stairs, but Othello grasped his wrist to steady him.

Isadora rolled her eyes and clicked her fingers to get Fletcher's attention.

'*Dearest* cousin, it has been far too long.' She smiled prettily and gave Fletcher an exaggerated curtsy. 'Why, it's been over a year, has it not? What *have* you been doing all this time?'

'You're no family of mine,' Fletcher spat, the memory of his long incarceration, and those behind it, still fresh in his mind.

'I couldn't agree more,' Tarquin replied, a vicious sneer on his face. 'Once a commoner, always a commoner. As long as the inheritance from Aunt Alice is still ours, I don't care what you call yourself.'

'You can keep your blood money,' Fletcher said. 'Just stay the hell away from me.'

'Gladly,' Isadora said, the pretty smile gone from her face. She lifted her nose in the air and sniffed pointedly.

'Come on,' she smirked, sauntering away. 'It stinks of dwarf here anyway.'

Othello reddened with anger, and Fletcher winced as the dwarf tightened his grip on Fletcher's wrist to stop himself from lashing out.

'Nice haircut by the way,' Tarquin called over his shoulder. 'You must tell me where you had it done.'

'That's it . . .' Othello growled, leaping to his feet. Fletcher followed suit, but the trio were gone and instead they found themselves staring at a startled Rory and Genevieve.

'Hello,' Fletcher said, unsure of himself. The three had not parted on the best of terms – he had almost killed Rory's Mite in the Tournament, after all.

'Hello. I see you got out then,' Rory said awkwardly.

'That's right,' Fletcher replied, scratching his neck.

'Good . . . good,' Rory said, avoiding Fletcher's gaze. 'I'm glad.'

They stood there in an awkward silence, until Genevieve stepped forward with a fixed smile.

'Welcome back,' she said, giving Fletcher a firm hug. 'Let's catch up later.'

She took Rory by the arm and they walked swiftly away.

'Well, that went . . . well,' Othello said.

'We just need some time,' Fletcher said. 'They won't forgive me all at once.'

'Aye,' Othello said. 'Though you'd think a year would be long enough, right?'

But Fletcher didn't reply, because Cress had clambered out of the arena and was making her way up towards them, brushing sand from her cadet's uniform.

Moments later, she stood with her hands on her hips before them, eyes sparkling.

'So you're the great Fletcher,' she said, flashing him a broad grin. 'I thought you'd be taller.'

'You're not so tall yourself,' Fletcher said, but he couldn't help but smile back. Her good humour was infectious.

'Cress and Atilla both made a good showing this year,' Othello said, smiling too. 'Beating that braggart Didric was the culmination of a lot of hard work and training. I can't tell you how unpleasant it's been studying with him. He and Atlas have been bosom buddies since they first met.'

'You can say that again,' Cress said.

She nodded across the room, and Fletcher saw Didric was

sitting on the other side of the arena, beside Tarquin, Isadora and Atlas. Though Didric wore the same black and yellow uniform Fletcher had seen before, Fletcher noticed that Atlas and the twins wore the uniform of the Forsyth Furies – black cloth with silver buttons and epaulettes.

'Why are they wearing their uniforms? Surely they've only just graduated?' Fletcher asked.

'Tarquin and Isadora were promoted to lieutenants after last year's tournament, Seraph too,' Othello said, following Fletcher's gaze. 'So the twins have been serving in their father's regiment all year. I guess they've brought Atlas his own uniform, now he's graduated too.'

With a year of fighting on the front lines, the twins would be more formidable than ever, Fletcher thought with dread.

'I know all about the mission, by the way,' Cress whispered, sliding into the seat beside them. 'Rook told us about it before the Tournament began. I want to join your team, if you'll have me. I think I've proven myself a worthy fighter.'

'Team?' Fletcher asked.

But before she could answer, Sylva squeezed in between them and sat down, still adorned in the green armour from the day before.

'What did I miss?' she asked Fletcher. 'Did Didric win? I would have stayed, but I went looking for you.'

'Oh. No, Cress here beat him,' Fletcher said, leaning forward awkwardly and pointing at the young dwarf.

'Well done,' Sylva said, holding out her hand. Cress took it with a hint of a frown, unhappy at being so rudely interrupted.

Fletcher felt strange sitting so close to Sylva, for they had not spoken since the council meeting. It was difficult for him, to swing between friend and diplomat so quickly, especially after her hesitation to support him.

'So, as I was say—' Cress began, but then stopped as Atilla stomped down the stairs beside them. He avoided her gaze pointedly, before nodding respectfully at Fletcher and Sylva.

'It's good to see you – Fletcher, Sylva,' he muttered, avoiding Cress's frank gaze. 'It has been too long.'

'Aren't you glad to see me too?' Cress said brightly, her tone bordering on the sarcastic.

Atilla reddened and turned his head away, then growled under his breath.

'It's bad enough among the students, but in front of all these people? It's . . . disgusting.'

Fletcher creased his brow, confused. What was Atilla talking about?

'Do I really look that bad?' Cress said, cupping her face between her hands and fluttering her eyelashes at him.

'Cover yourself,' Atilla said, his face darkening even further.

'Understand one thing, Atilla,' Cress said, her pleasant tone taking on a dangerous edge. 'Dwarf women wear the veil because *they* want to. It's for themselves, not for you. If I choose to reveal my face then that is *my* choice to make. You have no say in the matter.'

'It is immodest,' Atilla said, still looking away. 'You flaunt yourself for all to see.'

'And what about me, Atilla?' Sylva interjected. Her tone was calm, but Fletcher could see the tips of her ears had gone red, a sure sign she was angry.

'I don't understand,' Atilla said, confused.

'Am I immodest? Do *I* flaunt myself?'

Atilla spluttered, but could think of no reply.

'What about *you*, Atilla?' Cress asked, pressing home the advantage. 'You have a handsome face, a luxurious pair of moustaches. Why, I've seen you training bare-chested. You expose yourself to the world and to *me*. How *immodest* of you.'

Atilla stomped his foot in anger.

'I will not argue with fools. Cress knows what she is doing is wrong, even if you non-dwarves don't understand. You, brother, should not be so accepting. She is supposed to be an example to all dwarves, and everyone in the Hominum Empire will see her face if she joins the mission. Imagine if the other girls follow her example?'

Othello looked at Cress and gave her a tentative smile.

'I see nothing to complain about,' he said.

Atilla huffed and stomped away, making his way around the arena towards Seraph, who had just noticed them and was waving happily. He was wearing a gaudy amber uniform with a scarlet sash, and was armed with a scimitar and a holstered pistol.

As Fletcher and his friends waved back, Rook strode into the centre of the Arena, etching a spell as he did so. When he completed the etching, a tremendous bang echoed around the chamber, loud enough to hurt Fletcher's eardrums and leave a dull ringing sound in his head.

'Now that you have all shut up, we can begin the selection. Fletcher, Isadora, Malik and Seraph, come and join me in the arena.'

# 19

Sweat prickled Fletcher's back as he stepped into the arena, infusing Ignatius and Athena with a flash of his palm, for they were the only demons in the room. He could still sense both of them in his mind and, stranger still, a third connection, slowly forming between the two. Perhaps Athena and Ignatius were beginning to trust each other.

As he entered the pool of flickering torchlight, memories of the last time he had walked these sands swam to the forefront of his mind. The dangers he had faced then would be nothing compared with what was to come.

'You have all been told why you are here,' Rook announced, pacing back and forth along the sand. 'There are two objectives to your mission. The first, to destroy several thousand goblin eggs before they hatch. The second, to rescue Lady Cavendish, Rufus's mother.'

Rufus sat a little straighter in the stands as the students turned to look at him, and Fletcher could see his knuckles whiten as he gripped the hilt of his sword. The young noble had not impressed Fletcher last year, for the boy had fawned over the Forsyth twins. He hoped that Rufus would not be a liability on such a dangerous mission, especially with the added pressure of rescuing his own mother.

A flash of blue turned Fletcher's attention back to Rook. He had produced a wyrdlight, and the ball of light was slicing back and forth through the air. As it travelled, it left a trail of azure light in its wake, etching a shape as one might with a spell.

Soon, an enormous four-sided pyramid hung in the air, with a strange web of tubes surrounding a central chamber beneath it. It spun gently, casting the room in an eerie blue glow.

'Our intelligence suggests that the goblin eggs are located within the volcanic cave network beneath this ancient pyramid, deep in the heart of the orc jungles,' Rook said, jabbing his finger at the web of tunnels below the pyramid. 'Lady Cavendish is kept somewhere within too, and for good reason – it is the most secure place in the whole of Orcdom. The pyramid is their most sacred ground.'

This was all news to Fletcher, and his heart seemed to batter his ribs as his pulse quickened. He had thought they would be raiding a remote orc village, not losing themselves in the bowels of the earth.

'The Celestial Corps will drop you as close as they can, then you will make your way there on foot. You must – and I cannot stress this enough – you *must* meet at midnight, at the back entrance of the pyramid, three days after the drop-off. From that point, you will have a maximum of eight hours to complete your mission – that is as long as the Corps can wait on standby, halting their patrols of Hominum's skies. Remember, you place

161

the people of Hominum in jeopardy with every hour you take, for if the orcs notice the open skies they will send the Wyverns to raid helpless towns.'

Fletcher gulped, imagining the destruction a single Wyvern could cause to an unprotected settlement. It was a huge risk to take.

'The Celestial Corps will be watching through the scrying crystals and will try to arrive as soon as your mission is completed. If any team is not with the others at that point, it will have to find its own way home.'

Rook paused again, allowing the gravity of his words to sink in.

Fletcher knew that attempting to return home alone would be a death sentence. Around him, the others wore grim expressions. Even Tarquin and Isadora looked worried, the colour drained from their faces. They had been fighting on the front lines for over a year – and knew better than any what the teams would be up against.

'As you all know, scrying crystals are to be distributed around Hominum,' Rook said. 'Soon, every tavern, village hall and public square will each have four crystals, one for each team, where the populace can watch the mission's progress. You will not be given these yourselves, because if one team is captured, the orcs will be able to use them to track down the others.'

Rook snapped his fingers and the pyramid disappeared, leaving the room bathed in orange torchlight once again.

'In order to allow you to fully focus on your mission, each team will require a demon to act as the conduit for these stones,' Rook continued. 'As such, we have asked for sponsors to volunteer their own demons. These sponsors will also provide your team with an expert guide, to help you find your way through the jungle. You will find out who your sponsors and guides are soon enough.'

He clapped his hands and rubbed them together in anticipation.

'Now, let's all get into our respective groups. There are to be four teams of four, made up of three second-year students and one first-year volunteer. Volunteers, as soon as you set foot on this sand, there is no turning back . . .'

He allowed his voice to trail off as he watched the small group of first years across the arena.

'The captains have already been selected,' Rook continued, unravelling a long scroll. 'They stand before you right now.'

Fletcher felt a flush of pride and nerves, the two emotions sitting uncomfortably in the pit of his stomach. He had been out of the game for so long, had barely spoken to anyone but Ignatius for an entire year . . . and that was a pretty one-sided conversation. Was he really ready to lead a team on a deadly mission?

Rook cleared his throat, and Fletcher turned with baited breath to hear who his teammates would be.

'After careful consideration from the king's council and the teachers at the school, the teams are as follows. Please come and join your chosen captains as each name is called out.'

He cleared his throat.

'In Isadora's team, we have Tarquin and Atlas. In Seraph's team, Rory and Genevieve. In Malik's team, Penelope and Rufus. In Fletcher's team, Othello and Sylva.'

Fletcher breathed a sigh of relief as the students leaped down into the arena, joining their respective teammates. Sylva flashed him a smile as she stood beside him, and Othello gave him a light punch on the arm.

'Trust them to put a human in charge,' Othello whispered, but he winked to show he didn't really mind. 'Looks like they arranged us by friendships.'

'Agreed,' Fletcher said happily. 'Isadora's looking pleased. I bet when Tarquin lost the Tournament to me she was deemed the stronger of the two.'

As the rest of the students lined up, Fletcher saw four students left on the stands. Atilla, Cress and Didric, along with a dark-haired girl who Fletcher did not recognise. Rook swept his hand around the arena, pointing to each one.

'You will now have the option to select a fourth member on to your teams from the first-year students who volunteered for the mission. Isadora, you have been randomly chosen to go first.'

'Yeah right,' Sylva murmured in Fletcher's ear, and he suddenly became very aware of the soft touch of her hand on his waist. 'Not that it matters. We both know who she's going to pick.'

'The valiant Didric Cavell,' Isadora said, beckoning Didric over with a magnanimous hand. 'After his brilliant performance in the Tournament, robbed of his victory by rotten luck.'

'Luck had nothing to do with it,' Cress called, ignoring Rook's hiss of disapproval at her speaking out of turn.

Didric jumped down into the arena, staggering slightly with dizziness from what was probably a mild concussion. Tarquin shook his hand as Atlas and Isadora patted him on the back.

'Now, Fletcher,' Rook said, his eyes still on Cress, daring her to speak again.

Fletcher blanched. For some reason, he had expected to go last.

He paused, earning himself a glare from Atilla. It was obvious whose team the dwarf wished to join. Yet ... Cress had just won the Tournament. She had requested, politely, to be part of his team. Then there was Atilla's recent outburst against Cress's choice of dress. Fletcher wanted his team to be a shining example to the world – of solidarity, friendship and acceptance.

Atilla had a good heart and was a capable warrior, but Fletcher would not choose him, not for this. Now, he only needed a reason that Atilla would understand.

'I choose Cress,' he said, but held up his hand as Atilla began to protest. 'Othello and Atilla's parents would never forgive me, if their sons were in the one team that didn't make it, both killed in a single stroke of misfortune. Better to spread the risk. The king's army do not allow brothers to serve in the same regiment for that very reason.'

Atilla bowed his head, then gave the curtest of nods.

'I won the Tournament too, in case you forgot, Fletcher,' Cress said loudly, already walking across the sand. 'And it's Cress Freyja, by the way.'

'I had not forgotten,' Fletcher whispered as she took her place beside them. 'That is the other reason. Good to have you on board, Cress *Freyja*.'

'Seraph, your turn,' Rook said, turning his back on them.

Seraph gave the dark-haired girl a sidelong look, but only for a moment.

'Atilla Thorsager, of course. Come here, you grumpy bugger,' Seraph said with a wide smile, beckoning the dwarf over. Atilla rolled his eyes as he walked down the steps, but there was a hint of a smile on his face. The two must have become closer while Fletcher was away.

'And finally, Malik,' Rook said.

'I'm very happy to chose Verity Faversham,' Malik said, smiling as the dark-haired girl walked into the torchlight. 'I'm surprised she wasn't picked first.'

When the girl joined her team, Fletcher couldn't help but stare as she shook out a bundle of sable hair. She was beautiful, perhaps more so than any girl he had ever seen, with a heart-shaped face and large, expressive eyes that seemed to linger on him as she approached her team. For a moment, her name made no impression on him, and it took a growl of disgust from Othello to remind him.

'She looks just like her grandmother Ophelia, don't you think, Fletcher?'

Fletcher saw the resemblance, but found it difficult to associate her with the hard-eyed woman who ruled the Triumvirate with Zacharias and Didric. Even her Inquisitor father, Charles, seemed a long way from the girl, despite their shared pale complexions. Verity greeted Malik with a warm smile and embraced Penelope and Rufus with open arms.

Sylva elbowed him in the side, and Fletcher realised he was staring. He shook his head, trying to remember that the Faershams were enemies.

'She's a first year?' Fletcher asked.

'Aye,' Othello confirmed. 'Though I didn't see much of her

around. Kept herself to herself, spent most of her free time in her room studying or away in Corcillum.'

Fletcher watched as the rest of the teams lined up, waiting for Rook's next announcement.

'As you all know, the scrying stones that have made this mission possible were generously provided by Tarquin and Isadora's father, Verity's grandmother and Didric himself,' Rook said, nodding at the respective students. 'I think we should all take a moment to thank the Forsyth, Faversham and Cavell families for their generosity.'

He stared expectantly at the other students. The Forsyth twins and Didric grinned as Fletcher and his team muttered their unenthusiastic thanks, although Verity simply blushed and looked at her feet.

'Very good,' Rook continued. 'Now, I have an announcement for you all. There is a prize for this mission, to keep things interesting for both the participants and the spectators around the Empire. Whichever team succeeds in rescuing Lady Cavendish will receive one thousand sovereigns, to be divided equally among the team members. There will also be another five hundred sovereigns for any team that participates in the destruction of the goblin eggs. After all, there's nothing like some healthy competition.'

He grinned at the students as the room filled with furtive whispers. It was a king's ransom, enough to outfit a small army. The reward came as no surprise to Fletcher, though it mattered little to him. If, in the depths of the jungle, a team lost heart, the reward would be a strong motivator for them to do their duty.

'If you would turn around,' Rook ordered, pointing at the

doorway behind them, and Fletcher spun. Four demons stood in the entrance, three of which he instantly recognised.

'Teams, meet your new demons,' Rook said.

Lysander, Lovett's Griffin, walked proudly down the steps, beating the air with his wings to send a spray of sand in Isadora's team's direction. It was clear whose team he had been selected for, as he made his way straight towards Fletcher before pawing the ground beside them.

'She can't,' Fletcher whispered, his heart dropping at the thought of Lovett confined to a wheelchair, alone. 'He's her legs, her wings. He's her best friend. All she'll have left is Valens.'

'She wants to protect us, Fletcher. This is her way of doing that,' Sylva murmured. 'We'll bring Lysander back, safe and sound. And it will be as if she's right there with us. She can scry using her mind, practically inhabit his body like she did with Valens. I wouldn't be surprised if she's doing it now.'

Lysander gave Fletcher a nudge with his beak, as if to draw Fletcher's attention to the next demon that bounded down the stairs. It was a gesture that felt unusually human and, as Fletcher glanced down, he saw Lysander wink at him. Lovett was in there all right, and Fletcher grinned back at her.

Arcturus's wolf-like Canid, Sacharissa, scampered past, pausing only to give Lysander a playful nudge. The Griffin lashed out with a claw, but only succeeded in catching the end of the four-eyed Canid's bushy black tail.

'Looks like Arcturus was thinking along the same lines,' Fletcher said as Seraph welcomed Sacharissa with a strip of jerky, miraculously produced from a pocket in his jacket. Though

Griffins were more powerful and versatile than Canids, Fletcher wished that he could have both on his team. With Arcturus and Lovett's demons at his side, he would feel much safer in the gloom of the orc jungles.

'What the hell is that thing?' Cress asked, pointing, as an enormous, skeletal creature, roughly humanoid in shape, slunk down the stairs.

It had thick, branching antlers that swept out from either side of its head like tangled thorns. The head was like a hairless mix of deer and wolf, with hungry, black eyes that swept the room. Long, dangling arms knuckled the sand ahead of it, the hands tipped with razor-sharp talons. Its flesh was the mottled grey of a corpse, with a stench to match. Despite its rangy frame, the musculature shifted beneath the tight skin as it moved, like corded wire being stretched and tautened.

'A Wendigo,' Othello replied, his voice tinged with a mix of awe and horror. 'Level thirteen and rare to boot. That's Zacharias Forsyth's primary demon. Almost everything we know about the Wendigo was learned from studying that very creature – they're almost never seen in the ether.'

'No mystery where that thing's ending up,' Fletcher said, as the creature came to a stop beside Isadora's team. He grinned as Tarquin, the closest to it, wrinkled his nose at the smell.

'My Caliban shall be joining Malik's team,' Rook announced, beckoning the final demon over, his own.

It was Rook's Minotaur, a burly beast clad in a shaggy black pelt. It was powerfully built, all brawn and meat, where the larger Wendigo was sinew and hard bone. The bullish head snorted through its thick, piggish nostrils as it clopped down the

169

stairs on cloven hooves, each breath like the pumping of the bellows in Berdon's old forge.

'Thank you for sponsoring us, Inquisitor,' Malik said, bowing low.

'We can't let the Saladins' and Favershams' only heirs go unprotected,' Rook said, pointedly ignoring Penelope and Rufus, whose families, though noble, were not as wealthy as the rest. Rufus, however, seemed not to notice, grasping Rook's hand and shaking it emphatically.

'You won't regret this, Inquisitor,' Rufus said. 'My elder brother will reward you tenfold when we rescue my mother, I swear to that!'

'You shall be meeting your guides, who have been chosen for you by your sponsors, tonight,' Rook said, extricating his hand with a grimace. 'Malik's team, stay here with me. The rest of you, follow the demons.'

# 20

Lysander led them out of the arena and back into the atrium, with Sacharissa padding along beside him. Fletcher expected them to go out through the main entrance, as Caliban did, but the two demons continued up the western staircase instead.

It was a long climb, but he entertained himself by watching as the usually airborne Lysander slipped and slid on his way up, unused to having to mount steps, especially narrow winding ones such as these. Sacharissa waited patiently at the top of each staircase, her bright blue eyes keeping a protective watch over the struggling Griffin.

'Maybe you should have flown up and met us at the top,' Fletcher laughed, earning himself a stern glare from Lysander which could only have come from Lovett.

Fletcher had rarely entered this side of the building during his first year at Vocans, for the rooms were mostly the teachers' private quarters, servants' lodgings, a large launderette and storage rooms. It was no surprise then when they went right to the top floor's main corridor and headed for the north-west tower.

As they followed the two demons, Fletcher couldn't help but admire the paintings and tapestries that lined the topmost corridor, depicting ancient battles fought without gunpowder weapons. It was only when he passed an older painting, the colours faded and peeling from the canvas, that he paused.

It showed not orcs being vanquished, but dwarves. In the background, dwarven women had their veils torn away, while in the foreground, dwarven warriors kneeled in rows, their beards being clipped by heroically dressed men in shining armour. Around them, the corpses of the fallen dwarves were scattered about the scene, and above, flying summoners looked on, their lances bloodied from base to tip.

All three dwarves as well as Seraph and Sylva stopped beside him, while Rory and Genevieve wandered on, their eyes skimming over the painting as if it were no different from the rest.

'This is what we are fighting against,' Othello said, his voice barely above a whisper as he traced the fallen figures in the painting with the tip of his fingers. 'It could happen all over again. I have studied our historical texts, learned how swiftly the hatred can take root, on both sides. Four times the dwarves have rebelled, and failed. Four times our race was castigated, reduced to vermin in the eyes of humanity. We must break this cycle. Only through unity can we be truly free.'

Atilla strode away in disgust, and Fletcher could not blame him. The image was loathsome, not something to be glorified in the hallowed halls of Vocans. Seraph ran after him, but the arm he draped over the young dwarf's shoulders was shaken away.

'Come on,' Fletcher muttered. As he turned to walk on, there was a strange crackling sound. He looked over his shoulder to see that the painting's surface had been charred black, and there was an etched fire-spell symbol floating before it.

'Oops,' Cress shrugged, patting Fletcher on the back as she walked by, 'my hand slipped.'

They jogged to catch up with Rory and Genevieve, who had almost reached the top of the north-western tower. The stairwell had layers of dust coating all surfaces, broken only by a narrow pathway where it had been disturbed, as if only one person ever used it.

Finally, the two teams crushed together before a barred door, deeply embedded with iron mechanisms to keep it secure. Lysander lifted his front claw and tapped against it, a strange mix of scratches and knocks that were a code of some sort. After a pause, the locks began to twist and rattle. Then, with an ominous creak, the doors swung open.

The inside was as gloomy as the stairwell, the main lighting coming from a single chandelier in the high ceiling above.

'Come in, come in,' a gravelly voice called from deep within. 'Don't knock anything over!'

Fletcher and Sylva led the way, releasing wyrdlights from the tips of their fingers to illuminate their way forward. The blue light cast an eerie glow over a vast array of shelves, tables and workbenches, each one covered in glassware and tools.

To his left, Fletcher saw demons hanging suspended in jars of pale green liquid, just as the goblin had been at the council meeting. Many were missing limbs or heads, and the surfaces of the tables displayed their dissected remains. On the right there were potted plants instead of demons, as well as bubbling beakers of viscous liquid, slow boiled from below by miniature furnaces.

Each plant was stranger than the last. One had heavy, bulbous flowers that pursed and opened at them like kissing lips. Another was almost entirely comprised of tuberous roots that seemed to twitch towards the light as they passed by.

'Don't be shy, make yourselves at home,' the voice uttered, and a figure stepped out of the shadows.

Her skin was darker than Seraph's, with a cap of tight, greying curls on her head. She wore a long coat of white cotton, with blackened leather gloves extending over the sleeves. A bright, almost mad grin was spread across her face, and she peered at them through a pair of thick spectacles that made her eyes appear twice as large.

'You'll have to forgive the mess,' she said, motioning at the tables covered in vegetation and body parts around her. 'Jeffrey was supposed to clean up, but he snuck off to watch the Tournament instead.'

The group remained silent, and she shifted nervously, as if she expected them to speak.

'Cup of tea? Or was it coffee?' she asked, motioning to a simmering cauldron a few feet away. It was filled with an unidentifiable brown substance that shared the consistency of mud. 'Maybe ginseng? Cocoa? It was something tasty, anyway.'

'Umm, no thanks,' Fletcher said, politely. There was a *glop* as a large bubble burst on the surface.

She stared at them some more, the grin slowly leaving her face until Fletcher cleared his throat and asked what they were all wondering.

'Who are you? What is this place?'

Her smile returned and she motioned them over to the table beside her. It was better lit than the others, with a lantern suspended above it.

'I am Electra Mabosi, from the land of Swazulu across the Vesanian Sea. I am a botanist, biologist, chemist, demonologist. Little bit of everything really. Alchemist is probably the best word. But I am not your guide, if that's what you're worried about. Haven't left this room in four years and I don't plan on doing so any time soon.'

Fletcher looked around the gloomy room and tried to picture spending the past four years of his life in such a place. It was better than his prison cell, but not by much. What kind of person would want to stay there for so long?

'I've been doing secret research for King Harold and Provost Scipio since I arrived here. I keep them abreast of developments while I can, but they won't let me get involved in the teaching, no matter how much I ask. They say my time is better spent researching.'

She pulled a corked jar from a shelf nearby as she spoke, and removed a bedraggled demon corpse as large as a human hand from within. She lay it on the worktable in front of her and unravelled a leather roll of surgical tools beside it.

'See here. This is a juvenile Arach, found dead in the ether a few months ago. Fulfilment level six, rare but not uncommon. I've been saving it for this demonstration. Finally, I get a chance to teach.'

It looked like a large, hairy spider, with a glittering nest of eyes in its head, a pair of hooked fangs beneath and a spiky stinger like a bee's on its behind. Electra snipped each leg off with a pair of heavy scissors, as if she were trimming fingernails. She swept the amputated limbs into a bucket on the floor, leaving only the head and thorax. Genevieve shuddered and jumped away, for a leg missed the bucket and landed beside her feet.

'See this hole, below the stinger?' Electra asked, using a pair of tongs to hold it steady. 'The Arach is capable of shooting a sticky, mana-based substance from there, not unlike gossamer.'

She tugged the lantern above her closer and peered at the sodden specimen.

'We must be careful, the bristles on its body can become detached, floating in the air and irritating its victims' eyes and skin. Jeffrey tells me that Lord Cavell's own Arach has already caused a few problems in some of the first year's lessons, is that not so, Cress?'

'Aye,' Cress agreed, scratching at her wrist absent-mindedly. 'Didn't stop itching for a week.'

Fletcher shuddered, for the dead creature's eyes seemed to bore into him. He hated to think what a full-grown Arach would look like, though he had seen diagrams in his demonology lessons. It was poor luck that Didric had one of his own, for it would be a formidable opponent if it ever duelled with Ignatius.

Electra hummed a merry tune to herself as she pushed a tube-like instrument into the orifice beneath the demon's stinger, as if she were coring an apple. When she drew it out, she was left with a cylinder of slippery organs, which she spread out on the table with the tongs.

'That is repulsive,' Rory said, running his hand through his shock of blond, spiky hair. His face lost what little colour it had, and he went to join Genevieve on the edge of the group.

'Don't be such a baby,' Electra muttered, grasping Fletcher by a gloved hand and dragging him in beside her. 'What do you see there?'

For a moment Fletcher had the mad suspicion that she wanted him to divine the future, as orc shamans claimed to be able to do with the entrails of their enemies. But when he looked closer, he recognised a strange symbol, imprinted in one of the organs like a brand.

'It's . . . a spell symbol,' Fletcher said, shaking his head with confusion.

'Yes! Do you even know how spells and etching were first discovered?' Electra asked, turning so swiftly that the corer dashed a droplet of slime on to Seraph's cheek. He retched, pawing at his face with his sleeve.

'Demons have always used their special abilities by channelling their mana through organic symbols within them,' Electra continued, ignoring Seraph's moans of disgust. 'The first summoners must have realised that, dissecting their dead demons as I have just done and copying the symbols down. My mission here is to add to the roster of spells available to our battlemages through my research. It is a long forgotten art, which I have revived. I am not a summoner myself though, which does tend to complicate things.'

She turned to Fletcher and grasped him by the shoulders.

'Your Salamander, for example, will have the fire symbol somewhere within its throat. If they would just let me teach here, you would all know this!'

She sighed with frustration. Fletcher caught Othello's eye and they grinned at each other knowingly. Even compared to a zealot like Rook, Electra was obviously a little too eccentric to teach at Vocans.

'So what's with all the plants then?' Fletcher asked, pointing at a large pot with a fearsome looking plant within that resembled a thorny venus flytrap.

'They're demons too, technically,' Electra said, caressing the stem as if it were a long-lost pet. 'Plants from the ether. I haven't found a single symbol in any of them, but I have discovered one thing. The petals, roots and leaves of certain species can be made into an elixir which, when drunk, will have useful effects.'

She pointed to a wooden rack of vials nearby – corked test tubes full of red, blue and yellow liquids.

'Fortunately, Captain Lovett volunteered to test them. This one, when consumed, will heal the drinker of his or her wounds, just like the healing spell. It helped Captain Lovett partially recover from her paralysis.' She withdrew a vial, swishing the blood-red contents back and forth.

'And this one will replenish a demon's mana when its summoner drinks it,' she continued, pointing to one of the blue vials as she replaced the red one. There was an awkward pause as her hand hovered over the tubes filled with yellow liquid, then she shrugged and turned back to the group.

'I've only just started the plant research, but they're a good place to start!' she said brightly.

'I'll say,' Seraph exclaimed. 'That's going to give us a real edge!'

'What about the yellow ones?' Sylva asked. 'What do they do?'

Electra frowned and then shrugged with a shake of her head.

'I have no idea. I know it has *some* effect on *something*, but that's all. You drink it and feel the rush of something happening, but I haven't worked out what.'

She slapped Seraph's hand as he surreptitiously reached for one of the vials. Then the door behind them slammed shut and footsteps could be heard.

'Ah, Jeffrey's here,' Electra said, clapping her hands together. 'He's my eyes and ears, you know. Risks life and limb to collect orc demon corpses after there's a battle in the jungles. It's *their* species of demons we rarely see in our part of the ether, so they're more likely to reveal a spell we haven't discovered yet.'

Fletcher turned to see Jeffrey walking their way, his sunken eyes and unhealthy complexion compounded by the light around them. The servant boy smiled at Fletcher through a thick mop of shaggy brown hair, styled similarly to Fletcher's own.

'Of course, his asthma slows him down,' Electra said, 'but his knowledge of the jungles will be invaluable to you. I've been training him as an alchemist for the past two years too.'

'Hi everyone.' Jeffrey waved shyly. 'I look forward to working with you. I've always wanted a chance to contribute, but they wouldn't let me join, on account of my lungs. Now I can.'

'Wait, *he's* going to be our guide?' Seraph exclaimed.

'For one of your teams,' Electra said gruffly, raising her eyebrows at him. 'Captain Lovett selected him, but thought she would give both of your teams the option to take him. Arcturus has his own choice if you decide to turn him down.'

'Respectfully, I'm a little worried,' Othello said, shuffling his feet with embarrassment. 'If the military doctors said he wasn't fit for duty on the front line, how can he be ready for a mission this dangerous, deep in the jungle? I thought we would be getting a scout, or a tracker.'

'I was inclined to agree with you when Jeffrey suggested it to me,' Electra said. 'But I concocted him a herbal remedy that relieves his symptoms somewhat and, like I said, he knows the jungle better than even a scout would. He's studied its ecosystem, the same way I have the ether. Knows what plants to eat, which ones to avoid. He'll see you right, if you'll take him.'

'We have a choice?' Fletcher asked.

'Yes. Nobody is forcing you to choose him as your guide, but I know that Captain Lovett has yet to find a second option for your team. If you want my elixirs and the new spells I have discovered, you'll do it. That deep behind enemy lines, who knows what manner of demons you will encounter. I want an alchemist there,' Electra replied.

For a moment Fletcher stared at Jeffrey, who stood a little straighter, determination written across his face.

'I'll take him,' Fletcher said.

# 21

Fletcher and his team sat around the tavern table, examining the map in front of them.

'Why are they dropping us in so far from the mission target?' Othello said, pointing to the far edge of the map, where their drop zone was marked with an X. 'It will take us days to get there.'

'It's probably as close as they can get to the pyramid without being seen,' Sylva mused, tracing the distance from the front line to the mark with her finger. 'If we're spotted being dropped off, then we might as well set off some fireworks to announce our arrival.'

Fletcher watched the debate with his chin in his hands, too tired to add his own speculation. The cart ride into Corcillum had been miserable, drenching them with a thin drizzle that had kept them all silently huddled together, protecting the map and instructions that Rook had handed to them on the way out of Vocans.

When they finally arrived, Othello led them straight to a

boarded-up tavern, where he said they could bed down for the night, while Seraph's team followed Sacharissa, presumably to find whoever Arcturus had chosen as their guide. Lysander also took his leave, launching into flight without any prior warning. Fletcher guessed that Lovett had stopped scrying and the Griffin was eager to return to her side.

The tavern's rafters hung extremely low, as if designed for dwarves instead of men, and the inside looked as if it had not been disturbed for a long time, with tables and chairs scattered haphazardly around the bar. Othello had lit the few remaining lanterns, but the room stayed gloomy, relying mostly on the moonlight that filtered through the shuttered windows.

'Where the hell are we anyway?' Fletcher groaned, wiping his finger along the edge of the table and showing them the dust. 'It's filthy in here.'

'The Anvil Tavern,' Cress replied, pointing at a sign with the same name and symbol above the door. 'It's where the Anvils used to meet, believe it or not. The clue's in the name.'

She winked at him.

The name was familiar, and Fletcher had a hazy memory of Athol suggesting he go there on his first day in Corcillum, when he gave him the Anvil card that had been used at the trial.

'I used to come here,' Jeffrey spoke up, leaving the table and leaning on the bar. He'd barely said a word since they had chosen him as their guide. 'I was even a junior member, before they became arsonists and this place was shut down. Best beer in all of Corcillum. Worth joining up for that alone.'

'Dwarf-owned,' Othello said, his chest swelling with pride.

'My cousin's place actually. He said we could use it to prepare for the mission.'

'The instructions said that the mission starts the day after tomorrow,' Fletcher said, ignoring them. 'I'd rather get in some shuteye now, because I don't think we'll get much in the jungle. We can sort all this out in the morning.'

'Actually, Fletcher, you'll need to stay up a little while longer,' Othello said, a sheepish smile on his face. 'We have visitors coming. They'll be here any minute, with any luck.'

There was a knock on the door, the rat-a-tat-tat making Fletcher jump.

'Right on cue,' Othello grinned, running over to the door and throwing it open.

Two figures stood in the doorway. The closest wore long, flowing robes of pink and blue, with twisting flowers embroidered down the centre. Although she wore a veil, from the way Othello hugged her, Fletcher guessed it was Briss, his mother.

Beside her, Athol stood with his hands tucked deep in the pockets of his breeches, a tired but satisfied look upon his face.

'Would you give us a hand with the goods?' Athol said, motioning with his head to a boar-pulled cart behind him. It was piled high with packages, and the boar's sides were soaked with sweat from an arduous journey. 'Be careful, it's precious cargo. Might save your life.'

The swarthy dwarf winked at Fletcher, then laughed uproariously as they embraced. Fletcher pounded him on the back while Jeffrey, Sylva and Cress ferried the packages inside and laid them on the table. He had not realised how much he had missed Athol until now.

It did not take long for it all to be unloaded, and Athol gave the boar a slap on the rump with his hand. The animal gave a disgruntled squeal, then trotted away, the cart rumbling behind it.

'He knows his way back. Smarter than horses, boars,' Athol said, leaning against a table and plucking his braces with his thumbs. He gave a low whistle as he looked around him.

'Look at this place,' he moaned, picking up a discarded tankard from the table behind him and turning it upside down. A thin stream of dust trickled out and he wrinkled his nose.

'Used to be the best tavern in all of Hominum,' he grumbled. 'Soon as the first terror attack happened, it was boarded up and closed. Would have been burned down by some enterprising human otherwise. Damned shame.'

'What *did* happen?' Fletcher asked, trying to understand what had changed during his long incarceration. 'What do the Anvils have to do with these attacks?'

Athol sighed and rubbed his eyes.

'The Anvils were just humans who were friendly to the dwarves at first,' he explained, settling down on one of the low benches. 'Started with a few of them drinking in one of our pubs, because of our beer, of course. Soon we started handing out membership cards to keep out troublemakers, like some of the racist gangs who came looking for a fight. Didn't take long for them to become something of a gang themselves, making sure their dwarf friends got home safe, demonstrating at dwarven protests, that sort of thing. Nothing violent though. Nothing like what happened.'

Athol paused for a moment, gathering his thoughts.

'The first explosion was at one of the demonstrations, after a young dwarf lad was wrongfully arrested,' Athol continued, a grim expression on his face. 'Gunpowder and musket balls, packed in a barrel beside the Pinkertons and set off by a long fuse. Took out three of them and ten innocents. Could only have been an Anvil, the investigators said. The barrel had been left out days before to avoid suspicion, and the only people who knew the location of the protest was us and the Anvils. They might have pinned the blame on us dwarves, but a witness saw the bomber running from the scene. Too tall for a dwarf, they said.'

'But why?' Fletcher asked. 'What could that possibly achieve?'

'We'll never know,' Cress answered, her eyes closed, hands trembling with sudden anger. 'Their leaders all upped and vanished that very same day. But there were more attacks. One at the young dwarf's trial itself. Killed thirty people that time, including the dwarf in question. It was like they didn't even care. They left a calling card then, quite literally. Membership cards, the kind you couldn't fake, belonging to the leadership.'

'Like the one you gave me, the one they showed at the trial?' Fletcher asked.

'No, those were cards for junior members, if you can call them that. Most of the young girls and boys in Corcillum had a card at one point or another – they handed them out like candy,' Athol replied, shaking his head. 'Myself included, if you haven't forgotten. The only reason they would have brought it up at the trial was to confuse the jury, who wouldn't know that, so far north of Corcillum. It was little more than an entry ticket.'

'Rory and Genevieve had one,' Jeffrey agreed. 'Even some of the nobles. Plus most of the other servants, like Mr Mayweather the cook, used to come here. They wanted to try the beer, like me.'

There was silence then, the mood turning sombre as they realised how bad things had become. Fletcher wondered if this mission would make any difference at all, after what he had just heard. Would seeing teams of dwarves, elves and humans fighting together really bring about peace?

'Years of progress were gone in an instant,' Othello whispered, staring into space. 'Pointless, pointless, pointless. Everyone blamed the dwarves, of course. Said we were seducing young, impressionable humans with alcohol, brainwashing them and making them do our dirty work.'

'Tell them what Uhtred thinks,' Briss said, her face inscrutable behind the veil.

Othello rolled his eyes and shook his head, as if it was a waste of time. Cress kicked him and he yelped, rubbing his shin.

'I want to find out what's in these packages – get on with it,' she said, crossing her arms. 'And respect your mother.'

'Fine! It's a stupid theory, but it's no crazier than any other explanation I've heard,' Othello grumbled, sitting down and examining his ginger-haired leg for bruises. 'He thinks someone in the Anvil leadership was working for the Triumvirate. The new anti-dwarven sentiment is killing our weapons business. Quartermasters refusing to buy from us, rumours spread about us sabotaging our muskets to explode in their owners' faces.'

'Or it could just as easily be a fanatical dwarf who believes that we should rebel again,' Cress said, unimpressed by Othello's father's theory. 'Someone like Ulfr. He's the worst of us. Used to have Atilla under his wing too, until he met you of course, Fletcher.'

She smiled brightly at him, then turned to Athol and Briss.

'Now, I know you have both been working flat out all day on a top secret project, which is why you couldn't come and watch me win the Tournament,' Cress said, with a hint of admonishment. 'So let's see what the fuss is about.'

Briss clapped her hands excitedly, then reached behind and began to pass packages to the members of the team. Fletcher couldn't help but tear open his own immediately, the soft give beneath the brown paper wrapping telling him exactly what it was – a uniform.

He shook it out and held it up to the light, amazed by the deep blue of the cloth that it had been made from.

The jacket was chased with silver thread, with an open collar and wide lapels in white. It was long enough to go past his knees, just as his last jacket had been, but the material was thicker.

'It should be long and thick enough to keep you warm at night, and light enough to keep you agile,' Briss said, fiddling with her dress in embarrassment. 'It's wool, so it will breathe well, but I also rubbed oil in to keep it waterproof, though wool is naturally water resistant itself.'

Fletcher saw that the others were holding up identical clothing.

'It's perfect,' Fletcher breathed, 'and it's the blue and silver of the Raleigh house, right?'

'Yes,' Briss laughed. 'I'm glad you noticed! At first I was going to make it green, so it would blend with the jungle, but we need the world to be able to see you through the scrying crystals. Remember, this is about winning hearts and minds. A colourful uniform will help everyone identify your team.'

'That's so true,' Fletcher said, shrugging on the jacket and examining the matching trousers that came with it. 'I wouldn't have thought of that.'

'I also made you boots,' Briss said, pointing to a row of thigh-length moccasins that Athol had left on the table. 'Made with elven leather, soft but durable. The very best kind.'

Sylva smiled at that remark, bowing her head in cheerful acknowledgement. The team thanked her profusely, while Athol rocked back and forth on his feet, eager to open his own packages.

'My turn now,' Athol said, before Briss had a chance to respond. 'I know you already have a bow and falx, Sylva, so I'm afraid I don't have anything for you except for some blue-fletched arrows – your team colour.'

'That's OK,' Sylva replied, though there was a hint of disappointment in her voice. 'My weapons belonged to my father, so I think they'll do.'

'Good, good,' Athol said distractedly, rubbing his hands together in anticipation. 'Cress, I already made you the torq and seax for the Tournament, so you're all set with close-combat weapons, but I'll be providing you with a crossbow tomorrow, some blue crossbow bolts and a sword for Jeffrey. Didn't have room on the cart for them.'

'Bah,' Cress huffed, sitting down heavily. 'I was looking

forward to my new weapons all day!'

'Now, Othello,' Athol said, beckoning his friend over.

He pulled a package from the pile and Othello tore it open eagerly.

'This is a blunderbuss,' he explained, as the gun was extracted from an oily cloth. 'It's loaded with buckshot – small spherical balls that will spread out when fired. You won't get much accuracy from it, but you will have some serious stopping power. A berserk bull-orc might run through a normal musket ball, kill you and be halfway home for dinner before it realises it's been shot, same with arrows and crossbow bolts. It'll die eventually, sure, but that won't do you much good. Hit it with a handful of buckshot and it'll go down like it's been struck by a sledgehammer.'

Othello held the firearm up to the light, revealing a weapon that was very similar to a musket, but with a shorter barrel and a muzzle that flared open like a trumpet. The metal was burnished to a bronze sheen, and the wood was the dark grain of polished teak.

'I hesitate to give it to you in a covert mission such as yours, but if your cover is blown you might as well use it,' Athol said, stepping out of the way as Othello lifted the weapon and sighted down the barrel. 'Just be aware that if you shoot it, they'll be able to hear the gunshot from miles around.'

Othello's face was a picture of joy as he reverently laid the blunderbuss on the table. Athol's expression was identical, and he wordlessly handed him a leather gun-holster that could be slung over Othello's shoulder.

'There's also a battle-axe for you,' Athol said, pointing at a package beside him. 'I took it off the rack – one of your father's finest. No time to personalise it, unfortunately. I chucked a few hurlbat throwing axes in there too.'

'Thank you, truly,' Othello said, his voice hitching. 'You have outdone yourself with that blunderbuss. My father has taught you well.'

'Ah, well, he would have made it himself if he wasn't so busy with the council. Luckily, he managed to get your tomahawk back from the Pinkertons after the trial – he'll give it to you when he sees you off.'

Othello sat down, shaking his head with a rueful smile.

'Now Fletcher's turn . . . unless you want to go to sleep, Fletcher?' Athol winked. 'This can wait until tomorrow if you want.'

'Very funny,' Fletcher said, eyeing the pile of packages behind Athol. Could they really all be for him?

'I must admit, most of these are just me re-gifting you your possessions, courtesy of Arcturus,' Athol said, setting aside several large packages. 'He kept them safe for you while you were in jail. Your bow, khopesh, scabbard, scrying stone, money, clothes and arrows are all in these. He also wanted me to give you this.'

Athol handed him a familiar-looking package, and Fletcher laughed with delight when he saw what it was.

James Baker's diary and the spellcraft book had been neatly tied together with twine. Somehow, Arcturus had managed to rescue them from his cell. As Fletcher took it, he saw a note was pinned to the top:

*Fletcher,*

*I am glad these found their way to you last year – in all honesty I was not sure if I had bribed the prison guard enough. He sold them back to me at a hefty price. I'm sure you have the diary memorised by now, but I wouldn't want Didric to get his grubby mitts on it.*

*I suggest you give it to Athol for safekeeping. Good luck on your mission. I will be there in spirit (as well as in Sacharissa too).*

*Arcturus*

Fletcher grinned from ear to ear. The mysterious benefactor who had put the books in his cell had been revealed. Although he now knew that they were not half-brothers, Arcturus had done more for him than any brother could. Fletcher owed the man so much.

'I should have given that to you last,' Athol grumbled, noting Fletcher's joyous expression. 'Anyway, here you go.'

He held out a weighty package, which Fletcher set carefully on the table, then tore open.

A pair of pistols shone in the flickering light, one with an elongated barrel, the other with two shorter ones. The longer pistol had a Salamander engraved along the grip, the detailing intricate – more the work of an artist than a gunmaker. The other had a Gryphowl design of equal beauty, with a wing pointing down each barrel.

'Captain Lovett called on us earlier and helped me with the design. I hope you like it,' Athol said, rubbing his callused hands and watching Fletcher's face anxiously.

Fletcher hefted the Salamander pistol, careful to keep his finger off the trigger.

'It's amazing,' he breathed, rubbing the polished wood with his hand. It had a reddish tinge, and was smooth as silk.

'I'm so glad you think so,' Athol said, breaking into a broad grin.

Athol stepped forward, taking the weapon and holding it up to the nearest torch.

'This one's a prototype. The inside of the barrel is "rifled", with a groove that spirals down the inside and gives the bullet spin. You'll find it fires further and more accurately than any musket, but it's harder to load.'

Fletcher began to peer down the barrel, then thought better of it as Athol twitched it away and lay the weapon aside.

'This is another prototype,' Athol said, picking up the next pistol. 'Two barrels means two shots, but twice the reload time, so there's no rifling for this weapon. The barrels are smoothbore. Othello will show you how to load and fire these later down the line.'

'And you should name your guns,' Othello said, his eyes still focused on the gleaming metal of the blunderbuss. 'This one is called Bess.'

He reddened slightly, as Cress grinned at the name.

'Childhood crush,' he admitted, his ears slowly turning pink.

Fletcher laughed, then turned to his own brace of pistols. For a moment he considered naming them after his parents, but it felt wrong somehow. No, the engravings were the key.

'Blaze and Gale,' he said, brandishing each pistol. 'Blaze for Ignatius's fire and Gale for how Athena can glide on the wind.'

'Fine names,' Sylva agreed, nodding her head solemnly.

The guns weighed heavily in his hands, and he felt the power behind them. Capable of ending a life, just by pointing and shooting. Formidable weapons indeed.

'Aim for the head if it's an orc and be careful of the noise,' Athol advised, pushing Fletcher's hands down so the pistols pointed at the floor. 'Now, your final gift. I had to make some last-minute adjustments when Captain Lovett told me you had taken up Electra's offer, which is why we were a little late.'

Athol opened the package himself, revealing a long leather band, with a collection of straps, holsters and toggles along it.

'This is your harness,' he said, pulling it over Fletcher's head and adjusting the straps. He tugged and pulled here and there, then stepped back to admire his handiwork.

'That'll do just fine. Let's get you all set up. Holster those pistols, will you? You've got me all nervous pointing those things around.'

Fletcher slid his pistols into the holsters that were now at his sides, feeling the balanced weight of the two on his hips. Athol tore open the packages behind him, and Fletcher felt his bow and quiver clipped to his back, and the khopesh's scabbard added to his belt. Finally, the dwarf nipped around and slotted four of the vials that Electra had given them in a bandolier along Fletcher's chest.

'Perfect,' Athol said. 'You're armed to the teeth but you'll be able to slip through the jungle like a wraith with this thing on, nothing falling off or jingling.'

'It *is* perfect,' Fletcher said, looking around for a mirror to admire himself, but failing to find one. He contented himself with looking down at his chest, gripping the handles of his pistols and feeling the power behind them.

'I don't know how to repay you Athol, or you, Briss. I have some money – I won't be needing it in the jungles. Let me do that at least.'

'Not a chance,' Athol said, pushing his hands into his pockets.

Fletcher took the purse from one of Arcturus's open packages and tried to hand it to Briss, but she backed away with her palms in the air.

'Just survive,' she said simply, putting her arm around Othello's shoulder. 'And keep my boy safe.'

# 22

It was late afternoon when Fletcher awoke, the light from the sun filtering through the upper windows of the tavern. Ignatius purred softly on Fletcher's chest, his tail twitching as he dreamed. He had deliberately moved from his customary position around Fletcher's neck to deny Athena such a prime location. The Gryphowl had seemed annoyed by the little imp's antics, and Fletcher had wisely chosen to infuse her to avoid a confrontation.

Beside them, Othello snored loudly, his mouth open, nostrils flaring with every breath. Peering through the shutters and seeing the sun high in the sky, Fletcher gave Othello a gentle kick. The dwarf snorted awake and groaned, pulling the covers over his face.

'Looks like staying up all night to plot our route has meant we've wasted most of the day sleeping,' Fletcher complained, looking through the window. 'I told you we should have gone to bed.'

'Well, we've done all the leg work now,' Othello said, though he didn't sound convinced. 'We can spend the day shopping.

Don't you want to enjoy a day of freedom? You've been at it nonstop since you came out of that cell.'

Fletcher stretched and began to put on his boots, allowing Ignatius to slide off on to the floor. The imp remained on his back, legs akimbo, refusing to be roused despite a mental prod from his master.

'Trust me, there's nothing I would like more,' Fletcher replied, 'but last night Jeffrey suggested we go to the front lines, meet the soldiers. I've never been there – I want to see what it's like, what they're like.'

'Are you sure?' Othello asked, his apprehension obvious.

'Yeah.' Fletcher tiptoed past Jeffrey, who was still sleeping on the sofa across the room. 'We're about to go behind enemy lines and we don't even know what our own soldiers look like. I'm going to see if the girls are awake.'

He left their bedroom and knocked gently on the adjacent door. There was no answer, so he knocked a little harder. As he raised his fist to knock a third time, there was a bang as something heavy was thrown against the door, then a voice rang out.

'Bugger off!' Cress shouted.

Fletcher grinned and retreated from the door.

'Looks like it's just us three,' he said, prodding Jeffrey awake.

It was a long carriage ride to the front lines, so much so that the first orange tinge of dusk was already staining the sky when the driver knocked on the ceiling to let them know they had arrived. The journey had been a sombre affair, the realisation of the task the three would undertake the next day sinking in. Fletcher had even infused Ignatius halfway through their trip, as the demon

196

had caught their despondency and his mournful growls did little to lighten the mood.

'Come on,' Fletcher said, leaping out as the other two looked at the carriage doors with trepidation. 'Let's explore.'

The carriage had stopped at the top of a low hill, allowing him a view of the front line, which stretched for miles on either side of him. It constituted a single, wide trench that came up to a man's shoulders, with a wooden step built along the inside for the soldiers to stand on and aim their weapons over the top. Wooden bunkers with cannons emplaced within broke the line up at intervals, and Fletcher could hear the dull echoes of cannon-fire – an orc raid in the distance.

A few hundred yards away, beyond the trench, the green fronds of the jungle could be seen, with the ground between a barren wasteland, churned to mud after years of cannon-fire and pitched battles.

Fletcher had never seen the jungle before, and was fascinated by the intensity of colour and the thickness of the foliage, shrouding all but the edge of the jungle from view. Even as he peered closer, his stomach twisted. Soon he would be far beyond this border, cut off from the safety of Hominum's lands.

Behind the trenches on their side, red-uniformed soldiers milled aimlessly, walking among a mess of campfires and large tents, smoking, eating and drinking. Somewhere, a violin creaked out a mournful tune, then an angry bellow cut it short, the musician's efforts unappreciated.

'Great, Fletcher,' Othello grumbled, standing beside him. 'This looks like a fun place. Well worth the four-hour journey.'

'Give it a chance,' Jeffrey said, eyeing the largest tent, from where shouts and laughter could be heard. 'Let's see what's happening in there and have one drink, at least. We can sleep in the carriage on the way home.'

'Agreed,' Fletcher said, watching as a man was hurled from the entrance by two guards, landing in the mud with a spatter. Another staggered out behind him and retched violently, then collapsed on top of the steaming puddle he had left behind.

'Although, let's not stay too long,' he added, then turned to the driver of the carriage. 'Wait here for us and you'll have a fare for your journey back.'

'Right you are, sir,' the driver replied with a wink.

They trudged down, trying not to get too much mud on their brand new moccasins. As they walked by, some soldiers stood up straighter, tugging their forelocks or saluting. Jeffrey's walk turned into a swagger; the new uniforms they wore were clearly expensive, and identified them as officers of some sort. Even the two guards stepped smartly aside to allow them to pass, and soon they were within the confines of the tent.

It was devilishly hot within, the air steaming with the stench of unwashed bodies, pungent smoke and spilled beer. The place was full of men, swigging on tankards and puffing on cheroots, leaving a pall of smog to hang above their heads.

There was a bar to the right, which Jeffrey swiftly gravitated towards, joining a queue of men to secure a drink. Meanwhile, Fletcher and Othello saw a group crowded around what appeared to be a walled pit in the centre of the room. As they moved in to investigate, a gap-toothed man with a shaven head approached them, holding a grubby stack of papers in his hands.

'Place your bets, lads. Odds are five to one on all four of 'em.

Pick blue, red, green or yellow, 'tis all the same. Last one standing gets to live.'

They ignored him, pushing their way to the front of the crowd, with Othello just tall enough to peer over the lip and see what lay below.

A large crate sat in the centre of a bloodied sandpit, twitching and rustling with movement from within. Around it, four smaller crates were lined up against the pit's edge, each around the size of a small keg of beer and corresponding to the colours the bookie had named. All of them were connected to a rope that ran through a ring embedded in the awning above the pit, ready to lift them and release what was within. Animal bones were scattered among the sand like cheroots in an ashtray, while the ribcage of an animal, perhaps a large dog, lay mouldering in the corner.

All around, men were jeering, some spitting and hurling abuse at the unknown inhabitants of the four crates.

'Last chance for bets – anyone, anyone?' the gap-toothed man called out, but there were no takers. He leaped on to the barrier beside Fletcher and as the eyes of the crowd turned to him, Fletcher realised he was the organiser of the event.

'Release the gremlins,' he bellowed.

Slowly, the boxes were lifted, and out of the hinged flaps at the bottom fell scrawny, grey-skinned creatures, barely taller than a toddler and clad in ragged loincloths. They had long noses and ears, bulging eyes and nimble, pianist fingers that scrabbled at the boxes in their attempts to stay within. Each was daubed with a splash of paint across their backs, just as their containers had been.

Strangely, one stood out to Fletcher. While the others cringed and scampered into the corners, the blue gremlin stood proudly, triangular ears flattening along his back, eyes swivelling around, flicking from the large box in the centre to the crowd above. For a moment the gremlin's eyes focused on Fletcher, then it snatched up a broken thighbone from the ground, one end sharp and jagged, the other a thick double-club of bone.

'Looks like we have a fighter! Blue's got a bit of spunk in him.' The gap-toothed man laughed uproariously, slapping Fletcher's back as if he were in on the joke. Then his voice turned ugly and he gave Fletcher a sadistic sneer.

'They're usually the first to go.'

Jeffrey pushed his way between the two of them, much to Fletcher's relief. He handed a drink to both Othello and Fletcher, his eyes already glazed over with inebriation. Fletcher took one look at the foul-smelling liquid within his tankard and quietly handed it to the gap-toothed man, before Jeffrey could see.

The man winked with thanks and then, after a swig that spilled most of the drink down his shirt, roared, 'Unleash the rats!'

The largest crate was raised, and out came a mass of seething, wriggling bodies, a grotesque mix of tails, incisors and black, matted fur. There must have been a hundred of them, and wherever they scampered, they left little claw prints of blood.

The man threw his arm around Fletcher's shoulders, the drink buying his goodwill. 'We don't feed 'em for a while – gets 'em ravenous,' the man croaked with a conspiratorial nudge. 'Takes a while for 'em to resort to cannibalism, the sweet spot's three days. Looks like these ones started a little early.'

His breath stank, fetid in Fletcher's nostrils. He turned away in disgust, and his eyes fell on to the pit once more, unable to drag them away from the spectacle.

The rats had sensed movement now, though many were still extricating themselves from the pile. Blue, thighbone in hand, was chittering to his compatriots, giving them orders in a strange language, or so it seemed. But if he was, they ignored his pleas, instead hiding their heads between their legs, while one clawed at the pit's dirt walls, trying to find purchase in the crumbling material.

The first rat leaped for Blue, but he batted it away with a desperate flail. Again, he called to his friends, to no avail. Now two rats leaped, and he had no choice but to dive aside with a frantic roll.

The green gremlin fell, surrounded by a squeaking swarm of red-eyed rats. Blue cried out in alarm, but the sound was nothing compared to the screams and gurgles of pain as the teeth gnashed at the emaciated creature beneath them.

More of the vermin found their footing and Blue shuffled away, until his back touched the festering ribcage, pieces of fur still hanging from the bones, rotting tendons holding the structure together. The yellow gremlin was next to go, disappearing under a mass of black rats, its pitiful screams hollow in Fletcher's ears.

Of the others, only the red one remained, having somehow managed to scramble halfway up the pit. It hung there, suspended, unable to climb any further. Beneath it, the rats squealed and leaped, teeth snapping below the gremlin's kicking ankles. In the corner, Blue slipped beneath the ribcage, then pushed the sharp end of his bone through the gap and began stabbing at any rat that came within reach.

Fletcher watched in horror as a man leaned out and prodded the red gremlin, which fell screaming into the baying pack. There were yells of anger from some of the men, but they were only complaining because they had bets on it. Like a pack of piranhas, the rats stripped the tiny corpse until it was nothing more than a skeleton.

'Blue wins!' the gap-toothed man cried, greeted by a cheer from the men who watched. 'Now, who wants to bet on how long he will last? I've got two to one it's a minute!'

There was a surge of men, silver sovereigns held high as they rushed to take his bet.

'I thought the winner got to live,' Fletcher growled.

'The show's never been this good before,' the man whispered out of the side of his mouth. 'I ain't gonna let it go to waste.'

'I feel sick,' Jeffrey mumbled, gripping Fletcher's arm. 'I don't think this beer agreed with me. Take me outside, please.'

Below, Blue valiantly struggled on, a rat squealing as it was hit in the eye, another battering the ribcage beside it.

'Let's go,' Fletcher said, shoving his way through the crowd. The tent was suddenly too small, too hot. He needed to breathe again.

They burst through the entrance and Jeffrey staggered away, dragging Othello and Fletcher behind him. He began to vomit, and Othello rubbed his back, turning his head away in disgust. The darkness of night had fallen, the last vestiges of sun sinking behind the horizon.

'I took one sip of that stuff and poured it away,' Othello said. 'Like piss, fresh from the horse. Though drinking's no more than a coward's way to courage anyway.'

Courage. That was what Fletcher had just seen, from a little gremlin, fighting against insurmountable odds. As he pictured the struggling creature, his heart filled with resolve. He set his jaw and began to pace back to the tent.

'Fletcher, wait,' Jeffrey mumbled, spittle dripping from his mouth.

But Fletcher was already through the doors and barging through the crowd. He vaulted over the pit's parapet with a single leap, then blasted the rats aside with kinetic energy, sending their heavy bodies thudding into the earthen walls.

He summoned Ignatius with a pulse of mana and the demon came out fighting, slashing back and forth with his claws. A wave of flame from his mouth sent a dozen rats to their deaths, but the scent of cooking flesh was too much for the others – the remaining rats fell upon their burned compatriots with squeals of joy.

Blue was locked chest to chest with a monstrous rat that had wriggled inside the ribcage, stabbing it repeatedly in the side with his bone. Fletcher drew his khopesh and neatly spitted the rodent, using the sword and body to lift the cage away. Then, as the cries of excitement began to die, he sheathed his sword and gathered the little gremlin into his arms. Blue's skinny chest heaved in and out with exhaustion.

The crowd stared down at Fletcher in shock, then the gap-toothed man yelled.

'What the hell are y—'

But he never finished his sentence, for the world flipped upside down and an explosion tore through the tent, shrapnel ripping through the crowd of drunken men like a scythe through wheat.

Deep in the pit, the flare passed above Fletcher and Ignatius in a wave of roiling fire. His ears sang with pain from the thunderclap of sound and he was thrown to the ground by a shockwave that rippled through the earth.

Then he was clawing his way out of the pit and over the screaming bodies of injured soldiers, Blue still clutched protectively to his chest. He felt a hand grasp his ankle and he kicked it away, stretching and pulling forward like a drowning man heading for shore. Ignatius tugged at his sleeve, guiding him through the smoke. Then Othello's strong hands dragged him out and over the mud, until they collapsed together at the base of the hill. The dwarf's relieved face peered down at him.

'You're alive,' he breathed. 'It's a damn miracle.'

Fletcher stared at the carnage behind him. Frantic sergeants barked orders as soldiers dragged the wounded from the blackened, bloodstained ground and on to hastily prepared stretchers, made from spears and knotted jackets.

'This is no miracle,' Fletcher choked, for the air was thick with smoke, smaller fires spreading among the wreckage. Ignatius chittered fearfully and scampered on to Fletcher's shoulder, nuzzling his neck for comfort.

'We need to help them,' Jeffrey gasped, stumbling towards the ruined tent, but Fletcher grasped him by the collar and tugged him back.

'Othello, you shouldn't be seen here,' Fletcher said urgently, as angry voices mingled with the sounds of dying men. 'An explosion . . . a dwarf nearby.'

Othello's eyes widened in horror, then he was tugging Jeffrey up the hill with Fletcher, though the boy fought them every step of the way, demanding to be allowed to help the fallen soldiers.

It was not long before they reached the carriage, which by some miracle was still waiting for them.

'What the hell happened?' the carriage driver asked, his eyes widening as he took in the gremlin cradled in Fletcher's arm.

Fletcher shoved a fistful of coins from his purse into the driver's hands as Othello manhandled Jeffrey through the carriage doors.

'Take us back to Corcillum,' Fletcher growled. 'And quickly.'

# 23

'What the hell were you thinking?' Uhtred bellowed, slamming his fist on to the table.

They were in the cellar of the Anvil, getting the dressing-down of their lives. Uhtred had arrived a few minutes before and had dragged them down there as soon as he had heard their story, afraid that people would be watching the tavern for signs of movement after the Anvil attack.

'What if you had been spotted?' he growled, advancing on the three of them. 'The only dwarven soldier for miles around and you just *happen* to be there when the bomb goes off. We're in the *Anvil* Tavern, for pity's sake. You just got off on a charge of *treason*. If word gets out, your mission will do more harm than good – people will think you're traitors!'

'I think it's safe to say I was seen,' Othello muttered. 'But with my beard shaved, they might not have taken me for a dwarf, just a very short man. It was dark and crowded and everyone was drunk. Most of the people who saw me probably died in the explosion.'

'It was my idea to go,' Fletcher added, as Othello shrunk under his father's gaze. 'But how were we to know that there was going to be an attack? We just wanted a look at the front lines.'

Uhtred opened his mouth, then grimaced and closed it again.

'Be that as it may, you three are on very thin ice,' he said, though his expression had softened.

'Can you keep it down?' Jeffrey mumbled, clutching his head. 'I'm dying here.'

'Serves you right,' Uhtred grumbled, though he handed the boy a flask of water from his hip. 'Get this down you. We need you on top form for the mission tomorrow.'

Othello groaned aloud at the mention of the mission and Uhtred rounded on him again.

'Forgot about that, had you? The future of Hominum depends on you, both to unify the nation and to destroy the goblin threat. I dread to think what King Harold would say if he knew what happened tonight.'

Fletcher hung his head in shame, but part of his mind was busy wondering how Uhtred would react if he knew that a sleeping gremlin was in the rucksack now hanging on the bannister to the cellar stairs. He had no idea what he was going to do with the little creature, and Othello hadn't been much help. Jeffrey, on the other hand, was oblivious, having gone into a stupor immediately upon entering the carriage.

Uhtred glanced at Fletcher's pistols and then sighed, removing one from its holster and sighting down it.

'Did my son at least teach you how to load and fire these while you were out there?' he asked, though his tone suggested he already knew the answer.

'Well . . . with the explosion and everything . . .' Fletcher mumbled, avoiding Othello's eyes.

'You won't be able to practise in the jungle, they'll hear you miles off,' Uhtred said, exasperated. 'There won't be time tomorrow either. This place is soundproof enough, though it might hurt *our* ears a bit. Nobody on the street will hear us.'

At the far end of the cellar, a pile of broken furniture had been unceremoniously stacked against the wall. In the centre, there was a red-cushioned chair facing outwards, an ideal target.

Without hesitation, Uhtred pulled the trigger and a long tongue of smoke erupted out from the gun's end, the sound more a crack than a bang in the confines of the cellar. A smaller puff of smoke curled from where the flint had slammed into the gun, igniting the powder within.

The cushion simply vibrated slightly, but Fletcher could see a new hole in the threadbare fabric, just off the centre.

'Not bad,' Uhtred said, cocking the flint back again. 'Now, watch closely.'

He removed a small cartridge from his back pocket, a cylinder of yellow paper that was twisted shut at one end. He gripped the twist with his teeth and tore the top open, revealing a fine black powder piled inside it.

'You pour it into the square trough where the flint meets the steel of the pistol when it snaps down, known as the pan,' Uhtred said, trickling a small amount of the powder in. 'Hence the phrase *flash in the pan*.'

Fletcher watched with avid eyes as Uhtred pushed the remainder of the cartridge into the end of the pistol.

'Then, you put the whole thing into the barrel, and use the

ramrod to shove it down to the base.'

Uhtred pulled a slender stick of metal that poked out from the wooden stock of the pistol, just beneath the barrel. He rammed it down the end a few times, making sure that the cartridge was wedged tightly inside the gun. He replaced the ramrod in its holder, then pointed the barrel at the cushion once again. The whole process had taken less than fifteen seconds.

'Now, you have a go at firing. Remember, it has a bit of a kick!'

Uhtred handed the weapon to Fletcher. The gun was heavy in his hands, and his arm wavered as he raised it, sighting down the barrel. It was different to the bow, the point of focus too far ahead, the weight unbalanced, all of it on his one arm.

He fired, closing his eyes as the puff from the firing pan burst out, the clap of noise as loud as the Anvil attack had been. He could not see if he had hit anything, for there was too much smoke, but as his ears stopped ringing and the smog cleared, the cushion appeared as it had before.

'Where did it go?' Fletcher asked.

Slowly, a chair leg in the top right corner of the room wobbled, then broke away with a splintering sound, a bullet wedged in the joint. Othello chortled as it fell to the ground, far away from where Fletcher had been aiming.

'Well. Maybe aim for the chest instead of the head,' Uhtred laughed, slapping Fletcher on the back. Fletcher sighed and pushed the pistol back in its holster.

'Right, clothes off,' Uhtred snapped, clicking his fingers.

'What?' Fletcher asked. What was Uhtred talking about?

Then he looked down at his uniform. The front of his

brand new jacket and trousers were splattered with soot, mud and splashes of blood from the massacre. Even Othello's uniform was stained with the same, from when he had dragged Fletcher to his feet. In contrast, Jeffrey's was fine, despite his bout of vomiting.

Fletcher shrugged and slowly took off his weapons and clothing, until he and Othello were shivering in the cold air of the dusty cellar, wearing nothing but their underwear. Uhtred chuckled at their miserable faces.

'You're lucky that my wife is the best seamstress around. She'll replace what can't be cleaned and have these ready for you tomorrow.'

Before Fletcher could apologise for ruining his new clothes, there was a creak from upstairs. Then, before anyone could move, the door to the cellar burst open and a crossbow was aimed down the stairwell.

'Who's down there?' Sylva yelled, rolling out with her bow drawn, as Cress squinted at them over her weapon.

'It's just us,' Fletcher admitted sheepishly. Uhtred stomped up the stairs and pushed Cress's crossbow down.

'Get some rest,' he chuckled. 'I'll see you all tomorrow.'

For a moment the two girls stared at the half-naked boys, their faces marked with soot from the explosion, Jeffrey splayed drunkenly on the floor.

They burst out laughing, much to Fletcher's horror.

'Well, well,' Cress said, her eyes sparkling with merriment. 'Looks like we missed the party.'

# 24

The four teams stood on an expansive wooden platform, overlooking a sea of red-uniformed men, just beyond the trenches of the front lines. The soldiers stared back grimly, and the world was silent but for a whistling wind that left their jackets flapping in the air.

Fletcher felt a rustle in the rucksack on his back and froze. Blue had been sleeping, or at least pretending to, all night. The plan had been to keep him there and release him into the wild when they landed. Unfortunately, the gremlin's slumber seemed to be over.

As Fletcher prayed that Blue would go back to sleep, Provost Scipio climbed slowly up the stairs on the side of the stage, resplendent in the full uniform of a general. He nodded to each team, then turned to the crowd of soldiers.

'You all know me,' Scipio said, his hands clasped tightly behind his back. 'The Hero of Watford Bridge. Provost of Vocans Academy. I have fought in this war for a decade and defended the borders long before that. Many of you know me

211

personally. So when I tell you that what you are about to hear is the truth, I expect you to trust me.'

There were nods from the watching soldiers, tensed shoulders relaxing, even some smiles.

'You have heard about Lady Cavendish, suffering in captivity for all these years. You know of the goblins, and the thousands of eggs that are waiting to hatch. These four teams will be leading an expedition, deep behind enemy lines, to eliminate these threats. It is as dangerous a mission as I have ever signed off on. Each and every one of these young warriors is risking their lives to keep our country safe. I want you to keep that in mind when the dwarven and elven recruits arrive on the front lines.'

He paused, and Fletcher's eyes flicked to the blackened earth beyond the crowd, where the aftermath of the recent explosion was still visible.

'We lost forty-three good men last night, in a senseless, brutal attack. The men who did it are just that: *men*. The dwarven elders have condemned the attacks over and over again, pronouncing that these atrocities are not done in their name. I want you to remember that too.'

This last statement was met with frosty silence, some shaking their heads, others simply looking on impassively.

'The Celestial Corps will arrive soon, along with the teams' jungle guides and demon sponsors. I want you all to show them your appreciation for the sacrifice these young men and women make today.'

As applause broke out, tiny dots appeared in the clouds, at first circling like bees around a honeypot, then growing larger until they filled Fletcher's vision with enormous, flapping wings.

There were dozens of them, all powerful flying beasts that spiralled in perfect formation.

Lovett landed lightly beside them, the click of Lysander's claws barely making a sound. The Griffin folded his wings and kneeled beside Fletcher.

'I can fit two of you,' she whispered, pulling Fletcher up alongside her. Sylva slipped wordlessly behind him, a thin sheen of sweat on her forehead. She lay her head on his rucksack, grasping him around the waist tightly.

'It'll be fine,' Fletcher said, though unconvinced of his own words. There was no movement from Blue. It was as if the gremlin knew he should be silent.

Another demon landed alongside them, hooves clopping on the ground. It was an Alicorn, one of the rarer demons in Hominum's arsenal. Fletcher admired the beautiful white pelt and swanlike feathers, its body moving gracefully among the crowd of students. It looked like a large horse, but for its broad wings and a long cone of a horn that erupted from its forehead.

The rider's face was obscured by his leather cap and wide goggles, but he waved Cress and Othello aboard and then pulled them up beside him, their short stature making it difficult for them to mount themselves.

More demons followed, each landing accompanied by a cheer from the watching soldiers. Hippogriffs swooped in; like Griffins in physical form but with the body and back legs of a horse instead of a lion. Antlered Perytons clattered across the stage, appearing for all the world like elven elk but for their large, tawny wings, elongated tail feathers and the razor-sharp talons on their hind legs.

There was even the occasional Chamrosh, miniature Griffins but with a hawk's head and wings and a dog's body and mannerisms. These were too small to be ridden – only twice the size of Athena, perhaps. They instead provided much needed support and were excellent companions to the primary demons of the Celestial Corps.

Fletcher was amazed. He had never seen such an array of demons, especially such large and powerful specimens. He had become used to seeing the same demons at Vocans, and had almost forgotten the variety of species Hominum had at its disposal.

He was also glad to see no Gryphowls. Athena was a rarity, and he was looking forward to allowing her to stretch her wings on the flight. He had made sure that Ignatius and Athena were infused within him for as long as possible before the mission, so that they were well rested and had recovered as much mana as they could. Still, it felt strange to be without Ignatius for so long, and Athena's presence within his consciousness had taken some getting used to. Though she intruded rarely in his thoughts, as to be expected from a well-trained demon, Fletcher was still finding it hard to direct instructions to just one demon's consciousness at a time.

'Everybody ready?' Scipio shouted, watching as the final students mounted their respective steeds. At their head, Fletcher could see Ophelia Faversham mounted on her own Peryton, pale hair streaming in the wind. She carried Zacharias Forsyth behind her, there to see off his Wendigo when they reached the landing zone, or perhaps as added protection. Rook was also mounted, clutching the midriff of another officer and wearing a queasy look on his face.

Caliban, Sacharissa and the Wendigo were nowhere to be seen, but Fletcher knew they couldn't be infused or the connection to the scrying stones would be broken. Then he saw the soldiers pointing above them. He followed their gaze, and was amazed to see three large crates floating high in the sky, each one attached to two members of the Celestial Corps. It was small wonder that Rook looked so nauseous, for the boxes swayed pendulously back and forth and their owners would be able to sense the motion through their demons.

'Where's Arcturus?' Fletcher asked, noticing the absence of Seraph's sponsor, and Lovett pointed at the man on the Alicorn beside them. All of a sudden, Fletcher recognised the lower half of the man's face, and could see the edge of the scar beneath the goggles.

'A gift from King Harold!' Arcturus shouted, patting his Alicorn on the neck. 'I call him Bucephalus, or Buck for short! He'll keep me company while Sacha's away.'

Lovett turned to Fletcher and Sylva, a happy smile on her face.

'Arcturus will be part of the extraction team when you've completed the mission, or if you need rescuing. It will be nice to have a riding companion . . . once you've returned Lysander to me of course.'

Fletcher could see that all the others had now mounted, including Jeffrey, though it was difficult to see who was who with the milling demons and flapping wings in the way.

At a barked order from Ophelia, the Celestial Corps turned to face the jungles. Then, with a dry mouth and pounding heart,

Fletcher was launched into the air for the second time that week.

The ground dropped away faster than he thought possible, the sea of red uniforms shrinking into no more than a puddle, pooling against the dark bar of the trench. Still they flew higher, the clouds rushing to meet them. Before they broke through, Fletcher caught a glimpse of an endless, undulating blanket of green, broken only by the thick snake of a river that meandered towards their front lines before curving back in on itself.

'That was the river that boy, Mason, came in on,' Lovett shouted as they burst out of the clouds in a wash of mist. 'The one who brought back the body of the goblin. He's a brave soul – I wouldn't have the guts to do what he's doing.'

They were gliding above a great stretch of white mantle of cloud that extended as far as the eye could see. Now that they were above them, the sun blazed brightly in the sky, reflecting off the bank of clouds to give them a fierce glare. It was strange, for the sky had been overcast and grey before they flew through them.

'What do you mean, about Mason? Why is he brave?' Sylva asked, her voice breathy with excitement, hands clasped tightly around Fletcher's midriff.

'Why would he want to guide Malik's team?' Lovett replied. 'Remember the state he was in when he came back over the front lines? He's either mad or fearless to go back. I can't tell if it's out of loyalty to his friends who are still captives, or if he's after the money that comes with it.'

The formation of flying demons began to glide south, many just above the cloud line, their feet brushing along the tops. Fletcher stretched out his toes, hoping to feel something, but all he felt was the gradual soaking of his moccasins.

'I have something for you,' Lovett said, reaching into her saddle panniers. She withdrew a scroll, tightly bound with a red ribbon.

'If something happens to me while you're out there,' she said, pressing it into Fletcher's hands, 'this is Lysander's summoning scroll. I don't want him fading back into the ether in the middle of your mission if the worst happens.'

'Thank you,' Fletcher said, touched by the gesture. 'You will have it back when we return.'

He tucked it into the side pocket of his satchel, careful not to disturb the gremlin. If Lovett found out about the fugitive he was harbouring he wasn't sure how he would explain himself.

On they flew, the sun baking their skin, the wind watering their eyes with each gust. But it was not long before the exhilaration of flying wore off and the reality of where they were going sunk in.

'Why don't you let Athena stretch her wings?' Lovett suggested, sensing the tension.

Fletcher smiled and pointed his palm into the sky. Athena erupted into existence with a flash of blue light, spiralling in an elegant pirouette until she was gliding just ahead of Lysander's beak.

'You might want to move her,' Lovett chuckled, though Fletcher didn't understand the joke. He wracked his brains, confused, then Sylva whispered:

'Most of Hominum is watching this through Lysander's eyes. I don't think they'd appreciate a view of Athena's backside.'

'Oh!' Fletcher laughed, nudging Athena downwards with a swift thought. 'I forgot!'

'I won't be forgetting in a hurry,' Lovett grumbled, rubbing Lysander's tufted ears. 'Lysander spent most of yesterday being poked and prodded by crystals to be distributed around the Empire. We had to stand beside Hannibal, Zacharias's Wendigo, the entire time. That thing smelled riper than a gremlin's loincloth.'

Within Fletcher's backpack, Blue shifted, as if he recognised the word. Fletcher didn't even know if gremlins were capable of speech, but he changed the subject quickly.

'Why are we flying above the clouds?' Fletcher asked. 'Don't we need to see the lay of the land?'

'Actually, we're lucky the day is so overcast,' Lovett said, shaking her head at him. 'There are thousands of orcs, gremlins, maybe even goblins, going about their day-to-day business below us. This is their territory now. If even one of them happened to see us flying above them, this mission would be over before it has even begun. No, we'll be staying in cloud-cover until we reach the drop zone. You'll be pretty safe there – the Celestial Corps scouts tell us it's relatively uninhabited.'

Fletcher swallowed, the thick bank of clouds suddenly seeming an insubstantial barrier between him and the land below. Indeed, on occasion the mist thinned, giving him tantalising glimpses of mountainous terrain, all of it covered in an overgrown mass of greenery. He dreaded to think how long it would take them to make their way back, should the Celestial Corps fail to extract them. If they could even make it back at all.

For the first time, he noticed a short lance attached beneath

218

the side of the saddle. It appeared rather like a jousting pole of the knights of old, but a little shorter and more robust. This one was painted with stripes of white and blue, with a fearsome metallic tip that glinted in the sunlight.

'What's that?' he asked, pointing at it.

'A lance, what else?' Lovett replied, tugging it from its holder and demonstrating by couching it under her arm. 'When you're fighting a Wyvern, the lance is the only thing that will pierce its hide, and even then, you'll need some speed behind the blow.'

Fletcher shuddered at the thought of fighting so high up, riding on demons that clashed together in a flailing mess of wings and claws.

'Sometimes you'll get an unwelcome passenger drop in,' Lovett continued, replacing the lance and removing a blade from a scabbard at her side. 'Shrikes, Strixs or Vesps are the most common, smaller orc-flying demons, and if they get too close, you have to take them out with this.'

Fletcher recognised it to be a rondel dagger – a needlelike blade with disk-shaped guards on the top and bottom of the hilt to protect the wielder's hands.

'Of course, that's forgetting all the battle-spells flying around,' Lovett said, twirling the dagger with practised ease and returning it to her scabbard. 'If you thought spellcraft was difficult before, just wait until you have to do it in a dogfight.'

Fletcher shuddered, and for the first time resented how quickly he had been put through Vocans. One year was not nearly enough time to learn all that summoning had to offer, nor to perfect the techniques that he *had* managed to learn.

He had been told that orc shamans had weaker demons in

general, but he wondered if that was truth, or propaganda. After all, Wyverns were some of the most powerful demons in existence. Perhaps it was the demons that were sent against the front line that were weaker, and the more powerful demons were being held back. For now.

'We're following the river,' Lovett shouted as the wind picked up and snatched at her words. 'You'll be dropped in a swamp that feeds into one of its sources. Won't be long now!'

As if she had heard, Ophelia came to a halt at the head of the squadron. For a moment she hovered there, peering at the ground below, then she shot three wyrdlights into the sky in quick succession.

At the signal, Lysander folded back his wings and they dropped through the clouds like a falling arrow, hurtling through the air so fast that the wind tore at Fletcher's eyes and face. He took in a brief blur of green landscape, then leaves were slapping across his legs and arms.

Lysander seemed to leap from branch to branch, each one springing down like a bent sapling, slowing their descent to the point of breaking, only to be released as he moved on to the next. Finally, when Fletcher thought it would never end, there was a soft thud as the Griffin's claws tore into the soil, skidding along the top and leaving four furrows behind them. They came to a halt moments before hitting a tangled patch of thorny briars.

'Now that's what I call a quick descent,' Lovett whooped, punching the air with her fist. Fletcher felt Sylva slowly roll off Lysander's back, collapsing on the ground with her legs akimbo, still conformed to the shape of the saddle.

'That was awful,' she gasped, digging her fingers into the ground.

'I thought you'd be used to heights, what with the Great Forest and all,' Fletcher said, though his own heart was pounding so hard he could almost hear his pulse in his ears. He jumped to the ground and promptly collapsed beside her, his legs numb from gripping Lysander's sides for so long.

'It's not so much the height as the descent,' Sylva replied, slapping him playfully on the chest. They lay there, watching, as other riders glided more slowly through the canopy.

'Idiots,' Lovett grumbled, watching as one of the crates was lowered through the treetops by a pair of hovering Griffins. 'The longer we take to land, the more likely the orcs might spot us.'

Athena fluttered down and perched on Fletcher's chest, blinking as she examined him. She paddled with her paws at his stomach and legs, making sure he was still in one piece. He grinned and stroked her, revelling in the strange way her downy plumage blended with the soft fur of her chest and back.

He sat up and took in his surroundings. The woods were thicker and more abundant than the elven lands, which had consisted of massive trunks surrounded by a flat blanket of moss. In contrast, the jungle's ground was covered in a bed of mulched leaves, with thorny branches, broad-leafed plant-life and hanging vines filling the gaps between the gnarled, interlocking trees. The soil was dark and fragrant, fuelled by the constant fall of dead leaves to leave a rich, soft loam underfoot. Just beyond the clearing he and the others had landed in, pools of stinking liquid cratered the earth – brackish black water covered by a scum of moulding, rotting foliage.

'I'm *never* doing that again,' Cress declared, and Fletcher turned his head to see her face-down on the ground, hugging the earth for all she was worth. Othello seemed to be faring only slightly better, kneeling beside Arcturus's Alicorn with a relieved look upon his face.

'I'd rather walk,' Cress continued blithely. 'You can sod off with your flying malarkey, Arcturus. You and Buck can sleep in when it's time to rescue us.'

Arcturus laughed, removing his leather cap and shaking out a thick, untamed mane of black hair. Fletcher was sure he saw Lovett blush, glancing quickly up at Arcturus and then looking away. Fletcher caught her eye and grinned, but the stern look she returned him swiftly wiped it from his face.

'On your feet, all of you,' Ophelia's voice cracked out from the milling demons around them. 'We're leaving.'

The teams assembled and the crates unloaded, leaving Sacharissa, Hannibal and Caliban to stumble out and join the others. Arcturus lifted Lovett from Lysander's back and carried her to Bucephalus, cradling her like a sleeping child. For a while Fletcher had forgotten her loss of movement and he felt a surge of guilt for taking Lysander away from her.

Ophelia strode back and forth impatiently, eager to return to the safety of Hominum's front lines.

'I want you all to remember that the world is watching you through your sponsors' demons' eyes,' she snapped, her eyes roving across their faces. 'Comport yourselves in a way that would befit graduates of Vocans. Do not shirk your duty.'

Her granddaughter, Verity, raised a tentative hand, but after a glare from Ophelia, returned it to her side. It took a few more moments for Arcturus to remove Lysander's saddle and strap it to Bucephalus's side, then the Celestial Corps were mounted once again.

'Look after Lysander, would you?' Lovett called, raising her voice to be heard over the well-wishes of the other riders.

'Sacha too,' Arcturus echoed.

Then, just like that, they were in the air again, leaving the graduates to their fate. The teams stood and watched in silence for a while, until the corps had disappeared from sight.

'So,' Seraph said cheerfully. 'What do we do now?'

# 25

The four team leaders gathered in a rough circle, squatting on their haunches to avoid the wet ground. Seraph had spread his map on his backpack, with his planned route marked out along it.

The river followed a meandering path, the only real feature in an ocean of green. On one of the river's more curved bends, a red X marked the spot where the orc caves were, as well as a crude drawing of a pyramid. In the corner of the map was a more detailed diagram that delineated the orc encampment, made from Mason's memories of his time as a slave there. The square-based pyramid featured heavily, with a network of cave tunnels running beneath it – that was the location of the goblin eggs.

'We're going to follow the river on the west side, so we don't need to cross it to get to the camp,' Malik said, tracing his path with a finger. 'With Mason as our guide, we'll be able to avoid any patrols easily enough.'

'We're going on the east of the river and will cross in the

darkness,' Seraph said, shaking his head and pointing to the dotted line his team had already drawn along the river bank. 'The west side is nearer to the orc camps. I'd rather get wet than get killed.'

He nodded at his guide, a grizzled veteran who was armed with a heavy crossbow.

'Sergeant Musher was left for dead after a battle in the jungles last year. Evaded capture for twenty days, living off the land and navigating by the stars. He'll see we m—'

'You're both wrong,' Isadora interrupted, slapping Malik's hand aside and outlining a wider arc, further to the west. '*We* will cross like Malik, but curve around the west bank of the river. The river is a source of fish and water, that's where the orcs will congregate. It's more ground to cover but it will be safer.'

Fletcher felt strange, being so close to Isadora. Her father had worked hard to have him and Othello executed, not to mention the fact that she and Tarquin had planned Sylva's murder. Yet here they were, working together against the orcs.

'Fletcher,' Seraph said, nudging him. Fletcher glanced up and saw the other team leaders looking at him expectantly.

'I agree the banks of the river will be more populated,' he said, remembering the route he and the others had decided on. 'We'll do the same but on this side. We'll cross at night like Seraph but before that we will stay away from the river's edge.'

'Nobles on one side, commoners on the other,' Isadora smirked, nodding to herself with satisfaction. 'We'll see who gets there first.'

Seraph scowled at her words but rolled up the map.

'It's good we're splitting up,' Malik said, ignoring Isadora.

'If one team is caught, there will be three others to complete the mission. But there's a disadvantage too.'

'What's that?' Fletcher asked.

'It will be hard to arrive at the pyramid at the same time, like Rook said. If we don't, the first team to arrive will have to go in all alone and the other teams will be vulnerable when the alarm is raised. Then the Celestial Corps will have a hell of a time locating all four teams in the window before the Wyvern riders arrive.'

'He's right,' Isadora agreed, though begrudgingly. 'We'll just have to do our best. If one team arrives early, wait inside the pyramid. Mason tells me it's sacred ground that's used only for ceremonies, so we'll be safe inside. If you're late . . . you make your own way home.'

'That works for me,' Fletcher said, as Malik and Seraph nodded.

'We'll head through the swamp to where it joins the mouth of the river,' Malik said, standing up. 'Then we go our separate ways and reunite at the pyramid.'

As the team leaders returned to their respective groups, Fletcher was increasingly aware of the rustling gremlin in his rucksack. The little creature could obviously smell that he was back in the jungle and was making an attempt to break free. Fletcher needed a distraction.

'I have an idea,' he announced to the four groups, wary of raising his voice too much, in case it carried through the jungle. 'Each of our guides has expertise that the others don't. For example, Jeffrey has access to a new set of spells that have only recently been discovered and a knowledge of the local plant-life, all of which I am willing to share with you. Seraph's guide, Sergeant Musher, will know about avoiding detection and navigating in the forest. Yours . . .'

He looked over at Malik's guide, Mason, who was busy eating his way through a pile of jungle fruit.

'Well, we'll all have something to contribute I'm sure.'

'What about me?' growled a voice from among Isadora's team. 'Will I be of use?'

With all the excitement and the milling around, Fletcher had not had a chance to see who Tarquin's guide was. Yet, when the bulky frame revealed itself, Fletcher's breath caught in his throat. Grindle.

He was an ugly man, with the squashed face of a bulldog and a thick padding of fat all over his body, more even than Atlas, who stood beside him. He wore the black uniform of the Forsyth Furies, as did all of Isadora's team.

'I served as Lord Forsyth's man for many years,' he said, lumbering towards Fletcher. 'You know, getting my hands bloody, so Zacharias wouldn't have to. Couldn't let his kids go into the jungle without my watchful eye over them.'

Grindle winked at Sylva, whose face had gone ashen white. Almost two years ago, this man had put her head on a block and had raised the very same knobbled club that he now wore on his back, intending to kill her. Had it not been for Othello and Fletcher's intervention, she would now be dead, and Hominum would be in the midst of war with the elves.

Sylva nocked an arrow to her bow, but Othello tugged it from the bowstring before she could raise it.

'The world is watching,' he hissed, pointing at the Wendigo, whose black eyes were fixed on them with keen interest.

'You want to help them?' Sylva snapped, turning her anger on Fletcher.

'Maybe we'll just share with Seraph's team,' Fletcher said, his voice taut with the same fury. 'You seem like you have all the help you need.'

'What help would a filthy servant boy with ideas above his station and a soldier stupid enough to get himself lost in the jungle give us?' Tarquin said, inspecting his nails. 'Run along and share all you like. We'll be on our way now.'

Isadora grinned nastily at them, then hissed an order at the Wendigo. It knuckled its way through the underbrush, its claws spreading wide to tear a path ahead.

'Catch you later, Fletcher,' Didric called, tapping the rapier at his side. 'We'll be seeing you *very* soon.'

Then the Forsyth team walked nonchalantly into the jungle, their backs receding until all that remained was the distant snap of branches.

'Well, I don't want to know what that was about,' Verity said brightly, stepping forward. 'But we would be *very* willing to share. Mason can show you how to read the ground and leave no trail, a lesson that those idiots could have benefited from.' She pointed a thumb over her shoulder at the path of broken stems and disturbed ground the Forsyths had left behind. 'What do you say?'

She kicked Malik, who coughed and nodded in agreement.

'You're a Faversham,' Fletcher said bluntly, though he reddened as soon as the words left his mouth. He wasn't used to being so rude.

'And you're a Raleigh,' Verity replied sarcastically. 'I know my father prosecuted you at trial, but that's his job. I try not to judge people based on their families. Do you?'

Fletcher hesitated as she smiled at him, a hint of mischief in her big, dark eyes. She really was very attractive. He stuttered, tongue-tied – and the way Sylva was staring disapprovingly at him did little to help.

Fortunately, Seraph spoke before the silence went on for too long.

'Can't hurt,' he said, puffing out his chest. Seraph could never resist a pretty face. 'If one of us gets caught, it makes things harder for the rest. I say we spend the day here teaching each other and then camp overnight. It's already afternoon anyway. Should have done all this planning before we got here, but there you go.'

Fletcher looked to Othello for guidance, and after a pause, the dwarf gave him a curt nod. A faint scratching from within his backpack sealed his decision.

'Fine,' Fletcher said, pushing through his team and striding to the edge of the forest. 'Now, if you'll excuse me, I have some business with one of those trees out there.'

# 26

Fletcher hurried into the jungle, his face burning. Pretending to need the toilet. Couldn't he have thought of a better excuse?

He struggled through the tangled bushes, his skin itching as he brushed against a sticky cobweb. Around his head, the whine of mosquitos intermingled with the low buzz of common flies. Despite the abundant humidity in the air, the insects seemed attracted to the moisture in his eyes and mouth, and he spat and spluttered his way through until the others were out of sight.

Aware of his vulnerability so far from the others, he summoned Ignatius and Athena with two blasts from his palm. Immediately, Athena was fluttering to the top of the nearest tree, scanning the area for danger. Ignatius contented himself by scampering up Fletcher's shoulder, giving his master a remonstrative thwack of his tail for keeping him infused for so long.

With a furtive glance over his shoulder, Fletcher crouched among the bushes and slowly opened his pack. Within, Blue stared back through wide, fearful eyes. He had somehow armed himself with a fishhook, one of the many tools that Uhtred and

Briss had stowed in the leather satchels the dwarves had provided. It was a pitiful weapon, but the gremlin held it aloft as Fletcher stepped back, his arms raised to show he was no threat.

Slowly, his eyes never leaving Fletcher, the gremlin clambered out, until he was crouched on the ground, his scrawny chest heaving with anxious breaths.

'I shouldn't be doing this,' Fletcher said, and as he said the words, doubts began to plague him. Blue could go straight to his orc masters and tell them about the mission. But it was too late now, for the gremlin had shuffled out of reach. A flash of white from above told Fletcher that Athena had sensed his fears, and was ready to pounce. Then, the gremlin spoke.

'Thank you,' Blue trilled, dropping the hook to the ground.

He could speak! Fletcher's mind reeled as Blue darted into the thick of the jungle. Half a second later, Athena's paws thudded into the ground where he had been, and she hooted with frustration.

'Let him go,' Fletcher whispered, as Ignatius leaped down and nosed the bushes. 'He won't tell.'

He hoped.


As morning turned to afternoon, Fletcher was pleased that Malik's team had shared their guide's knowledge. Mason taught them to leave fewer footprints by avoiding the wetter ground and staying near the firmer soil beside tree roots. To remember, when they examined the prints of others, that wild cats walked with claws retracted and hyenas, the orcs' preferred pets, did not. How a few days of wind or a single night of rain would wipe it all away.

He showed them how to mask their scent and keep off mosquitos by rubbing wild garlic into their skin and hair. He told them of the natural highways of the forest, made more pronounced by years of passing animals. Some of this, Fletcher knew from his own hunting on the Beartooth Mountains. But to hear it said and taught, rather than just relying on his own instinctual understanding, was fascinating.

As Mason spoke, Jeffrey rummaged around the forest edge, collecting plant-life and stowing various specimens in his bag. When it was his turn to speak, it was his knowledge of botany that was most impressive, rather than the spells he revealed at the end.

'See here, the water vine,' he said, pointing to an unassuming liana that hung stiffly from the treetops. He sliced it at the bottom with a slim knife and held it to his mouth. Water flowed out, as easily as water from a tap.

'Fresh as a mountain spring,' he grinned, wiping his mouth. 'If you can't get rainwater or coconuts, this is the next best thing.'

He moved on to another plant nearby, a palm tree sapling. With some gentle sawing, he removed a core of white from behind the bark and crunched down on it with relish.

'Palm heart. Tastes like celery,' he mumbled through a full mouth. 'Nutritious though!'

He sliced the core into sections and handed them out. Fletcher found it to have a plain taste, with a hint of nuttiness he quite enjoyed.

Further out from the camp, Jeffrey showed them a flower with purple and white petals. He tore it from the ground to reveal a knobbly orange legume attached beneath.

'Sweet potato,' he grinned, shoving it into his pocket for later. For another hour he guided them around the jungle, all within one hundred feet of the camp. Papaya, guava, coconut and passionfruit hung from the treetops, only to be snatched down by the more acrobatic of demons. Malachi and Azura, Rory and Genevieve's Mites, snipped the various fruits from their stems to bring them to the ground with meaty thuds. Verity revealed her demon to be a Damsel, a demon that appeared as an iridescent dragonfly twice the size of a Mite. It had a sting and sharp mandibles to add an element of danger to the multicoloured insect swooping in and out of the trees. A low-level demon for a noble summoner, and Fletcher suspected it was not the only demon she kept in her roster.

But it was not all fun and games. Jeffrey stopped at a large, single-stemmed plant with heart-shaped leaves that grew close by. It didn't seem particularly impressive but for the translucent, bright pink berries that hung from it like bunches of grapes.

'This is the gympie tree. See here, the fine hairs that coat its fruit and leaves?' He held an arm out to keep them away, but lifted one of the leaves with his knife for all to see.

'Each fibre is infused with neurotoxin that will cause the fiercest pain imaginable. Worse still, the pain will linger for months, some say even years. Keep an eye out for it. Sergeant Musher, you will know of it?'

The grizzled veteran who was Seraph's guide shook his head sadly.

'Young lad of seventeen was caught short on patrol one night. Goes into the trees, does 'is business. Wipes with one of

233

them leaves there. The screamin' could 'av woken the dead. Definitely woke some orcs, 'cos we 'ad to get out of there sharpish. Took 'im back to camp, 'ad a doctor look, even 'ad a summoner heal 'im. Didn't make a blind bit of difference, the screamin' went on and on. Poor lad shot 'imself two weeks later.'

The mood took a sombre tone and Fletcher shuddered. The plant had not been far from where he had released Blue. This jungle was both a paradise and a death trap.

Again, Jeffrey led them away, this time stopping beside a larger tree, just as unassuming as any other.

'The manchineel tree,' he said, pointing at its branches. 'Burn its wood and the smoke will blind you. Stand beneath it when it rains and just one drop will blister your skin. Orcs coat their javelins in its sap to make the wound fester. They even tie runaway gremlins to the trunks for a slow death. Worse than burning, some say. The fruit is known as the death apple.' He pointed at the large green berries that hung from its branches. 'You can guess what happens if you eat one.'

There were many more revelations that afternoon. He showed them which woods would burn with the least smoke, so as not to signal their presence. He gathered sword grass with leaves so sharp that you could shave with them, the fleshy blades not unlike the spikes that lined Seraph's Barkling's back. There were even thorny vines that could be used as a rope-saw, so sharp and sturdy were the teeth of each spike.

Finally, Jeffrey held up diagrams of three new spell symbols. One, the leaf-shaped growth spell, could grow a seed into a plant within a few minutes, though none tried it out as Jeffrey warned them that the mana required was substantial.

The next symbol was a twisted line, which Jeffrey called the tangle spell. It would tighten and secure any knot or, by etching the inversion of the symbol, loosen it. The uses were limited, but Fletcher enjoyed testing it out on the lacing of Seraph's boots when he wasn't looking, much to the others' amusement. More than anything, Fletcher was relieved to see that Genevieve and Rory treated him well enough, apparently having forgiven him for the transgressions of the year before.

The final symbol was perhaps the most exciting – one that Jeffrey described as the ice spell, found within the carcass of a Polarion. Shaped in the crisscross of a simplified snowflake, it sent out a gust of frost that took hold of all it touched.

'A godsend in this heat,' Malik proclaimed, blasting the nearest pool of water. The surface crackled and froze solid, the moisture in the air between falling to the ground in a haze of icy flakes.

'A bit too powerful to cool yourself down with,' he declared with disappointment, 'but I'll be adding ice to my coconut water from now on.'

Fletcher wondered why the spells had been kept a secret for so long, for they would be useful to all battlemages. Perhaps they were Electra's only bargaining chips, and she had used them to allow Jeffrey to continue her research behind enemy lines.

Once the teams had tested the ice spell, it was Sergeant Musher's turn to demonstrate his knowledge. This was just as well, for the sky had darkened and the first stars were twinkling in the night sky. They settled in, huddling close as the heat of the day faded, leaving only the jungle's moisture to seep the cold into their bones.

Musher's voice washed over them in the darkness, describing the constellations and which directions they would take the follower. The Elven Arrow, pointing due north, or Corwin's Sceptre, which pointed east.

Nestled between the warmth of his friends, Fletcher dreamed.

# 27

Athena pawed at the baby's feet, careful to keep her claws retracted. He gurgled and watched her with wide, dark eyes.

'Athena! What have I told you about playing with the baby? He's barely old enough to sit up.' The voice was soft and pure, coming from above.

Tresses of blond hair descended over the child as hands lifted him out of the crib. Athena looked up from the bedsheets and took in the blue eyes of a noblewoman. She was smiling, despite the crinkle of a frown between her delicate eyebrows.

'Edmund,' the noblewoman called. 'Would you get this silly Gryphowl out of the crib?'

'I'm sorry, Alice, I wasn't paying attention. There's a house on fire in Raleightown. You can see it from the window.'

There were hurried footsteps and a man strode into view, beckoning Alice to follow him. Like Alice, he wore no more than a night shirt, open at the chest. His hair was swarthy and black, with a thick growth of stubble coating the lower half of his face.

Athena clambered out of the crib and settled on its wooden rail. The two nobles were huddled by the window of the nursery, watching a faint glow in the distance.

'Is it the baker or the blacksmiths?' Alice asked, squinting.

'Neither, they're both on the east side of the village. Wait . . . what's that?'

Athena sensed a pulse of sudden alarm from her master. There was a faint scream, cut short as quickly as it had begun.

She fluttered on to Edmund's shoulder and looked closer through the glass. The lawn of the manor house was neatly manicured, the edges lit by flickering lanterns. On the horizon, the flames of a burning village rose higher. Then, like the rising tide, a wave of grey appeared in the darkness.

'Heaven help us,' Edmund whispered.

They loped out of the gloom like a pack of wolves. Scores of orcs – lean, muscular giants with hunched shoulders and heavy brows, puffing great gouts of steaming breath in the chill night air. The short tusks jutting from their lower lips gleamed white in the lantern light, and they held their clubs and axes aloft as they ran. Athena could almost hear the thunder of their feet, yet the orcs did not howl or bellow, hoping to catch the occupants unaware.

'All the guards are at the mountain pass,' Alice whispered, clutching Edmund's arm. 'They would have raised the alarm if the orcs had attacked through there. We . . . we are betrayed!'

'Yes,' Edmund said, striding to the door of the nursery. 'Someone showed them the underpass.'

'Gather the servants and arm them as best you can,' Alice said, kissing the baby and laying him gently back in the crib.

'I'll hold them at the main doors.'

The orcs had reached the gravel around the manor house now. There was a bang downstairs, and then the din of horny feet and clubs battering the door.

Edmund ran from the room, but Athena sensed her master's desire for her to stay put and watch the baby. Though everything in her being drew her to him, she crouched on the edge of the crib and kept watch.

'Protect him, Athena,' Alice said. Then she was gone too.

Athena could only watch as more orcs streamed in from the village, bloodied weapons dripping on the lawns. The door downstairs unleashed a splintering sound as it gave way under the onslaught, then there was a shatter of glass as the nursery window imploded in front of her. A javelin whistled by, so close that Athena could feel the air flurry as it passed.

Then, as she looked out of the broken window, a blast from below hurled the mass of orcs into the lawn, like rag dolls thrown by an angry child.

Fireballs followed, flaring like meteors as each shot streaked into those left standing. They impacted with explosive force, knocking orcs down like flies.

But for every orc that fell, more took their places, crowding into the remains of the blasted entrance.

'Hold firm, the guards will come. They have to come!' Edmund's voice rang out clearly through the courtyard, even as the orcs began to bellow with fury.

Lightning crackled through the gathering orcs, leaving them twitching and spasming on the ground. Athena could feel the mana draining from her. It would not last much longer.

There was a dull thrum as a javelin was hurled through the doorway, then Athena felt a fierce pain on the edge of her consciousness. Edmund had been hit, but she could sense it was no more than a flesh wound.

A bull orc, larger than the others, charged through the doorway. Blood spattered on the gravel as a kinetic blast took its head off, but the orcs that followed it made it through.

More screams. A howl, from Edmund's Canid, Gelert, as the demon was unleashed upon the orcs. Alice's Vulpid, Reynard, must have been battling right alongside him, for the howls were accompanied by a high-pitched snarling.

Yet, even as Athena saw grey bodies hurled from the doorway, bloodied and burned, more and more orcs shouldered their way into the manor. The tide was turning now.

Pain. Fiercer this time. A shattered arm. Orders from Edmund, images sent down their connection with clear intent.

The memory of a great tree. An elf they had once met. Take the baby there. The child who was yet to be named. Don't stop for anything.

Athena grasped the newborn's arms with her paws. He was so heavy, and the destination so far. But she had to try.

A hoarse cry came from outside, cutting through the screams and snarls emanating from the horrors of the battle below.

Sir Caulder, grizzled and bloodstained, staggered on to the lawn in front of the house. He could barely stand from the exhaustion, for he had run there in full mail. Even so, the first orc to charge him was cut down at the knees, then kerb-stomped with an armoured foot. As the next orc turned to face him, it was thrown back by an arrow in its skull.

More soldiers stumbled out of the darkness, firing their bows.

But they were outnumbered – scores of orcs against a few dozen men. One by one, the exhausted soldiers were cut down by flying javelins or hurled axes, plucked away like puppets jerked from the stage. The closer men were battered to the ground by swinging clubs, as the grey giants ululated guttural battle-cries.

Sir Caulder fought on, even when a club shattered his arm. It hung limply by his side as he ducked and stabbed, making the orcs pay dearly for every step he took back. A blow from behind near severed his leg, the limb dangling at a sickening angle. He fell then, his eyes turned to the sky.

Athena launched into the night air, even as an explosion from below sent masonry hurtling across the lawn. The great building-stones were like a blast of buckshot, tearing through the massed orcs in clouds of red mist.

Edmund's connection was gone, just as he was. Athena could already feel the pull of the ether, tugging at her very essence. But the baby beneath her was crying, his arms stretching painfully above his tiny body. The night air grew colder as Athena flew higher and higher.


Darkness. Wingbeat after wingbeat. Unmoving stars shining above, glinting city lights passing beneath. The call of the ether, growing steadily stronger.


Hours pass.


Snow-capped mountains, rising from the earth like jagged teeth.

Body fading. The ether's wildness taking hold.

A village, far below.

No time.

No choice.

# 28

'Fletcher, wake up!'

Othello's green eyes looked down at him, matching the canopy above.

'Malik's team have left without us.'

Fletcher sat up, Athena's memory still vivid in his mind.

'Why?' he mumbled.

'They left a note, said they decided to make the most of the sunlight and leave early. They didn't want to wake us.'

'Fine with me,' Sylva yawned, stretching her arms. 'If there's trouble ahead, they'll run into it before we do.'

Seraph and his team were packing up. They had their demons out, and Fletcher was pleased to see that Rory now had a second Mite, smaller than Malachi, with a yellow shell.

Still, it was Atilla's demon that most surprised him, a dove-white bird with long tail feathers, perched on the young dwarf's shoulder. It was a Caladrius, a level seven demon with the ability to heal wounds by laying its feathers over them.

The demon was one of four rare, equally powerful avian

cousins, including the fire-born Phoenix, the icy Polarion and the lightning-powered Halcyon, with red, blue and yellow plumage respectively. He had a sneaky suspicion that it was not just Arcturus who had received a gifted demon from King Harold. Fletcher bet it was an apology to the Thorsagers for what had happened to Othello. He wondered what demon Atilla had before, and if he still had it in his roster.

'We should follow their example,' Seraph called, distracting Fletcher from his thoughts. 'We're heading off in a minute, with or without you.'

Sacharissa was already nosing the ground, eager to lead her team in the direction of the river. She whined as Fletcher hesitated, indicating that Arcturus wanted them to stay together.

It did not take long for Fletcher's team to get ready, the biggest delay being Cress, who did not take kindly to being woken at such an early hour.

'Can't you get Solomon to carry me, Othello?' Cress groaned, heaving her heavy satchel on to her shoulders.

'Carry you? Shouldn't it be the other way round?' Fletcher laughed.

'Actually, Fletcher, he probably could,' Othello said, flushing with pride.

He pulled a roll of leather from the side pocket of his satchel and laid it on the ground. Then, with a touch of his fingers, the Golem materialised in a flash of violet light.

Solomon had grown. He was as tall as Othello himself now, but wider and thicker-limbed. As soon as he caught sight of Fletcher, the craggy face split into a smile. The Golem surged forward with his arms open wide, and Fletcher had to skip back to avoid the bone-crushing hug.

'Solomon, no!' Othello remonstrated, then rolled his eyes as the demon hung his head in shame. 'He doesn't know his own strength yet.'

'So much has changed in a year. He'll be my height soon enough,' Fletcher marvelled.

'Aye, that he will. But let's not hang about, they're off.' Othello nodded at the forest behind Fletcher, where Seraph's team was already on its way out of the swamp and into the thicker jungle.

'We'll look like the lazy ones if we're not careful,' Sylva said, tugging Othello forward.

She nodded at Lysander, who was tactfully looking up at the sky. 'Remember, the world is watching. This is more than just a mission.'

Othello and Sylva hurried after the others, leaving Cress and Fletcher to trail behind them. Lysander walked sedately at their side, somehow managing to avoid the tangled undergrowth with feline grace. In contrast, Athena leaped from tree branch to tree branch above, showering Fletcher with leaves and dislodged insects. He did not mind, for he could sense the demon was missing the ether. After all, she had spent the past seventeen years there.

Fletcher's thoughts turned to his parents. He had spent so many years searching faces in Pelt, wondering what they looked like. Now, after Athena's vivid dream, he knew. He had his father's thick black hair, and the man's hazel eyes were just like his own. But he had the same pale skin and straight-edged nose as his mother.

He had been loved, once. He had felt it in that dream, so strongly that it made his heart clench with joy. But it had all been brutally torn away from him.

Soon the world turned dim as the canopy grew thicker, filtering the sun through its leaves into a darker shade of green.

The path was clear, for the thicker plants had been torn asunder by the Wendigo and then trampled underfoot by Malik's team. For now, the going was easy, and they fell into a comfortable pace that ate up the ground.

As they walked, Fletcher tried to commit his parents' faces to his memory, but he cursed himself as they blurred in his mind. It had all happened so fast.

'So . . . is this the first time you've seen a dwarven girl?' Cress asked, filling the awkward silence. 'Properly, I mean.'

'I saw Othello's mother once,' Fletcher replied.

He paused, unsure of what else to say. His mind was still on Athena's memory.

'Are we pretty?' she asked, grinning as Fletcher reddened. She was teasing him.

'As much as any other girl,' he replied, and as he looked into her smiling face he realised it was true. In fact, now that he had spent more time with her, Cress was beginning to grow on him. She reminded him a little of Seraph – blunt, even a little coarse, but charming in her own way.

'The dwarven boys tend to agree with you,' Cress laughed, after a moment's thought. 'It's not unknown for a young dwarven lad to run away with a human. I bet Atilla is worried I might do the same.'

She winked at him, and Fletcher couldn't help but laugh at

her forwardness. Her eyes twinkled with merriment and he felt the weight on his shoulders lift.

'Would that be so bad?' Fletcher asked. He realised he knew very little about romance between the races.

'Well, it's taboo, on both sides,' Cress said, shaking her head. 'Unseemly, so they say. It happens though, and it's the kids that have it the worst. Some get away with being short humans for a while, but they are always found out, especially if they follow the dwarven customs. Shunned by both races, the families travel to the lands across the Akhad desert, or sail the Vesanian sea to Swazulu.'

'I've heard of half-elves, but never half-dwarves,' Fletcher murmured.

'It's even worse for the half-elves, though it's rarer to come across one of them. The elves are very against mixing, even between the castes of high elves and wood elves. Half-elves' ears aren't as long as Sylva's, but they stay pointy.'

'You seem to know a lot about this kind of thing,' Fletcher said. 'I've never even thought about it before. I'm kind of ashamed of that, actually.'

'Don't be. I take a special interest in this stuff. My brother …' she looked away for a moment. 'He ran away from home to be with a human woman. I'm the only one in the community who will talk to him now.'

The pace ahead quickened as the morning turned to noon, and their conversation was cut short, replaced by heavy breathing as they jogged through the undergrowth. This time the silence was comfortable, even if the atmosphere wasn't. At the swamp it had been hot, but bearable. Now, it was sweltering, despite the breathable fabric of their jackets.

Even the sounds had changed. Above the chorus of whining insects, the fluty mating calls of birds filtered down through the trees.

'Shall we let our demons stretch their legs?' Cress asked, slipping a satchel strap from her shoulder and clutching it to her chest. 'It'll give me a chance to test out the battle-gauntlet Athol made for me.'

'Battle-gauntlet?' Fletcher asked, intrigued.

She rummaged within the satchel as they walked and pulled out a leather glove. The back had been armoured with bands of steel, extending down to the wrist, but that was not what made it stand out. The palm and finger pads had been branded with the same marks that were tattooed on Fletcher's hand.

'I'm not a fan of needles, so no tattoo for me.' She winked. 'I'm surprised these haven't come into fashion yet! Guess most summoners are stuck in their ways.'

Tugging on the glove, she pointed the pentacle at the ground ahead of her. To Fletcher's amazement, there was a flash of violet and a demon tumbled into existence.

It appeared much like a cross between a raccoon and a squirrel, with dark blue fur speckled with jagged dashes of teal. The demon's round, yellow eyes focused on Fletcher as soon as it materialised and the bushy tail whipped back and forth with excitement. Despite all of his studies, Fletcher had absolutely no idea what it was.

'It's a Raiju,' Cress said, patting her shoulder. The demon had padded fingers and hooked nails for climbing, allowing it to scamper on to the proffered perch with two, languid leaps.

248

'Almost as rare as your Salamander, or so I'm told,' Cress said, laughing at Fletcher's mesmerised expression. 'Level five too. Tosk can blast lightning from his tail like a storm cloud, so mind you avoid touching it. It can give you quite a shock.'

'That's amazing! I don't think I could have snuck that gauntlet into the Tournament though. How did you get such a rare demon?' Fletcher asked, as the Raiju preened his whiskers at him, almost flirtatiously.

'King Harold. He's quite the collector, being such a high level and all. When he heard two more dwarves were heading to the academy, he offered his Caladrius and Raiju to us. He really is on our side.'

Before Fletcher could pry further, there was a cry of excitement from ahead of them, and the group came to a halt. The jungle had opened up, and from the sound of rushing water, Fletcher could tell why.

The waters from the swamp and a dozen other streams beyond had come together into a network of inlets that poured out over a waterfall. Far below, water crashed and exploded in a haze of white mist that extended for miles around, until a great, snaking river emerged in the distance, carving its way through twin valleys on either side. At the very edge of their site, a triangular hump of dull yellow revealed their destination. The pyramid.

'So how are we going to get down?' Othello wondered aloud.

There was a steep climb to the ground on either side of the fall, but Fletcher was glad that he did not have to cross the river at this point, for the streams that fed the waterfall were numerous, with thin patches of soggy land between them.

'I guess Malik's and Isadora's teams have already crossed,' Seraph said with a hint of disappointment. 'I'd have liked to watch them wade through that mess.'

'Well, let's hope our crossing is as easy as theirs,' Fletcher replied.

They surveyed the land before them and it was soon clear that there were two ways down. One was a rocky path beside the waterfall itself, while the other was a thin forest trail that curved towards a hilly region to the east.

'Well,' Fletcher announced, slapping Seraph on the back. 'This is where we leave you.'

# 29

Fletcher shielded his eyes, gazing at the setting sun as its last light filtered through the tangled branches. He was glad they had chosen to make camp before it grew dark, for the moon was barely more than a slit in the sky and wyrdlights would attract too much attention.

Dusk's arrival was heralded by the gruff bellows of howler monkeys, echoing through the forest in the canopy above. The team settled down for their first night alone in enemy territory, choosing a clearing a safe distance from the forest trail.

As Ignatius scampered on to his neck and began to doze, Fletcher reflected on their journey so far. The natural trail had diverged towards the river on several occasions, but they made sure to head uphill, curving away from the water. Despite the incline, they had made good progress, and Fletcher felt confident they would reach their rendezvous at the pyramid in two days' time.

Sariel and Lysander had acted as rearguard the entire day's journey, watching for an ambush. Athena worked the canopy, occasionally fluttering above the treeline so Fletcher could make sure they were on course, using his scrying crystal. Meanwhile, Ignatius and Tosk protected their flanks, slipping through the thicker undergrowth with barely more than a rustle. It was Solomon who was left out, for he was too slow and clumsy. Instead, he became their pack mule, carrying their supplies on his stony shoulders when the weight became too much for them.

'Now that it's just the four of us summoners, it feels more real,' Sylva said, prodding their unlit campfire with a stick. 'I felt like we could take on an army when we were all together. Now I'm not so sure.'

'I don't know,' Fletcher said, tugging Ignatius from his neck. 'I think we're a pretty formidable team. We have two Tournament winners, and two runners up. If we encounter an orc patrol, I reckon we could take them.'

Ignatius mewled with annoyance at being woken and, after some mental cajoling, reluctantly spat a ball of fire at the pile of wood.

'It's not beating them that I'm worried about,' Sylva said, shielding her face as the sticks burst into flames. 'It's one of them getting away during the battle that scares me. If they raise the alarm, then the mission is over.'

'Well, Sariel and Lysander can chase them down,' Othello said, groaning as he removed his boots and socks. 'Because this great lump isn't going to be catching anyone any time soon.'

He rubbed Solomon affectionately on the head, and the demon rumbled with happiness. Just as he had back in the shed outside of Corcillum, the Golem dutifully held Othello's socks up to the flames. For the first time in what seemed like years,

Fletcher felt contented.

'So how's everybody feeling?' he asked, opening his pack and removing a wrap of dried venison. He spitted a piece on to a nearby twig and held it to the flames.

'About as good as I smell.' Othello grimaced. 'Which isn't great. This heat doesn't agree with me, or you lot for that matter.'

'You can say that again,' Cress laughed, holding her nose. 'The orcs can probably smell us from miles around.'

She rummaged around her pack for her own food, then paused.

'Hey! I'm missing some bolts from my crossbow.'

Cress frowned and showed them the quiver strapped to her satchel. It was no longer full, leaving the quarrels to rattle loosely within.

'Same here,' Sylva said, brandishing her own quiver. The fletching on her arrows, as well as Fletcher's and Cress's bolts, had been dyed blue, the team's colour. They were beautifully made and the points were slimmer and sharper than Fletcher's own, better than even his best efforts when he had fletched his own arrows in Pelt.

'Maybe they fell out?' Fletcher suggested.

He ran his fingers over his own quiver, but all the arrows seemed to be there.

Cress shrugged and laid the quiver back down.

'Still plenty left, but let's be careful. Orcs don't use arrows, but if they find one on the ground they'll know we're out here.'

Sariel and Lysander, who had been patrolling around the camp, returned and lay behind the fire, their broad backs making a comfortable pillow for the others. In fact, Fletcher saw that all but one demon had returned, with Tosk settling on Cress's navel, curled up like a dog.

Fletcher strapped his scrying glass to his eye, so he could see where Athena was, her view appearing as a pink-tinged overlay of half his vision.

Athena was standing vigil on a high branch, her owlish eyes able to see through the orange sunset as clear as day. Every few seconds she swivelled her head, like a sentinel standing guard. Fletcher urged the Gryphowl to come down with a thought, but sensed her desire to remain.

'Well, looks like we don't need to arrange a night-watch schedule,' Fletcher said. 'Athena intends to stay there all night.'

'Good,' Sylva yawned. 'I don't think I'd be able to keep my eyes open.'

They lay there in comfortable silence, allowing the campfire's heat to seep the ache from their muscles. The night sounds of the jungle had already begun, with the chirps of crickets adding a dull buzz to the quiet, interspersed with the occasional call of nocturnal birds. It was strangely soothing, reminding Fletcher of the sounds of Pelt's forests.

Jeffrey, who had been silent for most of the journey, spoke up for the first time that night.

'I don't know why I'm here,' he sobbed, the fear in his voice cutting through the cosy crackle of their campfire. 'All I have is the short sword Uhtred gave me. I'm only any good at biology and botany – we're not going to run into any dead demons out here and when the raid begins, dissecting one will be the last thing on my mind.'

'I'd take you as a guide over any of the others,' Sylva said generously. 'We're barely hungry with all the fruit and vegetables you gathered as we were hiking, and we've refilled our water-flasks from those vines all day. We don't need a navigator with that great big pyramid marking the way, and we have a map of their camp. Just make sure you hang back when the fighting starts and we'll deal with the orcs.'

'Thanks,' Jeffrey muttered, but it was obvious he was unconvinced. He rolled away with his back to them, and Fletcher thought he caught a glimmer of a tear on the lad's cheek, reflected by the firelight. Then the glimmer flashed again, and he realised it had appeared in the overlay of his scrying crystal.

'What the hell is that?' Fletcher muttered.

A fire had been lit, only a few hundred metres away, right on the forest trail. For a moment he'd thought Athena had been looking down at them, so close by was the light.

He removed his eyeglass and the others leaned in, squinting at the coin-sized crystal.

'Orcs?' Jeffrey asked, his voice trembling.

'I'll send Athena closer,' Fletcher said, conveying his orders to Athena with a flash of intent.

Soon, the crystal showed the rushing canopy below, as the Gryphowl glided over the treetops. It took but a few seconds for her to reach the place, and she landed with feline grace on a broad branch. It creaked under her weight – Fletcher could hear all that she did in his mind. He winced at the noise, but the figures below seemed not to react.

It was too far up to see their faces, but the monstrous creature standing watch beside them left no doubt as to who they were.

Isadora's team were following them.

'What are they doing here?' Sylva hissed. 'They're supposed to be on the other side of the river!'

'I don't know, but they're up to no good,' Othello whispered. 'Thing is, they can't do anything with Lysander watching. Not unless they attack in the dark . . .'

They paused for a moment, contemplating his words.

'Maybe they got lost, or decided against crossing the river,' Cress suggested.

'You don't know them,' Fletcher said. 'They're trying to sabotage us to prove that a team with dwarves and elves doesn't work. They could take us out with spells in the darkness. It would look like orc shamans had ambushed us.'

'That's incentive enough for them to ambush us,' Sylva said. 'Not that they need a good reason. They hate us enough as it is.'

Fletcher sat up, looking out into the gloom around their camp.

'We need to move at first light, put as much distance between us and them as possible. Athena will keep an eye on them, make sure they don't know we're so close.'

He looked at his team's bright fire, then began etching the ice spell in the air. With a pulse of mana, a stream of frost crystals enveloped the wood, casting the camp in pitch darkness.

'Get some rest,' Fletcher sighed, settling down against Lysander's soft underbelly. 'It might be the last we have for a while.'

As the others pulled blankets from their packs, Othello wriggled in beside him.

'Trust you to hog Lysander as a pillow,' Othello whispered. 'Move over.'

Fletcher shuffled to the side and Othello stretched out beside him. It was comforting to have the dwarf there.

'Hey,' Othello said suddenly. 'What did you end up doing with that gremlin?'

'I . . . Er . . . I let it go,' Fletcher said.

Othello sighed. 'I knew you would but . . . it makes me uneasy.'

Fletcher's stomach twisted with unease at Othello's words. He had almost forgotten about Blue, with everything else going on.

'I'm pretty sure it won't betray us. And anyway, it was the right thing to do,' Fletcher replied, not knowing who he was trying to convince more – himself or Othello.

'Well, I hope you're right,' Othello murmured, shifting on to his side. 'For all our sakes.'

Fletcher took a deep breath, trying to push the doubt from his mind. He already had enough to deal with, without the gremlin to worry about too.

'You've been brooding all day . . .' Othello said under his breath, so that the others couldn't hear. 'Anything else on your mind?'

Fletcher paused. He knew they should be sleeping, but he was sure he would be up all night thinking of Athena's infusion dream. Maybe it would help to talk about it.

'I saw my parents die,' Fletcher murmured.

'You remember it?' Othello asked.

'No . . . I saw Athena's memories. You know, from infusing her,' Fletcher replied, as tears welled in his eyes. 'They were so happy, and then . . . It was horrible.'

'Oh . . .' Othello whispered. He paused.

'I'm sorry.'

Silence. Then Othello spoke, his voice throaty with emotion.

'Did you know I had another sister?'

'No,' Fletcher said, creasing his brow. Had?

'Essie was born when Atilla and I were three, two years before my mother became pregnant with Thaissa and the laws were relaxed. We had to keep her hidden – dwarves were only allowed one child back then, and what with Atilla and I being twins we had already got away with two on a technicality. We kept her underground, hid her under the floorboards when the Pinkertons did their inspections. But when Essie was one year old she got sick . . . really sick. So we took her to a doctor, a human.'

Othello stopped, and Fletcher saw his friend's face was wet with tears.

'He called the Pinkertons, Fletcher, and they took Essie away from us. We don't know where. A few weeks later they told us she had died from the illness. Just like that – she was gone. They never even returned her body.'

Fletcher reached out and laid a hand on Othello's shoulder.

'I'm so sorry that happened to you, Othello. To your sister. To your family. I can't imagine how that must feel.'

'We never talk about it,' Othello said, wiping his tears with his sleeve. 'Thaissa doesn't even know. But if I had the chance to know what really happened to her – to hear her laugh, to see that smile one more time – I'd do anything for it.'

Fletcher knew he was right. It had been a blessing – to see his parents, know their voices, their faces. What had happened to them was a tragedy, and the truth of their death was painful to know . . . but necessary.

Above him, Lysander turned his head and stared down at Fletcher's tear-streaked face. Gently, he raised a talon and brushed Fletcher's cheek, the movement too human for the demon to do alone. Then he laid a wing on top of them, like a blanket. Fletcher knew that Lovett was watching over them.

'Thank you for sharing that with me, Othello,' Fletcher whispered. 'I'll remember it.'

# 30

It was early morning, and the team were moving at a fast pace through the jungle. They were even more careful than before to cover their tracks, but fortunately the trail they were on was regularly used by the jungle animals, confusing the ground with dozens of different claw and hoof prints.

Most disconcertingly, they had found the flatfooted prints of orcs there too, not unlike a human's but larger and with deep toe indents. It was difficult to say how long they had been there, but Fletcher was glad that Athena was watching from the canopy above, her view translating directly to the scrying crystal strapped to his head.

'Can . . . we . . . slow . . . down . . . yet?' Othello gasped, readjusting his pack with a bow-legged jump. Solomon had been infused within him, for the Golem was too slow to keep up and his weighty legs left deep impressions on the ground. Since then, the heavy satchels had once again been strapped to their backs, making the going even tougher.

Jeffrey's asthma made him take deep breaths through

a herb-filled cloth and Cress's short legs forced her to travel in short bursts of speed, as Othello did.

'Five minute break,' Fletcher announced, his heart thundering in his chest, sweat trickling down his back. After a year in captivity with no more exercise than a few press-ups, he too was struggling. In fact, only Sylva seemed to be faring well.

They stopped and collapsed to the ground, pressing their backs against tree trunks on either side of the path. There were a few minutes that were filled only with the gulping of water and the chewing of fruit and root tubers. Then Sylva pointed back down the path and groaned.

'Even at this pace, Isadora and the others could catch up with us by nightfall. We just can't travel as fast as they can.'

'Well, it's worth trying,' Othello groaned, laying his head on Fletcher's shoulder. 'We should reach the pyramid late tomorrow. If we can avoid them until then, all will be well.'

They continued to sit, and even though five minutes had passed, Fletcher let them rest a little longer. He had spent much of the previous night watching the other team through his crystal, hoping to hear their conversation. To his dismay, the Wendigo prowled the edges of their camp for most of the night, keeping Athena at a distance until he fell asleep.

Fear pulsed into Fletcher from both of his demons. Ignatius burst out of the jungle, and in the overlay of his scrying crystal he saw a disturbance on the path up ahead.

'Get off the trail!' Fletcher hissed, and then he and Sylva were scrambling into the jungle, while Othello, Cress and Jeffrey dived into the bushes on the other side of the path. Lysander and Sariel followed the others, pressing their bodies low to the ground and wriggling into the thicker vegetation. This was just as well, for it was not long before the new arrivals revealed themselves.

Three rhinos, long horns ploughing forward like the prows on a fleet of warships, emerged. Their skin was thick and leathery, the grey colour matching perfectly with that of the herculean giants that rode them.

Seven-foot bull orcs, matured to their greatest size, with three-inch tusks and bodies adorned with whorls of red and yellow war-paint. They carried great macana clubs, shaped like a flat wooden bat with rectangular shards of knapped obsidian embedded along the edges, sharper than even the finest blade. Fletcher imagined the damage those were capable of – they could probably decapitate a horse in one stroke. Baker's journal had described them as both mace and sword, crumpling armour and quartering flesh in equal measures.

Behind the orcs, loincloth-clad goblins rode in rows of two, armed with stone-tipped spears and misshapen clubs carved from tree branches. They appeared much like the specimen Fletcher had seen at the great council – shorter than him by a head and scrawny to boot, with long noses and flapping ears.

Their steeds were cassowaries, great ostrich-like birds with black feathers so fine they almost appeared like fur. The long featherless necks on their flightless bodies were a bright blue colour, and red wattles dangled from their chins. Strangest of all, they had humped casques cresting their heads, not unlike a short, blunt horn embedded in their skulls. Fletcher shuddered as their raptor talons ripped up the ground beneath them, each one capable of disembowelling a man with a single kick.

He knew from the findings in Baker's journal that cassowaries were only ever ridden by younger orcs, when they were small enough that the birds could bear their weight. With the arrival of the goblins, the orcs had found another use for them.

'My god, there are so many of them,' Sylva whispered. She was pressed tightly against Fletcher, their mad scramble leaving them practically on top of each other.

There were at least fifty goblins in the column, their frog-like eyes scanning the forest for movement. Trotting at the heels of the cavalcade were two spotted hyenas, their powerful, squat bodies ranging up and down the column, sniffing at the ground. For a moment a hyena paused by the trail, its keen snout snorting at the ground directly ahead of where they crouched, huddled in the bushes. They watched in silence as it moved closer. It began to growl, and Sylva grabbed Fletcher's arm in alarm . . . but a guttural bark from one of the orcs sent it scampering back to the front of the war-party.

Fortunately for the team, they seemed to be following the scent they had left down the trail. It occurred to Fletcher that they might be smelling something else, not far away. Perhaps the Wendigo?

It took no more than a minute for them to pass by, but it felt like an age before Fletcher gathered the nerve to step out on the path once more. As he did so, Athena swooped down and alighted on his shoulder, while Ignatius leaped into his arms and buried his head in Fletcher's chest. It had been a close call.

'Right, I say we get off this trail,' Fletcher announced, his voice trembling with nervous energy.

'Agreed,' Othello said, emerging from the forest with the

others. 'When the trail runs cold, they'll come back this way.'

'Those birds looked like demons,' Cress said, staring after them. 'I've never seen anything like them before.'

'Trust me, they're a real animal,' Jeffrey lectured. 'They're fast as hell and kick like a mule. You should see their eggs – giant green things, you'd take one look at them and think they could be a goblins' eggs. Try having one of those for breakfast—'

'You realise they're heading right for Isadora and the others?' Cress interrupted, looking in the direction of the column.

'That's perfect,' Sylva said. 'Maybe they'll take each other out.'

But Fletcher looked to Lysander, who was watching the retreating army with a concerned expression. Lord Forsyth would have one of Lysander's scrying crystals with him, so Hannibal would be able to relay a warning to Tarquin and the others. But he knew that with the Wendigo's size and stench, they would find it difficult to avoid the prowling hyenas. It was tempting. The thought of Didric or the twins being ambushed by orcs was an image he had pictured on many a lonely night in his cell, but then he felt a twinge of rebuke from Athena's consciousness. Fletcher sighed. She was right. He turned to his friends.

'Why are we here?' Fletcher asked, looking them all in the eye.

'To destroy a few thousand goblin eggs and rescue Rufus's mother, Lady Cavendish,' Sylva said, already swinging her pack on to her shoulders.

'No. Why are *we* here?' Fletcher asked again.

They stared at him silently, as if confused by the question.

'Our team is supposed to be a shining example to the world of cooperation between the races,' Fletcher said. 'We are to prove that dwarves and elves are worthy of humanity's respect. Now I want them dead as much as you; I'd kill them myself if I had a chance. But how will it look if we abandon Isadora's team, leaving them to be slaughtered?'

Othello and Sylva avoided his eyes, but they knew he spoke the truth.

'They're hunting us,' Sylva whispered. 'This is our chance.'

'We don't know that,' Cress replied stubbornly. 'They could just have changed their minds about their route.'

'If they're killed, that's one team fewer to join the raid. Even if they manage to escape, the orcs will raise the alarm,' Othello grudgingly admitted, lending Fletcher his support.

'But it's Didric, Tarquin, Isadora, even Grindle! They've all tried to kill every one of us. You're naive, Cress – the world would be a better place without them,' Sylva snarled, and Fletcher couldn't fault her words. Was he really going to save the people who had plotted his execution? He hesitated, but then Cress spoke again.

'What about Atlas? Does he deserve death just because we don't like the company he keeps?' she asked quietly. 'If we let them die, we would be no better than they are, putting our own ends before the safety of Hominum.'

Sylva exhaled with frustration, then turned back the way they had come, unslinging her bow as she did so.

'Let's get this over with,' she growled.

# 31

They shadowed the orc patrol for half an hour, using Athena's vision to make sure they stayed just out of sight. Fortunately, the riders were upwind of them, so the snuffling hyenas could not smell their approach.

'Wait,' Fletcher hissed, holding up his fist. 'They've stopped.'

From her vantage point above, Athena could see that the trio of rhinos at the front had come to a halt. Just ahead, the hyenas were yipping with a high-pitched cackle at the trees around them.

'No guns,' Fletcher whispered. 'Bows only. Loose on my signal.'

They took up positions on either side of the trail, keeping to the bushes. It had been a long time since Fletcher had used his bow, but as soon as it was in his grip it all came back, the string gliding easily along his fingers as he nocked a blue-fletched arrow to it. Beside him, Cress grunted as she wound her crossbow, the metal lever on the side slipping in her sweaty fingers.

'Jeffrey, stay back and cover our rear,' Fletcher ordered,

lining up his shot. 'If another patrol comes I want to know about it.'

He did not pull back just yet, for he knew that he shot better in a single, fluid motion. Instead, he concentrated on the orcs, as the first dismounted and peered into the forest.

A fireball took the orc in the chest, blasting him into the jungle. More sizzled through the air like meteorites, throwing the column into disarray. Isadora's team had prepared an ambush.

'Now!' Fletcher shouted, as the goblins at the back turned to flee. Two arrows and a bolt thrummed into the heaving creatures, plucking them from their mounts with deadly accuracy.

'Again,' Fletcher growled, and another volley followed the first, thumping into cassowary and goblin alike. At the head of the column, the Wendigo burst through the trees, slashing left and right at the two remaining orcs, while fireballs, lightning and kinetic blasts buzzed inaccurately through the air.

Miraculously, a goblin made it past their barrage of arrows, his cassowary hurtling them down the trail, away from the battle. Fletcher shouted a warning.

'Don't let him get aw—' A hurlbat axe whirled through the air and took the cassowary's right leg off, sending it head over heels. Then Othello erupted from the undergrowth, dispatching goblin and bird with two chops of his battle-axe.

Dozens of goblins shrieked with fury, and thundered towards the exposed dwarf. But a screech from above gave them pause. Lysander hurled himself out of the branches, bowling through the cassowary-riders in a whirlwind of wings and talons. But even as the goblins fell to the ground, the birds kicked and jabbed their beaks, and the Griffin roared with pain.

'Close in!' Fletcher ordered, and then he was running, khopesh drawn, heart pounding as hard as his feet did against the ground.

The first goblin swung his club, still dazed from being knocked off his mount. Fletcher parried and reposted, taking the goblin through the sternum and blasting it from the blade with a shot of kinetic energy. Cress's torq knocked another goblin to the ground, while Sylva decapitated a flailing cassowary with a sweep of her falx. Othello's hurlbat axes peppered the massed goblins from over Fletcher's shoulders, thrumming dangerously close to his ears.

It gave Lysander enough time to throw himself back into the air, sprinkling the ground below with droplets of blood. There was no time to assess the Griffin's injuries, for as the first row of goblins went down, another took its place, lunging at the trio with howls of anger.

'Back,' Fletcher gasped, as a club struck his left elbow, leaving his tattooed hand to hang limply by his side. Othello stepped in beside Sylva to protect the right of the trail, while Cress and Fletcher held the left.

Goblins and cassowaries crowded towards the thin line of summoners, spreading out into the jungle in an attempt to flank them. A gout of flame from the undergrowth sent a group of goblins scrambling back, one spinning away and screeching, as Ignatius scrabbled at its face. After one last slash, the Salamander dived back into the bushes, daring the goblins to leave the trail once again.

On the other side, lightning crackled into the massed

creatures, downing several and leaving them twitching on the ground. Cress's demon, Tosk, had joined the battle.

'Where's Sariel?' Fletcher shouted, sweeping his khopesh in a wide arc, and a goblin skittered back with a deep gash along its ribcage. 'Solomon?'

There was a splintering sound from behind, and half of Fletcher's question was answered. Tree branches arced overhead, slamming into the snarling goblins, and the guttural roar from behind told Fletcher that Solomon was making use of his great strength.

Then Sariel erupted from the bushes, snatching a cassowary by the legs and dragging it into the greenery. Sylva gasped with pain as the two creatures tore into each other, the crackle of broken branches accompanied by snarls and screeches.

'Battle-spells,' Fletcher ordered as the feeling returned to his arm once more. 'But conserve your mana.'

Sylva's etching was so fast that he had barely finished his sentence before her fireball buzzed into the nearest goblin, blasting it down to twist and wail on the ground, scrabbling at its chest. More followed from Cress and Othello, while Fletcher whipped a tongue of kinetic energy into the air, sending the few remaining riders tumbling.

Still the goblins pressed in, their gnarled clubs parrying Fletcher's thinner blade to jar his arm up to the shoulder. A hurled spear sliced past Fletcher's face. He felt a flash of pain as it caught his cheek, the trickle of hot blood mingled with the sweat pooling at the base of his neck. He shook his head and slashed a goblin across the face in return, sending it spinning away, clutching at its head.

A kick from a squawking cassowary hurled Cress back, but it failed to pierce her jacket. She responded with a bolt of lightning that took off its head in a spray of blood, and staggered back into the fight.

Flame flared from Ignatius, spiralling into the goblins as they surged forward once again, blinding them. Tosk added a jagged streak of electric blue, hurling the frontrunners into those behind in a tangle of limbs and clubs. In the brief respite, Fletcher took the opportunity to concentrate on his scrying crystal, the overlay showing him the full picture of the battlefield.

The two orcs were holding their own against the Wendigo, while Isadora's team stayed hidden in the bushes, keeping the goblins at bay with the liberal use of spells. It depleted their mana reserves, but was a winning strategy; dozens of the convoy's corpses littered the ground and the rest were huddled behind the bodies of the rhinos, which had already been dispatched. Of the fifty mounted goblins that had started, no more than a score remained. Even the hyenas were dead, their heavyset bodies splayed out in a macabre slumber.

That was when it all went wrong. One of the remaining orcs broke from the pack, bolting into the jungle. With Lysander out of the picture and Sariel locked in a life-and-death struggle out of sight, Fletcher had no choice but to leave his team.

'No survivors,' he yelled over his shoulder.

Then he was deep in the forest, following the sound of crashing branches as the orc tore its way through the undergrowth. The air was suddenly still and silent, disturbed only by a poorly aimed spell whiffling through the leaves above. He sensed Ignatius following behind but did not have time to wait for him.

Instead, he instructed Athena to remain above the battle and watch for more runaways. From her vantage point, he could see that Solomon had taken his place in the line, using a small sapling as a club to batter the goblins and cassowaries aside.

In the new quiet, the adrenaline began to leave Fletcher, his cheek stinging with each pulse of his rapidly beating heart. He was bone tired and his lungs burned in his chest. Still he staggered on, ignoring the flies that buzzed around his head, hungry for the salt in the blood and sweat that coated him.

He followed the crash and snap of the retreating orc, wishing he had thought it all through. The two orcs had battled the Wendigo without difficulty. Now he would face one alone.

There was a rattle of disturbed vegetation, then a grey-skinned orc appeared just ahead, cleaving at a thick patch of thorny branches with his macana club. Up close it was enormous, towering over him. He thought it as broad and muscular as Berdon and Jakov put together.

Fletcher didn't hesitate. He leaped with his khopesh in both hands, the point aimed squarely at the centre of the orc's back. It missed the spine by a hand's breadth, spitting the orc through its midriff, the resistance a fraction of what Fletcher had expected.

He yelled with triumph as the orc stiffened, a guttural bellow spraying heart-blood on the leaves ahead of it. Then Fletcher's head exploded with pain and his mouth was filled with the taste of rotting leaves and blood. The orc had spun, backhanding him into the ground and tearing the khopesh from his hands, leaving it impaled in its chest.

A callused foot slammed into the earth beside him as he rolled away, just in time. He fired a kinetic pulse, blasting himself from the earth to stand once again. No sooner was he on his feet than he was diving aside, the macana chopping through the air in a great, swinging arc. He sprawled into the thorny bush that had blocked the orc, his jacket caught on the hooked barbs, arms spread like a crucified man.

Bloody froth bubbled from the orc's mouth as it bellowed in triumph, lifeblood pumping from around the blade in its chest in dark gouts. It raised the macana, chuckling throatily as it lifted Fletcher's chin with the flat of the club. The obsidian shards on the tip dug into the soft flesh of his throat as the orc leaned forward, almost gently. His would not be a slow death.

Ignatius barrelled out of the undergrowth, a sweeping tidal wave of flame heralding his arrival as he landed on the orc's head. His tail struck like a scorpion's, stabbing madly at the orc's eyes, nose and mouth, while the flames flowed over its face in great pulsing waves. Fletcher tugged himself free, ripping the coat from the thorns' embrace after a few moment's struggle. It was just in time, for the orc chopped blindly at him, even managing to slice a button from Fletcher's sleeve. Then it was finished, the orc falling to its knees and keeling over, the last spurts of blood from its chest turning into a trickle.

Ignatius sprung into Fletcher's arms, mewling with sympathy and licking at the wounds in his throat. They stood like that for a while, basking in the glory of being alive. Fletcher's neck stung as Ignatius lapped his tongue along the wounds, but soon the feeling was strangely soothing. He ran his fingers along his neck tentatively, only to find the wounds had gone.

'Bloody hell,' he exclaimed. He held Ignatius up to his face and the demon yapped happily, licking the tip of Fletcher's nose.

'You must have a healing symbol hidden in that tongue somewhere,' Fletcher laughed, rubbing Ignatius's head affectionately. 'Even after all this time, you still manage to surprise me. Best not tell Jeffrey though, he'll have that tongue out and on his operating table if we're not careful.'

Ignatius wriggled in his grip and Fletcher set the Salamander on the ground. As he did so, he saw the orc's face and winced. It had been burned away, leaving only a blackened skull beneath, while the leathery grey skin of its belly and legs was covered with blood. Red and yellow whorls and stripes of war-paint adorned its chest and what was left of its cheeks. Without it, the orc would be practically naked, were it not for the rough-spun skirt that protected its modesty.

Fletcher's khopesh was stuck fast in the orc's flesh. He grimaced at the grisly sight and bent to tug it out.

A crossbow bolt hissed over his head like a striking snake, thudding into a tree behind him. Fletcher fell to the ground and pulled the orc's corpse on its side as a shield. Another bolt thrummed towards Fletcher a moment later, but it stuck into the orc's shoulder, the force of it so strong that it broke through, the tip stopping an inch from Fletcher's face. The accuracy and speed was astounding, that of a trained assassin.

Then, as Fletcher powered up his finger for a counterattack, the ambusher retreated, leaving the crash of broken branches in his wake. The grinning skull of the orc seemed to laugh at Fletcher as he shoved the corpse aside in disgust. He took a moment to catch his breath. If he hadn't bent to pull out his khopesh from the orc, he would have been skewered through the chest.

He tugged the crossbow bolt from the trunk and held it up to the dim light of the jungle. Blue fletching. Just like Cress's.

When Fletcher returned to the others, the battle was over. Solomon was busy digging a large grave, his great hands shovelling aside the dirt in a small clearing. It was good thinking; a pile of corpses would bring forth all sorts of carrion eaters and the clouds of vultures above would attract too much attention. Jeffrey was further up the trail, examining a goblin corpse and writing notes in a leather-bound journal. His hands were shaking with adrenaline, resulting in an uneven scrawl.

Othello had just healed Lysander, the last traces of white light dissolving from the bloodied feathers along the Griffin's side. Cress was nowhere to be seen.

'Where are Isadora's team?' Fletcher shouted, brandishing the bolts.

Sylva looked up from where she kneeled, in the middle of healing Sariel's wounds.

'They ran off,' Sylva said, her voice dull with exhaustion. 'Didn't even thank us for our help.'

'One of them tried to kill me,' Fletcher announced, holding up the blue-fletched crossbow bolt. 'With these.'

'Aren't those Cress's?'

'I don't think she lost them after all. I think they stole them.'

'You're joking,' Othello growled, unrolling his summoning leather for Solomon to stand on. He infused the demon in a burst of white light, for the poor Golem was staggering with exhaustion.

'I wish I was,' Fletcher said. He paused, realising the

274

implications. The attackers could have used a spell, or an arrow of their own. Instead, they had chosen ammunition that only Cress could have used. They wanted to frame her for the attack.

Othello had clearly been thinking along the same lines.

'If we had come across your body with that stuck in you, the whole of Hominum would think Cress had killed you,' the dwarf said, snatching the offending projectile from Fletcher's hand. 'They might even think Cress was working with the Anvils.'

'I don't know . . .' Sylva said, examining the bolt. 'We're jumping to conclusions. We barely know her. Maybe she *is* working for the Anvils.'

'Yeah, and I'm a goblin in disguise,' Othello scoffed. 'If she was a traitor, I'd know about it. The dwarven community is a small one; there are barely a few thousand of us left. I know who the trouble-makers are.'

Fletcher looked around.

'Speaking of Cress, where is she?' Fletcher asked.

'Right here,' came a voice from behind him.

Cress emerged from the jungle, Tosk perched on her shoulder. Her face was drenched with sweat and her crossbow hung limply in her hand.

'I see you caught the orc,' she said. 'Well done. I tried to catch up with you but got los—' She stopped as she caught the stunned expressions from the others.

'Where did you get that?' she asked, catching sight of the quarrel clutched in Othello's fist.

'You tell me,' Sylva said, standing up and narrowing her eyes at the dwarf. 'Someone just tried to kill Fletcher with it.'

Cress remained silent, her eyes still fixed on the bolt. Sylva motioned with her chin at the jungle behind the dwarf.

'In there.'

'I . . . I lost them,' Cress stammered, looking over her shoulder. 'Whoever it was must have taken them from my quiver back at camp, like I said earlier.'

'That's a convenient story,' Sylva said, crossing her arms and studying Cress's face.

'Your arrows are missing too,' Cress countered.

Something stung Fletcher's neck and he slapped at it irritably.

'It was Isadora's team, I know it,' he said, putting an arm around Cress's shoulders. He suddenly felt very weak, and it was a relief to lean against her. 'This is exactly what they want, for us to turn on each other. Now we know why they were following us.'

Sylva glared at him, then jumped up and slapped at her thigh.

'Damned insects,' she snarled, plucking something from her leg. But what she held between her fingers was not an insect at all. It was a tiny dart.

The projectile swam in Fletcher's vision and suddenly he was on his knees. The ground rushed up to meet him.

# 32

Their prison was made of sturdy, interwoven branches – more a spherical basket than a cage. It swung pendulously from a bough above, lurching from side to side as the wind tugged it back and forth.

'We are finished,' Jeffrey whispered, peering through the gaps in the branches.

They had woken there an hour ago, their clothes covered in soil from being dragged through the woods.

All thoughts of escape had already left them, after their first attempt. Othello had forced his arm through the branches, attempting to rip a hole for them to climb through. A few moments later and he was snoring loudly, another dart in his hand.

Of course, there was always the option of a shield, but their mana reserves had been depleted by the battle and their weapons had been taken from them. Not to mention the fact that they would be falling a good distance to the ground if they did blast the cage apart.

'What do you see?' Fletcher asked. He was pressed uncomfortably between Sariel and Lysander, their heavy bodies crushing him. Athena had settled on Lysander's neck, her tail curling lazily over his beak. Of all of them, she seemed to be the calmest, taking the opportunity to nap.

'Still gremlins. No sign of orcs yet,' Jeffrey murmured.

Fletcher twisted his body and squinted through the hole Othello had made.

They were suspended above a wide clearing in the deep jungle, the surrounding vegetation so thick it might take all day to cut through it. Deep burrows, not unlike enlarged foxholes, were cut into the earth all around. Gremlins patrolled the borders, carrying long blowpipes almost twice the length of their bodies.

'They look like miniature goblins,' Cress said, squeezing in beside him. 'Longer noses and ears though.'

Fletcher grunted in agreement, barely listening. He was confused by these armed gremlins. Everything he had learned about them had told him that they were little more than slaves, cowering creatures that were obedient to a fault. But these ones seemed far more hostile and he could see many of them pointing at the cage, deep in discussion.

'Mind if I have a better look?' Cress said, wriggling closer. In the darkness, Sylva coughed loudly.

Cress placed her eye against the hole, and Fletcher couldn't help but wonder how Sylva could possible think the dwarf was capable of trying to kill him. There was no way.

A cry like an eagle's call rang out from below. The gremlins ceased their patrolling, and then, in unison, the blowpipes were aimed towards the cage.

'Oh . . . balls,' Cress whispered.

Darts peppered the cage, many bouncing off, only to be plucked from the ground and used again. It was not long before most of the team had been struck. Fletcher had just enough time to examine a dart before he succumbed to the poison. It was fletched with tiny yellow feathers, like that of a budgerigar, while the tip was a sharp thorn cut from a tree.

This time, he did not feel consciousness slip from him. Instead, a cold numbness spread from his thigh, where the dart had struck. It felt much like when Rubens had stung him in the cell, but the effect was less powerful. He could still move his hands and legs, albeit slowly. Another few doses would probably have left him completely paralysed, but the bodies of Lysander and Sariel had protected him from the brunt of them. He might even be capable of a spell, if he could raise his hand in time. Then again, it would do little to help the situation.

Ignatius had used a great deal of mana when burning the orc, but he found that Athena's reserves, though smaller, had barely been touched. Fletcher's mana levels had virtually doubled the moment he had summoned her. Enough for a strong shield that might keep them alive a little longer, if the gremlins chose to kill them.

Fletcher felt a sickening lurch in his stomach, then there was a bone shaking thud as the cage hit the ground. The group groaned with pain, their bodies thrown into each other. Bony hands gripped the branches, while saw-toothed knives hewed them apart. They were made from what looked like shark teeth embedded in wooden daggers, not unlike the macanas the orcs used.

It took but a moment for the cage to split in two like a cracked egg, leaving the occupants blinking in the new light.

Frog-like eyes peered at them from above blowpipes, the hollow ends as threatening as gun barrels. There was arguing behind the crowd, the same clicking language that Fletcher had heard from Blue in the fighting pit. Fletcher raised his hands slowly, then cursed himself under his breath. Now they knew he wasn't paralysed.

'Stilnow, stilnow,' the nearest one chirred, kicking Fletcher in his chest with a webbed foot. It did not hurt, but he barely allowed himself to breathe. It was then that he realised that Ignatius had not been struck at all, his lithe body slotting easily between Fletcher and Cress. Was it time to make a move?

Even as the thought crossed his mind, a gremlin pushed its way through the crowd. He was somewhat larger than the others, with half an ear missing and a look of suspicion in his eyes.

'Waiyooheer?' he fluted, kneeling down and pressing a dagger of his own to the raw skin on Fletcher's neck. His voice, much like that of the other gremlin, reminded Fletcher of the way a bird might sound, if it could speak.

'We kill orcs,' Fletcher gasped, the cruel teeth digging into his throat. It was hard to speak, his tongue slow with the paralytic poison.

'Human keel gremlin,' Half-ear whispered, to the chittering agreement of the others around him. 'Human keel gremlin moar than orc.'

In that moment, Fletcher realised it was true. When the

military raided the jungles, the gremlins were often all they found. The poor creatures were slaughtered with impunity by the frustrated soldiers, eager to get a kill under their belts.

'I saved a gremlin,' Fletcher gulped, as the pressure of the knife increased. 'I saved the blue gremlin.'

At these words there was a hush. That was when Ignatius chose to act, vaulting out of the paralysed bodies of the others and tumbling Half-ear into the grass. His tail-spike hovered over the gremlin's eye and then he barked, daring the gremlins to make a move.

Fletcher eased himself into a sitting position, using the hump of Lysander's back as a prop. The clever Griffin had its eyes closed, or perhaps Captain Lovett was in control. If they were about to die, she wouldn't want the world to watch.

There was a commotion from the gremlins that crowded around them, somewhere at the back. One of them was shoving his way through, until he stood above Ignatius, his skinny chest heaving with exertion.

This gremlin was limping ever so slightly and he held a barbed harpoon in his hand, but that was not what marked him out from the others. No, it was the colour that still dyed the gremlin's back and shoulders – fading, but still very much there.

It was Blue.

# 33

Blue did not say a word to them. Instead, he knelt beside Half-ear and whispered in the larger gremlin's remaining lug. They bickered back and forth for a while, yet Ignatius never wavered once, his eyes flicking between the gremlins surrounding them.

After what felt like an age, Half-ear appeared to admit defeat. He sighed deeply and snapped some orders at the surrounding warriors. They paused as if confused, until slowly but surely they lowered their blowpipes.

In response, Fletcher directed Ignatius to get off Half-ear's chest, but to keep the tail poised above. They were still very much at the gremlins' mercy and he did not want to give up the last card he had left to play just yet.

'Thank you,' Fletcher said, bowing his head to Blue.

Again Blue ignored them, pushing his way out of the crowd and into the jungle. Strangely, the other gremlins did the same, disappearing into the burrows. Only Half-ear remained, staring at them with hatred in his eyes.

Sweat trickled down Fletcher's back as he waited, trying to ignore the gremlin's gaze. He noticed the sun was near setting and wondered how long they had been unconscious. If it had been a few hours, it mattered less. But if they had been unconscious for more than a day, they might miss their rendezvous with the other teams.

'So . . . what do we do now?' Sylva mumbled from behind him, recovering first from the darts.

She shuffled closer and laid her head on his shoulder, though whether it was the paralysis, exhaustion or something more, he couldn't tell. It mattered little to him why. He had not been so close to another person in a long time, and it felt right.

'Nothing,' Fletcher whispered.

He laid his own head on hers and they sat there, watching the setting sun filter through the leaves above. Despite their situation, his pounding heart stilled. Only Half-ear's unwavering gaze tarnished a perfect moment.

'You're bleeding,' Sylva said suddenly.

She lifted her head, and Fletcher saw a red stain on her temple.

'Your cheek,' she murmured, gently touching it with her fingers.

It was where the goblin spear had nicked him. The wound was deep, but somehow it did not hurt. A side-effect of the paralysis, perhaps.

'Let me,' she said, tracing a heart symbol on his face. It tingled strangely, as her mana merged with his skin. Then the cool, soothing pulse of healing energy began to seal his wound.

'Thanks,' Fletcher said.

She watched his face, her lips half-parted with concentration. Her wide blue eyes met his, and he felt a sudden urge to lean in closer.

Then Cress groaned from behind them, half lifting herself off the ground. Her elbows gave way and she collapsed in a spatter of mud, her face planting in Othello's backside.

'Uhhh, little help here,' she moaned, her voice muffled by his trousers. His moment with Sylva was gone, but still, Fletcher couldn't help but laugh aloud. He grabbed the back of Cress's jacket and pulled her off.

'Bloody hell,' she gasped, taking a breath of fresh air. 'I thought I was gonna suffocate in the worst possible way.'

Despite the headbutt to the behind, Othello snored even louder, completely oblivious to the world.

'And what about the blue gremlin?' Sylva asked, her face suddenly hard once again. 'What are you not telling us?'

'So . . . I might have rescued a gremlin from the fighting pits on the front lines . . .' Fletcher admitted, avoiding her eyes. He had preferred the girl he had been with a minute ago, but the wall she kept between them had returned once more.

'You what?' Cress exclaimed, so loudly that a gremlin poked its head out of the nearest burrow. She tossed a pebble at it and it ducked back once again.

'What do you mean, "rescued"?' Sylva asked, narrowing her eyes.

'I released him. Back into the jungle,' Fletcher murmured, and felt himself redden with a strange mix of embarrassment and shame.

'You're joking, right?' Cress said, hauling herself upright with a grunt. 'Are you a complete idiot?'

Sylva was even less impressed:

'We spend the past two days trying to avoid detection and you send them a damned messenger?'

'Well, he just saved our lives, so I guess it's a good thing I did!' Fletcher said, crossing his arms stubbornly.

'They came looking for us precisely because you let him escape,' Sylva replied, curling her lip with anger. 'They've probably been tracking us for days.'

Fletcher bit back a retort. What he had done was wrong, in almost every way. But watching that little creature refuse to give in against insurmountable odds . . . he couldn't have let it die. He would never have been able to forgive himself if he had. At the same time, he wondered if he would have made the same decision if he had known gremlins could speak.

'What's done is done,' Fletcher said, shaking his head. 'We can discuss this later. Right now we need to work out what's going on and how we're going to . . .'

He caught Half-ear's gaze and lowered his voice to a whisper, '. . . get out of here.'

A voice came from the hole nearest to them before the others could reply.

'You is not needing to do that,' it said. It had the same fluty tone of the voices of other gremlins, yet the intonation was clearer, if a little stilted and formal. A strange animal trotted out of the entrance, with Blue riding it bareback.

The creature looked a lot like a mountain hare, were it not for its slightly extended snout, shorter ears and long, coltish legs. It reminded Fletcher of what a hare might look like if it had the skeleton of an antelope and the hind-legs of a desert kangaroo.

'A mara,' Jeffrey breathed. 'I've never seen one in the flesh.'

'Is that a demon?' Cress asked, her eyes widening at the sight.

'No, it is a real animal,' Jeffrey replied, keeping his voice low. 'But an uncommon one.'

Blue halted the mara with a short tug of the fur on the back of its neck.

'How do you speak our language?' Sylva demanded, her voice laced with suspicion.

Blue dismounted and crouched beside Half-ear. He shook his head sadly.

'Many gremlins is learning it from humans, when we is captured. Many gremlins is escaping the pits. Me friend here, he is played dead after fighting a dog. He is being left to rot in a grave with the corpses. You is understanding why he wants gremlins to kill you, even if it is meaning death from your demon.'

'You learned to speak from that crass ringmaster?' Fletcher said sceptically.

'No. I is learning from another. A noblewoman, who is living in a cage. The human slaves are not being allowed to speak with she, so she taught I in secret. It was I who is being in charge of bringing woman food and water, changing woman's straw.'

'You know Captain Cavendish?' Sylva exclaimed.

'I do not know her name. She never trusted I enough to tell I. But she told I of you lands. How you hate the orcs like we. I did not believe the other gremlins, that you kill we like vermin.'

He trailed off for a moment, a wistful look in his enormous eyes.

'She is losing her mind, in the later years. So I is escaping and coming here. Then I is being captured when I is scouting. Bad men put I in pit. Then you save I.'

It was a lot to process. But one glaring question remained unanswered.

'Where the hell are we?' Fletcher demanded.

# 34

Blue did not reply. Instead, he unleashed a tirade of orders, all clicks and whistles.

In an instant, gremlins surrounded them once again, appearing as if from nowhere. Many had daubed their skin with green and brown ochres to blend in with the foliage. Others rode their own maras, their blowpipes firmly centred on Fletcher and the others. These were even more warlike, with bone-carved harpoons strapped to their backs and more of the deadly knives that had almost slit Fletcher's throat.

'We is taking you into the Warren, to meet leader,' Blue trilled, as the closest gremlins marched into the burrows. 'I warn you, we darts can make you sleeping, or freezing or dying. When we shoot this time, we use the dying ones. Do not make gremlins nervous. They eager to kill you, they is hating you as much as this one.'

Half-ear grunted and stood up as Blue prodded him with his blowpipe. The maimed gremlin's hateful glare never left Fletcher's face, but he backed away with his hands spread wide and empty. Fletcher did not blame him. After the cruelty he had seen in that tent just three nights ago, he would feel the same way.

Othello was still asleep, so they reluctantly left him with Solomon, as well as Athena – who kept watch in the trees above. Lysander continued to keep his eyes closed, so he remained too, while Sariel was too large to fit into one of the burrows.

Blue descended into the burrow he had come from, the largest of them all. Its mouth yawned dark and ominous but, far within, Fletcher could see the same glowing mushrooms that grew in the Great Forest.

Despite the burrow's greater size, Fletcher and the others had to crawl on their hands and knees to fit, with Ignatius and Tosk scampering ahead, ever wary of an ambush within. It was with great relief that the tunnel opened up into a large chamber, big enough to fit them all, if they stooped and pressed together. The luminous lichen was even thicker here, and they were all lit by an eerie green glow.

'Are we sure this is a good idea?' Sylva whispered.

'If they wanted us dead, we would already be in the ground,' Cress replied. She glanced at the earth above her and laughed. 'You know what I mean.'

'The dwarf is speaking truth. We will not be harming you if you do not give reason,' Blue said, nudging his mara into a tunnel that sloped even deeper. 'This way. Mother is being waiting below.'

They pressed on, their already filthy clothing stained further by the dark, moist soil. The temperature seemed to increase as they crawled deeper. They passed chambers on either side of the path they followed. Within them, furry mounds of mara pups suckled on their mothers' bellies, so young that they were yet to open their eyes. Piles of fruit, tubers and freshly cut grasses sat beside them, and the adult mara grazed on them as they passed.

The next room contained spherical green eggs, tended by gremlin matrons who splayed themselves over the grapefruit-sized objects protectively when they saw the intruders. They hissed as Fletcher peered in, and he hurriedly crawled on, whispering to Sylva, 'Gremlin eggs'.

Deeper still, Fletcher looked into another chamber, the rustle of insects distracting him from their path. A maelstrom of crickets, locusts and mealworms swarmed the walls, bouncing around the cavity with a mad energy. Fruit skins and husks were stacked in the centre of the room, while gremlins carefully plucked the largest insect specimens with their nimble fingers, putting them into tightly woven baskets at their hips. It was only when a gremlin popped one into its mouth and crunched down that Fletcher realised the room's purpose. He shuddered and moved on, though Ignatius licked his chops and had to be pulled away.

'They live as rabbits do, in a warren of sorts,' Jeffrey whispered from behind. 'Their eggs are kept safe from predators underground, and they farm insects to feed themselves. They have even developed a symbiotic relationship with the mara. See how their loincloths are made from mara fur and they ride them as we do horses, but the animals are protected and well fed by the fruit and grasses that are brought to them.'

Fletcher was fascinated, but he could not help but feel

constricted in the tight confines of the tunnel. It put him in mind of his prison cell, and he shuddered at the memory. Ignatius mewled in sympathy and slowed, so that he could rub his back against Fletcher's arm.

'Thanks, little guy,' Fletcher whispered.

On and on they went, until the side chambers ran out and the tunnel pitched forward so sharply it became more of a slide than a crawl. The earth seemed to become hotter still, and the sweat ran down his face and into his eyes. Even the frilled lichen became scarcer, until Fletcher felt like he was being swallowed down a black throat and into the belly of an enormous beast.

Finally, a glow of orange light told Fletcher that they had reached the end of their journey. Blue waited inside the entrance to the glowing chamber and tugged them out, one after the other, like newborns freshly birthed. 'Mother is here,' he said, reverently, when they were all through. 'You all meet Mother.'

Fletcher blinked in the glare, the heat so fierce his skin almost hurt with the force of it. A glowing stream of molten liquid flowed ahead, coloured the orange of heated metal. The lava trickled from a rent in the cave wall, wending along a deep channel and into a tunnel that stretched endlessly into the distance. Bubbles broke along the surface, spattering red-hot droplets with gloopy plops. He sensed a longing from Ignatius to approach the lava, but quelled it with a thought – now was not the time for curiosity.

Stalactites and stalagmites studded the floors and ceilings like snaggled teeth, while columns of those that had joined together held up the ceiling. They reminded Fletcher of the pillars of a great cathedral.

'The wild gremlins built their Warren here because of the lava.' A voice echoed from deep within the cavern, where the light of the magma did not reach. 'It kept the soil warm for them.'

It was a garbled voice, as if spoken through a mouth full of marbles. It sounded feminine somehow, despite the guttural intonation. The speaker had to be old too, for their speech quavered and cracked in their throat. Fletcher knew one thing for certain. It was not a gremlin.

'They need heat for their eggs, you see,' the voice continued, growing louder, 'the same way the goblins do. That is what you call them, is it not? Goblins? My spies have heard you call them such.'

There was the gentle tap of a cane on the ground and a presence appeared on the edge of the gloom. Fletcher squinted, but could see no more than a shrouded figure.

'Show yourself,' Sylva demanded, stepping beside Fletcher.

'Give me your word that you will keep the peace,' the shadow said. 'I do not wish to see any more death tonight.'

'I swear it,' Sylva said, looking around at the others for their nods of agreement. 'As do my friends.'

'Very well.'

The figure stepped out of the shadows, a long, blackthorn staff clutched in her gnarled hands. She was hunched like a vulture, the burden of her obvious age weighing heavy on her shoulders. Tangled black hair tumbled over her shoulders down to her waist, covering her nakedness, for all she wore was a feathered skirt and a broad necklace made from the small bones of a dozen unfortunate animals.

Her face and body were painted as if overlaid by a skeleton, the outline of a skull leaving her eyes as black holes, stark against the chalky whiteness. But one thing stood out more than anything else, jutting from her lower lips like the jagged stalagmites she stood among. Tusks.

Mother was an orc.

## 35

She stood there in silence, her eyes staring out blankly. Sylva's mouth opened and closed like a goldfish, while Fletcher could do no more than stutter. Despite her size, he did not feel threatened by her presence, for she was as frail as the withered staff in her hands.

'Who are you?' Cress asked, almost politely. She seemed respectful of the orc's old age rather than scared, even as Jeffrey shuffled behind Cress and tried, unsuccessfully, to hide behind her shoulders.

The venerable orc smiled, revealing a row of jagged teeth.

'You may call me Mother,' she croaked, stepping even closer. 'I have known no other name for the past half-century. Nor have I seen the light of day with my own eyes.'

Sylva's hand wandered to her back, as if her falx was still strapped to her shoulder. Mother noticed the movement, but did nothing more than cluck her tongue disapprovingly.

'With your own eyes?' Fletcher asked. His suspicions were confirmed when a green-brown Mite buzzed out of her hair, settling on the blackthorn staff and watching them through beady eyes. The demon was smaller than most Mites, almost the size of a normal beetle. It was then that Fletcher saw the milky whiteness of Mother's eyes, clouded by cataracts. The orc was blind.

'My Mites, Apophis and Ra, act as my eyes and ears. There is no limit to what I can see. I have more eyes now than I was born with.'

'A shaman then,' Sylva said, finding her voice again.

'I am a summoner, as you are,' the orc said simply.

Her demon buzzed into the air, hovering in front of their faces as she took them in. Clearly she had the same ability as Lovett, capable of scrying with her mind instead of a stone.

'Don't mind Apophis. He has been following you since I heard of your arrival. Just another insect in the trees. You should be more vigilant.' She chuckled to herself, her laughter throaty and guttural.

'Told you,' Sylva muttered, nudging Fletcher with her elbow.

Fletcher ignored her. The dark walls were bringing back memories of his captivity and his heart was racing. Enough was enough.

'Where are we?' Fletcher growled. 'Why are you toying with us like this?'

The orc bared her teeth, and it took Fletcher a moment to realise she was smiling.

'Come with me,' she wheezed, backing into the shadows once more.

Mother tossed wyrdlights over her head as she shuffled, sending them dodging through the maze of rock formations to cast myriad shifting shadows on the ground below.

Reluctantly, the others followed, while a vanguard of mara-riding gremlins kept a watchful eye. Only Blue remained close, his head bobbing just above Fletcher's waist as his mount hopped along beside them.

The newly lit space was deep and cavernous, the ceiling falling away into an open space. Their footsteps echoed, merging with the gloopy movement of the lava and dripping water from the stalactites above. Signs of inhabitation were scattered around. Mats made from woven reeds coated the floor. Pots filled with powders, mixing bowls, mortars and pestles were piled haphazardly in the corner and a cauldron simmered on the embers of a low fire, the contents a strange turquoise colour. Clearly she was an apothecary of some kind, healing the gremlins of their injuries and ills.

'Hurry, there's not much time,' Mother quavered from the gloom ahead of them. 'You took longer to wake than expected.'

'What's the rush?' Jeffrey grumbled, tripping over a discarded animal bone.

Mother came to a halt and the wyrdlights darted ahead to hover above her, revealing the end of the cave. It was a sight to behold.

Raw crystals emerged from the rock like multicoloured icicles. Some were oblong in shape, jutting out like the prow of a ship. Others seemed to blossom like flowers, sharp petals that glittered ruby red under the light. Mother stepped through them without hesitation, manoeuvring by memory alone.

But even the kaleidoscope of colours and shapes could not drag Fletcher's eyes from the gem embedded in the wall at the very end of the cavern. It was oval in shape, and it had been polished down to a gentle curve – not unlike the Oculus at Vocans, but three times as large. The clear, crisp image of a leaf sat in the centre, trembling on a breeze. It was an enormous scrying stone.

'This is where I teach the gremlin pups about the jungle, for only the foragers, fishers and hunters are allowed to leave the Warren,' Mother said, gesturing blindly at the stone. 'And now I shall teach you too. Please, sit.'

There was a smooth patch of rock, worn away by generations of gremlin backsides. It made Fletcher wonder just how old this orc was.

They settled down, though Ignatius and Tosk stood guard at their backs, keeping an eye on the warrior gremlins. Ignatius was especially energetic, prowling back and forth and hissing under his breath.

The image began to vibrate as the Mite in the crystal, Ra, took flight. The leaf fell away, revealing the world around it with startling clarity. In this part of the jungle, the vegetation looked thicker somehow, with the trees older and more twisted and the ground shrouded in deeper shadow.

'Long ago, I was an orc like any other. I came from a small tribe, far to the south. We did not even know humans existed.'

The image swung again. A village lay beyond, unlike any Fletcher had ever seen. Huts made from woven thatch and mud brick were scattered around a clearing. The broken canopy left it illuminated by a pillar of light from above, marred only by the billowing smoke of a fire in the centre. Figures were gathered around the flames, some swaying back and forth in a strange dance, others seated cross-legged in a semicircle.

Orcs. No more than a score of them . . . yet they were not as Fletcher had expected. Orc women combed out their hair with tortoiseshell combs, while others suckled their young on slings around their chests. Wizened elders puffed on long pipes, taking it in turns to pack tobacco and herbs in the bowls. Most were toothless, many with their tusks missing or broken off to stubs. There were but two males among these venerable members.

Meat was wrapped in banana leaves to steam by the fire. Those with teeth chewed for those without, spitting it in coconut bowls for the elders to slurp up with relish.

Far from being disgusted, Fletcher found himself smiling at the act. They cared for each other – something he had somehow never imagined of the orcs. It seemed a peaceful existence. Idyllic. Innocent.

Young orcs held hands and spun around the fire, their mouths opening and shutting in unison – they had to be singing! Fletcher wished he could hear them, so mesmeric were their stamping feet and rolling shoulders.

'I lived in a village just like this,' Mother whispered. 'A few families, nothing more. Once we were all this way, thousands of years ago. Before they came.'

Something was wrong. One of the old orcs had seen something. He stood and yelled, waving his arms in a frenzy. The younger orcs scattered, while the women cowered, covering their heads with their hands.

Mother jerked her head, and Ra followed her movement. Rhinos thundered into the encampment, their thick double-horns tearing a passage through the bushes. Bull orcs rode on their backs, swinging weighted nets over their heads. Others whirled lassos, snatching the youngsters' feet from under them and dragging them screaming in their wakes.

An old orc staggered from his hut, a simple club clutched in his fists. Before he could swing it, a javelin took him through the chest, flung almost casually by a nearby rider.

To Fletcher's dismay, the remainder of the villagers were tangled in the nets or herded back to the fire, even the younger ones who had made it to the edge of the jungle. It took no more than a minute, so expertly was the attack orchestrated. The riders were well practised.

'This family is what we were. These marauders are what we have become,' Mother said, her voice a throaty growl.

The young boy orcs were separated out from the others, leaving the elders and females to wail and cry by the fire. Great poles were removed from the backs of the rhinos, with loops of rope at intervals along them. They tightened them around the orc boys' necks. One was so young he had to stand on tiptoes to keep in line with the others. His tusks were little more than nubs, yet they manhandled him into position regardless. The poles were secured to the rumps of the rhinos. Then, with barely a word to the survivors, the riders marched their captives out of the village, disappearing into the gloom of the jungles.

'Why?' Sylva asked simply. She was unable to hide the tremor of sorrow from her voice.

'Soldiers for their armies. They take the boys young. Beat them until their minds are broken. Fill them with hate, teach them to kill. That is their way.' Mother's speech was garbled now, her mouth full of saliva. She swallowed and continued.

'They start with gremlins first. Make them hunt them down for sport. Slaughter most of them, enslave and breed the others. Then they force the boys to fight each other, weed out the weakest ones. By the end of it, those that remain only thirst for butchery and dominance. Their consciences are gone, their innocence lost.'

She lapsed into silence, the black nails of her crooked hands digging into her staff. Apophis buzzed mournfully to her cheek, wiping at the tear that trickled there with his forelegs. It stained the white of the skull beneath, a black fracture in the painted bone.

'So . . . how do you fit in?' Fletcher asked, twisting his hands awkwardly.

'When they attacked our village, I followed them. No . . . I followed *him*. The boy I loved.' She spoke in short bursts, as if she were on the verge of weeping in earnest. She blinked rapidly and took a deep breath. When she spoke again, it was not misery in her voice, but anger.

'I served as a shaman's servant girl in the hopes that he would lead me to the warriors someday. It was there that I learned to summon in secret, stealing one of my master's scrolls. I hoped that a Mite would help me find my love.'

She stroked Apophis's carapace, smiling in a toothy grimace.

'When I did encounter him a year later, the boy I knew had gone. All that remained was a cruel brute. I embarrassed him, walking into that camp, trying to save him in front of his fellow warriors. He beat me near to death and left me for dead. The gremlins found me and brought me here.'

It was all beginning to make sense now. The orcs' mindless

300

savagery, their pitiless slaughter. Even Baker's journal had not mentioned this strange enslavement of their own people.

Fletcher wondered what she was doing, hiding in the bowels of the earth? And who were these gremlins, that lived apart from the orcs? She answered him before he could ask.

'These are the wild gremlins, those that were never enslaved but still live in fear of the orcs. There are other warrens, littered around the jungle, but this is the largest of them. It is my hope to free all gremlins from their masters, and one day end the vicious cycle of hatred my people follow.'

'I still don't understand,' Cress murmured under her breath.

'What's that?' Mother asked, her hearing razor sharp.

'What's the point in all this? The soldiers, the armies? Why do you want to destroy Hominum?' Cress blurted.

'*I* don't want to destroy anything. They follow a prophecy, written on the walls of the ancient pyramid. That a white orc will lead them to conquer the known world. That one comes every thousand years. I know little else. Only the shamans know what is written, for only they can enter the pyramid itself.'

'And goblins,' Sylva added, raising her eyebrows. 'They seem to be allowed in there too, since they and their eggs reside in the cave network beneath it.'

'The goblins are something I know little about,' Mother sighed, lifting a fingertip and allowing Apophis to land there. 'In truth, I dare not send my Mites to look within the pyramid, for it is said that it is protected by demons. They might recognise my Mites for what they are.'

'Well, we'll find out when we get there,' Jeffrey said, then paused and looked at his lap. '*If* we get there.'

'I heard of your mission through Apophis, and I will help you. The noblewoman showed a great kindness to my friend here, as did one of you,' Mother pointed at Blue, who bowed his head solemnly. 'This gremlin, in turn, taught me the rudiments of your language, and the rest I learned as my Mites watched your troops in the front lines. This knowledge has saved many gremlin lives and for that I am thankful.'

'And the goblins?' Sylva asked. 'What of them?'

'An abomination, to be wiped from the face of our world,' Mother snarled.

She coughed suddenly, hacking and wheezing until she had to sit down, her back hunched and bowed. The orc was smaller than she had first appeared, shrunken and shrivelled by age. The paint hid the deep wrinkles in her face, but now that she was level with Fletcher, she appeared fragile and insubstantial.

'I grow tired,' Mother breathed, her voice barely above a whisper. 'Just remember what I have told you . . . we are not all monsters. Go with my blessing. My gremlins will guide you from here. You have only a few hours left.'

# 36

When they emerged from the Warren, Fletcher could not help but collapse to the ground and look up at the sky, revelling in the fresh air and dawn light. Already, the sun was setting, casting the clearing in a warm orange glow. He had no idea where they were, or how far the pyramid was. They needed to leave soon, but he could barely find the energy to sit up.

The gremlins remained within their Warren, except for Blue, who watched them warily from the main entrance. Others peered out curiously, their bulging eyes just visible over the lip of their respective holes.

Even the baby gremlins were present. One took a step out to get a better view, and was dragged back inside by its scolding mother. The yelps of protest within told Fletcher it was getting a sound spanking.

Fletcher let his head flop to the side and saw that Othello was still passed out on the floor, his nostril flaring with each snore. The dwarf smacked his lips and rolled over, clutching at Lysander's claw like a stuffed toy.

'Right, that's it,' Cress growled, brushing soil and slime from her uniform. 'Nap time's over.'

She straddled Othello's chest and tugged on his moustaches.

'Blargh,' he spluttered, slapping at her hands.

'That's right, wakey wakey,' Cress grinned. 'You've had enough beauty sleep.'

Othello shoved her off and sat up, rubbing his eyes.

'I feel like I've been smashed over the head with a rock,' he groaned. He caught sight of their surroundings and froze.

'Ummm . . . what's going on?'

He looked around, taking in the gremlin eyes that watched them.

'Come on,' Cress said, dragging him to his feet. 'I'll explain on the way.'

'On the way?' Fletcher mumbled. The soil was cool on his back, and he had no desire to get up just yet.

'Looks like we're heading out,' Sylva said, tapping him on the forehead and pointing at Blue's receding back. The gremlin and his mara were walking into the jungle, following a thin, barely discernible trail.

'Gather your packs,' Fletcher groaned, getting to his feet. 'Blue's on the move.'

Walking back into the jungle felt like being enveloped in a busy spider's web, the buzz and tingle of insects pervasive, the twigs, leaves and thorns tangling in Fletcher's clothes and hair.

The path had obviously been carved out for gremlins and their mounts – not for anything bigger. Fletcher reached for his khopesh to cut his way through, but found his scabbard empty.

'Hey, when do we get our weapons back?' he asked, raising his voice to be heard by the gremlin. Blue had not slowed down, and Fletcher would have lost him were it not for the fading stripe of blue paint on the gremlin's back, bobbing up and down ahead.

'They is waiting at the river.' Blue's singsong voice cut through the foliage. 'Patience.'

They struggled on, with Fletcher getting the worst of it. Lysander and Athena leaped in the less crowded branches above, while Sariel slithered on her belly through the undergrowth with surprising ease. Ignatius and Tosk ran ahead, wary of ambushes. The two were working well together, coordinating a crisscrossed passage that scouted a wide area.

Then Fletcher had an idea. 'Solomon, you take the lead,' he called. The golem tore through the undergrowth behind Blue, his stony body unaffected by the thorns. He lumbered ahead of Fletcher, carving them a wide path with his bulky frame.

Despite Solomon's efforts, when they finally broke through to the other side, Fletcher's forearms were covered in thin red scratches. Ignatius lapped at them, sealing the wounds, but Fletcher barely noticed. He had caught sight of the waterway.

The creek was almost a river itself, as wide as the moat at Vocans. The waters moved so slowly and placidly that it appeared they didn't move at all. Only the occasional leaf floating by told him otherwise.

A half a dozen gremlins were clambering out of the water. Silver-bellied fish had been threaded through the gills, which they carried over their shoulders in loops of cord. They were armed with simple spear-guns that shot harpoons attached to coils of tightly wound twine.

The guns were not unlike Cress's crossbow, but made from a single pole, a basic trigger and an elasticated band that was pulled back by hand. Not as powerful as a bowstring, but they appeared hardier and were obviously useable underwater.

'Blue, you must tell me more about these bands on your spear-guns,' Jeffrey said, marvelling at the weapons as the troop of fisher-gremlins walked past, avoiding their eyes. 'I assume they are made from the sap of the rubber tree – a fascinating material indeed.'

'Blue?' the gremlin turned his mara and crossed his arms.

'Sorry . . . that's what Fletcher called you earlier.' Jeffrey shuffled with embarrassment.

'What is your real name?' Fletcher asked hurriedly.

Blue paused for a moment, a bemused expression on his face. Then, he tilted his head back and unleashed a tumult of warbles, clicks and fluting breaths. He grinned at them as they stared at him, dumbstruck.

'I . . . I think I may have some trouble pronouncing that,' Jeffrey stuttered.

Blue grinned and dismounted his mara.

'Blue is being fine,' the gremlin laughed. He slapped his mount on the rump and the mara hopped off into the trees. For a moment Blue stood there, taking in the sights, breathing the air deep into his lungs. Then, he opened his mouth and unleashed a long, wavering trill. It sounded like something between an eagle's cry and a songbird's morning prelude.

At the signal, a score of gremlins swung from the trees that hung over the creek, landing in crouches among Fletcher's team.

306

They were armed with a strange mix of spear-guns, blowpipes and knives, and he recognised them as the gremlins that had surrounded them before, their bodies painted to blend in with the foliage. Not even Sariel had sensed their presence.

'We will go with you, to the pyramid,' Blue said, motioning down the creek. 'When you is attacking, we is raiding the orcs and freeing many gremlins.'

'Wow,' Fletcher said. 'That's very . . . generous of you.'

'It is helping both our causes,' Blue said simply. 'When the alarm is being raised, we is knowing you is discovered. That is when we attack.'

Fletcher could not tell if it was blind opportunism or a friendly alliance. Either way, a small army of gremlins to guide them was an advantage he could not pass up.

'Fine with me,' Fletcher said. He extended a hand, and Blue took it. The gremlin's fingers were coarse and thin, like clutching a bundle of dried twigs, but he gripped Fletcher's hand warmly enough.

'Take weapons.'

It was Half-ear – he had been one of the gremlins who landed among them. The braves flanking him threw two baskets to the ground. A clatter of metal revealed their contents, and Fletcher's team wasted no time in arming themselves. Sylva picked up Cress's crossbow, trying to get to her falx at the bottom of the basket. There was a tense moment as Cress held out her hand to take it. Then, reluctantly, Sylva passed it along.

It was a relief to feel the weight of his khopesh at his side once more, and Fletcher realised how naked he had felt without it.

No sooner had they finished, the gremlins were tugging them

towards the creek, impatient to move on.

'So, we float,' Blue said when they reached the bank, pointing at the shallows.

What Fletcher had first thought were enormous lily pads turned out to be strange, bowl-shaped vessels that floated on the water. Already, the braves were leaping into them, with four to each craft until they had all boarded. Still, a few vessels remained, including an especially large one.

'Will those things hold our weight?' Othello grumbled. 'We dwarves aren't known for our swimming prowess.'

Cress nodded in agreement, prodding at a boat with her toe.

'They will,' Jeffrey said enthusiastically, jumping into the nearest one. It rocked dangerously as he swayed on his feet, and water slopped in over the side. The gremlins twittered to themselves as he floundered, trying to prevent it from spinning with the tiny oar roped to its side. Still, it floated well, and he sat happily enough in the puddle of water at the bottom.

'Coracles,' Jeffrey said knowingly, rapping the side. 'The river peoples of western Hominum use them for fishing. Woven willow rods form the structure and tar-coated animal skins make them waterproof. Their flat bottoms mean they barely disturb the water and, by extension, the fish. Sometimes the simplest ideas are also the best ones.'

'As long as they get us there by midnight, they're good enough for me,' Fletcher said, stepping into his own and lowering himself to the floor. It was comfortable, like sitting in a large basket.

The others followed suit, though Lysander and Athena remained in the treetops, preferring to stretch their wings. There was a moment's struggle as Sariel splashed her way through to the largest coracle and tumbled in. From the smell of it, this bigger vessel was the one the gremlins used to store and transport their catch. She didn't seem to mind, snuffling at the bottom and lapping up the remains with relish, coating her tongue in flashing scales.

Sylva shuddered and then laughed aloud.

'You'd be surprised how good that tastes to her,' she chuckled, reaching over and ruffling the Canid's ears. 'I should probably infuse her but . . . she seems happy enough.'

There was a pause as the team manoeuvred their vessels downstream, then the gremlins slipped their oars into the creek.

'Onwards,' Blue fluted, stroking the water white as he propelled himself away from the bank.

They pushed into the centre of the river, where the gentle current picked them up. It tugged them along at a much faster pace than Fletcher had expected, in fact, they did not need to paddle at all. All he had to do was dip the oar in occasionally to keep the coracle from spinning.

'Can we go any faster?' Fletcher called over the rushing water. 'We need to be there before midnight. How long until we get there?'

'Plenty of time,' Blue said. 'Don't be worrying.'

Fletcher groaned and forced his anxiety away, hating that the fate of their mission rested on the word of one gremlin. Sylva caught his eye, and he saw she had an arrow nocked to her bow. Clearly, she trusted the gremlins a great deal less than he did.

He shrugged and settled back, allowing his spine to rest on

the shallow curve of the vessel. The gremlins chirruped among themselves, while the rest of his team watched the forest go by, their eyes half closed. It had been a long day, and the setting sun was already lulling them to sleep.

Ignatius pawed at his thigh and Fletcher saw him staring into the waters below. It was clear and placid as a sheet of glass; he could see the green fronds lining the bottom, swaying in the current. As he watched, a stingray glided past, as large as the coracle he sat in. Its undulating sides propelled it faster than the current, and it soon disappeared beyond his sight.

'Good meat,' Blue said, watching from his coracle. He ran his finger over the tip of one of the harpoons strapped to his back, and Fletcher saw it was barbed like the ray's sting. 'Useful tails.'

Even as he spoke, more rays emerged from the weeds below, drifting beneath in tandem. Wide-finned fish with green backs joined the procession, powered by the soft beating of their tails.

Something darted past, scattering them aside. It snatched a fish in its mouth and spiralled in a helix of bubbles, revealing itself to be what had disturbed the crowd from the shade of the underwater forest.

A dolphin, pink as a dahlia, swam beneath them. Its long beak gulped down the prey, then it thrashed its flukes, breaching the surface and splashing down in a burst of water.

All around, more rose-coloured dolphins leaped and dived, whistling and clicking with what sounded like laughter. The gremlins clapped their hands with joy, some even throwing titbits from the pouches at their waists for the dolphins to catch. Many replied, matching the dolphin sounds with their own.

It was strangely beautiful to watch, as if the two were singing to each other.

'The old men of the river is blessing journey!' Blue laughed, splashing the water beside his coracle to beckon one to the surface. 'It is being good omen!'

The dolphin rubbed its rosy flipper along Blue's fingertips, as close to a handshake as the two species could manage. Then, as if some silent signal had been passed between them, the dolphins shot off upstream, leaving the coracles to continue their journey alone.

'That was beautiful,' Sylva said, gazing after them. She turned to Blue. 'Could you understand them?'

'We is speaking many words while they is speaking few,' Blue said, smiling from ear to ear. 'Some say, long ago we is learning to speak from they. It is not the same, but we is understanding they meaning.'

As he spoke, his face darkened. Fletcher followed his gaze, peering through the dim light of the setting sun.

A crumbling statue lay on its side by the water's edge, layered with moss and vines. The head was partially submerged in the shallows, but there was no mistaking the creature it depicted, with its broken tusks and jutting brow. They were in orc territory now.

# 37

Night fell thick and fast, with barely a sliver of moon to illuminate their passage. They dared not produce wyrdlights, for the creek had widened into a tributary and the great river they had to cross flowed ahead, signalled by the sound of rushing water. The pyramid sat on the other side, the dark outline stark against the star studded sky. It was at least ten times bigger than Fletcher had pictured, larger than even Beartooth's peaks. He forced himself to stifle a curse of disbelief, in case there were enemies lurking nearby.

To keep them together, Blue had tossed them the end of a harpoon each, which they embedded in the rims of their coracles. Lysander and Athena had already flown ahead, to scout out their landing zone on the other side of the river. Even Sariel had been infused by Sylva, for the boat sat too low in the water with her inside. It now contained four gremlins, who deftly manoeuvred the unwieldy coracle into the centre of the fleet.

'Row, hard and fast,' Blue said in a harsh whisper. 'If current is taking you and you no keep up, we cannot save you. Your rope will be cut.'

Fletcher heard the sound of splashing and the coracles began to rock. He was sprayed as they entered the choppy rapids then, as he felt the boat lurch with the running water, he slashed over the side with his oar, desperately propelling the boat forward. Soon Fletcher was surrounded by grunts of exertion as they struggled on, and his world became a seemingly endless repetition of thrust, sweep, pull; thrust, sweep, pull.

The darkness obscured those around him. All his eyes saw was the pyramid against the skyline. Beneath it, thousands of goblin eggs were waiting to hatch, and a tortured soul waited for rescue. They were so close, he could taste it.

As the seconds ticked by, he despaired as the great silhouette slid from right to left, the current pushing them further and further down the river.

His arms burned but he dared not stop. On and on he rowed, snarling through his teeth with every thrash of his oar. Even Ignatius helped, cupping his claws and bailing the water that splashed into the bottom of the coracle and soaked Fletcher's trousers.

Then, unexpectedly, he felt the grate of sand beneath him. Blue's nimble fingers grasped his own, tugging him into the shallows of the river bank. The gremlin dragged the coracle behind them, until they had staggered to the edge of the jungle.

'Dig now,' Blue hissed, removing the harpoon with a tug and pushing Fletcher's hands into the soil. 'We is hiding the boats.'

Fletcher dug blindly at the ground with his hands. Despite his exhaustion, it was surprisingly easy to push aside the earth, for it was loose and dry. Athena fluttered down beside him and helped, as did Ignatius. They pawed the loam between their legs until the hole was deep enough to stash the shallow bowl of a boat, making sure to place it upside-down so it would be easy to remove should they need to return. He could hear the others in the darkness, burying their own coracles. No sooner had they finished, than Blue reappeared.

'You friends is being ready,' the gremlin whispered, pushing the harpoon and its coil of rope into Fletcher's hands. 'Follow. We eyes see better.'

Fletcher gripped the harpoon and trudged into the blackness, the water squelching in his boots. Every now and again there was a tug on the harpoon's rope and he would adjust his direction. Twice he stumbled, stifling curses as he grazed his knees on the pebbles that lined the shore. He was not the only one to trip over, judging from the occasional thud and gasp of pain from behind him.

Fletcher wished he'd had the foresight to put on the scrying crystal, for Athena and Ignatius's night-vision were better than his. Instead, he had stashed it inside his pack in case it fell in the water, and now he was too occupied to delve inside and find it. Even the cat's-eye spell was out of the question – the yellow light of the spell would reveal their presence, exposed as they were on the river bank.

Despite the pain twinging through his knees, he was glad the gremlins were there to help them. He could not imagine how the other teams would cross the river, not without being swept half a mile downriver before reaching the other side. He hoped that all the teams would make it in time.

'Stop here,' Blue hissed.

They were at the base of the pyramid, where the forest had been cleared away to leave a clear path to the stony base of the giant structure. The building towered above like a sleeping giant, and Fletcher was filled with dread at the awesome sight. Shaking his head with resolve, he strained his eyes in the darkness. He was just able to make out the entrance, yawning like a cave mouth.

'This is being where we part,' Blue said, his voice low and urgent. 'We is hiding among our brothers and is attacking tomorrow.'

'Good luck,' Fletcher whispered.

'I is thinking it is you who is needing it,' Blue replied. 'The gremlins is living further down the river.'

He paused and lay his fingers across Fletcher's palm.

'May we paths cross again, Fletcher.'

With that, the harpoon was jerked from Fletcher's hand, followed by the fading patter of feet. He looked out into the darkness, hoping to catch another glimpse of the brave little creatures, but they had disappeared into the night. Fletcher's team had been lucky to find such formidable allies.

After a moment's pause, Fletcher positioned Athena on his shoulder and pulled the scrying stone from his bag. Swiping her wingtip with it to begin the connection, he strapped it to his eye and took in the scene.

The others were crouched in the dirt around him, their wide eyes unseeing as they glanced around fearfully. Even Lysander seemed nervous, his claws digging a furrow in the earth as he waited for their next move.

'I can't believe we made it,' Fletcher said, looking at the

position of the moon in the sky. 'It's almost midnight. Let's see who else is here.'

'We can't be the only ones,' Cress whispered.

Fletcher crouched low and scuttled towards the pyramid, Ignatius loping ahead with his nose to the ground and Athena keeping watch from above.

As they moved closer, Fletcher took in the enormous building. Despite the threat of the foreboding treeline on either side, he could not help but focus on Athena's view of the structure.

It was larger than anything he had ever seen, even more so than Vocans itself. It was made from a series of square levels that narrowed as they neared the top. Athena's night-vision showed that the stone slabs it was comprised of were a dull yellow in colour, and their outsides were coated in tangled vines and creepers.

Then they were in the shadow of the pyramid itself, and suddenly they were not alone.

'Is that you, Fletcher?' Seraph's voice called from the entrance, accompanied by the click of a pistol's flint being pulled back.

'Put that thing away,' Malik hissed, and there was a clatter as a gun was knocked to the floor.

The two leaders were crouched in the entrance. Both were soaking wet, their shaggy black hair plastered to their foreheads. They looked miserable, terrified and exhausted.

'It's us – no need to go shooting up the place,' Othello said, picking up the gun and handing it to Seraph. 'That thing wouldn't have fired anyway, it looks like the powder's wet.'

'Well, that's what half drowning yourself in the river will get you,' Seraph groaned, wringing out his hair between his fingers.

'The others are drying off in the entrance chamber. Don't worry, you can't see the fire from outside.'

'There might be demons guarding the place in there,' Cress remarked, peering into the entrance. It was a bare corridor that stretched into darkness, with a small chamber to the left. Fletcher could see the hint of the glow of flame from within it, but wasn't unduly worried. Any guard demons would most likely be deeper inside, if there were any at all. Even so, Seraph shuddered and shuffled away from the entrance.

'Why are you wet?' Fletcher asked Malik, remembering the route his team was supposed to have taken.

'We changed our minds,' Malik muttered. 'When Isadora's team switched to your side of the river, we thought they knew something we didn't and followed. We met up with Seraph's team just before crossing.'

Fletcher froze. So, Malik's team had been on their side of the river too. Was it possible it was one of them who had tried to kill him?

'Speaking of which, have you seen Isadora's team?' Seraph interjected, breaking up Fletcher's thoughts. 'Our window for the raid closes in eight hours.'

'Are they not here yet?' Cress exclaimed. 'We need them!'

'What do we do now?' Fletcher asked, his heart pounding. He had not really considered what they would do if another team were late.

'I'd rather wait for Isadora's team.' Malik yawned. 'If we attack now, their chances of rescue are much lower.'

Sylva snorted, as if Malik had made a joke.

'Wouldn't that be a shame,' she muttered under her breath.

'I say we hole up here and hope they make an appearance,' Malik continued, already moving to the fire-lit chamber. 'The orcs won't be expecting anything.'

'The Celestial Corps are on standby right now,' Seraph warned, looking into the night sky. 'Every minute we waste is a minute Hominum's skies go undefended.'

'Be that as it may, we're all exhausted,' Malik replied. 'We might as well wait until morning.'

Fletcher was bone tired … but they only had eight hours to complete the mission. Who knew how long it would take for them to find their objective in the labyrinth of tunnels ahead?

'Maybe we *should* attack now,' Fletcher argued. 'We're about to bed down in the most sacred place in Orcdom, while Hominum's only air defence waits for us on the ground. Does that not sound crazy to you?'

But support for Malik came from an unlikely source. Seraph had changed his mind.

'Look, we're a team down right now,' Seraph sighed. 'I know you have issues with Isadora's lot – hell, I do too – but whether you like it or not, we have a better chance of success with them fighting alongside us. Malik's team and mine expended a lot of mana crossing that river, we had to use the telekinesis spell to help propel ourselves through that current. We need to rest.'

Malik chimed in.

'We can go in half-cocked now, or wait a few hours and do it properly. Remember, we only have one shot at this. Let's make it count.'

'Easy for you to say,' Rufus's voice snarled from within the pyramid. 'My mother might not last another night.'

Malik winced, but ignored the outburst and beckoned Fletcher's team to follow him through the entrance.

'They don't use this place other than for rituals, right?' Malik said over his shoulder. 'Mason says only shamans are allowed in the pyramid. We're safer hiding here than out in the jungle.'

As whispered greetings were made, Fletcher looked at his team through his scrying lens, Athena's eyes cutting through the gloom. They were all damp and exhausted from the trip across the river and most had barely slept since the night they had encountered Isadora's team – unless poison-induced unconsciousness counted. Othello and Atilla were already dozing, their arms around each other's shoulders. It was true, a night's rest would do them all good, but was this the right call? Hundreds, if not thousands, of people could die if the Wyverns attacked Hominum that night.

'All right team, infuse your demons and get some shuteye,' Fletcher said, slumping to the ground in defeat. 'I have a feeling we're going to need it.'

# 38

Fletcher woke to the sound of drums. They pounded with a deep, incessant throb, booming low and loud across the pyramid.

He was not the only one awake. Mason, the escaped slave, watched him through half-closed eyes. The boy remained silent, but nudged Malik with his foot until the young noble groaned. Moments later he was as awake as Fletcher was, the pulse of noise startling away the vestiges of sleep.

The room was a dim, bare cube, with sleeping bodies surrounding the remains of a fire now reduced to cold ashes. The light of dawn glowed from the corridor outside. They had slept through the night. He looked over and saw Malik was clutching a pocket watch. He peered at it. They had two hours left . . . was that enough time?

'What the hell is that noise?' Jeffrey mumbled from behind Fletcher.

Fletcher turned to see most of his team were awake too, as well as Lysander, Sacharissa and Caliban, who had stayed up all night on watch, in order to wake them in time and to let them know if Isadora's team arrived. Evidently, they had not.

'We need to find out what it is,' Sylva said, peering out of the chamber furtively. She jerked her head back in immediately, her eyes wide with shock.

'There are orcs out there,' she whispered. 'Fetching water from the river. We can't risk going outside.'

'That's not the plan anyway,' Malik said dismissively. 'This is the safest place we could be. But yes – we need to find out what that sound is. It could be some sort of ceremony involving the pyramid.'

'I don't care what it is,' Fletcher said. 'We've waited long enough – the sponsors should have woken us earlier. We have to start the raid. Now.'

'I know what it is.' Mason spoke for the first time. His hands trembled ever so slightly, and his eyes were closed.

'It's the end of the orc trainin',' he continued, taking a deep, quavering breath. 'Where they separate the weak from the strong. 'Appens every year. This is terrible timin' – the area'll be crawlin' with orcs.'

'Will they come into the pyramid?' Fletcher asked.

'They might,' Mason replied, his eyes still closed. 'The shamans'll test the young 'uns for the ability to summon today, just as 'Ominum's Inquisitors do. If there're any adepts, they'll be takin' 'em into the pyramid. They come in through this back entrance and leave through the front. That's all I know.'

'And that's all we'll know, if we don't go out and check.'

It was Verity who had spoken. She was sitting in the corner, watching her Mite crawl over her hand. It was black, and small for a Scarab, just as Apophis had been.

'Nobody will notice Ebony here, if she flies out and takes a look.'

As she spoke, she rummaged in her satchel before tugging out a flat rectangle of crystal the size of a dinner mat. Its edges were reinforced with a steel band to prevent it from shattering, though one edge was already beginning to crack.

'A gift from my grandmother,' Verity said, holding it up for all to see. Ebony alighted on it, and Fletcher was amazed at the clarity of the image as the Mite's view came into focus. Even the Oculus back at Vocans had not been so crisp and clear.

'Glad it will be of use,' Verity continued, tossing her hair. 'I've been lugging it about this whole trip without using it once. I'd rather have one like yours, Fletcher.'

She turned her big brown eyes on him, and Fletcher smiled at the compliment. Sylva rolled her eyes.

Ebony swooped past his head, flicking a spindly leg against the lens strapped to his face. The overlay of Ebony's view appeared, and he felt dizzied as the Mite zoomed around the room. Athena's view was a lot more stable and less prone to sharp turns.

'Any objections?' Verity asked.

'None,' Malik said, admiring Verity's scrying stone.

He turned to Fletcher, since Seraph was still sleeping beside Othello and Atilla on the floor, his own snores adding to the bass chorus. All the others were awake now.

'Let them sleep,' Malik said, grinning. 'Fletcher, what say you?'

Fletcher paused, listening to the ominous throb of the drumbeats.

'We need to know when the coast is clear, so we can find somewhere better to hide in the pyramid,' Fletcher said, tapping his chin. 'We're sitting ducks in here. It can't hurt to do a bit of investigating.'

Before he had even finished speaking, Ebony had buzzed out of the chamber and into the light, the image blurring as the demon jinked left and right. Higher and higher she flew, Fletcher's overlay filled with clear blue sky and the glare of the blazing sun. Then, just as the others began to grow restless, Ebony turned and looked to the ground.

Beyond the pyramid, a teeming metropolis spread out below. These were not the grass huts that Fletcher had envisioned, but squat, heavy buildings of carved sandstone, with small ziggurats and monoliths surrounding a central plaza. It was all built around the great pyramid, except for a thin strip of beach between the pyramid's back entrance and the river – where they had travelled last night.

'Holy hell,' Cress whispered. 'There're so many of them.'

Thousands of orcs milled in the square, waving pennants and banners of stretched cloth, bird feathers and animal-skin. Brightly coloured body paint separated the crowd into a patchwork quilt of different tribes. Even their hairstyles were different, a strange mix of shaven patches, topknots and bowl-shaped mops.

But they were not alone. Smaller orcs cringed beside each group, wearing heavy wooden yokes around their necks, like oxen. They had been daubed with blue ochre from head to toe, and the stone floor was stained by their footprints.

'The weaklings, chosen from among the captives after a year

of indoctrinashun',' Mason said, tapping the scrying tablet where the blue patches were. 'They'll take part in the games for a place among the warrior elite.'

There was a great stairway on the side of the pyramid, leading down into the plaza, and Fletcher could see that the balustrades that lined it were carved in the likeness of interwoven snakes. A squat, rectangular block sat at the flat zenith, with a shallow basin hewn into the stone and a dark hole in the centre.

Mason leaned in and squinted at the tablet.

'There,' he said, prodding to the right. 'Go there.'

The image magnified as Ebony flew closer, shaking as the wind buffeted the demon. In the end, the Mite settled at the top of a tall obelisk to watch the proceedings below.

'The pitz ball game,' Jeffrey murmured. 'I've heard about this.'

As had Fletcher, for Baker's journal had waxed lyrical on the subject.

In between two sloping stone bleachers filled with cheering spectators, two teams of blue orcs leaped and dived across a long field of sand. On either end, a stone hoop was embedded in a wall, almost twelve feet off the ground. The hoop was turned sideways like a perfectly round ear, and Fletcher knew that the aim of each team was to get the ball through the opposing team's to win the game.

He had seen many sketches of these pitches from Baker's study of orc villages, but had never imagined how the game itself was played, nor that there would be more than fifty players battling up and down the pitch.

Most fascinating was the ball itself: a heavy sphere of rubber, the same material the gremlins used for their harpoon guns. It was bounced from orc to orc as they batted it around with wooden clubs, which they also used to batter aside their opponents. Blue dye and red blood spattered the sand, the two colours blending together as they did on the neck of a cassowary bird.

'It's brutal,' Sylva whispered as an orc's tusk was knocked from its mouth in a spray of crimson. The crowd jumped to their feet with a roar that reached even the confines of the chamber.

'Nah,' Mason said, pointing to the edge of the next pitch along. 'There're far worse things than the pitz. Look. The venatio.'

Ebony's eyes turned to the next pitch, where the red on the sand far outweighed the blue and the watching crowds were much thicker. Three orcs were chained together by the ankles, surrounded by a pack of hyenas. A fourth was being savaged on the ground not too far away. Armed with nothing but spears, they stabbed and whirled at the baying animals.

In the corner of the field, a pile of blue bodies had been left for the vultures. Among them, the corpses of animals could be seen, including big cats such as jaguars, tigers and lions. Hyenas and wild dogs seemed to be the most common, with crocodiles and even baboons appearing here and there.

'The pitz 'onours the wind god. The venatio 'onours the animal gods. And then there's the skin-pull, for the god of fire and light.' He pointed at the next pitch, and Ebony's view swung once again.

There could have been a hundred blue orcs on the next pitch, though there was no blood on this one. Instead, a great pit of flames burned fiercely in the centre, dividing the grounds in half. A great rope of knotted animal skins was stretched above the fires, while two teams of orcs strained, slipped and staggered in the sands in a desperate tug of war.

'Surely they wouldn't . . .' Jeffrey whispered as the front row of one side stumbled, their feet scrabbling frantically against the edge of the pit.

'It's for their gods,' Mason said dully, averting his eyes. One after the other, the defeated orcs were dragged into the flames, falling away until all that came out of the other side was a blackened rope of skin.

More pitches stretched out into the distance, where other games were being played. The nearest was a pool filled with water, where orcs in canoes beat each other with oars. Stone weights were tied to their ankles, so that the losers would drown if they fell. If that was not bad enough, the black bodies of crocodiles were thick in the pool, and already the water was tinged red around the remains of an upturned canoe.

'That's called naumachia. It's to honour the water god,' Mason whispered.

'Who needs to kill orcs?' Sylva said, shaking her head with a mix of wonder and disgust. 'They're doing the job for us.'

A cheer filtered through the walls of the chamber and Ebony's eyes flicked back to the pitz. A team had managed to score. The winning orcs fell to their knees in gratitude, chests heaving with exhaustion. Many embraced each other, while others simply lay on their backs, tears streaming from their faces. The losers were swiftly rounded up by the crowd and marched away from the pitch and into the plaza. Spectating orcs hounded them on their way with leashed hyenas, until the animals nearly choked themselves to death in their attempts to attack.

'You'd think they'd just lost more than just a game, the way some of those boys are going on,' Verity said, for the losing orcs were sobbing bitterly as they were pushed to the base of the stairs. 'Not so tough after all.'

'They *'ave* lost more,' Mason murmured, shaking his head. 'You'll see. This is where we find out if there're any adepts this year. Let's 'ope that . . .'

He stopped. The shouts and drums had silenced. On the scrying stone, the crowds no longer milled to and fro. They began to part like a multicoloured curtain, as a parade entered the plaza from a ziggurat opposite the pyramid.

'Here they come,' Mason uttered.

A great litter was carried aloft by a herd of rhinos, their great heads tossing as they strained under the weight. It was like a carriage without wheels, and had been carved to look like an enormous orc skull. The outside was painted gold so that it shone fiercely beneath the blazing sun. It stood nearly as tall as the monolith Ebony was perched on, but it was impossible to see anything more than darkness from within.

An escort of orcs surrounded it, larger specimens than any Fletcher had seen before. Their skin was splashed with red war-paint, coupled with stripes of yellow along their chests and faces. Each was armed with a macana and wore a quiver of javelins on their backs. Jade stone-plating covered their chests, elbows and knees, ceremonial armour that shone bright green in the sunlight.

'They must be the albino orc's bodyguards,' Fletcher

whispered. 'He has to be inside that carriage.'

'If Lovett sent Lysander to take him out . . .' Cress said, gripping Fletcher's arm.

'Don't even think about it,' Mason muttered. 'If the legions of orcs around us won't put you off, look behind 'em.'

There was another group of orcs at the rearguard of the parade, wearing enormous headdresses of gaudy feathers. They were clad in nothing but bone jewellery, just a belt of human skulls protecting their modesty. Most had ritualistic scarification on their bodies and face, while others had thick plugs through their noses and ears. Despite their fearsome appearance, it was not this that marked them out from the rest.

'They're shamans,' Sylva breathed.

Demons walked beside the orcs, monstrous creatures of every kind. Some Fletcher had no trouble recognising: Felids, Lycans and even a Minotaur. But others he only knew from his lessons at Vocans or the illustrations in Baker's journal.

The two Nanaues were the most fearsome. Like Felids, they shambled along with the posture of a jungle ape, but that was where the similarity ended. Their species were as close to sharks as Minotaurs were to bulls, with great gaping mouths filled with razor teeth, a large fin cresting each of their spines and swishing, rudder-like tails.

'Level nine,' Jeffrey whispered, his finger brushing along their outline. 'I wouldn't mind dissecting one of those.'

Three Onis lumbered beside the shamans, matching them in size and form. Fletcher might have confused them with orcs, were it not for the giant horns erupting from their foreheads and their hunched-over gait. Their skin was a stark crimson red, and

328

they snapped bestially at the crowds, with overdeveloped fangs. Though they looked humanoid, Fletcher knew them to be less intelligent than an average Mite.

The largest of all was a Phantaur, an enormous, two-legged elephant standing at nine feet tall, with great flapping ears, a grasping trunk and serrated tusks as long as its heavily muscled arms. Smaller demons scampered and buzzed around its feet, but the distance was too great to identify them.

'Nobody has ever captured a Phantaur before to know what level they are, but I reckon that big bugger must be a level twenty at least,' Jeffrey theorised.

'So much for orc demons being weaker.' Rory shuddered, holding Malachi close so that the Mite could see. 'They must keep their strong demons back, only send their low-level specimens against us. Just think, half of Hominum is watching this. No one's going to volunteer for the military after seeing them!'

'Speakin' of, we need to get the 'ell outta here, before they come in,' Mason hissed, crawling to the doorway and poking his head outside. 'The coast's clear, for now.'

'Move Ebony further back before she's recognised by a shaman,' Malik ordered Verity, grabbing his pack. 'We must find somewhere to hide, deeper in the pyramid. The jungles aren't safe and neither is this room.'

'Agreed,' Fletcher said, prodding Othello and Atilla awake. 'But leave Ebony outside. We need eyes on what's happening.'

Othello stretched and yawned, then froze as he caught sight of Verity's tablet, the parade emblazoned across its front.

'What did I miss?' he groaned.

# 39

They descended into the gloom as soon as they were packed, their footsteps echoing softly around them. The slim rectangle of light from the back entrance shrunk as they walked deeper into the bowels of the pyramid, until it was little more than a glimmer of light. Ignatius and Tosk led the way, while Athena rode on Fletcher's shoulders, giving him the sight he needed through the darkness. Meanwhile, Caliban, Lysander and Sacharissa followed at the rear, watching the back entrance for movement.

There was a thud and a groan from ahead.

'Ow,' Seraph said, and Fletcher could see he had collapsed on the ground in front of him. 'There's a wall here.'

Ignatius licked Seraph's face in sympathy, eliciting another groan.

'Screw it.' Verity flared a wyrdlight into existence. 'If there are demons guarding this place, they're going to hear us, light or no light. At least this way we can see them coming.'

More wyrdlights erupted, until the walls were lit with ethereal blue light. As the gloom rushed away, Fletcher saw that Seraph had walked into the wall at the end of the corridor. Two identical paths diverged on either side, narrower and more dusty.

'We need to split up,' Malik stated, sending a pair of wyrdlights down both passageways. The path curved back towards the centre of the pyramid, out of sight.

'Verity, Mason and I shall go to the left with you, Fletcher,' Malik murmured, stepping into the east corridor. 'Penelope and Rufus, go with Seraph's team on the right.'

'Who said you make the rules?' Atilla growled, throwing his arm around Othello's shoulders. 'I'd rather stick together.'

'Realistically, we're not going to find a hiding place for all of us in one spot,' Malik replied, raising his palms in peace. 'Splitting up is inevitable.'

'Malik's right,' Fletcher said. 'The map says there's a passage to the caves somewhere in here – right, Mason? Do you know where?'

'It's just what I 'eard,' Mason said, scratching his head. 'Never been allowed in 'ere, just the caves. Only ever seen a passage from the caves to the pyramid, but dunno where it comes out.'

'We have a better chance of finding it if we spread out,' Seraph said, propelling Atilla down the passage on the right. 'Remember, the pyramid isn't the target. The caves beneath it are.'

'We'll see you on the other side,' Genevieve said, tossing Azura into the air to scout ahead. 'Come on, Rory.'

Sacharissa whined and nudged Fletcher's arm, forced to go with Seraph's group. 'We made it, Arcturus,' Fletcher whispered. The Canid gave Fletcher a playful headbutt to the chest, then pattered after her team.

Rufus paused beside Fletcher as he followed Penelope down the other passageway.

'Fletcher,' the noble said, gripping Fletcher's wrist. 'If you reach the caves before us, save my mother first. Please.'

'I'll do my best,' Fletcher replied, though he avoided Rufus's eyes. His heart went out to Lady Cavendish, but in Fletcher's mind the goblin eggs were the real threat. Every one destroyed was one fewer goblin sent against Hominum.

'Thank you,' Rufus whispered. 'I would be forever in your debt.'

Then he was gone, jogging after the others.

Just as he began to move, Fletcher was slammed against the wall. Caliban had barged him aside, stooping so that his horns didn't scrape the ceiling.

'Looks like Rook isn't missing you.' Othello winked, following.

The next passageway was as long as the last corridor had been, but it ended far less abruptly. After a few minutes of walking, the passage opened up, revealing an antechamber as large as the summoning room at Vocans.

Stranger still, the place was full of sacks, some of which had burst, scattering freshly picked yellow flower petals haphazardly throughout the room. The petals lay upon a thick layer of dust which coated the floor of the room, disturbed only around the edges, where whoever had brought the sacks had walked by.

'What is this place?' Othello asked. The dwarf sent wyrdlights skimming around the room, darting into the corners until the entire chamber was lit. They revealed hieroglyphs and etched scenes on the walls, all of which were painted in fading dyes.

'Can you read these?' Fletcher asked Jeffrey, who was already busy copying them into his notebook.

'No,' he murmured, his fingers tracing along the symbols. 'I don't think even the orcs could. This is ancient stuff here. A culture pre-dating theirs by millennia.'

'You're saying orcs didn't build this place?' Verity said, not looking up from her tablet.

'I have no idea,' Jeffrey said, his pencil scribbling back and forth across the pages. 'There are pictures of orcs on the walls, so I would think they did. But these hieroglyphs are in an entirely different language. Whichever civilisation built this place, they died out a long time ago. That would explain the difference in size and architecture of the ziggurats that surround the pyramid. No wonder it's so important to the orcs, I bet they think this place was built by their ancestor-gods.'

Fletcher examined the hieroglyphs closest to him. The symbols depicted the jungle's animals and plants, a sort of alphabet based on the natural world. They bore no resemblance to the orc runes that he had seen on Ignatius's summoning scroll, which were formed from jagged lines and dots.

It was impossible to decipher their meaning, so he turned his attention to the sacks of petals by his feet. After Jeffrey's warnings of the jungle plants he avoided touching them, but a deep sniff revealed them to smell similar to tobacco, with an alcoholic tinge. What the petals of a plant like that were doing within the pyramid was a mystery.

'Guys, I think you need to take a look at this,' Verity said, looking up from her scrying stone with wide eyes. 'They've reached the pyramid.'

So they had. The tablet showed the skull-shaped palanquin being lowered, the rhinos kneeling before the great stairs. Fletcher also noticed drums had begun to beat again – even this deep into the pyramid the dull thump could be heard, as if the ancient building had a pulse of its own.

That was when Fletcher saw him. The albino orc, leaping out of the skull to land on the steps, his body a perfect symmetry of power and athleticism. His appearance triggered roars and the stamping of feet from the crowd, until their fervour shook the very ground.

It was true that the albino orc was taller than the other orcs, standing at what must have been eight feet. He wore little more than a plain skirt, his white skin greased to gleam like polished ivory. In contrast to the plethora of stylings from the orcs around him, a simple mane of ashen hair fell over his shoulders, as long and thick as Sylva's. He was less bulky than those around him, with rangy musculature suited more for speed than strength.

He raised his arms, welcoming the adoration of the spectators. Nodding and smiling through his savage tusks, he walked like a dancer up the steps, his pace fluid and controlled. Two shamans flanked him, their Nanaues vaulting back and forth along the stair with excitement.

Before they had reached the top, the crowd's roar turned into a chant, a single word repeated over and over, muffled by the walls of the pyramid. The drummers punctuated the mantra with the beat, redoubling their efforts to keep in time with the masses.

'What are they saying, Verity?' Fletcher asked, trying to make out the word.

'Khan,' Verity said, her eyes closed with concentration. 'It sounds like Khan.'

'That's his name,' Mason said, shuddering. 'That's what they call him.'

The three orcs had reached the top of the steps by then, and as Fletcher watched, Khan withdrew a jagged, obsidian knife from a scabbard at his waist.

The crowd went mad, howling and screaming in a fanatical fervour. Only the score of blue orcs who had lost the pitz contest remained silent, kneeling at the base of the steps. Then, one by one, they were shoved up the stairway, making the long walk to the top.

'This is too weird,' Cress murmured. 'There's nothing up there. What are they doing?'

'You'll see,' Mason said grimly, shuffling away from them. 'But I'd rather not watch if it's all the same to you.'

The first blue orc reached the flat top of the pyramid. Even though Ebony was far above him, Fletcher could see that the orc's hands were shaking. He shuffled forward until Khan jerked him on to the altar. The blue orc lay there, spread-eagled, while the albino orc raised the knife. Fletcher looked away just in time.

Verity retched and handed the tablet to Sylva, running to heave in the corner. The rest looked on in horror. Only Jeffrey had been spared the scene, too fascinated with the etchings on the wall to pay attention to the tablet.

'Sacrifices for the old gods, the forgotten gods,' Mason murmured. 'Orcs are scared of 'em, reckon they're inside this 'ere temple. So they give 'em the most blood – more than they give to any of the others.'

The blue orc's corpse was hurled down the steps, to tumble past the remaining victims and into the crowds below. The onlookers cried out once again, scrambling for the body then raising it above their heads and passing it backwards in a macabre celebration.

Another sacrifice lay down on the altar, his chest heaving with fear. The knife rose and fell once more. Khan held the still-twitching carcass by the ankle, crimson spurting from the gaping chest wound and on to the altar.

The group in the pyramid stood there for a while, watching the blood drip with grim fascination. Until Jeffrey spoke up.

'Guys. You're not going to believe this.'

# 40

They stared at the wall Jeffrey was pointing at, unable to believe their eyes. Malik snuffed out the nearest wyrdlights and replaced them with a ball of fire, so that the faded colours were not tinged with blue light.

An orc in white was drawn there, the spitting image of Khan. There were orc warriors behind him, painted in the red and yellow of the bodyguard outside. But what was astonishing were the humans on the other side of the painting. They were drawn roughly, but their features and bodies were unmistakeable. One figure led them, mirroring the position of the albino orc.

'Every thousand years,' Fletcher murmured. 'I bet that's what the hieroglyphs say. A marked messiah, sent to defeat mankind. That's what an old soldier once told me, anyway.'

'More like a natural mutation that occurs in every species . . .' Malik said under his breath. 'It may be that albino orcs are larger and have a higher summoning level than others, making them natural leaders. The rest is superstition, nothing more.'

'Be that as it may, that's not the strange part,' Sylva said, looking at them as if they were all blind. 'It's the humans. They shouldn't be drawn here.'

'Why not?' Cress asked.

'Because humans arrived here two thousand years ago, when your ancestors crossed the Akhad Desert,' Sylva explained. 'This pyramid was built long before humans even set foot in these lands. Elven texts as old as five thousand years have mentioned this place.'

'There's something else,' Jeffrey said, wiping away a layer of dust with his sleeve.

The outline of a demon appeared between the orcs and humans, the paint that had coated it long peeled away. 'A Salamander,' Fletcher breathed. Ignatius chirruped with excitement and pawed at the wall below.

Set above this image were two separate scenes. One, where the orcs stood victorious over the bloody corpses of the humans, and another, where humanity were the victors.

Fletcher thought back to his first infusion dream. He knew from this dream that Ignatius's summoning scroll had been originally intended for an albino orc, over a thousand years ago. Perhaps the orcs who had drawn the images here had been trying to recreate this prophecy. What was obvious to him now was that, according to both the carvings and his infusion dream, the orcs believed that a Salamander was the key to their victory . . . or doom.

'We need to copy this all down,' Fletcher said, pointing at the wall. 'Maybe we can translate it later.'

'Already done,' Jeffrey said, showing Fletcher his sketch book.

'Guys,' Sylva interrupted, holding up the tablet. 'We need to move, now. The sacrifices are over and Khan is walking towards the back entrance. He has a bunch of his shamans with him, plus a group of orcish youths. They must be adepts.'

'Damn it,' Malik growled. 'There's nowhere to hide in here – we'll have to move on. Follow me.'

He snuffed out his fireball and jogged to the other end of the antechamber, where the passage continued. Fletcher and the others had no choice but to go after him.

'Looks like we've waited long enough,' Othello whispered, trying and failing to hide a smile. 'Isadora's team missed their window.'

They jogged until the passageway split once again. There was no time to decide who went where; in the rush Fletcher ended up taking the right passage with Othello, Sylva and Lysander. This time, the floor angled up sharply. They seemed to be heading to the central point of the pyramid.

'Hey,' Fletcher gasped, their feet thundering along the passageway. 'We left Cress and Jeffrey.'

'We'll catch up with them later,' Sylva replied, leading the way with a glowing fingertip. 'The orcs will be here any min—'

Sylva cut her words short as the passageway ended abruptly, opening up into a massive room. It was vaulted with great beams of rusted metal, while a network of pipes flowed from the ceiling and out into the walls.

A pit fell into darkness around the platform, so deep and cavernous that they could not see the bottom. A wide plinth sat in the middle, with a pentacle deeply engraved in it. There was a hole in the very centre, though how deep it went Fletcher could not tell.

The only way to reach it was four stone bridges, crisscrossing from the four entrances to the room.

'Where the hell are we going to hide?' Othello asked, his eyes scanning the room. 'There's nothing here!'

'Look – stairs,' Sylva said, pointing to the plinth. It was supported by a wide pillar of equal width beneath it. The column had a rough stairway carved to go around it, the stone a fresh white, as if it had been cut recently.

Fletcher tossed out a wyrdlight, sending it spiralling into the depths below. It was deep, almost half as deep as the pyramid was tall. But at the very bottom, Fletcher could make out a tunnel leading into the earth.

Strangest of all, a clutch of several hundred eggs could be seen, piled in a trench around the base of the pillar. They were bottle green and perfectly spherical, with the size and appearance of unripe oranges.

'Those must be gremlin eggs,' Fletcher said, recognising them from the Warren. 'Goblins' eggs would have to be much bigger, because Mason said goblins hatch from their eggs as fully formed adults.'

'I don't want to know what those are doing there,' Othello said. 'But I guess we'll find out in a minute – that tunnel's our hiding spot. It might even go to the caves.'

'Who knows where it leads,' Fletcher said, peering into the depths. 'I bet that's where Khan and his shamans are headed, down those steps. If it's a dead end it'll be us three trapped down there against . . . how many orcs?'

'Ten,' Sylva said, counting the shamans and adepts on Verity's tablet. 'Their demons have been infused though. We'd better

340

hurry – they're walking in through the back entrance right now.'

Fletcher wracked his brains. They could take one of the other three passages leading into the room, but there were no guarantees that the shamans wouldn't come that way. They couldn't go down . . . an idea formed in his mind.

'Lysander, can you fly us up to those beams?' Fletcher said to the Griffin, looking at the vaulted ceiling. 'They're broad enough to hide us.'

Lysander squawked in agreement, then gave Fletcher a wink, confirming that Captain Lovett was in control. He grinned back, her support steadying his resolve.

'Are you sure?' Othello said, staring up at the beams. 'They look rustier than a fisherman's bucket.'

'It's that or take our chances in the caves,' Fletcher said, putting Ignatius on his shoulder and then mounting Lysander. Othello and Sylva squeezed on behind, and Fletcher felt Sylva's hands slip round his waist. He, in turn, gripped Lysander around the neck. Without a saddle, Fletcher's seat was made up of the ever-shifting back muscles of the powerful beast, and the Griffin's feathers were slippery beneath his breeches.

Fletcher opened his mouth to give the order, but before he had a chance, Lysander launched them from the bridge with one powerful thrust of his wings. For a heart-stopping moment they dropped like a stone, then the bottom fell out of his stomach as they swooped upwards in an arc that hurled them into the rafters above.

Lysander skittered his talons along one of the broad beams in a screech of rusted metal until they came to a standstill. For a moment Fletcher took some deep breaths to calm himself, his face buried in Lysander's glossy neck feathers. Then he felt the others dismount and he followed their example, careful to plant himself in the very centre of the rafter.

From this view, he could make out the eggs at the base of the pit quite clearly, as well as the platform below. The largest pipe was just beside his head, and the sloshing of liquid could be heard from within. He shuddered and extinguished his wyrdlights, casting the room into pitch darkness. He was just in time, for he could already see the glow of light coming from the entrance they had used.

Then, clutching a crackling torch in his hands, Khan ducked into the room. Up close, his size was even more stark in contrast to the shamans that followed him. His brow-ridge was less defined, and his tusks were somewhat smaller than most orcs'. But that was not what made him stand out the most to Fletcher. It was the demon perched on his shoulder, peering around the room with amber eyes.

Khan had a Salamander with him.

# 41

The Salamander was black as pitch and twice as large as Ignatius. It even had stubs of wings on its back, where Ignatius's shoulder bones were. But despite these anomalies, it was indisputably a Salamander, from the spiked tip of its tail to the toothless beak on the end of its snout.

Ignatius seemed to think so too, for he chirred quietly as he watched the demon preen itself on Khan's shoulder. Fletcher quelled him with a thought and watched as the shaman retinue marched behind, following the albino orc over the bridge. One carried a sack of yellow petals from the antechamber.

None had their demons with them, nor did they have summoning leathers but, even from the rafters above, Fletcher could see that all of them had pentacles and other symbols tattooed on their hands, just as he did. Even the new adepts had them, though several held their hands gingerly, as if they had only recently been marked.

Up close, Fletcher could see that these adepts were smaller than the others, with underdeveloped tusks jutting from their lower lips. They wore little more than grass skirts, but their bodies had been dusted with white powder, perhaps to emulate the albino's skin.

A shout from Khan made Fletcher jump. He gave orders in guttural barks, pointing at the five corners of the pentacle. The shamans that had accompanied him took their places there, while the adepts kneeled behind, watching intently.

More orcish speech followed, and in unison the shamans began to etch complex symbols that intersected in the air above the star. It was mesmerising to watch. For some reason, Fletcher had always imagined orc shamans to be the most rudimentary of summoners, barely capable of controlling anything more than a low-level imp.

He had to remind himself that orcs had been summoning long before humans, and though he daren't suggest it to Sylva, possibly before the elves had too.

Khan bellowed another order when the etching stopped. A strange ring of double helix hung in the air above the pentacle, and the shamans' hands glowed blue as they pumped mana into the symbol. Soon, the ring became a disk of spinning blue light, moving faster than Fletcher could follow.

The orc shamans began to wail and chant, raising their voices against the roar of the spell. As their voices reached a crescendo, Khan knelt on the floor and pressed a small knob on the platform. It sank into the stone and a rumble echoed throughout the pyramid. The clank and screech of machinery echoed from the ceiling just above Fletcher's head. For a moment Khan stared up at the noise and Fletcher ducked behind the beam, his heart fluttering in his chest like a caged bird.

It was only when he heard the slosh of liquid in the pipe beside him that curiosity compelled him to peek again. What he saw was sickening.

Blood gushed from the pipe and into the hole at the centre of the pentacle, pulsing like a severed artery. As the fluid passed through the spell it frothed and sizzled, the consistency becoming viscous, the colour verging on black. Far below, the liquid clotted and congealed over the gremlin eggs, oozing out of holes at the base of the pillar and into the trench. Then, the eggs began to throb, palpitating in the water as they grew in size, spilling out of the trench and filling the pit right to the edges.

A whispered curse from the darkness beside him told him he was not the only one who had seen it. Soon the blood from the pipe had reduced to no more than a trickle. The spell flickered and faded, the shamans collapsing to the ground with exhaustion. Fletcher's palms prickled with sweat as he contemplated the gruesome ritual. The blood from the blue orcs had a purpose after all.

Khan grunted with approval, reaching into a pouch at his waist and slipping a hunk of meat into his Salamander's mouth. It gobbled it up greedily, gulping it down with two birdlike jerks of its head.

The albino orc snarled another order and the adepts scrambled to queue up behind him, stringing themselves out across the bridge. Each took a bunch of the yellow petals from the sack, and even Khan snatched a fistful. Together, they stuffed them into their mouths, chewing and swallowing with audible gulps. The younger orcs grimaced at the taste, one even dry heaving before forcing it down with a swig of water from a gourd at his hip.

Fletcher wondered whether it was some sort of drug or poison, to numb their bodies or dull their senses. They certainly seemed to sway on their feet, though whether it was out of fear or the effect of stimulants, he couldn't be sure.

After a moment's pause, Khan spoke again, his rough speech bringing the shamans to their knees. They bowed their heads in deference, avoiding Khan's eyes. Each dipped their fingers in the pentacle's blood, one hand in the key on their point of the star, another in the star itself.

'The orc keys!' Sylva whispered, just loud enough for Fletcher to hear.

Fletcher's heart leaped, and he had to cover his mouth to stop himself from gasping. The coordinates to the orcs' part of the ether were below – their best-kept secret revealed for all to see. He hadn't noticed until the carvings had filled with blood.

Fletcher waved his hand frantically at Lysander, until he caught the Griffin's attention. He motioned below, miming the symbols, and the Griffin leaned out from his perch, risking all to get the best view of the scene below.

Fletcher knew that all over Hominum, people would be carefully copying them down. Even if they failed in their mission, it would not have been in vain. They had achieved something that Hominum had long given up on.

With the coordinates to the orc's part of the ether, Hominum's summoners would be able access an entirely different ecosystem, with new demons to capture. It would change the war irrevocably in their favour, and it was Fletcher's team that had made it happen.

The symbols in question began to glow blue, as did the pentacle, the blood within them sizzling and popping as the mana flowed into it. It was not long before a glowing sphere expanded in the air, a spinning portal to the ether. The ball was enormous, far larger than any Fletcher had seen before. As he watched it rotate, a dull throb filled the room, ebbing and rising with every revolution of the orb.

Spitting yellow pulp from his mouth and holding his torch aloft, Khan strode forward, until he stood but an inch away from the portal. He scowled at the adepts, his red eyes flicking from one to the next. Then, without a moment's hesitation, he disappeared into the portal.

Fletcher heard Sylva gasp as, one by one, the adept orcs followed, vanishing into another plane of existence. The remaining shamans chanted in low voices as they pushed a constant stream of threaded blue light into the bloody channels of the pentacle.

In the darkness above, Fletcher watched incredulously as the minutes ticked by. They had been taught that the ether's air was poisonous, causing paralysis and often death. Summoners had to enter it dressed in an airtight suit – Captain Lovett's visor had barely cracked when she had gone in almost two years ago, yet the poison had left her paralysed.

The seconds ticked by excruciatingly slowly; the only change in the scene below was the thin sheen of sweat gradually forming on the shamans' backs. The team above were forced to hide in silence, barely allowing themselves to breathe.

Fletcher watched as Sylva stifled a sneeze, her eyes watering as she clamped her fingers down on her nostrils. His heart somersaulted as she swallowed it down, her shoulders heaving at the effort.

Almost a full half-hour had passed when the white orc stepped out of the portal, his black Salamander riding high on his shoulders. The adepts emerged but a moment later, many tumbling out as if in a great hurry. The white orc laughed aloud as they scrambled behind their shaman masters.

As soon as the last adept was free, the shamans allowed the portal to close, casting the room in darkness. The only source of light came from Khan's torch, which had survived the journey into the ether.

With one last barked order, Khan led the other orcs across the pentacle and through to the opposite passageway. Exhausted, the shamans stumbled after him, panting hoarsely with exertion.

Even when the room was pitch black, Fletcher and the others remained silent, for they could not be sure whether the orcs would return. It was only when a cheer from the crowd outside filtered through the stone that they knew it was safe to move.

'What the bloody hell was that?' Othello growled, shuffling over to Fletcher and Sylva. 'Orcs are immune to the ether's poison?'

'It looks like it,' Sylva whispered, tossing a wyrdlight into the empty space beneath them. 'But we have their keys now. It was our team that did it – a dwarf, an elf and a human.'

She beamed with pride, and to Fletcher it felt as if that smile lit up the room more than a wyrdlight ever could. Just for a moment, he allowed himself to bask in the joy of their achievement. The orc keys were guarded jealously, so much so that the objective of discovering them had not even formed a part of this mission. His team had exceeded expectations a thousandfold.

In the minutes that followed, Lysander flew them down one by one, until they stood on the platform for the first time.

'Get a good look at each key, Lysander,' Fletcher said, pointing at the blood-filled symbols on the floor.

He peered over the lip and dropped a wyrdlight to the bottom of the pit. The eggs were still there, each one now swollen to the size of a keg of beer. They throbbed and pulsed like living things, the gelatinous shells slippery with mucus.

Othello crouched and examined the pentacle. Within the carving, a crusty black residue remained, still steaming from the mana that had coursed through it. Wrinkling his nose, he pushed himself upright using a nearby protrusion in the rock.

There was a sloshing from above the pentacle and Othello looked up, only to receive a splatter of blood from the pipes.

'You've got to be kidding me,' Othello wailed, stepping aside and frantically wiping at his face with a sleeve.

'Organic material for pentacles,' Sylva said, crouching down and examining it as more blood trickled out of the pipes to pool within the lines of the pentacle. 'Just like our summoning leathers and Fletcher's palm. There must be a pipe coming from the bottom of the altar.'

'You don't say,' Othello said sarcastically, splashing his cheeks with water from his hip-flask. Fletcher couldn't help but chuckle at the miserable dwarf.

The room felt different now: they had discovered so much, yet it had left many unanswered questions.

'So what was that, some induction ceremony for orc novices?'

Sylva said, pacing around the pentacle. 'Their first taste of the ether, perhaps?'

'Probably,' Othello sighed. 'Well, now we know how the goblin eggs are made.'

'Yes, some horrific spell that makes the orc blood mix with the gremlin eggs,' Fletcher grunted.

He used his toe to test the first step into the pit, dizzied as he looked at the spiral around the platform's pillar.

'Speaking of which . . . let's go and have a look at what we're dealing with.'

The step felt firm enough, so he continued until his head was level with the platform.

'Shouldn't we be looking for the others before going down there?' Othello suggested, eyeing the stairway with trepidation.

'If there's an entrance to the goblin caves, this is it. The others'll be along soon enough, their sponsors will have seen that the coast is clear from Lysander's scrying crystal, and will guide them to us with their demons.'

Fletcher trudged on, running his fingers along the coarse stone as if it might give him some purchase against the long drop to the ground below. The walls seemed to press in, and he was reminded of the stairwell Didric had taken him up on their way to the courthouse. Dread pervaded his skin, prickling him with cold sweat. They were vulnerable on the stairs, with nowhere to hide if an enemy appeared below . . . or above.

Only the comfort of Ignatius's warm skin against the back of his neck strengthened his resolve, even as he descended deeper into the belly of the beast.

The trench around the bottom of the stairs was filled with

eggs, as well as a slick coating of the clotted blood. Fletcher had no choice but to wade through them, groaning with disgust. His breeches were coated with the stuff by the time he clambered out on to the soil of the other side.

Sylva and Othello had the good sense to leap from the stairs above, their feet barely splashing the bank of the moat-like trench. Lysander glided down without any trouble, and Fletcher realised he could easily have hitched a ride. This time it was Othello's turn to chuckle as Fletcher wiped away the foul jelly with the back of his sword.

'It looks like they add a few hundred new eggs to their reserve every time they have the ceremony,' Sylva said. 'I wonder why we're only encountering these goblins this year. They must have been secretly building an army.'

She removed her falx and speared the nearest egg through the middle. A gush of opaque fluid spilled from within, and the green ovum deflated to a withered sack. The stench was foul, like a putrid sewer.

'Thanks for that,' Othello said, giving the empty egg-sack a wide berth. 'Now we have to wait here with that stink in the air.'

Sylva rolled her eyes.

'Well how was I supposed to—'

A crossbow bolt thudded through Fletcher's shoulder. He stared at it, the blue fletching protruding from him like some strange new appendage. Another took him in the thigh, and he fell to one knee. There was no pain, only the dull numbness of shock as his arm hung uselessly by his side. The khopesh slipped from his fingers.

Sylva roared and fired a bolt of lightning at the platform

above, where the attack had come from. It shattered against the roof of the pyramid in a puff of dust and masonry.

Othello was already on Lysander's back, the Griffin powering them upwards with berserk thrusts from his wings. The echo of fading footsteps told Fletcher it was useless. The assassin was already gone.

'No, no no,' Sylva whispered, catching Fletcher in her arms as he fell back.

The pain came then. It felt as if he were being torn apart. The downward trajectory of the first bolt had taken it through his back and into his upper chest. It hurt to breathe.

'Take it out,' Fletcher croaked. He could taste metallic blood on his lips and knew he had been lung-shot. 'We need to heal . . .'

He gasped as Sylva snapped the steel tip from the shaft between her fingers and drew out the bolt in one fluid motion. Then he choked as his lung began to fill with blood.

The procedure was repeated on his thigh, with Sylva first pushing the shaft further through so she could grip the steel tip.

As Fletcher gurgled, Sylva etched the healing spell in the air, the white threads of light flickering around his wounds. Ignatius joined the effort, his tongue lapping at the wound as he desperately tried to staunch the flow of blood.

It was slow, too slow, and Fletcher's thigh was gushing crimson into the earth. His artery had been hit.

He watched it all in grim silence. He didn't want to die in this fetid pit, with the whole world watching. He would be a failure, and a symbol of the disunity of Hominum. A martyr to everything he hated.

Then he remembered. Electra's potions, strapped to his chest.

Unable to speak, Fletcher tugged one from its slot and popped the cork with a flick of his thumb. He gulped it down, the taste as metallic as the blood that stained his teeth. For a moment he felt nothing but the life draining from his body. Then . . .

'Woah,' Sylva gasped, her healing spell flickering out of existence.

Fletcher felt a cold sensation rush over him. The pain was gone, almost instantly. He looked at his leg to find no more than a patch of bloodstained skin through the tear in his breeches. His chest was much the same.

Ignatius bounded on to his shoulder, wrapping himself around Fletcher's neck. Beneath the Salamander's skin, he could hear the hammering of the terrified demon's heart.

'Easy there, buddy,' Fletcher murmured. 'I'm still here.'

'I thought I'd lost you,' Sylva whispered, pressing her forehead to his, gasping with emotion. For the briefest of moments, so quickly that Fletcher couldn't even be sure it had happened, he felt her soft lips brush his own.

Then Othello landed beside them with a thud, and they were wrapped in a bear hug.

'That was too close,' Othello sobbed, squeezing them so hard Fletcher thought his ribs might crack. 'Don't you *ever* do that to me again.'

# 42

They hunkered down in the lee of the pit's tunnel, out of the line of fire. Only Lysander remained, hiding among the beams once again in case the assassin returned.

'Either Isadora's team are here, or it's Cress,' Sylva argued, her arms crossed defiantly. 'Isn't it weird that she wasn't here both times you were shot?'

'No, I can't believe it,' Othello said, just as stubborn. 'She wouldn't do that to us. To Fletcher. Truth be told, I think she has a soft spot for him.'

Sylva reddened at his words, but set her jaw and stared Othello down.

'She could be a fanatic. Maybe she wants a war, and the not wearing a veil thing is just for cover. She could be just like Atilla was.' Sylva's eyes were wild as she spoke. 'I . . . *we* almost lost him!'

This was a different girl to the one he knew. She was still pressed close against him, and Fletcher couldn't help but wonder if something had changed between them, in that fleeting moment together.

She had even summoned Sariel, who was watching the dark tunnel intently. Sylva absently ran her hands through the Canid's fur, and the demon whined miserably.

'Lysander saw me get shot,' Fletcher whispered, his back propped up against the wall.

'If Cress wasn't in view of Caliban or Sacharissa when the attack happened . . . the whole of Hominum will think it was her,' he continued. 'The crossbow bolt has blue fletching.'

'It probably was her!' Sylva exclaimed, exasperated. 'How many times do I have to tell you? We can't trust her.'

'Don't you get it? I don't care if it was or wasn't,' Fletcher said in a low voice. 'All the goodwill we just earned by discovering the orc keys is gone.'

'Lysander barely saw it,' Othello said generously, 'he and I shot off so fast. Plus, from his angle, they wouldn't be able to see the colour of the fletching.'

'Maybe . . .' Fletcher muttered despondently. 'But a dwarf trying to assassinate a human would cause an uproar all over Hominum.'

'Not just a human, you're a noble now.' Othello sighed, then turned back to Sylva. 'Anyway, it's not as simple as that. Malik's team were on our side of the river the entire time too. He could be harbouring a grudge after you defeated him in the Tournament. Verity is in his team: she could be working for the Triumvirate – her grandmother's one of them after all.'

'You really think it could be Verity?' Fletcher asked, trying to picture those large eyes peeping out from behind a crossbow, levelled at him.

'Why not? Just because she's pretty?' Sylva glared at him.

'It could be Rory, or even Genevieve, still angry after you almost killed Malachi last year,' Othello continued. 'Don't forget Seraph's team were nearby too.'

Fletcher wondered how he had acquired so many enemies! It seemed like half of Vocans had a reason to kill him.

'If you're too blind to see it, I'm not going to argue with you,' Sylva snapped, shaking her head. 'I won't say anything when she shows up. But I'll be watching her.'

As an ill-tempered silence descended, there was a squawk from above. The team were instantly ready – Fletcher and Sylva with their bows drawn, Othello with a fire spell etched. They waited with bated breath, aiming at the platforms above.

Didric poked his head out.

'I told you it smelled like dung in here,' he said jovially. 'Look Tarquin, I found the source.'

Othello whispered out of the corner of his mouth, 'See?'

Sylva scowled but remained silent, her bow firmly centred on Didric's face.

Tarquin's head appeared, and he frowned at the sight of them.

'Well well,' he drawled, holding his hands up in mock surrender. 'You made it after all. I guess we only have ourselves to blame, after we saved you from that patrol.'

'*You* saved *us*?' Othello growled, incredulous. 'If we hadn't come back for you, you'd be a brown stain at the bottom of an orc latrine by now!'

'Oh pish posh, what utter drivel,' Isadora's voice echoed down. 'Grindle darling, be a dear and carry Atlas down for us.

He looks positively ghastly.'

A shadow passed over them, then Fletcher saw the Wendigo, Hannibal, lead the way down the stairs, his great gangly frame navigating the narrow steps with difficulty. Grindle appeared behind him, with Atlas slung over his shoulder. He grinned at the others, and was followed by a daintily skipping Isadora. Somehow, her black uniform appeared as clean as the day they had arrived in the jungles.

Fletcher and the others were forced to lower their weapons as the Wendigo made his way down, his black eyes fixing on them intently.

Tarquin and Didric were not far behind. When they reached the bottom, they followed Grindle in leaping over the moat as Othello and Sylva had done, while the Wendigo waded into the trench and lifted Isadora over the water. Fletcher rolled his eyes. A true gentleman . . .

'What happened to Atlas?' Fletcher said, eyeing the near-unconscious boy.

'He ate some berry or other that didn't agree with him yesterday, after we crossed the river,' Isadora said, examining her fingernails. 'The fat lump scoffed everything in sight. I doubt he's going to make it. Pointless bringing him with us – he's slowed us down the entire way. But Tarquin seemed to think it would look bad if we left him behind.'

Fletcher knelt beside the stricken boy. He had a bloodless pallor, and his breathing was shallow and erratic.

'How long have you been here?' Fletcher asked, tugging another health vial from the slot on his shoulder strap. 'We waited for you by the back entrance.'

'We just arrived,' Didric croaked in his burned-out voice, prodding an egg absently with his rapier. 'It took us forever, we had to carry this idiot most of the way. We were lucky most of the orcs are on the other side of the pyramid.'

'We waited for you, you know,' Othello growled. 'A thank you would be nice.'

'Nobody asked you to,' Tarquin said, shrugging.

Fletcher ignored them and considered the vial. He only had two left and the last one had saved his life. Could he really sacrifice it to save this treacherous boy's life? It was only a remonstrative look from Lysander that swung his decision. The world was watching.

He popped the cork and trickled some of the liquid into Atlas's mouth. The boy licked his dry lips and swallowed it down.

'You're wasting your time with him – we tried the healing spell. He's a goner for sure,' Grindle said. He turned to Sylva and winked. 'Nice to see the she-elf made it. Would be a shame to let an orc deny me the pleasure of killing her myself.'

Sylva's knuckles tightened on her falx, so firmly that it wavered in the air by her side. Despite this, she replied with a cool, level stare.

'Please, try. The pleasure would be all mine.'

As the last of the elixir drained from the vial, Atlas's colour began to return. He coughed and sat up, looking blearily around him.

'The healing spell did nothing,' Isadora said, incredulous. 'We wasted a huge amount of mana trying it.'

'Looks like the elixir's an anti-venom too,' Fletcher said,

checking his shoulder strap. He had only one red health vial left, but there were still three of the blue mana ones. They should come in useful when it came to destroying the eggs.

Atlas eyed Fletcher, a look of confusion on his face. He began to speak, then hesitated as Tarquin cleared his throat. Atlas turned at the noise, and after a brief pause, hoisted himself up and walked resignedly over to the others.

'You're welcome,' Fletcher said sarcastically.

Another squawk from Lysander echoed down, announcing the arrival of the others. Fletcher's eyes landed on Cress and he briefly considered whether Sylva's suspicions could be right. But one look at her smiling face convinced him that she was innocent. Fletcher shook the suspicion from his mind and looked down the dark passageway. Hot, fetid air seemed to waft in and out, like the breath of a slumbering giant. This was it. All that they had risked, everything that they had gone through, had led to this moment. They had reached the goblin caves with half an hour to spare, and the raid was about to begin.

# 43

The teams kneeled at the entry of the passageway, examining the crude map that Mason had mocked up of the cavern. Their demons crowded the tunnel ahead, watching for movement.

'I have no idea 'ow this tunnel links to the caves, but I'll know it pretty well when we get inside,' Mason said, using his sword to point at a large central chamber in the middle. 'This is the main cavern. I've only been in there once, but I know it's where they store the goblin eggs. It's a magma chamber, so it keeps 'em warm. From what I've seen, the oldest batch 'atches right around the time a new one is brought in, so we need to be careful.'

He looked warily over his shoulder down the tunnel, then down at the swollen eggs in the moat.

'Some goblins could be comin' to collect 'em at some point, so we'd better move soon.'

'What about the prisoners?' Cress asked, hunkering down beside him. 'Where are they kept?'

As she spoke, Sylva watched her face intently, her hand on the handle of her falx.

Mason pointed to a chamber connected to the main cavern by a long, thin tunnel, with another branching off it to the surface above.

'That's where they kept the prisoners sometimes. I dunno if my mates'll be in there at this time of day.'

'Is that where my mother is?' Rufus asked, his eyes wide.

'Yeah. She was kept in a cage. They never let 'er out, or let us speak to 'er,' Mason said, shaking his head. 'We weren't even able to speak to each other in there – there were goblins in the room all the bloody time, it's where most of 'em sleep, especially when there's a celebration time, like today. They'll have drunk themselves into a stupor by now, but we'll still 'ave an 'ell of a time gettin' 'er out without bein' spotted.'

Rufus drew his sword at these words and went to stand beside his demon, an otter-like Lutra, at the end of the tunnel. Fletcher knew how the boy felt. He would give anything for a chance to see his mother again.

Isadora clapped her hands together, making them all jump.

'Right, here's how it's going to play out,' she said, pointing down the tunnel. 'We take out the eggs in the main cavern quietly, until we're discovered and the alarm is raised. When that happens, it's about destroying as many as possible. Gunpowder, fireballs, lightning, it doesn't matter how loud it is, we need to take out their reserve eggs and get out safely. Anyone have a problem with that?'

Fletcher shook his head. Despite his misgivings, he couldn't ignore the sense of Isadora's orders. That was what he would have done. Isadora continued, unfazed by the silence from the others.

'As soon as they see us reach the eggs, the Celestial Corps will take off and make for our rendezvous at the back of the pyramid, giving us around twenty minutes to complete our objective. When they're almost here, our sponsor demons will let us know it's time to go. We'll have ten additional minutes to get back to the extraction point at the back of the pyramid from then on. Arrive later than that, you're on your own.'

'How are we supposed to get back if half of Orcdom is armed to the teeth in front of the pyramid?' Verity said, taking her tablet from Sylva and holding it up for the others to see. The image showed thousands of orcs milling around outside, with the various games still being played through sunset.

'It won't matter.' Mason peered at the tablet. 'They won't all come in 'ere. Only orc adepts can enter the pyramid, so we'll only 'ave goblins, shamans and their demons to deal with when we get back to this point. But I reckon we oughta move quick-like when the alarm sounds. The caves'll be flooded with orcs pretty sharpish.'

'Good,' Fletcher said, loosening his pistols in their holsters. 'Now, unless there are any more questions, let's get moving.'

'Aren't we feisty today?' Didric said, giving him a lopsided grin. 'You're forgetting there's a batch of eggs right here. Why don't you stay back and deal with them, while the big boys do the real work?'

Fletcher ignored him, but Didric's words gave him pause. He turned to Jeffrey, who was holding his short sword in front of him as if it were a dangerous snake.

'Jeffrey, you stay here and destroy these eggs,' Fletcher said, pointing at the sticky globes that crowded the area around them.

'Someone has to. I'd rather you stay in the pit and keep watch, out of the way. You can warn us if any shamans come back. Can you do that?'

Jeffrey nodded gratefully. 'Honestly, I would just slow you down. I'll examine these newly fertilised eggs more closely, see what I can find out.'

He sliced into the nearest egg with a wild swing. The foul stench in the air grew thicker, eliciting a collective groan from the others.

'Idiot,' Didric said. 'All right, let's get out of here.'

And just like that, the mission had begun.

The demons led the way, following a single wyrdlight that cast a dull glow around the cave. The walls and ceiling were made of a strange mix of soil, shale and roots that to Fletcher appeared as unstable as a three-legged chair. Every now and again dust would trickle down on to their heads, disturbed by the passing of so many.

'Here,' Fletcher said, handing a mana vial to Cress, Sylva and Othello, keeping the one remaining health vial for himself. After two assassination attempts, he wasn't going to take any chances.

As he handed it to Cress, Sylva pulled a face, still distrustful of the young dwarf. But at this point it mattered little to Fletcher. All he cared about now was protecting Hominum, and he couldn't afford to be distracted by anything else. Despite all of the lies and trickery, his enemies would not dare do anything in full view of the four demon sponsors, for all the world to see.

With all of their demons present, Fletcher felt a sudden confidence in their chances. They had at least a dozen demons in all, varying in size from Tarquin's Hydra, Trebius, to Rory's yellow-shelled Mite.

He was able to observe Verity's third demon, prowling just beneath her hovering Damsel. He eased his nerves by examining it.

It was an Enfield, a distant cousin to the Vulpid. It was smaller, only the size of a large dog, but with the head of a fox, forelegs of an eagle, the narrow chest of a greyhound and the hindquarters of a wolf. Its front talons were dangerously sharp, with tawny brown feathers interspersed among the red fur of its front and the grey of its back. An elegant demon on all accounts – just like its owner, Fletcher mused.

There was a light at the end of the tunnel, a dull red-orange glow that reminded Fletcher of the cave beneath the Warren. Mason, walking just behind the demons, held up a clenched fist. The summoners halted the advance, and Mason paced towards the light in a low crouch.

He stayed there for a moment, then returned, wild-eyed.

'We've 'it the motherlode,' he whispered. 'Bloody thousands of 'em, piled up willynilly.'

'Any goblins?' Tarquin asked.

'Not a one,' Mason replied with a grin. 'We'll 'ave a few minutes to ourselves before we're disturbed. Like shootin' fish in a barrel.'

'Let's get this over with,' Othello growled, hefting his battle-axe. 'The rescuers will have taken off by now. Twenty minutes – in and out.'

With those words, the four teams charged towards the light.

# 44

They ran into an enormous cavern, larger even than the Atrium at Vocans. A pool of lava sat in the very centre, bubbling and seething like a boiling cauldron. Four rivers of molten rock, offshoots from the fiery lake, seeped away and into the walls, splitting the room into four quarters of solid rock. Each quarter had its own tunnel to other chambers, and the patches of solid ground were all connected by precarious bridges made of misshapen stones, crudely held together by crumbling mortar.

And there were eggs. Not just hundreds, but thousands and thousands of them, some piled so high they almost reached the ceiling. Many were covered in dust and cobwebs, while those closer to them appeared fresher. The dried-out husks of those that had already hatched littered the floors. There were almost as many of them as there were eggs.

'There must be a legion of goblins hatched by now,' Fletcher murmured, prodding a nearby husk with his khopesh. 'We may already be too late.'

'Last time I was in 'ere was three years ago,' Mason said, his mouth flapping open like a fish on dry land. 'There weren't 'alf this many then.'

'No time to worry about that now,' Isadora said, burying her blade in an egg. 'Leave the big piles – we'll burn them last in case there's too much smoke.'

Already her Felid, Tamil, was slashing apart the nearest eggs, hissing as the alluvium within coated his claws. The other demons followed suit, except for the Mites, who were too small to do much damage. Instead, they hovered by the three other entrances to the cavern, to watch for patrolling goblins.

'Let's get cracking,' Fletcher said, raising his khopesh. In seconds the room was filled with the acrid smell of rotting meat, the stench so strong, Fletcher could taste it.

Then he felt a sudden sense of comfort and satisfaction that made him start. It took him a moment before realising it was coming from Ignatius.

The Salamander was swimming to the centre of the pool of lava, where the molten rock was white hot. The demon felt no pain, only a sense of yearning and purpose, and even . . . familiarity. Fletcher wondered if the place reminded the imp of his home in the ether, wherever that might be.

'What the hell is Ignatius doing?' Othello growled, kicking a pair of eggs into the lava. They sizzled and blackened, emitting a whiff of burning hair.

'I have no idea,' Fletcher said.

As the stubborn imp reached the core of the lake, Fletcher felt a sudden jolt of power. Something was changing.

The seconds ticked by and, despite the changes in his consciousness, Fletcher could do nothing but hack away at the eggs, keeping an eye on Ignatius as he swam circles around the heart of the lake. All the while, pulses of mana seeped from Ignatius's body for no apparent reason. It was like a leaking tap, and Fletcher wished he had kept back a vial of mana for himself.

He was sure it was something to do with the lava. He tried to call Ignatius back, but his demonic control didn't seem to work, almost as if the little Salamander wasn't even aware of him. Fletcher could do nothing but hope that when it was time to leave, Ignatius would heed his call. He concentrated on destroying the eggs, ignoring the jolts of power that flooded from his demon.

Even with nonstop work, no more than a few hundred eggs had been destroyed once five minutes had passed. Some of the eggs even had half-grown goblins within, which had to be quickly dispatched as the poor deformed creatures were brought into the light.

Fletcher took stock, and saw that the teams had barely cleared their quarter of land, and that didn't include the large central pile that was to be burned.

'What about the prisoners?' Rufus panted, looking at Malik beseechingly. 'My mother?'

'We'll get this done first,' Malik replied, grunting as he bisected an egg with a slash of his scimitar.

'Get on with it, Rufus. It'll take all of us to destroy these in time,' Didric snarled, shoving Rufus towards the nearest egg.

Rufus stumbled, then turned back, his shoulders stiff with anger. There was something in his eyes Fletcher hadn't seen before. The mousy-haired boy was shy and unassuming at the best of times, yet now he was filled with a steely resolve.

'I'm going to get my mother. I'll be damned if some pleb with ideas above his station thinks he can tell me otherwise.' Rufus spat at Didric's boots, and Fletcher couldn't help but grin as Didric's face fell at the insult.

Before anyone could stop him, Rufus sprinted over the nearest bridge, dodging through the eggs to the closest tunnel. Fletcher didn't hesitate. He charged after him, with Mason hard on his heels.

'Rufus, stop!' Mason said in a half-shout, half-hiss. 'You'll give us away!'

But Rufus was fast and had a head start. By the time Fletcher had crossed the bridge and reached the tunnel, the young noble had disappeared into the darkness.

'At least the bloody idiot's goin' the right way,' Mason groaned, catching up behind him. 'The other tunnels lead to the surface.'

'We'd better follow,' Fletcher said, listening for sounds of disturbance ahead. 'He can't do it alone.'

Mason hefted his sword, a large, cleaver-like weapon known as a falchion. It looked almost comical next to the boy's emaciated frame, which was already weighed down by a large crossbow. He was still skinny from his long incarceration, but he handled the sword well enough. After all, the boy had once been in the Forsyth Furies, a fearsome regiment by all accounts.

'Let's go then,' Mason said, leading the way.

Fletcher paused. He knew the pain of losing a parent, and his heart went out to the scrawny young noble.

But was this really what Hominum needed? There were thousands of eggs that were yet to be destroyed. How would rescuing a mad old noble change the fate of the war?

Still, he could not let Rufus run into danger blindly, not least because he might raise the alarm.

Torn, he left Athena to continue destroying the eggs. Pacing into the tunnel, he sheathed his khopesh and drew his bow, an arrow ready on the string in case of sudden attack.

'We come back in fifteen minutes,' Fletcher murmured to himself. 'With or without them.'

The tunnel sloped upwards, so much so that Fletcher began to breathe heavily from the climb. In the dim light, he could just make out Mason ahead of him. The boy was moving stealthily, keeping to the shadows and avoiding the stream of light from the exit at the end. This glow was of a different kind – natural. They had to be near the surface.

There was a final slope before the tunnel opened up, blocking their view of the cavern beyond. Mason crawled up to the edge and Fletcher followed his example, making sure to keep himself pressed firmly to the ground. His chest was soaked from the damp soil by the time he reached the top, but this small discomfort was swiftly forgotten as he took in the scene within.

'Bloody hell,' Fletcher breathed.

## 45

There were thousands of them, sprawled across the rocky ground like toys in a spoilt child's playroom. Goblins, sleeping in the warm shade of the cavern. Their numbers were so many that there was more grey skin than ground, their limbs splayed out on top of each other as if they had fallen dead where they stood.

Above, the light filtered through openings in great beams, cutting through the darkness like solid blocks of ice. It did not appear that there were any guards, which was just as well. Rufus was on the move.

'Bloody lunatic,' Mason muttered, watching as the young noble picked his way through the sleeping goblins. 'He's lucky they get blind drunk on fermented coconut during the festival.'

Fletcher followed Rufus's direction and found his target. It was a bamboo cage, abandoned against the wall of the chamber like an afterthought. Within, Fletcher could make out a bedraggled figure, hunched over in the corner.

Something else caught Fletcher's eye. There were a dozen young men dozing on the other side of the cavern, as well as a handful of gremlins. The boys wore no more than loincloths, as did the gremlins, and they were all tied together by cruel leather straps.

'Your friends?' Fletcher asked, nodding at the group.

Mason shuddered as he saw them, his face losing its colour.

'Three years I spent there,' he said, his voice quavering. His hands trembled as he unslung his crossbow and quiver, laying them on the ground.

'I'll get them,' he muttered. He stood up and swayed unsteadily, his breathing reduced to short sharp pants. The boy was having a panic attack.

'No, I'll go,' Fletcher said, removing his weapons belt. If Mason stumbled just once . . . they would all fall.

'I'll cover you,' Mason said, the relief clear on his face.

Fletcher tugged off his boots and socks, to better navigate the maze of tangled bodies ahead. He also left his bow, pistols, quiver and scabbard, taking only his sword to cut the prisoners free.

Rufus was making slow progress, his way blocked by a particularly thick patch of slumbering goblins. Fletcher watched as he was forced to turn back and take a more indirect path.

Hoping not to make the same mistake, Fletcher tried to work out the best route around the sleeping goblins.

Then he was walking among them, slotting his feet between the crooks of elbows and knees, holding his khopesh low and straight for balance. A goblin beneath him snorted in its sleep, so close that he felt the rush of air against his ankle. Fletcher froze, his heart in his mouth. For a moment the goblin's nose rested against his bare skin, wet and cold like a dead fish. He could feel the mucus bubbling on his shin with every breath.

After what felt like an eternity, the goblin swallowed and rolled over, its elbow briefly knocking his leg. The slumbering goblin barely noticed. In fact, it was now splayed over the body of another. Both remained dead to the world.

Emboldened, Fletcher increased his speed, skipping from bare rock to bare rock with careful but swift steps. He knew that it would take just one to open its eyes and see him – then all hell would break loose. He had to get through them quickly.

As Fletcher looked up to check his progress, he saw one of the boys was awake. He was skinny to the point of skeletal, with skin as dark as Electra's and a wild tangle of tight black curls on his scalp. He watched Fletcher make the last few leaps through half-closed eyes, too tired to react to the figure approaching him. Perhaps he thought Fletcher was a dream.

It was only when Fletcher cut through the straps holding him to the wall that he moved, staring up at Fletcher in awe.

'Wh-wh . . . ?' was all he managed. Fletcher silenced him with a finger to his lips, then moved on to the next prisoner. It was not long before they had all been freed, many of them scrambling away from him as if he was some kind of ghost. The gremlins barely moved. There was no life in their eyes, and many of them had crooked arms and legs, the result of broken bones, poorly set. Fletcher plucked one of them from the ground and pressed it into the tangle-haired boy's hands. He motioned at the others, until all the gremlins were safely ensconced in a slave boy's embrace.

A scraping sound came from across the room. Fletcher looked up to see Rufus sawing at the cage, his short sword making swift work of the ancient bamboo. There was no door on the structure. Disturbingly, the orcs had built it around the noblewoman, with no intention of ever letting her out.

Mason waved the boys over, and they began the dangerous journey to the tunnel entrance. Fletcher remained where he was, watching Rufus's progress. The young noble had managed to cut two bars from the cage, enough for his mother to crawl through. But she remained hunched in the corner.

Gritting his teeth with frustration, Fletcher picked his way across the cave. The light from outside was dimmer, tinged with orange from the sunset. Their time was measured in seconds now, and every second was another that could be spent destroying eggs. In his overlay, the image shifted as Ebony flew back and forth outside the pyramid, exacerbating his struggle to place his feet in the darkness. He winced with each step. It did not help that the mana pulses from Ignatius were becoming more frequent.

There was a moment of pure panic as a goblin stood by the entrance. It staggered into the light of the outside, clutching its belly and crooning. Fletcher stood frozen, still as a statue. He held his breath, gritting his teeth. Then, the goblin was gone.

Soaked in a cold sweat, Fletcher continued on, moving his feet as quickly as he dared. By the time he made it to the cage, Rufus had resorted to frantic whispering, his arm outstretched to the huddled figure within.

'Mother – Mother, it's me. Take my hand. Take it, damn you!'

He was sobbing, tears streaking his grimy face. His shoulders shuddered violently with each breath and his hands trembled as they grasped for her.

But the woman refused to move. She simply stared through him with vacant eyes. Blue had not been lying when he'd said her mind was gone.

'I'll get her, Rufus. You go on back. You're no good to her like this.' Fletcher laid a calming hand on Rufus's shoulder.

The young noble gulped and stood aside, but shook his head when Fletcher pushed him gently back towards the tunnel.

There was no time to argue, so Fletcher squeezed himself into the cage, the sharp ends of the broken bamboo scraping harshly across his abdomen as he wriggled through the hole. Inside, it appeared even smaller.

It was half the size of his old cell – he would only be able to lie down diagonally with his head touching one corner and his feet touching the other.

The woman remained unmoved, even when he crawled towards her. There were old signs of her former comprehension. Notches made on the post above her, more than a dozen. A rough comb made from a tortoise-shell, clutched in her hands. Even her threadbare clothing had been neatly stitched and patched – a whittled bone, sinews and dried animal skin acting as needle, thread and cloth, piled in the opposite corner.

The encrusted blood staining her mouth and the boards beneath him confirmed what the piles of bones and offal suggested. They had never bothered to cook her food, or even clean out her surroundings. He covered his nose with his sleeve at the smell, stronger somehow within the confines of the cage. The stench was like that of a rotten goblin egg, and his stomach lurched with both pity and revulsion.

The lady wore a uniform Fletcher could not recognise, though little remained of the original fabric. It might have been white once, but now it was a sullied yellow. Her hair and face were filthy beyond recognition. Only the eyes stood out from the dirt, the whites clear, the irises a pale blue. They suddenly flicked to his face.

Fletcher started and stifled a gasp. She stared at him, then held out a hand, palm up like a beggar asking for alms. He took it gently, for the wrist was so skinny he felt like he might break it with the slightest pressure. She struggled to her feet, forced to stoop beneath the roof of the cage. Fletcher saw her knees give way just in time, and he caught her as she fell. It was like holding a bundle of bones, her body insubstantial and weightless.

'Give her to me,' Rufus said. His voice was too loud, but it was clear he was beyond the point of caring. Fletcher passed the woman through the hole, her head lolling against his shoulder. She was so emaciated that he could lift her like a rag doll.

Rufus snatched her from his arms and left without a word. He rushed through the slumbering bodies without looking down, taking great strides and leaps in his haste, his mother clasped to his chest like a long-limbed baby. It was a miracle no goblins were woken in his mad rush to the tunnel.

Ahead of him, the slaves had gone, sent on earlier to the main cavern. Only Mason remained, scanning the room for signs of movement. Rufus barely gave the boy a glance as he stumbled past with his burden.

As soon as the two were clear, Fletcher followed in Rufus's footsteps, carefully darting between the goblins, his heart hammering in his chest with every pace. Still the goblins slept on, dead to the world in their drunken stupor.

It was when he was halfway across that he saw it. Mason. Taking careful aim with his crossbow, the point firmly centred at Fletcher's head.

Fletcher stopped, dead in his tracks. He whipped up his hand to make a shield, but nothing came out. His blood chilled as realisation dawned on him – there was no mana left. Ignatius had taken it all.

Mason squinted down the stock of the crossbow, his tongue poking out between his lips. Fletcher could do nothing but stand there, waiting for the end. He would not jeopardise the mission by leaping aside, even if it meant his own death. How stupid he had been, to trust the boy. Once a Forsyth Fury, always a Forsyth Fury.

The dull thrum of the release hit his ears as the bolt whipped by him. Behind him, a thud and a squeal.

Fletcher turned in time to see a goblin collapse to the ground, the quarrel skewered through its neck. It spasmed and flapped at its throat, but the only sounds it made were quiet gurgles.

'Get on with it,' Mason hissed, waving him on. 'Before another one wakes up!'

# 46

They reached the main cavern to the sounds of arguing. To Fletcher's shock, Didric was standing over the tangle-haired slave, the tip of his blade drawing blood as it pressed against the boy's heaving chest, the injured gremlin still clutched in his arms. The other teams stopped their destruction of the eggs to watch. Only half the room had been cleared.

'There's no room for you,' Didric snarled.

His spider-like Arach scuttled between his legs, its cluster of eyes turning to Fletcher as he ran to the scene.

The Arach had bound the boy's ankles with glowing gossamer, the white threads unspooling from a hole beneath its fearsome stinger. Fletcher wasted no time in slicing through them with his khopesh.

'What are you doing?' Fletcher demanded of Didric, pulling the slave upright. 'They're on our side!'

The gremlin in the slave's arms chittered nervously, and the boy jiggled it as if he were silencing a baby.

'You've done it now, Fletcher, you complete idiot,' Didric

exclaimed, shaking his head in disbelief. 'There are a dozen slaves here. How do you expect the Celestial Corps to fly all of us out now?'

Fletcher's heart sank as understanding dawned on him. Didric could be right. The rescue party would be well on its way by now, and there would be no time for reinforcements.

Didric shoved the slave to the opposite tunnel, where Rufus was still cradling his mother. The others followed, cringing away as Didric aimed a kick at them.

'There will be enough demons to carry them,' Fletcher said, more hopeful than certain.

'There will be three to a demon, if you're wrong,' Didric growled. 'How are they supposed to outrun the Wyverns with all that weight on their backs? I can tell you now, I won't be taking one of them on *my* ride.'

'We'll deal with that later, Didric,' Malik ordered from across the room. 'They land in five minutes. Get back to work.'

'I'll get back to work when I'm good and—' Didric began, but stopped as his eye caught sight of something near to the entrance.

Fletcher turned to see a grey torso squirming out of an egg, clawing apart the translucent sack that coated it. Beside it, another egg fell on its side, then a grey fist punched through its outer layer and scrabbled at the ground.

The new-born goblin's eyes turned to them, pale globes that swivelled back and forth. It opened its mouth and gave an ear-splitting shriek, the cry echoing around the cave and down the tunnel. Cress put an arrow through its skull.

More eggs began to shake and split, hundreds of them,

scattered around the ground they stood on. An answering call came echoing down the tunnel – a tumult of screeches that set Fletcher's teeth on edge. The slumbering goblins had woken.

'Burn them. Burn them all!' Othello bellowed. He unleashed a whirlwind of flame that billowed through the nearest pile of eggs. It tore through them like rice paper, shrivelling and charring them until they were no more than withered black sacks. The rest of the team followed suit. Lightning bolts crackled throughout the cavern, eggs exploding left and right, splattering the air with their mangled contents.

'Sylva, your vial – I'm out of mana!' Fletcher yelled, as the first goblin charged out of the tunnel, brandishing a war club. Sylva hurled the vial from across the room and Fletcher caught it by the tips of his fingers. In the same moment, he parried the goblin's flailing club.

Athena swooped in and buried her claws in the goblin's head. It spun away, squealing, giving Fletcher time to gulp down the bottle. It tasted sickly sweet, like honeyed lavender water.

The mana spilled from his core like a tide of white light, roiling through his veins and down his connection to Athena and Ignatius. Supercharged, Fletcher blasted a ball of fire through the goblin's chest.

Almost immediately, the pulses of mana began to drain from Ignatius, but Fletcher had had enough of the disobedient Salamander.

'That's it! You're getting out of there.' He whipped a kinetic lasso into the lake and tugged the demon out, sending him tumbling through the air to land steaming at his feet.

Ignatius shook his head, as if to dislodge an unwanted

thought. The demon seemed larger somehow, but there was no time for a thorough examination. More goblins erupted from the tunnel, screeching their war cries, and the bass roar of orcs echoed behind them.

'Back to the pyramid,' Fletcher ordered, sending a crackle of lightning through the frontrunners. As he turned, a new-born goblin gripped his ankle, tripping him to the floor. Ignatius slashed its face to the bone with a swipe of his claws and it spun away, squealing.

Then they were up and running. As he neared the entrance, Fletcher saw the others were well ahead, with Othello and Sylva acting as rearguard.

A kinetic ball blurred over his shoulder, the yelp of the downed goblin behind dangerously close. Othello arced another over Fletcher's head, the explosive force showering him with soil and screams. He glanced back to see the first wave of goblins in disarray, many of them screeching in agony as they burned in the lava they had been blasted into.

'Come on,' Sylva yelled as Fletcher sprinted by.

The three barrelled headlong down the tunnel, with Ignatius and Athena scampering behind. Ahead, Sariel and Solomon waited at the base of the pillar. The others were well on their way up the stairs, Jeffrey included.

'Up, up!' Fletcher yelled, and they sprinted up the steps. It would not take long for the goblins to regroup.

Solomon went first, for he was the slowest, his stumpy legs struggling to mount the steep steps. Fletcher and Sylva protected the rear, while Othello removed the blunderbuss from his holster and aimed it at the tunnel entrance.

'What do you see, Fletcher?' Sylva asked breathlessly, as they backed up the stairs. 'Are we gonna have a welcoming committee at the top?'

Fletcher allowed his sight to align with the scrying crystal over his eye, still showing Ebony's point of view.

'The orcs aren't entering the pyramid, and the shamans are too far away,' Fletcher answered with relief. 'Looks like Mason was right.'

'Well, the goblins will have no such qualms,' Sylva said, as the yowls of hatred echoed down the tunnel. 'Watch out, here they come.'

The goblins stampeded out of the tunnel, brandishing javelins, spears and clubs. The first projectile whistled between Fletcher's legs and he scrabbled to throw up a shield spell. It was just in time, for a dozen others clattered against it not a moment later.

The first handful of goblins mounted the steps, tripping over themselves in their bloodlust. There was a snarling veteran leading the charge, its shoulder scarred from an old bullet-wound. Ignatius took it down with a well-placed fireball, sending it tumbling into those behind in a tangle of limbs.

Forced to hold the shield in place with his left wrist, Fletcher fenced one-handed with his khopesh. Sylva backed him up with great sweeps of her falx, rending the goblins apart to send them tumbling back into the pit below.

'Firing,' Othello bellowed, and Fletcher ducked instinctively.

There was a thunderclap, followed by a gout of sulphurous smoke. The spray of buckshot scattered into the horde below, a furrow of dead hurled to the ground as if a giant invisible fist had slammed through them.

'Loading,' Othello yelled, as the ranks closed and more goblins lunged from the tunnel to take their places.

A blue crossbow bolt whipped into the goblins still on the stairwell, taking one through the shoulder. It plummeted down, wailing and flailing until it hit the baying masses below with a sickening thud. A second quarrel followed in its wake, plucking another goblin from its perch.

'You're almost there,' Cress called from above. 'I've got you covered.'

Fletcher took the brief respite to look up at their progress. Othello was frantically reloading his gun, his hands shaking as he poured the gunpowder down the barrel. Cress kneeled on the bridge just above them, firing her bolts with deadly accuracy. Lysander remained beside her, unable to join the fight. He was too large to avoid the javelins that still peppered them from below.

'Watch out,' Sylva yelled.

Fletcher turned just in time, sucking in his stomach to avoid a spear thrust that would have gutted him. He slammed it down with the flat of his blade and lashed out with his sword's hilt. It caught the offending goblin squarely in the face, and the creature spun to teeter on the edge of the stairs. Athena swooped by with a screech of fury, tugging it into empty space.

A flare of pain across Fletcher's abdomen told him the spear had left its mark. Emboldened, the goblins charged around the pillar once more, swinging their clubs over their heads.

'Firing,' Othello bellowed again. This time, he shot directly down the staircase, the acrid smoke billowing between Sylva and

Fletcher's faces. The devastation was concentrated into an expanding cone of shrapnel, leaving a charnel house in its wake. The blood-soaked remains sickened even Fletcher, and sent the survivors screaming back down the stairwell, fighting to get past the more eager goblins behind them.

In the lull that followed, the team staggered up the final steps and on to the platform, while Cress kept the immediate stairway clear with her crossbow.

'Screw this,' she said suddenly, slinging her weapon. She popped the cork of her mana vial and gulped it down. Shuddering as the mana flooded her body, she pointed her battle-gauntlet at the stairway. A wave of flame erupted out, spiralling down the stairs and sweeping them clear of the goblins arrayed along it. It was brutal to watch, like a tidal wave flushing the rats from a piece of flotsam. The inferno pooled at the bottom of the pit, seething and roiling like liquid fire. Those that did not throw themselves back down the tunnel were incinerated, their squeals of pain harsh in Fletcher's ears.

Silence descended, broken only by the sizzle of the cooking corpses below.

'I'm out of mana,' Cress said, peering down and wincing at the sight. 'But they don't know that.'

'Me too,' Sylva said, scraping the blood from her falx against the edge of the platform. 'Used it all up burning those eggs.'

Fletcher's reserves were low, but he reabsorbed the shield back through his fingers to replenish them. Just enough for a few more spells.

'I've saved my vial,' Othello said, frantically reloading his blunderbuss. 'And I've still got some mana left over. Solomon's mana levels increased with his size.'

The Golem rumbled at hearing his name, his face splitting into a craggy smile.

Then, as the first goblins began to venture into the pit once more, a howl echoed around the room. It came from the passageway on the other side of the platform. Fletcher looked in his scrying crystal, to see Ebony was hovering above the pyramid. Below her, dozens of creatures streamed by the waiting orcs and into the front entrance.

'Demons,' Fletcher breathed, his eyes widening with horror.

# 47

They backed down the passageway as the roars of the demons grew louder and louder.

'The rescue party are here,' Fletcher said, looking in his crystal. 'They're waiting for us by the back entrance.'

He could see scores of orcs attacking the waiting Celestial Corps, though many of them lay dead in the land between the river and the pyramid. Arcturus and a few other riders were the only ones still fighting, with most of the rescuers already disappearing on the horizon with the other teams. Fletcher could see puffs of smoke and fireballs streaking across the overlay as they battled to hold their position. Even as he watched, Ebony turned away, following her mistress back to civilisation.

The team were halfway down the passage now, and the antechamber with the hieroglyphs lay directly ahead of them. The wail of goblins joined the uproar, and as Fletcher glanced back, he saw the first of them following down the tunnel.

He fired a ball of flame, illuminating the long dark passage. It took the nearest goblin in the chest, blasting it head over heels.

Those behind simply trampled it into the ground, screeching their battle-cries.

The team ran on, with Lysander barrelling into the room ahead as Solomon's slow pace held them up. Moments later, they burst into the antechamber.

A flickering torch on the far wall was the only source of light, lit by Khan and his orcs on their way in. Rufus lay in the corner, clutching at his stomach, blood slowly spreading in a pool around his body. His Lutra lay beside him, its head half severed. Jeffrey was cradling the boy in his arms, while Lady Cavendish sat hunched in the corner, rocking back and forth.

'Help me,' Jeffrey begged, holding up his hands. They were bloodied to the elbow, where he had attempted to staunch the wound.

'It's too late,' Othello said, kneeling beside the stricken boy. 'There's nothing we can do for him.'

Lysander groaned, then collapsed to the ground.

'What the hell?' Cress cried, rushing to the demon's side. There were no wounds, yet he was completely unconscious, his beak gaping open like a chicken with its neck wrung.

'Solomon, pick him up,' Othello ordered, pointing at the inert demon. 'I'll get Lady Cavendish.'

'Heads up, we have company,' Sylva yelled, shooting an arrow down the passageway. The thunder of footsteps approached and the first goblins came barrelling out of the gloom.

'Take Bess,' Othello yelled, throwing the blunderbuss across the room.

Fletcher caught it and fired from the hip, the force of the blast staggering him as half a pound of shrapnel ricocheted down the corridor. The slaughter was instantaneous, cutting the goblins down like wheat before a reaper. Those that avoided the initial salvo scrabbled to return the way they had come.

But the goblins were not alone. Two Nanaues were racing past them, leaping from floor to wall to ceiling, their claws digging into the stone as easily as tree bark.

Fletcher resisted the mad urge to hit them with the last of his mana, knowing that spells were ineffective against demons. Instead, he drew his pistol, Blaze, the long single barrel trembling as he squinted down the sight. Even as he aimed at one, an arrow from Sylva pierced its shoulder, knocking it to the ground.

Fletcher switched targets and fired, seeing the musket ball hit the other Nanaue in the chest before the pall of smoke obscured his view. The creature skidded and tumbled along the ground in its momentum, knocking Fletcher's shins with its body. Its wet black eyes gave him a thousand-yard stare of death, but there was no time to be sure.

The injured Nanaue behind tore the arrow from its shoulder, the great gaping mouth flapping open as it roared and continued its charge. Twenty feet. Ten feet.

Fletcher drew Gale, and fired both barrels in quick succession. The first musket ball took it through its knee and the Nanaue continued in a lopsided stampede. The second missed completely, no more than a puff of dust and broken masonry from the ceiling above.

Then Fletcher was knocked to the ground, the pistols clattering from his hands. He scrambled, punching left and right, hitting nothing but air. Sitting up, he saw Sylva wrestling with the demon, its rows of teeth buried across her chest. She screamed with pain, even as Solomon battered at the demon with his stony fists.

Fletcher looked around desperately for a weapon, only to find Cress lying on the ground beside him, her eyes staring blankly. Tosk lay beside her, his twitching tail the only sign of life.

Then Sariel was on the scene, clamping her claws on either side of the Nanaue's maw and levering them open. Sylva wriggled free and Sariel hurled the creature back down the corridor, before following it into the darkness with a snarl of hatred.

As the two demons tore at each other in the passageway, Othello staggered beside Sylva, pulsing healing energy over her. The row of bloody bite wounds closed slowly, and Fletcher added his own healing spell, giving it all he had as Sylva gasped in pain.

'She pushed you out of the way,' Othello said in a tight voice.

The wounds were only half healed, but the dwarf's healing spell flickered and died. His brow creased with confusion.

'Something's wrong,' he muttered, his head lolling drunkenly against his chest. His eyes rolled back into his head and he slumped over.

'Solomon, I need you,' Fletcher cried, dragging Sylva upright. 'Get them out of here.'

The Golem wailed at the clumsiness of his rough hands, as he struggled to pick Cress up from the ground. Ignatius and Athena were dragging Othello by the arms.

'Jeffrey, move!' Fletcher yelled, but all the alchemist could do was cower in the corner with Lady Cavendish.

Sylva pointed down the corridor with a gasp. Behind Sariel,

scores of demons were bearing down upon them, their shadowed forms illuminated by the fire elemental in their midst – an Ifrit, a humanoid fire-demon that burned with roaring flames.

Sariel looked into their eyes. Her opponent was dead, though the brave Canid had paid dearly for it. There was blood dripping from a horrific wound in her hind leg, torn to the bone. She inclined her head and gave a gruff woof, her soft eyes wet with tears. Ignatius lapped at her wounds, but the Canid gently pushed the Salamander aside.

'No, Sariel,' Sylva sobbed, sensing her demon's intent.

The Canid turned and limped into the darkness, howling a challenge to the approaching demons. She was buying them time.

Fletcher raised his hand as Sariel slammed into the ranks of the demons, slashing left and right with her claws. As the Ifrit took Sariel by the throat and hurled her aside, Fletcher roared, unleashing a huge kinetic blast into the ceiling of the corridor. Dust billowed out and the stone imploded, scattering razor shards. An avalanche of rubble followed, burying the corridor and its inhabitants with a rumbling crash.

Then he sensed it. Ignatius and Athena, filled with fear. He turned to see their bodies spread-eagled on the floor, unable to move. A dart was buried in each of their backs, injecting paralytics through their veins. Sylva yelped as she was struck, her head flopping as the poison took hold.

As Fletcher searched wildly for the perpetrator, a sharp stab of pain emanated from his shoulder, and he tugged out another dart. Instantly, he felt the cold spread of paralysis disseminate through his body, leaving his arm hanging uselessly by his side.

He had just enough time to snatch the red vial from his belt before his other arm numbed, but he did not have time to bring it to Sylva's lips. The crash of Solomon's body as it hit the floor told Fletcher the Golem had fallen too. He lay there, his eyes flicking around the room for their hidden enemy. He did not have to wait long.

'I can't even begin to tell you how long I've been waiting for this,' Jeffrey chuckled, walking out of the shadows. He checked that Lysander's eyes were closed, then squatted beside Fletcher and twiddled a blowpipe in front of his face.

'Very useful, these poisons,' he said. 'From the curare plant, if you didn't know. Got the blowpipe and darts from Blue, bless his heart. Far too trusting, the both of you.'

'Why?' Fletcher managed to gasp. It was becoming hard to breathe, the poison spreading across his chest.

'I'm a patriot, Fletcher,' Jeffrey said, 'pure and simple. I love my country and my race – more than life itself. But look at what is happening to Hominum. Dwarves and elves mixing with humans, tainting our bloodline with half-breeds. The king elevating them to our equals, allowing them to join our exalted military. It makes me sick to my stomach.'

He spat at Othello's frozen body, the mask of the scared servant boy gone. The face of a mad fanatic was all that remained.

'As soon as you befriended that dwarf, I knew you were trouble. Such a shame, we did hit it off so well. Didn't you ever wonder why I was avoiding you? Or did you forget me so quickly?'

In truth, Fletcher had barely given Jeffrey a moment's thought since that first week at Vocans, what with everything else that had been going on. He had barely seen the boy for the rest of the year.

He glanced at Sylva and was relieved to see her wounds were almost gone. She would live, for now. Jeffrey gripped his face, turning it back to him.

'I have to say, it hasn't been easy. Joining the Anvils, rubbing shoulders with dwarf-lovers, gaining their trust, drinking their disgusting beer. I wouldn't have managed it without the Forsyths – it was their idea after all. We've been working together for years, ever since I told them what I'd overheard about the dwarven war council. Didn't you ever wonder how they knew where and when it would take place?'

Fletcher concentrated on breathing, his tongue too numb to reply. He attempted a spell, but his mana would not respond. The poison did more than affect the muscles. Only his feet and sword-hand seemed to have any semblance of control – he was still able to feel the smoothness of the vial against his fingers. It gave him an idea … He just had to be patient.

'I do like framing the dwarves,' Jeffrey said, smiling at the memory. 'It's so easy, everyone hates them already. People just need an excuse, which I was happy to provide. You'd be shocked at how easy it is to make a bomb, and nobody suspects a barrel left on the side of the road. Kidnapping the Anvil leadership was easy too, with some help from the Inquisition, of course. They even planted the bomb at that dwarf boy's trial – King Alfric and the Triumvirate see eye to eye when it comes to the lesser races.'

It had been Jeffrey who had suggested they go to the front lines, even the gambling tent itself. It had been Jeffrey who had pushed for Electra to bribe his way into the team. Jeffrey who had hung back during the ambush, waiting for an opportunity to strike. How had he not seen it?

Then Jeffrey's face fell, and he turned on Fletcher with a curled lip.

'You did almost ruin it though, running back into the tent after I set the fuse, even with me spilling my guts outside. You weren't meant to die yet, my little sacrificial lamb. Not before the whole world saw your corpse with Cress's crossbow bolt in its belly. Or Sylva's arrow. Maybe even Atilla's tomahawk in Seraph's back, if you had turned down Electra's offer.'

He laughed aloud as Fletcher choked and spluttered with anger.

'I was so sure I got you that second time. If only Electra hadn't given you those vials. Such a gullible woman. Still, I'll settle for this: the three-race team, dying pitifully at the last hurdle. Shows the world that we should each keep to our own.'

Fletcher attempted to spit at Jeffrey, but he only managed a weak dribble down the side of his mouth. Jeffrey dabbed at it with his sleeve, cooing at Fletcher sarcastically, as if he was a baby.

'You were so concerned for poor, sickly Jeffrey. It's not hard to shoot a crossbow, Fletcher, or conceal one in a satchel,' he continued. 'I can't believe you thought it was Isadora's team. They would never take such a risk, with so many watching. No, I shouldered that responsibility.'

The alchemist glanced at Rufus's dead body and shook his head sadly.

'It's a shame I had to kill the boy, but I needed *something* to distract you. There's an older brother to carry on his line, so no harm done.'

As Jeffrey turned, Fletcher opened the vial with his thumb, wincing as the cork rolled along the ground. Jeffrey didn't seem to notice.

'I really should be going,' Jeffrey said, looking over his shoulder as the *pop pop* of gunfire from the back passage intensified. 'They won't wait for much longer.'

His face dropped with mock fear, and he hunched his shoulders.

'It was a terrible accident, Arcturus!' he cried mockingly. 'There was a cave-in! They're all dead – we need to get out of here!'

He laughed again and slapped Fletcher across the face, just because he could.

'I'll let the orcs finish what I started.'

Jeffrey turned and began to jog to the exit. It was now or never. With a colossal effort, Fletcher raised the vial and spilled it across his lips. A thin trickle made it into his mouth, and he gulped it down as fast as he could.

It was not enough. The paralysis dulled somewhat, but he could barely twitch the fingers of his tattooed hand. He lapped desperately at the spillage on his face, spooning it with his tongue.

The paralysis faded with every second, until he could flex the fingers again. Gritting his teeth, Fletcher growled and lifted his hand, pointing it at the boy's retreating back. He didn't hesitate. Jeffrey deserved a traitor's death.

A lightning bolt speared Jeffrey's spine, hurling him down the corridor to slam into the wall. The boy lay broken on the ground, his eyes staring blankly, mouth gaping in a macabre parody of shock. Death did not become him.

Fletcher forced himself to sit upright, looking at the frozen bodies of those around him. They were so close. Arcturus and his team were just out of sight, around the bend of the corridor.

He staggered to his knees and began to crawl. The seconds ticked by as he dragged himself towards the room's exit, his legs still incapable of carrying his weight. But it was slow. Too slow.

He snarled through his teeth and managed to stagger a few steps, before collapsing to the ground once more. The corridor was just ahead . . . if he could just reach the back entrance, Arcturus would help carry the others out.

But then the howls began again. The demons had found another way through the pyramid. Even as he watched, the first rounded the corner. It was an Oni, its red skin gleaming in the flickering recesses of the torchlight. It grasped Jeffrey's head as easily as a grapefruit, lifting his body like a carcass hung out to dry.

Another demon skidded in behind it, a leopard-spotted Felid. There was no way Fletcher could fight his way past them. He had one choice open to him.

Gathering the last of his mana, Fletcher cradled a ball of seething kinetic energy, hiding it behind his back. He waited as more demons spilled out into the corridor. They took their time, knowing he was trapped. Still they hesitated, remembering their buried comrades in the other tunnel.

'Come on!' Fletcher yelled, beckoning them closer.

A Kamaitachi hissed and clattered towards him – a fanged,

weasel-like demon with serrated bone-blades replacing its paws. Two piebald Canids jostled to be first into the antechamber, snapping and snarling at each other. Sweat stung Fletcher's eyes. Not yet. Not just yet.

Then he saw it. The glow of the Ifrit, pushing its way through the jockeying creatures. In the new light of its fiery flesh, Fletcher could see dozens of demons following, from common Mites to tentacled monstrosities. It was time.

He hurled the spell into the corridor's ceiling, blasting the stone with every last trace of mana he had. The explosion threw him back, catapulting him head over heels. Stars burst across his vision as he cracked his head against the paving.

He lay there, choking as the dust-laden air filled his lungs. In the dim light, he saw the corridor was gone, replaced by a mass of broken rubble and masonry. The screams of buried demons echoed through the antechamber, and Fletcher smiled grimly. He'd taken most of them with him.

As he listened to the fading cries, he realised the gunfire outside had stopped. He checked his scrying crystal and saw it was blank – Verity had severed the connection.

His grim acceptance of their abandonment turned to despair as the torch spluttered in the dust from the explosion, then died. They were cast in total darkness.

Trapped.

# 48

Fletcher lay in the blackness, the back of his head sticky with blood. It was over. Already he could hear the goblins in the corridors, digging at the rubble and screeching at each other. They could break through in a few minutes, or a few days.

He wondered absently if dying of thirst was a better alternative to capture. Not that he had any choice in the matter. He closed his eyes and waited for the end.

Hours passed.

Othello was the first to move, forcing a tiny wyrdlight from his frozen fingertips. It moved determinedly around the room, flitting to each of them as the dwarf checked they were all in one piece.

A groan from Cress announced her own tentative recovery. She tried to speak, but all that came out was a numb-tongued garble. Silence resumed, as the team waited patiently for the paralysis to wear off.

Time went by and, slowly but surely, the others gradually

regained their faculties. Othello was the first to speak, his words slow and deliberate.

'Well done,' he said. 'Under the circumstances things could be a lot worse.'

'A lot worse?' Cress grumbled, slurring her words, but quickly warming to her theme. 'We're buried alive, surrounded by what looks like the entire orc and goblin army, a hundred miles deep in enemy territory and all of Hominum probably thinks we're dead. We have about as much chance of getting out of this as a one-legged man in an ass-kicking contest.'

Fletcher couldn't help but snort with laughter. Then he heard a sob from Sylva.

'Hey . . . are you OK?' Fletcher asked, crawling over to her.

He shone wyrdlight from his finger, and saw her half-healed shoulder and upper chest still bore the marks from the Nanaue bite, a jagged half circle of scars. He lay his hand on her arm, but she jerked away.

'Don't touch me,' she hissed.

'Sylva . . . I'm sorry about Sariel,' Fletcher murmured.

'You killed her,' Sylva whispered, her blue eyes filled with tears. 'I saved you and then you killed her. I felt the rocks come down, her spine snap. It took hours for her to die – did you know that, Fletcher? Body broken, barely any air to breath. Alone, in the dark.'

'She gave her life so you could live,' Fletcher said, though Sylva's account sickened him to his stomach. 'She knew it was the only way.'

'It wasn't your choice to make!' Sylva yelled, shoving him away from her.

'You're right, Sylva. It was Sariel's,' Fletcher said simply.

Sylva did not reply, curling into a ball with her arms over her head. Her shoulders shook with silent sobs.

Ignatius, Athena! Where were they? Fletcher looked around desperately until he saw their inert bodies on the cold ground. Ignatius was still frozen on the floor – but to Fletcher's relief his amber eyes were flicking back and forth, and he could sense no pain from the paralysed demon. Athena was faring better, though she had only managed to awkwardly roll over on her front.

Othello lurched to his feet and staggered over to Cress and Lysander, motioning at Fletcher to join him. Fletcher dragged himself across the room, still too dizzy to stand. A bag of yellow petals got in his way, and he slapped it aside, spilling the contents across the floor.

Othello helped pull him the last few feet, and they pressed their backs against the Griffin's side, the effort of sitting up too much for them.

'Best to leave her in peace,' Othello said in a hushed voice. 'I'd be a wreck if I had lost Solomon.'

'Yeah,' Cress replied. 'Don't worry, she knows you did what you had to. She just needs to blame someone now, and you're them.'

She prodded Tosk with her gauntlet. The creature was still completely frozen, like Ignatius and Athena. Only Solomon seemed capable of movement, tottering unsteadily around the room.

'Solomon's skin must have stopped the dart going in too far,' Othello suggested, as Cress pulled the Raiju on to her lap. 'Plus he's bigger than the others.'

'So's Lysander, though,' Fletcher mused, looking at the spread-eagled Griffin. He was as still as a corpse, the only sign of life the gentle stirring of dust where his breath disturbed it.

After a moment's thought, Fletcher swiped his arm along Lysander's side, knocking several darts to the floor. The tips were still slathered in a black residue.

'Looks like he got a large dose, being first into the room and all,' Fletcher said, lifting the incapacitated demon's paw. He let go and it flopped to the floor. 'I wonder if Captain Lovett can even hear us.'

The demon remained unresponsive. In fact, Fletcher could barely hear a pulse as he laid his head against the demon's side. He hunted for more darts in the fur and feathers, but found nothing.

'So what are we going to do about her?' Othello murmured, floating his wyrdlight over to Lady Cavendish. She was still huddled in the corner, madly rocking back and forth. A corona of blood lay around her son's body, and Fletcher shuddered at the sight.

'I'm going to get her out of that corner,' Fletcher said. He walked unsteadily, avoiding Rufus's forlorn corpse. He lifted her from where she sat, and was surprised when the woman stopped rocking and placed her arms around his neck. He lay her beside Cress and collapsed back in his place.

'You're a state,' Cress said, seeing Lady Cavendish's filthy exterior for the first time. She sloshed some water from her hip flask on to her sleeve and dabbed at the woman's face. Lady Cavendish closed her eyes, accepting the dwarf's ministrations wordlessly.

'We're screwed, aren't we?' Othello whispered, nodding at the exit. There was a rumble as the rocks shifted, and a goblin screeched in pain. Then a thud from the other side, and dust cascaded from the ceiling as the room shook. The orcs were blasting the rubble apart.

'When they break through, we kill as many of them as we can,' Fletcher said, closing his eyes. 'We should have some more mana by then – I've already recovered enough for a few fireballs.'

'Aye, and there's the last vial of elixir. One gulp each,' Othello said, flexing his numbed fingers. 'Let's hope the demons are recovered by then too.'

Fletcher nodded in agreement, too tired to answer. He let his fingertips trail through the dust on the ground. It was smooth to the touch, but a strange indent curved beneath the fine powder. He swept the area with his sleeve and created a wyrdlight to see.

They were sitting on the edge of a pentacle, just like on the platform in the centre of the corridor. It was smaller, barely larger than a carriage wheel, but serviceable nonetheless. The black residue of centuries-old blood remained within, and the orc keys were stamped on each corner of the star.

'Would you look at that,' Othello said, peering at it. He glanced up to see a short black pipe embedded in the ceiling above, and shuffled nervously aside.

'If we were orcs, we could go into the ether,' Fletcher said wistfully. 'Not that it would be much better than here.'

'I never thought I'd hear you wishing you were an orc,' Othello chuckled. 'But you have a point. Better than dying here, or being captured.'

'Maybe the air in their part of the ether isn't poisonous,' Cress suggested, looking up from her work. 'Maybe they're not immune after all.'

Lady Cavendish's face was pretty beneath the dirt, though gaunt and malnourished. She looked about Arcturus's age, in her mid-thirties, with the beginnings of crow's feet at the edges of her eyes. How old was she supposed to be again? There was definitely something familiar about her, as if he had seen her not long ago. Were those Rufus's eyes that stared back at him?

Cress clicked her fingers.

'Hello? I said maybe their ether isn't poisonous at all,' she repeated.

'You're welcome to test it out,' Othello said drily. 'If you want to be our guinea pig, be my guest. Personally, I'd rather take a few orcs with me.'

Cress shrugged and turned back to Lady Cavendish, teasing the knots in her hair with a comb.

Another boom shook the cavern, and a loose boulder tumbled from the pile of rubble blocking the passageway.

'They're impatient,' Fletcher said.

'I wonder if they'll tie us to that manchineel tree,' Othello wondered morbidly. 'Worse than burning, isn't that what Jeffrey said?'

'Who can trust what that traitor said,' Sylva's voice cut through the darkness.

Fletcher was glad to hear her voice. She was sitting up now, her face cold and furious. Sylva had turned her anger on the right person.

'Maybe we can chew on some of these, to numb the pain,'

Cress said, picking up one of the scattered petals and brushing off the dust.

She popped it in her mouth and chewed thoughtfully.

'You know, it's not too bad,' she mumbled. 'Makes my mouth tingle.'

'Are you sure that's a good idea?' Othello asked, picking up a petal himself and giving it a sniff. He wrinkled his nose and tossed it away.

'If I'm gonna die anyway,' Cress said, shrugging. She paused and raised her eyebrows.

'Hmmm,' she mused, shaking her head slightly. 'It's doing *something*. No idea what, though.'

Fletcher frowned. He had heard someone say that before. Electra.

'Wait,' he said, looking at the petals. They were yellow, just like the vials Electra had shown him. In his mind, something clicked.

'These petals are from the ether,' Fletcher continued, holding a petal up to the light. 'I bet you a hundred sovereigns this is what goes into those yellow vials Electra showed us. The ones which seemed to have no effect.'

'So?' Cress asked, munching on another petal.

Othello gave her a disapproving stare.

'What?' she said, grinning. 'I like the way it tingles.'

Another boom from the corridor, so loud it shook the very ground. Fletcher could hear the bass voice of orcs, shouting guttural orders. He raised his voice.

'It *means* that this isn't just some drug the orcs use to get drunk – if Cress's reaction is anything to go by. Maybe it simply makes the user immune to the ether's poison?'

Othello stared at him for a moment, his brow creasing as he mulled over Fletcher's words. Then he whooped and seized his friend by the shoulders.

'You bloody genius,' he said, shaking Fletcher back and forth. 'That's got to be it!'

'I think you're right, Fletcher,' Sylva said begrudgingly. She shuffled over to them and examined the pentacle.

'Now we just need to fill the pentacle's grooves with something organic, so we can use the damned thing. Any ideas? Because I don't see any blue orcs waiting to be sacrificed around here.'

Fletcher scanned the room. For a moment he settled on the pool of Rufus's blood, but shook his head, disgusted with himself. Not that. Never that.

'Didn't Khan press some kind of button?' Cress said, sweeping the thick layer of dust with her hands.

She grinned and pointed at a small nub in the ground in front of her.

'Good thing I didn't step on this earlier, or Othello would have had another bloodbath.'

'All right, everyone eat,' Fletcher said, stuffing a handful of petals into his mouth. The taste was mildly bitter, but not completely unpleasant. It reminded him of sour whisky.

He watched as Cress gently coaxed the noblewoman to eat one. She was so hungry that she gulped it down like a half-starved animal, barely chewing before swallowing it.

'Well done, Cress.' Fletcher smiled.

A huge blast juddered through the room. Through the rubble

of the back exit, a tiny chink of light could be seen from the goblin torches outside. The voices of the orcs could be heard distinctly now, their harsh monosyllabic speech so loud it was as if they were in the same room.

'We'd better hurry,' Fletcher said, shuffling with Othello away from the carving. 'Go ahead, Cress.'

She pressed the button, hissing through her teeth with exertion until it sank into the floor. For a moment nothing happened. Then, as panic began to take hold, the first drop of blood dripped on to the pentacle.

The droplets became a trickle, red liquid so dark it looked almost black. It spread slowly, splitting and merging until the star and the keys along it were fully formed.

'Pass me the mana vial, Othello,' Fletcher said, holding out his hand. 'Unless you want to do it?'

'By all means,' Othello said, handing it over. 'Your paralysis is almost gone, thanks to that health potion. I don't think Cress or I could do it, the state we're in.'

Fletcher nodded and gulped down the sickly liquid. A moment later, he was revelling in the feeling of his body pulsing with mana once again.

'Listen to me,' Fletcher said, dipping his fingers into the blood. It was still warm, and he stifled an involuntary shudder. 'Sylva, I need you to throw as many of these bags of petals through as you can – we don't know how long the effects of the plant will last.'

Sylva closed her eyes and nodded.

'Good. Now, Cress, I want you to gather the rest of the supplies, including my pistols, Rufus and Jeffrey's packs and anything else of use; we're going to need it all. Put it through the portal, then take Lady Cavendish through with you, she seems to trust you the most. Solomon will carry Lysander into the ether, while Othello takes Tosk, Ignatius and Athena.'

The noblewoman stirred, looking up.

'Lady Cavendish?' Fletcher asked, hopeful for another reaction.

She stared back blankly, and he sighed and continued.

'I'll have a few seconds from when my finger leaves the blood to jump into the portal before it closes, so I'll be last. Go, now!'

With those words, Fletcher pumped mana into the pentacle, the liquid glowing with a fierce violet light. He gritted his teeth and strained as the first pinprick of a portal appeared, growing to the size of a grapefruit.

'I can't carry them all, but I think Athena's almost recovered,' Othello shouted.

'Not now, Othello,' Fletcher growled, blasting another pulse of mana into the pentacle. The portal grew and spun until it hung in the air like a miniature sun, filling the room with a dull roar.

'Athena,' Lady Cavendish repeated, so softly that Fletcher thought he had imagined it.

Sylva began to hurl the bags of petals into the portal, as the others struggled under the weight of their respective charges. The packs soon followed, Rufus's spilling open as it spun through.

Solomon was the first to the portal, staggering under Lysander's weight. He charged headlong into the light, disappearing in an instant.

Sylva staggered up next, more petal bags cradled in her arms.

'I hope this works,' she muttered, then jumped into the glowing sphere. She vanished just as another blast tore through the chamber. This time, a barrage of pebbles showered them, the pile of rubble beginning to crumble.

'Othello, go!' Fletcher yelled.

The dwarf sprinted into the portal, Tosk and Ignatius clutched to his chest. Athena flew in after him, her flight erratic under the paralysis. For the briefest moment, Lady Cavendish raised her hand, as if to touch the Gryphowl.

'Cress, take Lady Cavendish, now!' Fletcher shouted, as another explosion rocked the room. The first goblin appeared, jamming its head through a gap in the blockade. It screeched as it tried to push through, clawing at the rock.

Cress grabbed Lady Cavendish's hand, but the noblewoman was suddenly responsive once again. She struggled with the dwarf, pulling away.

'Athena,' she yelled hoarsely. 'Where's Athena? My baby!'

In that moment, Fletcher knew. Her face was just like Lady Forsyth's, when he had seen her at his trial. He had seen her younger self in his dream, standing over his crib.

'Mother,' Fletcher breathed, his heart pounding. 'Alice Raleigh.'

At the sound of her name, the fight went out of her. She turned her eyes to Fletcher.

'Follow Athena,' Fletcher said, smiling through his tears. 'Cress will take you to her.'

Then he was alone, Cress dragging his mother into the portal. One more detonation blew the rubble apart, the shockwave rushing over him like a hailstorm. He took one last look at the world.

And threw himself into the ether.

# DEMONOLOGY

# DAMSEL

An insect-like demon, akin to a giant dragonfly, with an
iridescent carapace and four wings. These deceptively
fast creatures are highly manoeuvrable in the air, capable
of changing direction on a penny. They are a close cousin
to the Mite, with a sting that is three times as potent.
These demons are common throughout the known ether.

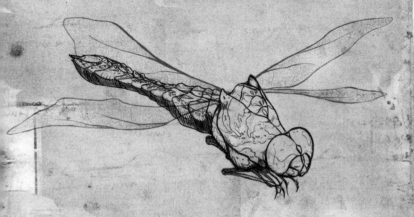

SUMMONER MASTER: *Verity Faversham*

CLASSIFICATION: *Arthropidae*
SUMMONING LEVEL: *3*
BASE MANA LEVEL: *21*
MANA ABILITIES: *None*
NATURAL SKILLS: *Flying, Agility*
RARITY: *Very Common*
DIET: *Herbivore*
ATTACK/DEFENCE 1: *Paralytic sting*

# KAMAITACHI

A demon that appears similar to a large, fanged weasel, with serrated bone-blades replacing its paws. Relatively common in the orcish part of the ether, these expendable demons are regular attackers of Hominum's front lines.

CLASSIFICATION: *Rodentia*
SUMMONING LEVEL: *3*
BASE MANA LEVEL: *20*
MANA ABILITIES: *None*
NATURAL SKILLS: *Climbing*
RARITY: *Common*
DIET: *Omnivore*
ATTACK/DEFENCE 1: *Bone-claws* 2: *Bite*

# VESP

Appearing much like an overgrown wasp or bee, these demons are often difficult to capture because of their tendency to travel in swarms. Armed with a sting just as deadly as a Damsel's and a pair of potent mandibles, these demons are a favourite among orc shamans.

CLASSIFICATION: Anthropidae
SUMMONING LEVEL: 4
BASE MANA LEVEL: 28
MANA ABILITIES: None
NATURAL SKILLS: Flying
RARITY: Very Common
DIET: Omnivore
ATTACK/DEFENCE
1: Paralytic Sting
2: Mandibles

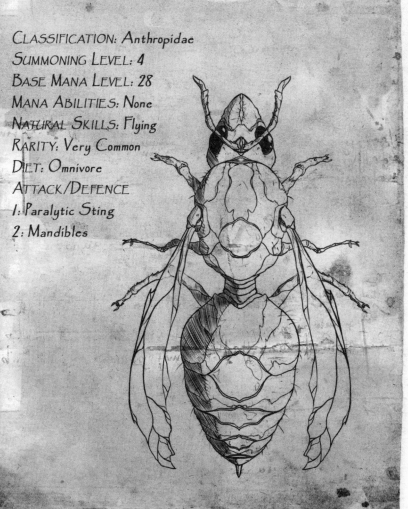

# STRIX

Often mistaken for the Gryphowl, the Strix appears as an owlish bird with four limbs. Their feathers are tipped with red, giving them a fearsome appearance. They are common in orcish parts of the ether, and are valued by orcish shamans for their vicious nature. It is not unknown for a Strix to kill and eat its siblings when they reach maturity.

**SUMMONER MASTER:** Inquisitor Damian Rook

**CLASSIFICATION:** Aves
**SUMMONING LEVEL:** 4
**BASE MANA LEVEL:** 29
**MANA ABILITIES:** None
**NATURAL SKILLS:** Flying, Eyesight
**RARITY:** Common
**DIET:** Carnivore
**ATTACK/DEFENCE 1:** Beak 2: Talons

# GRYPHOWL

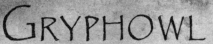

This demon is a combination of cat and owl, and is closely related to the Griffin and Chamrosh, though it is far rarer. Their sharp retractable claws and beak are their best weapons, but it is their keen intelligence and agility in the air that make them such a desirable demon. The Gryphowl is a loner by nature, but will often form a close bond with its summoner and fellow demons, if treated well.

## SUMMONER MASTER:
Fletcher Raleigh

CLASSIFICATION: Aves, Felidae
SUMMONING LEVEL: 4
BASE MANA LEVEL: 30
MANA ABILITIES: None
NATURAL SKILLS: Flying, Climbing, Eyesight
RARITY: Rare
DIET: Carnivore
ATTACK/DEFENCE 1: Beak 2: Claws

# RAIJU

The Raiju is so rare that only five have ever been captured in Hominum's history. Appearing much like a hybrid of squirrel, racoon and mongoose, this mammalian demon has large yellow eyes and dark blue fur that is emblazoned with whorls and jagged stripes of teal. It has unusually high mana levels and at its most powerful, the Raiju's lightning-bolt attack is capable of killing a bull orc. Strangely, this demon enjoys sleeping on its summoner's stomach, curling around its master's navel.

## SUMMONER MASTER: Cress Freyja

CLASSIFICATION: Rodentia
SUMMONING LEVEL: 5
BASE MANA LEVEL: 40
MANA ABILITIES: Lightning
NATURAL SKILLS: Climbing, Immune to lightning
RARITY: Endangered
DIET: Omnivore
ATTACK/DEFENCE 1: Lightning-bolt

# ENFIELD

The Enfield is both rarer and smaller than its cousin,
the Vulpid, and is the size of a large dog. It has the
head of a fox, the forelegs of an eagle, the narrow chest
of a greyhound and the hindquarters of a wolf. Its front
talons are dangerously sharp and it has tawny brown
feathers interspersed amongst the red fur of its front
and the grey of its back.

**SUMMONER MASTERS:** *Verity Faversham*

**CLASSIFICATION:** *Canidae, Aves*
**SUMMONING LEVEL:** *5*
**BASE MANA LEVEL:** *35*
**MANA ABILITIES:** *None*
**NATURAL SKILLS:** *Acute scent,*
*Acute hearing, Agility*
**RARITY:** *Rare*
**DIET:** *Carnivore*
**ATTACK/DEFENCE**
*1: Bite 2: Talons*

# CHAMROSH

This hawk-dog hybrid is a quarter of the size of its closest cousin, the Griffin. The Chamrosh is renowned for its loyal and loving nature, and will often become lonely when separated from its master. The preferred support demon of the Celestial Corps, this companion is a favourite among summoners.

CLASSIFICATION: Aves, Canidae

SUMMONING LEVEL: 5

BASE MANA LEVEL: 35

MANA ABILITIES: None

NATURAL SKILLS: Flying, Eyesight

RARITY: Uncommon

DIET: Carnivore

ATTACK/DEFENCE 1: Beak

# ARACH

The Arach appears as an enormous spider, almost as large as a wild boar. Its eight dextrous legs are capable of skilful manipulation, allowing the demon to jump as high as ten feet and grasp its opponents by the face. The Arach has three powerful abilities. The first is the gossamer spell, shooting a luminescent web that puts one in mind of the silk of a glowworm – an adhesive that fades out of existence after a few hours. The second is its vicious sting, the venom of which is capable of killing a grown man – if the impalement of the spike does not do the job first. Finally, rather like some breeds of tarantula, the Arach is capable of releasing the bristled hair from its back to float in the air, scourging its opponents' skin and even blinding them. Only its summoners are immune to these bristles, as well as the Arach's venom.

SUMMONER MASTER:
Didric Cavell

CLASSIFICATION: Arthopidae
SUMMONING LEVEL: 6
BASE MANA LEVEL: 45
MANA ABILITIES: Gossamer
NATURAL SKILLS:
Climbing, Jumping
RARITY: Rare
DIET: Carnivore
ATTACK/DEFENCE
1: Venomous Sting
2: Gossamer 3: Bristles

# CALADRIUS

One of four elemental bird-like demons, the Caladrius
is cousin to the fiery Phoenix, the icy Polarion and the
lightning-powered Halcyon. With the white feathers and
gentle features of a dove, this demon's high mana and rare
healing powers are highly desired, even if its relatively
small talons are not. These demons are rumoured to spend
most of their time high above the cloudscape of the ether,
where the air is too thin for other demons to find them.

## SUMMONER MASTER: *Atilla Thorsager*

CLASSIFICATION: *Aves*
SUMMONING LEVEL: *7*
BASE MANA LEVEL: *52*
MANA ABILITIES: *Healing*
NATURAL SKILLS: *Flying*
RARITY: *Very Rare*
DIET: *Omnivore*
ATTACK/DEFENCE 1: *Peck* 2: *Healing*

# PHOENIX

A large bird with red-orange plumage and long tail feathers like that of a peacock, the Phoenix is the rarest of the four elemental avian demons. High in mana and capable of breathing fire like a Salamander, these demons are said to inhabit the rims of active volcanoes in the ether.

CLASSIFICATION: Aves
SUMMONING LEVEL: 7
BASE MANA LEVEL: 52
MANA ABILITIES: Flame
NATURAL SKILLS: Flying, Immune to fire
RARITY: Very Rare
DIET: Omnivore
ATTACK/DEFENCE
1: Peck 2: Talons 3: Flame

# Halcyon

The Halcyon is thought to be the most common of the four elemental avians, with bright metallic feathers that make it shine brilliantly when it flies. With razor-sharp talons, high mana levels and the ability to fire lightning from its elongated tail feathers, its conspicuousness is its only disadvantage.

CLASSIFICATION: Aves

SUMMONING LEVEL: 7

BASE MANA LEVEL: 52

MANA ABILITIES: Lightning

NATURAL SKILLS: Flying, Immune to lightning

RARITY: Very Rare

DIET: Omnivore

ATTACK/DEFENCE 1: Peck 2: Talons 3: Lightning

# POLARION

Polarions are believed to inhabit the clouds above the ether's seas, using their abilities with ice to hunt any small demons foolish enough to leap out of the water. Rare sightings report the demon to be built much like a kingfisher, with blue-black plumage and a white belly. They are unusually high in mana and have the extremely rare ability to freeze their enemies, making them a fine addition to any summoner's roster.

CLASSIFICATION: Aves
SUMMONING LEVEL: 7
BASE MANA LEVEL: 52
MANA ABILITIES: Ice
NATURAL SKILLS: Flying, Immune to frost
RARITY: Very Rare
DIET: Omnivore
ATTACK/DEFENCE
1: Peck
2: Talons
3: Ice

# ALICORN

A horse demon with swan-like wings and a single horn growing from the centre of its forehead. These equine demons are notoriously difficult to capture, thanks to their speed both in the air and on land. Alicorn herds migrate across Hominum's part of the ether once each decade, and those that are slow enough to be captured tend to be the sick, injured or young.

**SUMMONER MASTER:**
Captain Arcturus

CLASSIFICATION: Equine, Aves, Caprid
SUMMONING LEVEL: 8
BASE MANA LEVEL: 56
MANA ABILITIES: None
NATURAL SKILLS:
Flying, Agility,
RARITY: Migratory
DIET: Herbivore
ATTACK/DEFENCE
1: Gore 2: Kick

# HIPPOGRIFF

The Hippogriff is a hybrid of eagle and horse.
Though fast on the ground, it lacks the fierce claws
of its more powerful and rarer cousin, the Griffin,
relying on strikes from its beak and hooves. It is a
popular choice of demon for members of the Celestial
Corps, second only to the Peryton.

CLASSIFICATION: Equine, Aves
SUMMONING LEVEL: 8
BASE MANA LEVEL: 57
MANA ABILITIES: None
NATURAL SKILLS: Flying, Agility, Eyesight
RARITY: Migratory
DIET: Carnivore
ATTACK/DEFENCE 1: Peck 2: Kick

# Nanaue

This humanoid, land-dwelling shark demon is a favourite among orc shamans, thanks to its vicious jaws, sharp claws and impressive agility. With a posture more akin to a chimpanzee than a man, these demons are excellent climbers and are capable of jumping great distances.

They come in the various breeds of their animal counterparts, with the great white, the hammerhead and the tiger shark being the most common.

CLASSIFICATION: Aquarine

SUMMONING LEVEL: 9

BASE MANA LEVEL: 61

MANA ABILITIES: None

NATURAL SKILLS: Climbing, Agility

RARITY: Rare

DIET: Carnivore

ATTACK/DEFENCE 1: Bite 2: Claws 3: Tail-swipe

# PERYTON

The most favoured demon of the Celestial Corps, Perytons appear as winged, horse-sized stags, with majestic antlers branching from their foreheads. Their front legs end in hooves, yet their back legs are clawed like a falcon's, complete with deadly talons that can do serious damage. Instead of the traditional bobtail that most deer possess, these demons have long, elegant tail feathers. Their herds migrate sporadically across Hominum's part of the ether, and they are considered the most common of the flying steeds available to Hominum's summoners.

## SUMMONER MASTER: *Ophelia Faversham*

CLASSIFICATION:
Aves, Caprid
SUMMONING LEVEL: 9
BASE MANA LEVEL: 62
MANA ABILITIES: None
NATURAL SKILLS: Flying, Agility
RARITY: Migratory
DIET: Herbivore
ATTACK/DEFENCE 1: Gore 2: Talons 3: Kick

# ONI

Oni appear similar in size and stature to orcs and are a favoured demon among veteran shamans. They are characterised by their crimson red skin, a pair of horns erupting from their foreheads and overdeveloped upper and lower canines. Though they appear bright, Onis are thought to be unusually slow-witted, with less intelligence than the average Mite.

CLASSIFICATION: *Apeish*
SUMMONING LEVEL: *10*
BASE MANA LEVEL: *70*
MANA ABILITIES: *None*
NATURAL SKILLS: *Strength*
RARITY: *Rare*
DIET: *Omnivore*
ATTACK/DEFENCE
*1: Gore 2: Bite 3: Punch*

# MANTICORE

This rare demon has bat-like wings and forelimbs, a
scorpion tail and the body of a lion, though the dark fur
is interspersed with sharp spines. The Manticore's
leonine face can sometimes appear almost human, and
its features are capable of expressing complex emotion.
Its venom is so potent that one droplet will kill a man
within minutes. Members of the Raleigh family are
said to be immune.

## SUMMONER MASTER: *Charles Faversham*

CLASSIFICATION: Felidae, Arthropidae
SUMMONING LEVEL: 12
BASE MANA LEVEL: 85
MANA ABILITIES: None
NATURAL SKILLS: Flying
RARITY: Very Rare
DIET: Carnivore
ATTACK/DEFENCE
1: Venomous Sting
2: Bite
3: Claws
4: Spines

# IFRIT

The Ifrit is an elemental akin to the Golem, aligned with fire rather than stone. A close cousin to the ice-powered Jotun, its skin appears to be made of blazing lava. This fire elemental is immensely strong and is even capable of breathing flames from its mouth. It is one of the more powerful demons that orc shamans are able to capture from their part of the ether.

CLASSIFICATION: Elemental
SUMMONING LEVEL: 13
BASE MANA LEVEL: 91
MANA ABILITIES: Flame
NATURAL SKILLS: Glowing, Immune to fire, Strength
RARITY: Endangered
DIET: Omnivore
ATTACK/DEFENCE 1: Flame

# JOTUN

Jotuns are only known from a fleeting mention in a single ancient elvish scroll, though Hominum's scholars dispute the authenticity of this text. Described as giant humanoids that appear to be hewn from ice, they are said to be capable of freezing all that they touch. These demons are suspected of living in the snowy icecaps of the ether's tallest mountains.

CLASSIFICATION: Elemental

SUMMONING LEVEL: 13

BASE MANA LEVEL: 91

MANA ABILITIES: Ice

NATURAL SKILLS: Immune to frost, Strength

RARITY: Endangered

DIET: Omnivore

ATTACK/DEFENCE 1: Ice

# WENDIGO

The Wendigo is a rare demon that is known to follow the Shrike migration across the ether, eating the carcasses of its fallen victims. Despite its role as a carrion eater, the Wendigo is a powerful beast in its own right, with corded muscle lining its skinny frame. Standing as high as eight feet tall, it has branching antlers, a wolf-like head and long arms that it uses to knuckle the ground like a gorilla. It is known to have the mottled grey skin of a corpse and the stench to match – most likely from its regular consumption of rotting flesh.

## SUMMONER MASTER: Zacharias Forsyth

CLASSIFICATION: Caprid, Canidae
SUMMONING LEVEL: 13
BASE MANA LEVEL: 90
MANA ABILITIES: None
NATURAL SKILLS: Agility, Strength
RARITY: Very Rare
DIET: Carnivore
ATTACK/DEFENCE
1: Gore
2: Bite
3: Claws

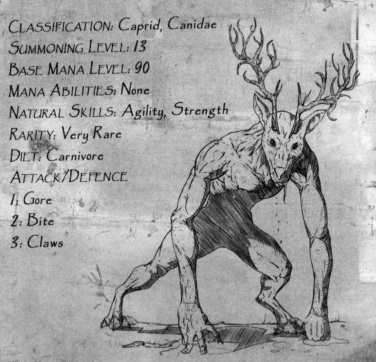

# WYVERN

The Wyvern is the orcs' main counter to the demons of the
Celestial Corps. These enormous, scaled creatures have
bat-like wings, long, spiked tails and horned, crocodilian
heads. Their skin is so tough and cartilaginous that only a
lance or well-placed musket ball can pierce it. Other than
their jaws, the Wyvern's main weapons are their powerful
legs, which are tipped with the hooked hind-claws of a raptor.

They are slower than most flying demons and are often
backed up by the more agile Shrikes, Strixes and Vesps.

CLASSIFICATION: Reptilia
SUMMONING LEVEL: 15
BASE MANA LEVEL: 105
MANA ABILITIES: None
NATURAL SKILLS:
Flying,
Thick-skinned
RARITY: Very Rare
DIET: Carnivore
ATTACK/DEFENCE
1: Gore
2: Bite
3: Talons
4: Thick-skinned
5: Tail-swipe

# PHANTAUR

The Phantaur is as much an elephant as a Minotaur is a bull. With its serrated tusks, sturdy fists and a height of over ten feet, it is a force to be reckoned with. Thought to be the rarest and most powerful demon available to orc shamans, only one has ever been seen. Little is known of its behaviours and habitats. It is thought that the one Phantaur to have been captured has been passed down through thousands of generations of shamans, its origins lost to the mists of time.

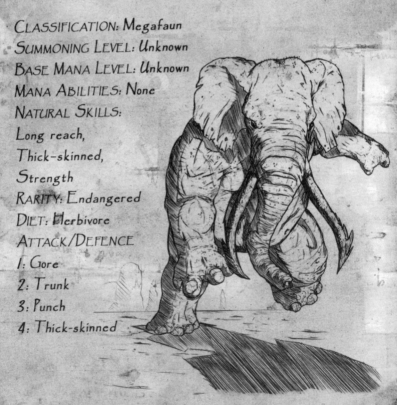

CLASSIFICATION: Megafaun

SUMMONING LEVEL: Unknown

BASE MANA LEVEL: Unknown

MANA ABILITIES: None

NATURAL SKILLS:

Long reach,

Thick-skinned,

Strength

RARITY: Endangered

DIET: Herbivore

ATTACK/DEFENCE

1: Gore

2: Trunk

3: Punch

4: Thick-skinned

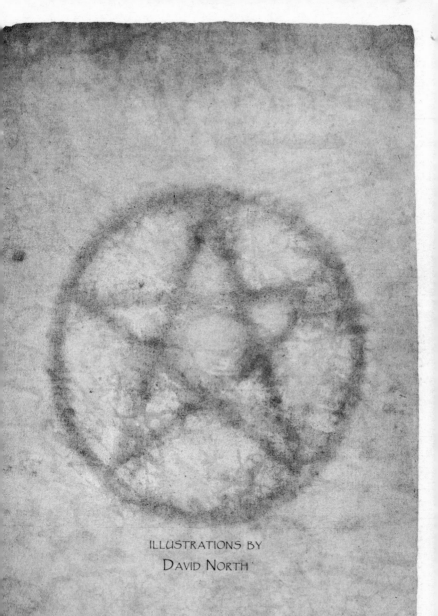

ILLUSTRATIONS BY
DAVID NORTH

# SUMM✪NER

# The Outcast

MORE DEMONS

MORE BATTLES

MORE ADVENTURE

## COMING SOON
in 2018

F MAT